NEXT

ALSO BY JAMES HYNES

Kings of Infinite Space

The Lecturer's Tale

Publish and Perish

The Wild Colonial Boy

NEXT

a novel

JAMES HYNES

A REAGAN ARTHUR BOOK
LITTLE, BROWN AND COMPANY
NEW YORK BOSTON LONDON

Reagan Arthur Books / Little, Brown and Company
Hachette Book Group
237 Park Avenue, New York, NY 10017
www.hachettebookgroup.com

First Edition: March 2010

Reagan Arthur Books is an imprint of Little, Brown and Company, a division of Hachette Book Group, Inc. The Reagan Arthur name and logo are trademarks of Hachette Book Group, Inc.

The characters and events in this book are fictitious. Any similarity to real persons, living or dead, is coincidental and not intended by the author.

Library of Congress Cataloging-in-Publication Data
Hynes, James.
    Next : a novel / by James Hynes. — 1st ed.
      p. cm.
    ISBN 978-0-316-05192-7
    I. Title.
    PS3558.Y55N49 2010
    813'.54 — dc22   2009008490

10 9 8 7 6 5 4 3 2 1

RRD-IN

Printed in the United States of America

In St. James Street there was a terrific explosion; people came running out of Clubs; stopped still & gazed about them. But there was no Zeppelin or aeroplane — only, I suppose, a very large tyre burst. But it is really an instinct with me, & most people, I suppose, to turn any sudden noise, or dark object in the sky into an explosion, or a German aeroplane. And it always seems utterly impossible that one should be hurt.

Virginia Woolf, *Diary*, 1 February 1915

She would not say of any one in the world now that they were this or were that. She felt very young; at the same time unspeakably aged. She sliced like a knife through everything; at the same time was outside, looking on. She had a perpetual sense, as she watched the taxi cabs, of being out, out, far out to sea and alone; she always had the feeling that it was very, very dangerous to live even one day.

Mrs. Dalloway

Comes an age in a man's life when he don't want to spend time figuring what comes next.

James Coburn in *Pat Garrett and Billy the Kid*, screenplay by Rudolph Wurlitzer

PART ONE

The Battle
of
Bertrand Russell

AS THE GROUND rushes up to meet him, Kevin thinks about missiles again. One missile in particular, a shoulder-fired anti-aircraft missile, blasted from a tube balanced on the bump where some guy's clavicle meets his scapula. What guy — a Saudi? An Egyptian? A Yemeni? Some pissed-off Arab anyway, kneeling in the bed of a dinged-up pickup truck with Texas plates, or crouching on the springy backseat of a rented convert- ible on a dirt track just outside the airport fence. One of those portable weapons from Afghanistan, back when Afghanistan was somebody else's problem, called...something, a Slammer or a Tingler or something like that. Kevin recalls that it's the same name as a cocktail — a Whiskey Sour? A Tom Collins? A shoulder-fired Banana Daiquiri? No, a *Stinger*, that's it! Four parts brandy to one part crème de menthe in a cocktail glass, *or* a fat olive-green tube that farts flame out the back while the missile erupts from the front, its backside trailing a wobbly spi- ral of smoke until the missile gets its bearings and climbs like a sonuvabitch in a long smooth curve into the heat-hazy Texas sky toward the sleek underbelly of Kevin's plane, a Pringles can with wings, packed full of defenseless Pringles.

Trouble is, Kevin's seen his fair share of movie air disasters. Used to be they just shook the camera and Ronald Colman or whoever would grit his teeth and bug his eyes and dig his fingers into the armrests, and then a wobbly model airplane would plow up a miniature of a mountainside in the Hindu Kush, breasting snowbank after snowbank like a speedboat. Now of course they rub your nose in it, and you see planes split apart *from the inside:* the skin peels away like foil, the cabin fills with flying magazines and gusts of condensation, oxygen masks dance like marionettes. Then there's the money shot, no movie air disaster these days is complete without it: the awful, thrilling, gut-wrenching cum of the whole sequence when some poor extra still strapped in his seat is sucked out of the plane, or a whole row of seats is yanked as if by cables out the ragged gap where the tail used to be and spins ass over tit into a freezing, fatal darkness.

But now it's broad daylight, and Kevin's flight from Michigan is coming down in Austin, Texas. He was even more worried about missiles during their predawn takeoff from Detroit Metro. How could he not have been, what with the security check-in line running out of the terminal all the way to the parking structure, and with every ceiling-hung TV along the concourse tuned to CNN or Fox, still streaming images from the bombings in Europe last Thursday? Crumpled subway cars, rows of bodies under sheets, cops and paramedics in orange vests, deltas of blood on pale, wide-eyed faces. The usual images — for all he knows they could be running file footage from earlier catastrophes: London, Madrid, Mumbai. Not to mention the usual grainy CCTV images of the usual round, dusky, beard-fringed faces of pleasant-looking young men — *those people,* Kevin can't help thinking, against his better nature — guys only just out of adolescence, with a death wish and a remarkable talent for synchronization. Moscow, Paris, Berlin, Amsterdam, all within a few minutes of each other. And Bern — who bombs Switzerland? And Glasgow! If the first, botched attempt on Glasgow was farce—a couple of pissed-off professionals torching a Jeep Cherokee, not quite enough to bring Western civilization to its knees—this new attack was tragic, but it still felt unlikely to Kevin. Who knew Glasgow even *had* a subway system, and now Kevin remembers the name of Buchanan Street Station (a place he's never heard of before) as indelibly as if he'd ridden through it every day of his life. Creeping in the check-in line through the terminal, he passed a Wayne County sheriff every thirty feet posed like a Cylon centurion in Kevlar vest and riot visor. At the checkpoint itself, he saw the surest sign of Orange Alert, a couple of paunchy Michigan National Guards in fatigues and combat boots, carrying automatic weapons and eyeing Kevin with a caffeinated gaze as he stood crucified in his stocking feet while a TSA drone swept him with a wand. Have a nice flight, sir!

And it didn't help that Detroit Metro is a ten-minute drive from Kevin's favorite Lebanese restaurant in Dearborn, where no doubt some deeply disgruntled dishwasher dreams of airliners dropping from the sky like ducks in duck season, or—who knows?—where some Al Qaeda sleeper out of an episode of *24* is waiting tables and biding his time for a chance to sneak out to a two-track behind the airport with a piece of cast-off American ordnance and blow one of his better customers—and Kevin's a big tipper, he used to wait tables himself—out of the sky. But now, deep in the privacy of his brainpan, in the plane descending over Texas, Kevin feels guilty for thinking this. *Those people*—what a thing to say! In the cozy, progressive cocoon of Ann Arbor, where he's lived nearly all his life, you don't openly speculate about terrorists in Dearborn, not in polite society you don't, not even four days after a six-city European bombing spree. And if you do, it's only to concede that it serves us right for looking the other way while our government handed out Stingers to radical Islamists in Peshawar like a corrupt Indian

agent handing out Winchesters and firewater to angry Coman-
ches in some glossy fifties western. Read your Chomsky, friend,
we're only reaping the whirlwind, and anyway, Islam's a big,
complicated religion like Christianity, it's not a monolith, it's
not like every Muslim in the world wants you dead. Apart from
the waiters in Dearborn, Kevin doesn't even know any Muslims, or at least he doesn't think he does. In college he slept a
couple, three times with a girl named Paula who called herself a
Sufi, but probably only to *épater les père et mère* back in Grand
Rapids, and anyway that was thirty-some years ago, and who
knows where she is now. Probably not shooting down airplanes,
is a safe bet.

And *those people,* it turns out, can be guys just like Kevin.
Just this morning, keeping an eye on CNN as he dressed for
the flight, Kevin learned that the Buchanan Street bomber,
according to the surveillance footage, was a pale, green-eyed,
red-haired Celt—another Kevin, in fact, a young white Scots-
man named Kevin MacDonald, who'd changed his name to
Abdul Mohammed—SLAVE OF MOHAMMED read the helpful
caption beneath his grainy visage—and who carried a backpack full of plastic explosives into a crowded Glasgow subway
car. The cable ranters are already hyperventilating about the
Glasgow bomber's ethnicity, parsing his motives—whatever
they may have been—and either blaming the grinding poverty
of his upbringing for his desperation, or blaming permissive
Britain for allowing radical Islam to infect the white working
class. Kevin, to his mild shame, understands how unsettling this
other Kevin is, how each new attack seems to strike closer to
home. The first Glasgow terrorists were *doctors,* for chrissakes,
sworn to do no harm, but at least they were, you know, *for-
eigners,* or at least foreign to the country they were attacking.
Not to mention inept, especially the one idiot who managed
to set only himself on fire, thus scoring one for the other team.

But how much scarier is it if it's a guy who looks just like you? Kevin's half Polack, so this morning he can cling to his mother's heritage for consolation, but the fact is, looking at the guy's ID photo on the television as he pulled on his dress trousers, Kevin thought, he could've been my cousin on my father's side, or my nephew, if I had any nephews. Twenty-three years old was Kevin MacDonald, says the CNN caption, and Kevin thinks, hell, if I'd ever gotten lucky in Glasgow—where, thank God, he's never been—this kid could've been my son.

So the lingering images of Buchanan Street, the blunt Celtic face of the Other Kevin, and the prospect of sudden, violent death on takeoff worried our Kevin enough to distract him from his pretty seatmate, a long-limbed Asian American girl some twenty-five years younger than he who had already curled next to the window with youthful limberness, and who had plunged into a fat paperback even before Kevin got on the plane at Metro. He folded his suit coat and laid it flat on somebody's garment bag in the overhead, and settling into the aisle seat he exchanged a glance and a smile with the young woman, who was reading, it turned out, a mass-market edition of *The Joy Luck Club*. An Asian girl reading Amy Tan—at first this seemed kind of predictable to Kevin, and then kind of redundant, a coals-to-Newcastle kind of thing. What could Amy Tan tell this girl that she didn't already know? Then his Ann Arbor brainpan brimmed over with guilt again and he thought, maybe *I* should be reading Amy Tan, what do I know? He's never read the book, but he's seen the movie, a glossy melodrama—he saw it with Beth, years ago—and mainly what he remembers is a series of yuppie young women whining about their jobs and their boyfriends, until they're flattened by their no-nonsense immigrant mothers, who say things like, hey, you think *you* got it bad, back in China I had to *drown my baby*.

But as the plane lurched back from the gate and rumbled

slowly out to the runway, thoughts of the Other Kevin and of terrorist Lebanese busboys from Dearborn drove Kevin to ignore the girl and peer anxiously past her instead into the predawn gloom beyond the glare of the runway, where of course he couldn't see a thing. She glanced at him a couple of times, probably thinking that he was just another melancholy middle-aged guy checking her out, and maybe he was, just a little bit. She wore jeans and a green camisole top with teensy little straps, and she had kicked off her sandals to tuck her heels under the tight denim curve of her rump. While scanning the bright amber-and-green circuit board of suburban Detroit below — I-94 streaming with white lights one way, red the other — for the telltale flash and blinding streak of a shoulder-fired missile, Kevin managed to admire how the straps of her camisole angled over her collarbone, how the jagged cut of her hair brushed the long, smooth slope of her shoulders, and, when she fixed him with a clear, brown-eyed gaze, how the golden nose stud twinkled in her left nostril.

"Do you want to switch?" she said to him in a flat, midwestern accent like his own.

"It's okay," he said, forcing a laugh. "It's just that I don't like to fly." Especially not today, he almost added, but why belabor the obvious?

"Then maybe you shouldn't look out the window," she said evenly, her thumbs keeping *The Joy Luck Club* pried apart in her lap.

"Well," he said, "you're right." He shifted his backside in his seat. He folded and refolded his fingers over the buckle of his seat belt. He refocused his gaze down the aisle. "That's a good idea."

But now, enduring an ear-popping descent into Texas, where there may or may not be fewer Arab terrorists — fewer Lebanese restaurants, perhaps, but more Middle Eastern students of petroleum engineering—Kevin shifts uneasily in his seat. During the flight, out of Stinger range at thirty thousand feet (or so Kevin hopes, he really has no idea), his imagination had shifted again to the Other Kevin, the baby-faced Scottish jihad- ist, the freckled Islamo-Celt, and Kevin found himself profiling every person who walked past him down the aisle to the bath- room: every young guy in jeans, to be sure, especially the dark or swarthy or bearded ones, but also pale guys his own age in polo shirts and Dockers, and even the weary blond steward- ess with the crow's feet. Who knows what she might be embit- tered about? High over southern Illinois or Missouri, Kevin wasn't thinking of Stingers, but of rogue bottles of shampoo and mouthwash, holding household chemicals that the guy in Dockers could mix in the tiny bathroom sink and then spark with the battery from his iPod or his cell phone, blowing a hole in the plane, sucking everybody out one at a time through the toilet like Goldfinger at the end of *Goldfinger*. Still, perhaps because the latest bombs in the news were backpack devices in subway cars, Orange Alert this time around hasn't meant the confiscation of personal grooming products, but in the last year or two, Kevin has been on flights whose passengers were relieved of shampoo, mouthwash, toothpaste, shaving gel, sunblock, cologne, perfume, moisturizer, not to mention any implement for the care of one's nails: clippers, scissors, nail files, emery boards. On those flights Kevin saw a vision of a new world in the sky, a dirtier, scruffier world with planes full of passen- gers unshaven, unwashed, unscented, untanned, undeodorized, unmoisturized, and unmanicured, their untrimmed nails inch- ing over the armrests they gripped so tightly.

But right now, descending into Austin, Kevin's thinking is old school: he's thinking that whatever gets them is going to be a good, old-fashioned, shoulder-fired surface-to-air missile, and he glances once more past Ms. Joy Luck and through the sun glaring in the scratches across the little oval of window. All he can see is a dull silver expanse of wing, dinged and dented and streaked, and beyond the wing a little wedge of desiccated brown ranch land sectioned by white dirt roads and fence lines and littered with tin-roofed houses and metallic trailers and oblong stock ponds full of greenish water. Even if the plane splits open like a piñata, he won't have far to fall. He angles from side to side, wondering what's the point of these fucking little windows if you can't *see* anything, and his heart begins to pound almost as if he's actually glimpsed the silver streak of the Stinger atop its billowing gush of smoke. Joy Luck was right—he's better off on the aisle, where he won't be able to see anything, where he won't know what's coming until it's too late. Even if he were able to watch the entire, fatal, rising arc of the missile, he's just another Pringle in the Pringles can gliding belly down out of the sky, with no control over the plane, no say over his fate. What would he do if he actually saw it coming? Clutch Joy Luck's hand for that last moment of human contact? Tighten his seat belt? Put his head between his knees? Pray?

His seatmate lifts her eyebrow at him. She's barely moved for three hours, except to shift her knees from one side to the other. The thick sheaf of pages in her lap has shifted inexorably from right to left, unread to read. She says, "Maybe you *should've* sat here. You'd have felt less, you know." She wobbles her hand in the air.

"Maybe," gasps Kevin. "Maybe not. Partly it's just..." He curls his arms over his head, evoking the long, enclosed, hermetically sealed tube of the plane. "And the way we're all..." He pushes his palms toward each other at an angle. Pringles in a Pringles can, he nearly says.

"Yeeaah," she drawls, sympathetically. "You're all..."

"Yup," gulps Kevin, his hands curled in his lap. His heart

pounding, his fingers numb, his stomach rolling over and over. He hears the windy thunder of descent, the anxious hiss of ventilators, the electric whine of the landing gear. Down the aisle of the tube he sees the fragile crowns of every defenseless Pringle's head—black, gray, blond, tousled, kinky, curly, straight, buzz-cut, cowlicked, and pinkishly bald—none of them potential terrorists anymore, but his fellow innocents, the people he's going to die with. Earlier in the flight, a cherubic infant was propped up in his seat looking back at Kevin with the twinkly, ruddy-cheeked smile of a bemused old man—Winston Churchill without his cigar—and now the kid is out of sight, wrapped up and belted in. Who's going to save that baby, he wants to know, who's going to save us all, who's going to save *me* from the furious Stinger whizzing closer and closer to the belly of the plane, now only an inch away, now half an inch, now a quarter of an inch? The only thing that'll save us is Zeno's paradox—Kevin was a classics major once, for about three weeks—all we have to do is trust in the pre-Socratics and that sonuvabitching missile will never catch up. Though of course if you follow that line of reasoning, the plane itself will never reach the earth, the fat black wheels will come closer and closer to, but *never…quite…touch,* the tarmac, the fat-bellied plane and the shark-nosed little missile will streak together forever at a hundred and sixty miles an hour, never coming in contact, never coming to earth.

Then they do, or anyway the plane does, the wheels screeching and smoking against the runway as all the Pringles lurch forward against their lap belts. (Some breakage may occur in shipping.) Kevin feels the jolt through his backside and up his spine, and he grunts in alarm. The braking engines scream, the overhead bins rattle, the whole plane shudders with relief. Joy Luck rocks in her seat but never lifts her eyes from the book, and out the window Kevin sees the flat Texas horizon looking greener edge on, while the strange little growths between run-ways—junction boxes on metal stems and unlit yellow lights like tulip bulbs and arcane little signs that say G3 or E1—glide by. Behind the plane the angry Stinger sputters out in exhaustion, shark-nosed no more, but red-faced with bulging cheeks and eyes rolled white like Thomas the Tank Engine or the Little Engine That Could, only this is the Little Missile That Couldn't, doubled over gasping in midair, pooting out a last couple of comic little puffs of exhaust, comedy clouds for a cartoon rocket, before it tumbles fuelless and unfulfilled, bent and blunted, end over end down the runway behind the plane. Meanwhile the pickup full of glowering Saudi engineering students simply evaporates.

Kevin sags into his seat like a sack of meal. From the tiny speakers overhead comes the pilot's syncopated Chuck Yeager drawl: "*Wel*come to Austin, folks, it's *eight* forty-eight in the ay em, we're juuust a tad early, the *temp*erature is a balmy *eight*-tee-two degrees," blah blah blah. Enough with the Right Stuff already, thinks Kevin, just park the fucking plane. All around him the other passengers rustle restlessly in their seats, stretching, collecting, cell-phoning, watch-glancing, yawning, all except Joy Luck, who *will not* lift her eyes from her book. Beyond the girl's admirable clavicle he glimpses the low half shell of Austin's terminal, blanched with morning light, airliners nosed up under the tall tinted windows, an accordion jetway affixed to each plane like a remora to a shark. Thrust up behind, the tail fin of each aircraft shimmers in the heat.

At last, at last, at last Kevin's plane bumps to a stop, and with the clacking of unbuckled seat belts passengers surge into the aisle. Kevin's one of the first up, tipping back on his heels from the swing of the overhead door, then rocking forward to snatch his suit coat. Waiting now with chin tucked to breastbone, Kevin finds himself looking down the front of his seatmate's camisole. She's already flipped up the armrest and stretched across both seats, her finger still stuck in the paperback, while reaching behind with the other to pull on her sandals. In the cool green shadow where the camisole droops away on its straps, Kevin can see her nipples, and perhaps even the shadow of a tattoo snaking up from under one of her velvety breasts. Her eyes are hidden under her bangs. Now he *is* the melancholy middle-aged guy copping a look, and as she scootches up onto the aisle seat, tucking one knee under her, Kevin drapes his jacket over his clasped hands and rolls his eyes upward, an altar boy contemplating a prank.

Inch by inch the snake of passengers unkinks up the aisle, making the floor panels thump. Kevin steps back to let Joy Luck ahead of him, and she unfolds herself into the aisle, still holding her place in the paperback. She's nearly as tall as he is, and she pops open the next overhead compartment and, still holding the goddamn book, effortlessly hoists out a fat, cylindrical, olive-green duffle. It's so big Kevin's surprised they counted it as a carry-on, but she swings it over her shoulder and sways up the aisle like a sailor. Kevin treads right behind her, his nose a couple of inches from the bulging round bottom of the duffle. He shuffles up the aisle past the flight attendant with the crow's feet, and he follows the girl through the gap between the plane and the jetway where the Texas heat leaks in like steam. Then they're walking faster up the slightly cooler slope of the ramp, where he can encompass Joy Luck from head to toe in one glance. She's long-waisted and slim-hipped, and she sways up the jetway with one bare arm curled round her duffle and her other arm swinging at her hip, the paperback pinched around her middle finger. The abbreviated hem of her top reveals the matching dimples at the small of her back and the small tattoo of a green apple between them, just over the beltless waistband of her jeans. Kevin cannot help but admire the enormously fetching way she moves, a sort of well-lubricated slouch by which she lets her shoulders droop and leads with her hipbones. It's not an aggressive catwalk strut, it's much less self-conscious and much more feral, and as Kevin follows her into the filtered light and cathedral echo of the terminal itself, into the delta of debarking passengers fanning across the carpet and onto the cool marble, he thinks, *I know* that walk, I've *seen* that walk before. And for one thrilling moment, his heart swells with the possibility that *I know that girl!* But of course, he couldn't possibly—she's twenty-five, maybe thirty years younger than him, he's never seen her before in his life, and if he had, he'd have remembered. But by God he knows that walk, someone else used to walk that way, he's felt that walk up close, he's curled his fingertips around those hipbones from behind, and then his heart fills up again, only this time with honest-to-God, hundred-proof middle-aged melancholy. It's Lynda, he realizes, Lynda used to slink like that, Lynda used to glide away from his touch just like that. Lynda on the dance floor, Lynda *à la plage*. Lynda on the railing.

Then something tangles round his ankles and he staggers forward, the fat treads of his shoes sticking at the icy floor. In that pre-accident moment of crystal-clear slo-mo, he realizes that his jacket has slipped off his clasped hands and fallen to the floor between his feet. In a desperate little tap dance he kicks the jacket free, and it slithers across the marble floor like the cloaked shadow of a Ringwraith. He hops and pirouettes and catches himself with both hands on the top of a trash bin, while the other folks streaming out of the jetway step briskly around him as if he were a dog chasing its tail. He's blushing, he can feel the heat rising off his face, and he pushes himself erect from the trash can, stiffening his back and lifting his chin. Then he stoops to the limp jacket, which is laughing at him from the floor, and jerks it into the air. Of course the carefully assembled contents of his left inside pocket all tumble to the floor: his notebook with a loud *slap,* the letter inviting him to the job interview gliding like a paper airplane, his pen and sunglasses skittering end to end. Clutching the jacket to his chest, he stoops red-faced again to snatch everything up, smiling sheepishly at no one in particular. A young mother pushing a slack-jawed infant—young Winston at rest—twists the stroller in a sharp angle to avoid him. The terminal's arctic air-conditioning clamps around him then, and he shakes the jacket out by the collar as if disciplining a child. His heart hammers from embarrassment, his hands tremble a little as he slots the notebook, the pens, the glasses, and finally the letter back into the jacket's inside pocket. He puts the jacket on and glances around to see if anyone has noticed his spastic little routine, but all he sees are a couple of men dozing in the black leatherette chairs and an old woman paging through a magazine. By now the plane is empty behind him and the rest of the passengers are trailing away down the long cathedral arcade of the terminal through the pillars of light streaming in the windows: silhouettes fat and lean, major and minor, limping, striding, slouching, swinging briefcases, dangling backpacks, towing wheeled suitcases, in twos and threes, or weaving through the crowd, alone. None of the silhouettes ahead is swaying. None of them is carrying a duffle. None of them is dangling a book at her hip and holding her place with a finger. Kevin can no longer see his slinky seatmate, Ms. Joy Luck Club, the girl in the camisole, the girl with the tattoos, the girl who walks like Lynda.

On the concourse Kevin allows himself only one glance at a dangling television, where a soigné, cheekboned überblond on Fox mouths silently over a banner that reads, with characteristic subtlety, 666: IS THIS THE END? Christ, thinks Kevin. Then, worried that he's going to see the round, abstractly familial face of the Other Kevin once more, which will only rattle him further, he resolves not to look at a TV again, not until he's back home in Ann Arbor. He has enough to worry about, and anyway, he's on the ground in Texas, and Austin doesn't even have a subway. Get thee behind me, Osama.

In a men's room halfway down the concourse Kevin micturates, his nerves thrumming like wires. As relieved as he is to be on the ground and not in pieces all over central Texas, he's still anxious about the interview this afternoon. He's taking a flyer here, after all, applying for a private-sector job he picked almost at random out of the back pages of *Publishers Weekly;* to his astonishment, they responded by inviting him down to Austin for a brief interview, rather than interviewing him over the phone. "We'll pay for your ticket," said the woman on the phone, Patsy something of Hemphill Associates, whoever they are, and Kevin was too surprised to ask if maybe they could put him up for a night in Austin. He knows that businessmen and women fly twenty-four hundred miles roundtrip in a single day all the time to take an hour-long meeting, but this is sort of new in Kevin's experience. Still, here he is, twelve hundred miles from home at 8:30 in the morning, draining his bladder into a Texas urinal, with no luggage or traveler's checks, just his interview suit, a little extra cash in his wallet, and a pair of e-ticket boarding passes. Welcome to the global economy.

His middle-aged bladder at last more or less empty, he shakes, tucks, and zips up. Then he takes off his jacket again, carefully, and hangs it on a hook as he washes his hands and face. The dazzling white tiles of the lavatory are studded with colorful intaglios of Texas iconography—an armadillo, a cactus, a bright green jalapeño pepper—and the Muzak here isn't Muzak, but Texas swing: Asleep at the Wheel, playing "Miles and Miles of Texas." Kevin was a record store clerk once, back in the age of vinyl, at Big Star Records in Ann Arbor, and peering at his dripping face in the mirror he remembers how, whenever it was Mick McNulty's turn to pick the music, it was always Asleep at the Wheel, until everybody on the afternoon shift knew all the words whether they wanted to or not, or could imitate the singer's sleepy bass-baritone drawl. "Ray Benson's a genius," McNulty'd say in his own sleepy, midwestern mumble, "the new Bob Wills." McNulty had a gift for stating the obvious about an artist as if it were revealed truth, though everything he knew was culled from the liner notes. Kevin blots his face with a couple of paper towels, then runs the damp towels under his collar and over the back of his neck. He lifts his jacket off the hook and watches himself in the mirror as he puts it on. Meanwhile the goddamn song penetrates his lizard brain: "I saw miles and miles of Texas"—now it'll be stuck in his head all goddamn day—"Gonna live here till I die."

Where's McNulty now? he wonders as he steps out onto the echoing concourse again. Whatever happened to McNulty? Back when Kevin knew him, McNulty had been in his early forties, a tall, slope-shouldered guy with a round little belly and a slouching, easy, keep-on-truckin' walk. He had wispy blond hair turning already to gray, which he kept short like a Beach Boy's, and heavy-lidded eyes, and his manner was part aging stoner and part aging athlete. Improbably, for his age and general lassitude, he was the best player on the Big Star softball team, where he played first base with his glove on one hand and a cigarette in the other. Somehow, whenever the ball wafted into his general vicinity, he managed to pull it into his gravitational field by sheer karma, reeling it into his mitt without even stepping away from the bag. Then he'd put the smoke between his lips, throw the ball unerringly wherever it needed to go, take a drag on his cig, and return to his original slouch. He could make a double play without even losing the ash from his Marlboro. Not a great employee, though, Kevin recalls. McNulty took fewer shifts at the register than everybody else because the manager knew he'd screw up every third or fourth transaction. Instead he spent a lot of time restocking, which he did very, very slowly, with obsessive but idiosyncratic accuracy, lingering for ten minutes at a time over a particularly difficult decision.

"Fairport Convention," he'd say. "Not really rock. Not really folk." He'd shake his head slowly. "I just don't know."

"The sixties were very, very good to Mick," the manager told Kevin once, when they were taking a break in the alley behind the store. Though the circumstances of the observation strike Kevin as ironic now—they had been sharing a joint at the time—the disjunction between the remark and its context went unnoted back then. In a hip, regionally famous, independent record store in Ann Arbor in the late seventies—long gone now, of course, strangled by the chains and the Internet and iTunes—reliability and even competence weren't necessarily the first things you looked for in an employee. Entertainment value counted for a lot, and McNulty had entertainment value to burn. During the long reaches of slow, midweek, midsummer days when Big Star was nearly empty, Kevin would stand with McNulty behind the counter or in the back of the store by the jazz section, and McNulty would smoke and slouch and, from the depths of a heavy-lidded midafternoon coma, relate fantastic stories from his youth.

Like the Battle of Bertrand Russell. In 1960, McNulty had been stationed at Althorpe Air Force Base near the east coast of England, and one day the base had been besieged by the Campaign for Nuclear Disarmament, the gate stormed by the cream of the British left: doughty old pacifist women wearing sensible shoes and wielding signs; ruddy, strapping vegetarians who wore socks with sandals and sported fantastic beards like William Morris; humorless, porcelain-skinned Communist girls in black turtlenecks; their scrawny boyfriends with unkempt hair and toggle coats covered with badges; reedy academics in woolen waistcoats and baggy trousers; and in the vanguard the elfin philosopher himself, a wave of white hair atop an elegant black overcoat. The assault had all the menace of a warm spring rain, but the base went on full alert anyway, with klaxons blaring and jeeps roaring everywhere and all personnel recalled to duty. Except for McNulty, who was off duty at the time and didn't hear the klaxons because he was in his favorite spot at the far end of the runway with his shirt off, vainly trying to get a tan from the pale English sun. As the base, unbeknownst to him, hustled to repel the gentle barbarians of the CND, McNulty alternated between dozing and reading *Naked Lunch* and watching B52s lumber over his head.

"*Naked Lunch*," he'd said, his eyes almost shut. "It was a new book at the time." And Kevin, who was twenty-two or twenty-three when McNulty told him this story, almost swooned with admiration. This was the apotheosis of cool for him, and it still is, even now, as he trudges middle-aged down the concourse in Austin past the food court. It had the all elements to awe an impressionable young dilettante of a bohemian bent: irreverence, contempt for military authority, catching some rays while bombers glided overhead, and the happy conjunction of William S. Burroughs and Bertrand Russell. Even better (at least for the purposes of the story), once McNulty's inadvertent dereliction had been discovered, he had been busted from sergeant back down to airman, and McNulty had turned the demotion to his advantage, boldly walking in uniform into a local pub (The Frog and the Scorpion) to chat up one of those intense, porcelain Communist girls, telling her that he'd offered up his career in the United States Air Force as a sacrifice to nuclear disarmament.

"Did it work?" Kevin had said, as wide-eyed as a kid. Daddy, tell me about the sixties again.

"God, yes," said McNulty, almost energetically, and he went into some detail about a bloodlessly pale girl named Judy who had led him through a twisting maze of redbrick houses set close as teeth, each street narrower than the last, the raw night air full of coal smoke, until they came to Judy's bedsit, where they took off their shoes and crept up the stairs past her landlady. In her tiny, unheated room they grappled silently on her narrow, swaybacked bed while she whispered to him about Althusser and Lukács and E. P. Thompson and he tried to peel off her black turtleneck. She consented at last, not so much out of lust as out of a grim determination to show that she wasn't bourgeois, but even so she dug her ragged, bitten fingernails painfully into his shoulders whenever she thought the bed was creaking too loudly. She had a point, McNulty told Kevin; the floors were so thin they could hear the landlady snoring directly below them, but once again McNulty made lemonade and turned Mrs. Allenby's honking to his advantage, murmuring to Judy that as long as her landlady didn't *stop* snoring, they were probably all right. Soon McNulty was balling—that was his word for it, *balling*, Jurassic-era hipster slang—in that lovely, loose-hipped American way the English girls loved (said McNulty).

"But my mind wandered," McNulty told Kevin, "it always does when I'm balling, I can't help it." Propped up on his strong American arms over the self-consciously ardent Judy, he started to think about the names of the streets they'd passed on the way to her bedsit: General Gordon Road, Gallipoli Lane, Sebastopol Row. "Nobody celebrates their own military disasters like the British," McNulty said, and he told Kevin he'd begun to laugh, right there in the saddle, as it were. Judy looked more puzzled than hurt, perhaps she wasn't used to laughter during sex, McNulty didn't know, but he said "Sebastopol" out loud, puzzling her even more, and to make it up to her he began to thrust in a breathless, galloping, Tennysonian rhythm — *half* a league, *half* a league, *half* a league onward, *forward* the Light Brigade! Judy went stiff as a two-by-four when she came, her eyes wide, her lips a wordless *O*, and for an awful moment McNulty thought he'd killed her or something, because at the same moment, eight feet below, Mrs. Allenby stopped snoring, and in that instant he seemed to be the only one in the house with a beating pulse. Then Judy melted with a whimper, Mrs. Allenby began to trumpet again, and McNulty collapsed happily in Judy's pale, undernourished arms. Afterward, she explained Gramsci's theory of hegemony to him while he stretched out and lit a cigarette and silently recollected how the French called an orgasm *le petit mort*. Into the valley of death rode the six hundred, thought McNulty, blowing smoke rings at the oppressive floral wallpaper and trying not to laugh.

That's the coolest story I ever heard, Kevin thinks, and it occurs to him with a pang that he's older now than McNulty was then. Trudging around the gleaming glass cube of the airport's newsstand, instinctively ignoring the alarming headlines, Kevin wearily wonders if admiring McNulty has done him any good at all. Back in his twenties, it had never occurred to Kevin to ask what a guy McNulty's age had been doing working for four dollars an hour in a record shop, where even the manager was fifteen years younger. Kevin cringes at the memory, partly out of pity for McNulty — who knows where he is now, he'd be in his late sixties at least — and partly out of fear that he, Kevin, may not have much more to show at fifty than McNulty did at forty. He has a much better job than McNulty ever did, of course, and a mortgage and a retirement plan, and good friends he's known since his Big Star days and before. But no kids, no *career*, really, no overriding passion in his life, and an ex-girlfriend who at long last heaved him over the side to have children with a man younger than Kevin — and certainly no happy memories of balling English Marxists and being the first American in Lincolnshire to read *Naked Lunch*.

GROUND TRANSPORTATION declares a sign, and a fat arrow points to the left, where Kevin joins a narcoleptic conga line shuffling toward the down escalator. The line is watched by a fierce-looking, heavily armed young woman in camouflage fatigues, another harbinger of Orange Alert. She's a Hispanic girl with a lot of Indian in her (thinks Kevin), a woman warrior, an Aztec Amazon. She stands with her legs apart, her black jump boots tightly laced, a semi-automatic pistol bulging at her hip. She holds her ugly black automatic rifle diagonally across her chest, the corner of the butt propped on her shoulder, the fierce muzzle pointed at the marble floor. Her fine, inky hair is drawn tight into a bun under her beret, sharpening the raptorish edge of her cheekbones and her nose, making her black-eyed glare even fiercer. While she may be a reservist or a National Guard, this young woman is a real soldier, this woman is no McNulty, she's no irreverent, Beat-reading shirker, probably no seducer of earnest young Englishwomen (though you never know). No, in work and in play, this young woman is clearly all business; this girl is on the job. This girl would empty a clip into Bertrand Russell without a second thought.

Even for an Ann Arbor liberal like him, Kevin's glad to see the young woman, especially today. Four days after Buchanan Street — funny how quickly a name becomes iconic and needs no further explanation, like Watergate or Guantánamo — there are no bleeding hearts on public transportation, and he's grateful for the guard's sacrifice in that dutiful way mandated by the White House, network anchormen, and country music stars. But even so, Kevin wants to know, is this the best use of her time? Wouldn't she be more effective patrolling the perimeter of the airport in a jeep, looking for suspicious characters in rented cars, dusky and not-so-dusky guys watching planes take off and land through binoculars? Shouldn't she be looking for wired-up bottles of shampoo in checked luggage? Mysterious vials of white powder? Stingers in the grass? Not to tell you your job, soldier, I'm just saying, if something's going to happen, is it really going to happen here, in the terminal? Then the soldier swivels her head and meets Kevin's gaze, and Kevin jerks his eyes away.

And nearly stumbles getting on the escalator. The corrugated step splits under the soles of his shoes, and he shuffles back and catches himself on the rubbery handrail. But when he glances back, the woman warrior is already watching someone else. Kevin sighs and descends into the cool, gray atrium of baggage claim, into a magnifying, mall-ish echo of voices, an oceanic murmuring. A diffuse crowd mills around the steely hippodrome of a baggage conveyer, and for a moment his heart lifts at the prospect of catching another glance of Joy Luck and her tattoos. But she was already carrying her luggage; she's long gone by now. Kevin feels like a movie director riding the camera crane down into a crowd scene — he was a film major once, for half a semester — John Ford or William Wyler chewing the stem of his pipe, his feet dangling from his trouser cuffs and showing a pair of tartan socks and a little pale shin. This gives Kevin the momentary illusion of control, the feeling that he could bark at the crowd below and they'd all look up at him as one, waiting for direction. Hey, maybe he's even some *young* director, a veteran of hip-hop videos making his first feature, a chunky white kid in a Raiders jersey and a vast pair of cargo shorts and a backward ball cap, watching his milling extras with a critical eye and calling out, "Where's our star, yo? The fuck's my leading lady? She in this shot, or what?" Ms. Joy Luck in the role of Lynda — Lynda *à la plage,* Lynda on the railing. "She's in her trailer, Mr. Quinn." *Mister* Quinn — Kevin likes the sound of that. "Well, go ask her if she'd like to join us this morning, dog.

We're losing the fucking light." But as the crane descends, the people below become less and less foreshortened, less and less under Kevin's control, until with a gentle bump the escalator deposits Kevin sole to sole with his own dim reflection in the dully gleaming floor. Now he's at eye level with everyone else, just another arriving passenger, just another guy in the crowd, just another extra in somebody else's movie.

He passes through the sliding doors into his first real embrace by the Texas heat. It's not so bad; the air presses warmly against his skin, that's all. Plus he's in the shade of an overpass, under a ceiling of massive rectangular beams held up by squat, square pillars of dirty white concrete. The Texas sunlight leaks in from the far ends, where the passenger pick-up lanes curve beneath the overpass. Vehicles coming out of the glare dim as they roll into the shade, a slow parade of SUVs and pickup trucks inching over speed bumps and braking impatiently for the crosswalks. Beyond a median, shuttle buses with broad foreheads line up nose to tail like baby elephants, and beyond that rises the cliff face of the parking garage, each pier embossed with a big, five-pointed Texas star, just in case the armadillo tiles in the men's room and Asleep at the Wheel over the public address have left him in any doubt as to where he is.

Truth is, he feels like he's not just in another state, but in another country. He knows no one in Texas; the folks waiting to see him this afternoon have never laid eyes on him. And no one in Ann Arbor even knows he's here. He could hardly tell the folks at the Asia Center where he was going, so he took a personal day—annual checkup, he told Mira, the center's administrative associate and his immediate superior—and to be on the safe side, he didn't tell any of his friends, either. Even Stella doesn't know he's gone. Especially Stella. He plans to be back in Ann Arbor by eleven p.m. tonight, and Stella won't be back from her sales conference in Chicago till late tomorrow. Unless the folks today offer him the job and he decides to take it, no one will ever know he was here. When he was a young backpacker, feeling invulnerable and immortal, he'd loved the thrill of knowing that he could step off a cliff in Donegal or fall down a sinkhole on the North York moors and no one would ever know what happened to him. But now his anonymity pierces him like a hook and hauls him up short. It's not too late, he thinks, I could go back inside, change my ticket, and be back in Ann Arbor by midafternoon.

He realizes that he's stopped walking. Other passengers step around him, the little wheels of their suitcases clacking over the joints in the pavement. He hears the mutter of the PA, first in English—"Due to heightened security, knives are not allowed on planes"—and then in Spanish—*"Debido a la seguridad aumentada, cuchillos no se permiten en los planos."* The guttural grind of buses, the hiss and squeal of brakes, the slam of car doors reverberating off the concrete all around. A tepid breeze full of diesel exhaust brushes by him, and Kevin realizes he's not even *in* Texas yet. The airport doesn't count; it's only an island in an archipelago nation of glassed-in atolls where everybody speaks a sort of English and lives off warm cinnamon buns and day-old turkey sandwiches.

He joins the pedestrians funneled into the crosswalks by concrete security barriers. (Just because you're on the ground, says his lizard brain, doesn't mean you're safe.) Under his clothes the sweat prickles out of his skin. At the median he joins the queue at the taxi stand, behind a large woman in a broad-beamed pair of jeans and a voluminous shirt who is talking to herself in short, disjointed bursts and with much frantic gesturing. There is nothing in her hands. Time was, on the Diag in Ann Arbor where the homeless congregate, Kevin would circle around someone talking to herself in public, but now everyone does it. He feels aged by the fact that he's still surprised to see people conducting phone conversations in public.

"I know that," the woman says. "Don't *think* I don't know that." From behind, Kevin watches her shake her helmet of hair. "Listen, I've been saying ex*actly* the same thing." She lowers herself into the next cab. "Doggone it, Pearl, that's what *I've* been saying." She's shaking her head as the cab pulls away. "Dog*gone* it, Pearl."

Kevin approaches a green Chevy Lumina with JAY'S TAXI printed unceremoniously along the side; the cabbie's already reached back to open the rear door.

"Luggage?" he says hoarsely, peering through the purple tint of his aviator glasses. A long, gaunt face. Scooped-out cheeks, pale, slack skin.

"No," says Kevin. He lifts his knee to slide into the seat and the cabbie says, "Close that trunk for me, willya, bud?"

Kevin pushes back from the car and walks around to slam the trunk with both hands. Then he slides grumpily into the backseat of the Lumina—the meter's already running, he notices—and the cab starts to roll even before he's pulled the door shut. That's when he sees Joy Luck in the crosswalk, swaying up to a shuttle bus with her duffle on her shoulder and the paperback dangling at her hip, her finger still holding her place.

"Whoa," Kevin says involuntarily, and the cabbie hits the brake. Kevin rocks forward, and the door slips from his hand and bangs all the way open.

"You okay?" The pale cabbie levels his gaze at Kevin, an edge of irritation in his voice.

"Yeah." Kevin reaches for the door again. Up ahead Joy Luck stands her duffle on end and shares a smile with the shuttle driver, a bull-chested Hispanic with his uniform shirt tucked into bulging bicycle shorts. He slings the duffle up into the shuttle, and Joy Luck pauses at the door, one long leg bent on the bottom step. She twists her hair one-handed off the back of her neck, just like Lynda used to. Oh Lynda, Lynda, Lynda, thinks Kevin, where are you now?

"Meter's running, sir," says the cabbie. "We comin' or goin'?"

"Go," says Kevin. He lunges for the door and slams it. Joy Luck is swallowed by the shuttle as the cab hauls away from the curb.

Kevin's more aware of the noises a car makes when he's not driving: the crepitation of tread against pavement, the throaty roar of acceleration, the galloping slap — *thump-thump, thump-thump* — of tires over the joints in the road.

"Where we headed?" The cabbie watches Kevin in the rearview mirror. The AC vents are whooshing; the dispatch radio spits unintelligibly; voices on the car radio mutter in an unidentifiable language, something rapid-fire and vehement. The meter ticks relentlessly, and the dull red numbers already register $2.75. Pasted across the dash is a SEMPER FI bumper sticker in scarlet and gold; a small medallion, silver and black, dangles from the rearview, twisting in the breeze of the AC. Kevin finds one end of the seat belt and digs for the other in the crack of the seat. It's not too late to go back, he's thinking, it's not too late to get on the shuttle with Joy Luck, or even to offer her a ride in his cab, anywhere she wants to go, his treat. She's hooked him somehow and she's holding the other end of the line, and any second now all the slack will be played out and he'll be yanked like a tuna right out of the cab. Then he snags the blunt end of the belt and claws it two-fingered out of the seat, and the cab shoots out of the echoing cavern of the underpass into the light. Even behind the tinted windows of the taxi, Kevin squints against the Texas glare. *Thump-thump,*

thump-thump go the tires. The line tugging at his heart tautens and snaps. Too late.

"Downtown," says Kevin, yanking on both ends of the belt until they connect. "One Longhorn Place." Three twenty-five, and they haven't even left the airport yet. Together Kevin and the cabbie ride in a Lumina-shaped bubble of dank air-conditioning, the air tainted with the farting of the dispatch radio and their own mild, mutual ill will. Kevin notes the cabbie's dirty white hair combed straight back over a sun-reddened bald spot, his raggedly trimmed beard, his long-boned arms, his big-knuckled hands on the wheel. He wears a faded Hawaiian shirt that hangs off his shoulders as if off a wire hanger. Kevin pulls out his sunglasses.

"Street address?" says the cabbie.

Kevin grunts and reaches into his jacket for his notebook; he sets the sunglasses on the seat. The details of his interview are buried in the middle, of course, and he hunts past grocery lists; Stella's cell number; instructions on how to jump a battery; Stella's e-mail; prices for a new battery; directions to a brunch in Dexter; a list of chick-lit authors Stella wants him to read, none of whom he's ever heard of; a Michigan license number for a red Toyota pickup, he can't remember why; Stella's cell number again, this time in her own hand; a list of cities where he'd be willing to live, none of which is Austin.

"Ummm," he says, stalling, "is there a Congress Street?"

"Congress Avenue?" Kevin can hear the smirk in the cabbie's voice. "I reckon I can find that."

Kevin gets right away that asking for Congress Avenue is like asking for Times Square or Picadilly Circus. He lowers the notebook for his first proper look at Texas, a rolling, yellowish savannah under a cloudless sky. Miles and miles of Texas. The sky really is bigger here, though it isn't the deep cerulean you see in Michigan this time of year; even this early in the morning it's bleached like an old blue sheet left out in the sun. There's too much light for the sky to soak up and it glitters everywhere, off the cars in long-term parking, off the light standards bent at the neck over the roadway, off the pavement itself.

"You from up north, right?"

"Ann Arbor." Then he adds, thinking the name may not mean anything this side of the Mississippi, "Michigan."

"Go Blue," drawls the cabbie. "You here for a meeting, right? Just for the day?"

"Job interview." The dangling rearview medallion twists this way. It's a pair of nestled black-and-white spermatozoa, yin and yang.

"My next guess. No luggage, that's how I can tell."

What are you, Sherlock Holmes? Kevin nearly says, mouthy as a New Yorker, but his midwestern reticence buttons his lip. A Michigander can be every bit as prickly as a New Yorker, just not out loud. The midwesterner's credo: keep it to yourself.

"What's the job?" says the cabbie. "Don't mind my asking."

Kevin never knows what to do with his hands in a taxi—fold them in his lap? Cross his arms?—and he lays them flat on the seat to either side. Thus he rediscovers his sunglasses, and he puts them on. The bleaching glare becomes a warm, amber, sunset glow. WELCOME TO AUSTIN reads a sign, silver sans serif against limestone.

"I'm not sure," he says. Another midwesternism—someone asks you a question, it's impolite not to answer, even if you don't have one.

"Oh yeah?" Guy's watching him again in the rearview. "Kind of a mystery job, or what?"

"Well, no, the *job's* not a mystery," says Kevin, at once eager to explain and hating the eagerness in his voice. "It's an editing job, they're looking for an editor."

"Oh yeah," says the cabbie, knowingly. "Like a proofreader, that kind of deal?"

"Well, there's a lot more to it than that." He hates the defensiveness in his voice, too, but the cabbie's touched a sore spot. For the last twenty years, Kevin's made his living as an editor at the Publications Program for the Center for Asian Studies at the University of Michigan, the last eight as the Pubs Program's executive editor, and even now, after all those years and all the monographs he's acquired, edited, designed, copyedited, proofread, and marketed, he still has a hard time getting anyone to understand that editing is a *profession* and that he is a *professional*. Too often, when Kevin has been introduced as an editor at the university, he's had to append so many qualifications that it sounds like he's backpedaling. No, he doesn't work for the U of M Press. No, he's not an academic himself. No, he has no background in Asian studies—or any interest either, though he'd never say that. No, he doesn't speak Japanese, Chinese, or Korean. No, he's never been west of the Golden Gate Bridge. And no, he has no final say over what the Pubs Program publishes—that rests with the publications committee, the publications director, and the center director, all of them academics in Asian studies, and all of them as amiable and collegial as scorpions.

"Oh sure," the cabbie's saying. "You gotta find the books and read 'em and all that stuff, right?" They're on an access road now and the ride is rougher, the tires thumping arrhythmically over potholes and cracks. They pass a low, mean, flat-roofed building called Club Vaquero, whose sign features a silhouette of a big-assed, big-titted woman with a wild mane of hair. It's the same sort of business he sees around Detroit Metro, but here the light's sharper and dustier, the bold colors of the sign both brighter and bleached somehow. Here, in this steeply angled light, even shade is for rent, Kevin notices, as they pass a private long-term parking lot where travelers can leave their cars under enormous blue canvas pavilions.

"That's right," says Kevin. *And all that stuff*—guy doesn't know the half of it. Much of the job experience Kevin's acquired over the years isn't the sort you can put on a résumé. His only credential is an utterly useless bachelor of General Studies from Michigan—he never did settle on a major—but he has a frigging Ph.D. in bureaucratic savvy, with another fifteen years of painstaking postgraduate work in the survival skills of the midlevel university staffer. So far he's survived eight different directors of the Asia Center, five pubs directors, and two dozen iterations of the pubs committee. He knows the taxonomy of academic rank the way a physicist knows the periodic table, and he knows the infinite gradations of academic condescension the way an oenophile knows Bordeaux. As recently as five years ago, when he was already running pubs, one pubs director, a Napoleonic little poli-sci professor, introduced Kevin to a new pubs committee as the Center's "editorial assistant."

"Executive editor, actually," Kevin said, giving his official title.

"Of course," said the director with an insufferable wink, as if humoring an eight-year-old. An equally insufferable murmur of laughter went round the table, and Kevin simply swallowed his rage. For one thing, it wasn't like he had any choice, and for another he had broken his own rule, which he had written out years before on an index card and taped to the slide-away typing table on his old Steelcase desk. KYMS read the card. Keep Your Mouth Shut.

"If you want to understand the workings of an academic department," a slightly less condescending pubs director, a Marxist with a graying ponytail and a leather jacket, had once told Kevin, "study *The Sopranos*." To which Kevin nearly replied, "If you want to understand the life of the university staffer, study *The Remains of the Day*." But he knew better not to. Even with a Marxist—perhaps especially with a Marxist—you KYfuckingMS.

But there's a limit, thinks Kevin, which is why he's sitting in a cab in Austin, Texas, this brilliant Monday morning, on his way to a job interview when everybody at the Asia Center back in Ann Arbor thinks he's gone to the doctor. The muttering on the car radio, which he thought was something foreign, suddenly resolves into English, spoken rapidly and forcefully, in the unmistakable manner of talk radio. "Buchanan Street," he hears the radio voice say, using the already-iconic shorthand. "I mean whattaya do with people like that?"

"Freakin' animals," says the caller, in a tinny cell phone voice. "Round 'em up, is what I say."

Could you turn that off, please? Kevin almost says, but doesn't, because he's afraid of drawing the cabbie's attention to the subject. But not to worry, the cabbie's not listening, the cabbie's off on another topic of his own.

"You know, a few years back?" the cabbie's saying, speaking up over the radio and the noise of the car. "I had an idea for a book. It was when I was in rehab? This'd be eight, nine years ago, I was sitting out on the patio, you know, thinkin'. I'm a deep thinker sometimes, I just like to sit and *think*. Anyway, I was wondering, what if we're all just computer programs? I mean, this goes against my beliefs—I'm a Buddhist? Since 1969?—but I was just thinkin', what if we're all just computer programs, and the world's not the world, you know, just some computer programs runnin' into each other?"

"Huh," says Kevin. The cab muscles its way, engine straining, across three lanes of freeway traffic toward an exit. Kevin rocks in his seat and steadies himself with a hand on the window. The glass is warm to the touch.

"Then a coupla years later, that *Matrix* movie comes out? Before I had a chance to..."

"Yeah, you shoulda jumped on it," Kevin sighs.

"Yeah, I reckon." The cabbie's narrow shoulders rise and

fall. "But it's okay. It's not my kinda thing. I prefer your classic themes, you know, the classic struggle of good and evil. Like *Blade*. Or them *Rings* movies. You know?"

Kevin's not really listening anymore. He's tuned out the cabbie and the ranters on the radio, watching through the windshield for the Austin skyline, but all he sees are giant airport hotels on a bare, treeless ridge, looking gaudy and flimsy, fodder for some apocalyptic Texas tornado that will reduce them to kindling, suctioning splintered lumber and shredded drywall into the bleached sky like straw. And I want to move here, Kevin thinks, I *want* to put myself in the path of that biblical weather, I *want* to endure the blistering heat and the titanic thunderstorms. Seven months ago, in the crepuscular gloom of a Michigan November, leaving Ann Arbor had seemed like a pretty good idea. Especially after his inaugural meeting with Eileen Burks, the day she took over as the new director of the Center for Asian Studies. He knew her slightly already, as a member of the pubs committee and a rising star of the history department. He had seen her from time to time at the university rec center, where she came to run and he came to play pickup basketball two or three days a week on his lunch hour. She'd trot past him up the stairs in filmy shorts and a sports bra, sheened with sweat, and they would exchange a collegial nod. Kevin didn't delude himself — there wasn't a flicker of electricity between them, and anyway, he'd assumed she was gay — but even so, in the middle of his game, lifting his eyes from the slap and screech of the court to the running track above, he'd steal a glimpse of her at full throttle and admire her long-legged stride and the glide of muscles in her back.

Now she was his boss, and Kevin looked forward to a working relationship unpoisoned by testosterone. Male academics were as hierarchical as dogs, sniffing the assholes above them and snarling at the lesser mutts, and a mere staffer like Kevin was expected to roll over and bare his belly to anyone with a graduate degree. This unavoidable humiliation was compounded by the awkward fact that Kevin was the same age as or even, in recent years, older than most of the men he had worked for. A couple of the younger ones had even shown a moment of uncertainty—but only a moment, because arrogance and ambition always trump age and experience—when they realized that Kevin had been editing monographs for the center while they were still in high school. For his part, meetings like this made Kevin sympathize with Hillary Clinton, or even John McCain, at the spectacle of a seasoned veteran losing out to some jug-eared upstart.

But Eileen Burks was not that much younger than Kevin, and he knew from working with her on the pubs committee that she was brisk and straightforward. He also knew that she was more feared than respected, especially by the male junior faculty, who secretly considered her gender an unfair competitive advantage. And her grad students, a couple of whom had worked for Kevin as freelance copy editors, told him she was notorious for blowing off her office hours and taking her own sweet time reviewing dissertation chapters. Eileen Shirks, they called her.

Still, she'd always been pleasant enough to him, and coming into the director's office for their first meeting after her appointment, Kevin had helped himself to a seat before she'd offered him one. Thus he found himself sitting while she was still standing behind her desk, sorting through carpet swatches. After a moment Kevin made as if to stand again, but she cocked an eyebrow at him and said, "No, stay," like she would to a dog.

She continued to stand and sort through swatches while he delivered his little State of the Pubs Program address, complete with a spreadsheet printed out that morning from Excel. She scowled at the carpet samples the entire time he was talking, and when he offered her the spreadsheet she lifted her sharp chin toward a corner of the desk. He lay the folder gingerly on the desktop. The only sound he heard was a thin whine, which was all the good will and high hopes he'd brought into the office escaping into the air at a pitch that only he could hear. He also had the sinking feeling that the new carpet she was busy selecting was going to be paid for, at least in part, out of the publications budget.

"I've seen you at the gym," she said, still standing.

"Yes." Kevin brightened — she remembers me!

"I assume that's your lunch hour?" Still she wouldn't meet his eye, but instead glanced from a wine-red swatch in her left hand to a blue one in her right.

"Yeah," he said casually. "I play a pickup game with some guys two, three days a week."

"So," she said, laying down the blue swatch and picking up a bluer one, "the game itself lasts, what, forty-five minutes?"

"Maybe a little less." Uh oh.

"So by time you walk over there, change your clothes, warm up, play the game, shower —"

And sauna, thought Kevin, but he knew better than to say so.

"— and walk back to your office, that's what? An hour and a quarter? An hour and a half?" Still she wasn't looking at him.

"Come on, Eileen," Kevin said, collegially. "I see you at the gym all the time."

"I'm not on the clock." She let both swatches fall from her hands in disgust, and then said, with icy politesse, "May I call you Kevin?"

"Of course." He could feel himself dwindling in the chair.

"Kevin." Eileen fixed him with glacially blue eyes. "You're not salaried like I'm salaried."

His feet dangled above the carpet, his head shrank into his collar.

"Do we understand each other?" Eileen said.

"Perfectly," said Kevin, the Incredible Shrinking Man.

The meeting was over. "I'll look over your budget," she said as he walked, vibrating with rage, across the crummy old carpet to the door, "and we'll have a talk about it, soon." On his way through the outer office, he heard her call for the center's administrative associate.

"Mira!" cried Eileen. "Call Building Services. These can't *really* be the only swatches they have. These are just *unacceptable*."

Two minutes later, in his own office up under the eaves of Willoughby Hall, Kevin had dropped into his chair, slapped the latest issue of *Publishers Weekly* onto his desk, and begun to pore through the job postings at the back of the magazine. His *PW* subscription was like his long basketball lunches, a little perk he allowed himself on the Center's nickel, buried deep in a sub-sub-basement of Excel. The bitch slap he'd just received from Eileen wasn't the worst humiliation he'd ever endured from an employer—the manager at Big Star had called him "adolescent" to his face, and the speedfreak manager at Central Café had fired him for being too slow—but as he began to limn likely jobs with an orange highlighter, he decided that it was going to be the *last* humiliation. And it wasn't just petulance or wounded pride, he told himself. The state of Michigan was dying all around him, leading the nation in unemployment and mortgage foreclosures. The auto industry was in its last throes, Detroit itself slowly reverting to nature, Flint was such a wasteland no one but Michael Moore went there anymore. Five years ago, Kevin would have said that his own job was as secure as you could get without actually having tenure—the academics he worked for loved the idea of having their own little publishing unit—but now the legislature was cutting the money for higher education year after year, and the U itself was trimming budget lines in every department. Even his profession didn't look so secure anymore: young academics still needed to publish or perish, but now they could distribute their monographs worldwide instantly, and pubs programs like Kevin's were beginning to look as quaint as floppy discs or newspapers.

Reflecting on all this, Kevin highlighted an intriguing if mysterious ad from Hemphill Associates in Austin, Texas. Hemphill offered "innovative and effective outsourcing solutions" in booming Austin, according to their *PW* ad, and while Kevin's tender Ann Arbor heart trembled at the implications—wasn't it outsourcing that was killing the Michigan economy?—they did want a managing editor—to edit what exactly, they didn't say—for 20K more than Kevin makes now. He knew better than to think that the private sector would be any less stressful, but at least it would be straightforward, no-bullshit stress: meet the deadline, work under budget, earn your keep. The iron fist is there for all to see, without the velvet glove of "collegiality."

"It's all about chi, brother," the cabbie's saying. He lifts a big-knuckled hand off the wheel and flicks the yin-yang medallion with his fingernail. It spins, glittering: yin-yang, yin-yang, yin-yang. "Hot and cold," says the cabbie. "Moist and dry. Shit like that."

"What?" Kevin is suddenly alarmed. Did I say out loud that I work for the Asia Center? God forbid he should incite an exchange on Eastern spirituality with some half-crazy old Texas Buddhist, some self-taught syncretist who mocked up his own religion out of a split-backed *I Ching,* a dog-eared *Portable Nietzsche,* and a lot of Thai stick. Just like McNulty, Kevin thinks, and then his heart nearly hammers to a stop. What if this guy *is* McNulty? Austin's just the sort of place a guy like McNulty would wash up, kind of a Southern-fried Ann Arbor, an Ann Arbor with bigger portions. Hailfire, son, ever'thang's bigger in Texas. Guy's the right age, that dirty white hair could have been blond once, and McNulty had big bones and power-ful hands just like the guy's hands on the wheel.

But the cabbie's gaze behind his aviator lenses, framed in the rearview, isn't heavy-lidded, only watery and weak. And the name on the license, which Kevin can't read without leaning forward, is shorter than McNulty. And this guy sounds like a native Texan. In the mirror, his glance shows that he knows Kevin hasn't been listening. His skeletal shoulders sag. They ride without speaking, and as if to fill the awkward silence, the radio voices seem to speak louder, all on their own.

"Turns out one of these guys was a white guy," says the host, with a deep, old-school radio voice like Rush Limbaugh, or that Canadian guy who used to be on CKLW out of Windsor.

"Kevin something," says the caller. It sends a chill through Kevin to hear his own name on the radio in this context.

"MacDonald," says the Limbaugh clone, who adds, with leaden sarcasm, "Oh, *excuse me*, I mean 'Abdul Mohammed.'"

"They're calling it '666,'" says the cabbie, lifting his voice over the radio and raising his gaze to the rearview again. "You heard that?"

"What?" says Kevin, though he knows exactly what the guy's talking about. 666 said the Fox banner. IS THIS THE END?

"Last Thursday? All that shit in Europe?"

"Sure," says Kevin.

"They're calling it 666."

"Huh."

"Six bombings, on June 6."

"I hadn't heard that," Kevin says.

"They search you at Metro?"

"Sorry?" says Kevin. The cab has angled off the freeway onto a four-lane road between scruffy tin-roofed houses on the left, and on the right a new subdivision of oversized houses on freakishly green lawns. The meter's already up to $11.50.

"Fella traveling alone? No luggage?" The cabbie's rearview gaze interrogates Kevin. "They didn't take you aside and search you?"

"Yeah, actually," says Kevin. "They did." They'd wanded him, anyway. Does that count?

"Funny, you don't look Muslim." The cabbie drops his gaze to the road. "I mean, you're blond, right? Though that don't mean you're not a Muslim. I mean, look at that one guy in Buchanan, Scotland, or wherever."

Kevin's Irish and his Ann Arbor instincts kick in simultaneously, and at the same moment he glimpses the Austin skyline for the first time, blurred and dull like a painted backdrop, like the Emerald City of Oz. In between the squarish skyscrapers, Kevin glimpses thin, skeletal spires like radio masts. Then the road dips and the skyline sinks behind a screen of trees.

"You think they should search Muslims?" he hears himself say. "For being Muslim?" What does he care? He secretly believes the same thing himself.

"I'm just saying, you got all these guys blowing themselves up and a lot of other folks, too. I seen their pictures on the news, and they ain't Southern Baptists. Except maybe that Scotch guy, I don't know what religion they got over there." The cabbie's watching the rearview for Kevin's reaction.

Behind his amber lenses, Kevin is speechless. McNulty would never have been a bigot, but then who isn't anymore? Watching the display of mugshots on TV over the weekend, he had the same thought himself. He can't help thinking that if Muslims had been banned from Glasgow public transit, no matter what they looked like, no matter what their ethnicity, Buchanan Street Station wouldn't have become a charnel house. Sometimes, though, in order to be decent, you have to fight your own instincts, and at last he says, "A lot of Muslims died in those bombings."

He's only guessing, of course, he actually doesn't know if this is true. In Amsterdam, Berlin, and Paris, it probably is, but he doesn't know about Glasgow or Moscow. And how many Muslims are there in Bern? In the whole of Switzerland?

"Well, hell, search everybody then." The cabbie sounds peeved and resigned; he watches the road again. Christians, Muslims. Moist, dry. It's all about chi, brother. "It's only fair. I mean, why single anybody out, right?"

Why, indeed? thinks Kevin. Life goes out of its way to single you out, it doesn't need any help from the Department of Homeland Security. Take Eileen Burks, for example—five weeks after she lowered the boom on Kevin's lunchtime hoops, she collapsed in a seizure on the rec center running track. A few days after that she was diagnosed with an inoperable brain tumor. She returned to work for a few weeks wearing colorful headscarves like a fortune-teller, then went home for good to be nursed by her husband—Huh! thought Kevin—and by finals week, she was dead.

The Austin skyline pops up again behind the screen of trees, a little sharper this time. Kevin sees the narrow nipple of the Texas capitol dome. The skeletal masts are construction cranes, each one tall and spindly and one-armed like a carpenter's square; they hover over narrow tower blocks in various stages of construction, which rise in silhouette like the uneven bars on his stereo equalizer. Condominiums, Kevin guesses, counting five of them before the skyline dips out of sight again. Now the cab's rolling by an anonymous apartment complex, a herd of dirty-pastel boxes with peaked roofs like Monopoly hotels, their tiny balconies crowded with lawn furniture and Weber grills and potted plants. A limp banner slung between two palms—palm trees!—says $99 MOVE-IN and FREE CABLE. Never mind those pricey downtown high-rise condos, thinks Kevin, that's where I'd be living if I moved here, or someplace just as bleak and anonymous. At least at first. That would be my bicycle upended on a hook on the balcony, that would be my forlorn cactus hanging in the stifling heat. That would be my palm tree, sort of. Say he comes to Texas, say he sells his house in Ann Arbor right out from under Stella. What would freak her out more, her boyfriend moving to Austin, or her landlord selling the house? In the back of the cab Kevin closes his eyes. Stella—not now. He opens them again behind his sunglasses, sees nothing. That's assuming he could even sell the house on Fifth Street—he knows people who live in nicer parts of town, Burns Park or the Old West Side or out on Geddes Avenue, who have had their houses on the market for months. He'd be lucky to get what he paid for it. And what do houses cost in Austin? Today, even after the housing bubble's burst, probably more than he can afford. Christ, they're *still* building luxury high-rise condos here, even now. So, move to Austin and be a renter again. Move to Austin for a fresh start, and start from scratch. He can see Beth, his ex, bouncing one of her children on her hip and shaking her head; he can see the ironic twist of her lip, hear her saying, "At your age."

Kevin nearly groans aloud. He's on the very horns of the dilemma, damned if does and damned if he doesn't. Six of one, as his father used to say, and half a dozen of the other. Settle for senescence, or pull his life out by the roots. It's not a real choice so much as it's a choice between two equally risible clichés: Count Your Blessings, or Follow Your Dreams. The fact that his dilemma is so predictable, so utterly and laughably banal, doesn't make it any less pointed. Look it up (\mid-lif kri-ses\ *n*) and find a line drawing of Kevin Quinn in a sporty little convertible, with his perky young—well, young*er*—girlfriend beside him, her hair loose in the breeze. See MIDDLE-AGED MAN.

"I think that's Longhorn Place right there," says the cabbie, and Kevin leans forward for his first real view of Austin's skyline, shockingly close. It's like a beautifully crafted and intricately detailed miniature for a film, shot in slow-motion to make it look massive. It's the city of the future from *Metropolis* or *Things to Come,* all it needs is a silvery biplane buzzing between the buildings. Several of the older buildings are neo-deco, broadchested and square, the color of concrete and topped with blunt little Masonic pyramids. Sprouting like saplings among them are three or four construction cranes like T squares and more new condo towers.

"Which one?" Kevin says.

"The tall one," the cabbie says, "with the pointy top."

One building is much taller than the others, sleek and narrow and straight-sided, clad in ice-blue panels; on top, four sharp steel and glass triangles tilt toward each other, like a pyramid left slightly ajar, or a grasping, four-fingered mechanical claw. The tower glints icily in the sun, looking slightly unreal and miniature and menacing, the lair of a Bond villain. Kevin can imagine those four sharp panels slowly flowering with an almighty Dolby rumble and the doomy, minor-key blare of horns to reveal the blunt red foreskin of some rogue nuclear warhead purchased from bristle-jawed Russian mobsters, all set to hoist itself atop a billowing gush of smoke and dazzling flame. Or perhaps it's a corporate Barad-dûr, the four icy panels concealing a huge, fiery red eye with a slit like a cat's, ready to cast its baleful light on the hapless residents of Austin.

"There's your future, huh?" says the cabbie.

"My future?" Kevin's leaning far enough forward to read the cabbie's name now. *Kidd* it says on his license, next to an overlit ID photo that makes him look drunk.

"If you get the job," says Kidd the Cabbie. "That's where'll you be. Top of the world."

Kevin sits back against the stiff seat. Top of the world, ma. That's a different movie altogether, with a different sort of explosion. He's not so sure he likes that. He sees the fare click over to $15.75.

"Huh," he says.

The traffic thickens as they cross over a freeway, and the cabbie breaks off to watch the road. Kevin closes his eyes, but that only seems to make the radio louder, and he hears the caller—the same one? A new guy?—declare, "Nuke Mecca, dude. I'm serious. Nuke it from the air."

"C'mon, caller," says the Limbaugh-resonant voice. "Do you really think that would solve anything?"

"It's like *Aliens,* man," sputters the caller. "You try to kill 'em one at a time when they come at you, you're never gonna win. You gotta wipe out the nest."

"No no no," the host is saying over this—apparently even talk radio ranters draw the line at genocide—but even so, Kevin says, without opening his eyes, "Could you turn that off, please?"

"What's that?" says the cabbie.

"The radio. Would you mind turning it off?"

The cabbie says nothing, but a moment later the voices are gone. Kevin sways in the darkness behind his eyelids, bumping against the padding under the window. He senses the cabbie's anger, but fuck him. The older he gets, the less eager to please Kevin feels. After Eileen Burks went into the hospital, Kevin returned to his basketball lunch as soon as he was sure he wasn't going to run into her at the gym anymore. He was guilty over this for about ten minutes, until he missed an easy layup and one of his teammates, a perennial ABD with a single ginger eyebrow like a werewolf, snatched the ball away and growled at Kevin to get his head in the fucking game. Then, when he heard she had died, he thought—for one awful moment for which he's still ashamed—I win! He didn't say it out loud to anyone, thank God, but even so his conscience began to throb, and a moment later he was wondering, win what? The right to ninety-minute lunches? Freedom to read *PW* at my desk? The woman's dead, and I'm still just the pubs guy, the editorial assistant, and if the economy continues to tank, maybe not even that. When times were fat, when Lansing was generous, he had an assistant editor and a typist, and now he's lucky to get a work-study student for ten hours a week to help with the packing and shipping. He doesn't even hire freelancers anymore, but does most everything himself. The only line left to cut in his budget is himself.

Kevin can feel the car turning, and he opens his eyes. Now they're galloping over the expansion joints of a six-lane bridge, *thump-thump, thump-thump, thump-thump,* the Austin skyline looming ahead. Over the low rail of the bridge he sees glassy, greenish water, and away to the left, beyond more bridges in diminishing perspective, low green hills dotted with pastel boxes and red roofs, picked out by the sun and blurred by haze. More condos under construction rise along the river, the lower floors already sheathed in glass, the middle floors in bright yellow Tyvek sheeting, the top floors open to the sky and sprouting tufts of rebar. Straight ahead the squashed ziggurats loom on either side, and Congress Avenue rises slowly between them toward the state capitol at the far end. The dome has a creamy limestone tint, like French vanilla, while the slanting morning light casts a curl of shadow in the scoop of the capitol's portico. Even though the office towers are taller, some trick of perspective or some quality of the morning haze makes the capitol look improbably massive, like a predator resting on its forearms and lifting its bald head.

As they reach the end of the bridge, Kevin notes the fare—$20.50! Jesus H. Christ! He should've taken the shuttle with Joy Luck. He has to press his temple to the warm glass of his window to see the blue claw now. The giant tower—Long-horn Place, the Ernst Blofeld Building, Barad-dûr, whatever—is partially obscured by a couple of intervening buildings, but its four panels still look as if they're just about to rub their cold, razor fingertips together.

Twenty-one seventy-five now. Hurry up, thinks Kevin, mentally inventorying the cash in his wallet. In front of the ziggurat on the right, a businesswoman in a tight silk suit—a bust like a figurehead and an ass like two dogs fighting in a sack—marches up the sidewalk; Kevin can almost hear the sharp tattoo of her heels. Her black hair's drawn painfully back like the Aztec warrior's in the airport, and Kevin turns to watch her as the cab passes. The red nails of one hand swing a chic leather brief-case down by the straining, shimmering fabric of her thigh, while the claws of her other hand press a cell phone to her ear. She's fleshier than the fierce girl in the airport, but she has the same bronzed aspect, the same raptorish nose and cheekbones, the same brown-eyed gaze fixed fiercely ahead. She might be the Aztec's mother, and he realizes that he would never see a woman like that striding up State Street in Ann Arbor. Hispanics are pretty thin on the ground in Ann Arbor, and even a full professor at Michigan wouldn't dress like that. You might see a tailored suit on a law professor—Kevin was glared at once on the Diag by Catherine MacKinnon, who caught him staring at her—or on an administrator, but even they don't march with the triumphal strut of this magnificent woman. He's both thrilled and terrified to think he might find himself in the same city, maybe even in the same office, with a woman like that.

Then the cab crosses an intersection and he's blinded by the sunlight falling steeply down the side street. He shields his eyes. A shadow sweeps alarmingly across the windshield and he presses his temple to the window in time to see one of the construction cranes sweeping overhead, a massive red pulley swinging free. Up ahead, between the looming office towers, the state capitol gets smaller the closer Kevin comes to it.

"Longhorn Place," announces Kidd the Cabbie, as he pulls up to the curb.

The cab accelerates away, and now Kevin's well and truly in Texas, feet firmly on the pavement. The breathless heat is a pressure around Kevin's chest, as though he were wrapped in bandages. He associates this kind of heat with the dull rattle of locusts on a August afternoon in Ann Arbor, when the trees droop over the sidewalks and stunned midwesterners wade through the humidity as if through water up to their waists. But here the heat is *noisy* — Kevin's startled by the grumbling of buses, the rush of cars from light to light, the reverberating tap of hammers from a construction site. The heat clings to his skin the way it never does in Michigan; even in the long shadow of the office tower, he feels the sweat prickling under his arms, and it's not even ten o'clock in the morning! Meanwhile a trio of trim young Texans in crisp khakis and unwilted polo shirts, carefully barbered behind their mirrored sunglasses, laugh at something one of them just said. An enormous Hispanic guy lumbers by, not a drop of moisture on his bulging jowls or even the hint of a stain on his Tommy Hilfiger jersey. Even the fat people here don't sweat, marvels Kevin.

Could I live in heat like this? he wonders. Could I stand the constant glare? The light bleeds even into the blue shadow of the office tower, and the autumnal tint of his sunglasses doesn't seem to make much difference. He wades through the heat toward the wide bank of doors, where a middle-aged guy in a billowy shirt and a gaudy tie, his slacks cinched under his paunch, dangles a Diet Coke by four fingers of one hand and lifts a smoke mechanically with the other. His whole face puckers as he inhales, and the smoke just hangs around his head in the heat. He catches Kevin looking at him and shrugs, Kevin doesn't know why. He looks like he's about to speak, too, but then both men are distracted by the tattoo of a woman's heels, and both gazes swing to watch the Aztec in silk striding toward them. Three blocks after Kevin first saw her, she's still on her cell, briskly nodding and staring fiercely ahead, swinging her chic little briefcase alongside her flashing thigh. Even in the tower shadow the sheen of her skirt glimmers, and she strides purposefully toward the lobby doors at the same time as Kevin, who's still wading in molasses. The three of them — paunchy smoker, silk-suit Amazon, sweating Michigander — are drawn together as if by a seine, the eyes of the two men tracking the dogfight bustle of the woman's silken backside. Without breaking stride she lifts her briefcase hand to grasp the door handle, and both men galvanically leap to open it for her. The midmorning smoker is closer and quicker, grinding the pavement with the ball of his foot and hauling at the ice-blue door with his cigarette hand. The door opens with a satisfying bass *pong* like the ring of a bell, and Ms. Silk Suit, for all her bulk, shimmies through the widening gap. Her tight little bun of black hair swivels as she rewards the smoker with a glance, and the smoker shrugs again and hauls the door wider for Kevin, who trots after the woman into a gust of frigid air.

The sudden clamp of cold air almost stops him gasping in his tracks, as if he has plunged into freezing water. The lobby of Barad-dûr is air-conditioned like a meat locker, instantly chilling the sweat on his forehead and tightening his skin. He pauses to fold his sunglasses into his jacket pocket, and Ms. Silk Suit's magnificent booty recedes from him under the cavernous vault of the lobby, two stories of creamy marble and herringbone teakwood panels and mild, recessed lighting. He

follows her progress in the blue-green diamonds of the glittering marble floor, where her bustling, inverted reflection meets
the sharp points of her heels and toes. Even with the teak to
soak up the echo, her heeltaps sound like pistol shots, and the
fat treads of his own shoes—a pair of $150 Cole Haan oxfords
which Beth would have told him were too young for him, but
Stella said were *way cool* when he tried them on at Macy's in
Briarwood—send a screech ricocheting against the unbroken
curve of the ceiling, into the elevator alcoves, and off the tall
outer windows.

He has no idea where he's going—his interview isn't until
two—but he can't resist following the lubricious vaudeville
bump-bumpa-*bump*-bumpa-*bump* of Ms. Silk Suit's old-time
ecdysiast strut, and when she stops short and laughs out loud, he
nearly blunders into her from behind. She cants all her weight on
one sharp heel and tosses her head back; her laugh, an artificial
squeal, bounds all around the lobby, followed by a rapid burst
of Spanish. Kevin swerves around her and heads for the security desk, a rounded island off to one side of the lobby. On the
teak wall above the desk a flatscreen TV is showing Fox News,
still blazing its red BREAKING NEWS tab as a pair of commentators
in split screen—heavy woman with blond hair, balding dark-
skinned man—dissect the life of the late Kevin MacDonald, or
so Kevin assumes from the white-on-red caption: HAS JIHAD COME
TO SCOTLAND? He can't tell for sure because the sound is turned
off. He turns to the prow of the security desk, where a wide-
screen video monitor shows a bright Texas flag waving endlessly
against a flawlessly blue sky. Across the flag in red letters is the
message TOUCH TO START. Ms. Silk Suit's heeltaps are receding,
the echo of her Spanish diminishing, and by time Kevin turns
she's already disappearing into an elevator alcove.

"Help you?"

Kevin snaps to attention, wide-eyed and blinking. "Pardon?"

"Can I help you?" The security guard, a bored black woman, looks up from behind the breastwork of the desk. She's bulky and dark, with gold hoop earrings and blood-red lipstick and a sleek, striated helmet of ebony hair. She wears a white shirt buttoned to the top with no tie, and a shapeless blue blazer. "Who you looking for?" she says, folding her hands.

Kevin wonders, is this standard operating procedure, her demanding so abruptly that he account for himself, or is it an Orange Alert thing? Do bombings in Glasgow subway stations resonate all the way down to lobby guards in Austin, Texas? Is there a photo display of suspicious types taped to the inside of her desk? Is one of them a picture of the Other Kevin, aka Abdul Mohammed, prompting the frowning guard to suspect all Celtic-looking guys who wander past her desk? Moments like this, Kevin turns motormouth. Maybe it's an authority thing, or just his midwestern eagerness to please, but he always explains way more than he needs to.

"Um, yeah, right, I'm Kevin Quinn? From Ann Arbor, Michigan? Just flew in this morning for a job interview with uh...that is, I have an *appointment* here, this afternoon with uh, just a sec, with uh..." Christ, he's spaced on the name, so he digs inside his jacket, pulls out notebook, sunglasses, pen, everything but the letter, which he fumbles out at last. "Hemphill Associates?" He lifts his eyebrows at the woman, tries to fold the letter back into his pocket.

"Touch the screen, sir."

"Beg pardon?"

She lifts her chin. "Big screen there? With the flag on it? Touch it."

"Ah." The letter's all sharp corners for some reason and won't go back in his jacket, so he folds it roughly and thrusts it into a side pocket. "Of course." He touches the screen, the flag vanishes, replaced by a luminous green alphabet. Kevin touches the *H* and up pops HEMPHILL ASSOCIATES, 52 ONE LONGHORN PLACE.

"Fifty-two?" Kevin peers hopefully at the guard.

"Fifty-second floor," she enunciates slowly, as if to an idiot. "Right up at the top."

"Do I need to sign in or anything?" He plunges into his inside pocket again, feeling for his pen. "Do you need to call them and let them know?"

The look on her face, and he lets the sentence dwindle away.

"No, hon." She slowly shakes her head. "You just go on up. When's your appointment?"

Kevin grimaces sheepishly. "Two?"

"Two!" The woman puckers her lips. "You a little early, ain't you?"

"Well, I just flew in from Ann Arbor? Michigan?" Motormouth again. "I wanted to make sure I knew where I was supposed to go."

"Mission accomplished." The security guard refolds her hands.

Kevin tiptoes slowly back from the desk.

"So," says the guard, "you got someplace to go for the next"—she glances to the side—"four and a quarter hours?"

"Ah." Stops. "Thought I'd, you know, take a walk on the riverwalk or something."

The guard goggles at him. "*River*walk!"

"No?" Kevin balances on his toes.

"You in Austin," says the guard. "Ain't no riverwalk here."

"Oh."

"Riverwalk, that's San Antonio."

"Ah." Even in the arctic AC, Kevin can feel himself blush.

"What *we* got is a hike and bike trail." She says "hike'n'bike" like it's one word, and her eyes glide up and down. "But you ain't exactly dressed for it. I tell you what." She unfolds her hands and places her pink palms on the desktop and slowly presses herself up. The security desk stands a little higher than the lobby floor so that she looms over Kevin. "They's a Starbucks right across the street." She slices the air with her hand, across the lobby. "Have you a cup of coffee or whatever, buy you a newspaper, figure out someplace cool to go till"—she smiles—"one thirty, anyway."

Kevin gives her a double thumbs up and backs away. "Starbucks."

"Starbucks be catty corner, right across the street." She slices the air again.

Kevin pivots on his squeaking toe, nearly blunders into the paunchy smoker, who's slouching back to work across the lobby. They do a brief Alphonse and Gaston dance, side to side in the arid air, and the smoker gives Kevin another shrug. Kevin sidles round him at last, through his faint tang of tobacco, then hits the blue door with both hands—*ponggg*—and steps out again into the heat.

Crossing Sixth Street, Kevin passes through a cascade of sunlight. An old, round clock on a lamppost, some restored relic of old Austin, tells him it's coming up on ten; he instinctively starts to set his watch back an hour, then decides not to. He's here less than twelve hours, might as well stay on Michigan time. Now he's got the walk signal, so he veers left across Congress. In harsh sunlight at the end of the avenue, framed by office towers and a row of exhausted trees on either side, the capitol looks shrunken now and faded, like a dusty model in a museum, the Texas statehouse rendered in matchsticks or sugar cubes. Everybody else in the crosswalk—more khaki businessmen, a pair of bare-shouldered girls in camisoles and jeans (oh, Joy Luck! Oh, Lynda!), a shuffling homeless guy in a huge Minnesota Vikings T-shirt and sandals worn down to his bare heels—each moves more slowly than Kevin, metabolically adjusted to the heat. Halfway across, he pauses and takes a deep, calming breath of the viscid air. He's sticky under his shirt; sweat prickles out of his hairline. Starbucks is just ahead, the cornerstone of a big, blond, vaguely deco office block. Against Kevin's inclination—progressive, Ann Arbor, buy local—Starbucks looks like a haven, and instantly he's irritated at himself for falling for the mendacious seduction of the chain store: reassurance, familiarity, a spurious homecoming. Near campus in Ann Arbor there's a Starbucks at the corner of State and Liberty, a ninety-second walk from his office in Willoughby Hall, but he's never been inside, not once. Of course he's been in other Starbucks—who hasn't?—but this one supplanted his favorite local coffeehouse, Gratzi, where he used to run into other university staffers every midmorning and midafternoon, where behind the counter the cute girl (not always the same one) remembered his preference, where he bought his coffee every day in his own Gratzi cup, which collects dust now on his desk up under the eaves of Willoughby, as forlorn an artifact as a big-haired troll or a pet rock. So he won't set foot in the State Street Starbucks, out of his stubborn and admittedly useless nostalgia for the funky Ann Arbor of song and story—which, to be honest, he only caught the last act of. He came to Ann Arbor too late for Tom Hayden at the *Daily,* for the Black Action Movement strike, for the torching of the ROTC building, for John and Yoko at Crisler Arena, for the first Hash Bash where a state representative fired up a spliff in public on the Diag right in front of the A-Squared pigs, man. Kevin was half a generation behind the town's heyday, but even so, during his undergraduate days and his years as a waiter and a record store clerk, he caught the scent of it like the last April Fool's whiff of Panama Red. He heard all about it after work from old-timers like McNulty and others, sitting breathless at their every word over pizza in Thanos Lamplighter (gone now, too), over a beer at the Del Rio (also gone), or over a plate of fries at the Fleetwood (still there, but not the same), listening to world-weary guys only five years older as if they were flinty old veterans of the Ardennes or Guadalcanal.

These days, where he buys his coffee depends on which way he walks to work. Say he comes up behind the Union and along Maynard under University Towers and through the Arcade, in which case he stops at Expresso Royale and carries his cardboard cup steaming along State Street. That's his route on cloudy days. When it's sunny, though, he walks all the way up Fifth to Liberty, then straight up Liberty into the rising sun, because one of his favorite sights in the world is the view up Liberty on a brisk autumn morning or on a mild spring one, under a scrubbed blue midwestern sky, with the Michigan Theater's black marquee soaking up the slanting light and Burton Tower printed against the sky at the end of the street, limned in astringent northern light. Here, at least in Kevin's youth, was once the epicenter of funky retail Ann Arbor, the heart of elvendom on earth. Within two minutes walk of each other were three world-class record stores: Liberty Music, where a middle-aged clerk in a tie escorted you to a booth so you could listen to six different recordings of Shostakovich's Fifth; hip Big Star, where if you didn't know what you wanted, you were in the wrong place; and Discount Records, where Iggy Pop once worked. And five bookstores: overlit Follett's, fussy Charing Cross, overstuffed David's, bohemian Centicore, and the original, independent, prelapsarian Borders, whose clerks had to pass a book test to get the job and afterward strutted the carpeted aisles as arrogant as Jesuits. "Romance novels? We don't sell *romance* novels. Why don't you try Walden's? At the *mall*."

Not to mention a shoe store and a barbershop and a pharmacy and a five-and-dime and a declining old midwestern department store. And two Greek diners, a gourmet hot dog stand, a vegetarian restaurant, a five-dollar steak house, a Japanese restaurant, two or three sub shops, an ice cream shop, a cookie shop. And Drake's, where he first met Beth, not long after he started at the Asia Center as an editorial assistant. As an undergraduate Kevin had never liked Drake's, with its sickly green decor and cramped, unpadded, wooden booths, unupholstered since 1935. The place survived on nostalgia—misty alums on football Saturdays sharing a pot of weak tea, and the rest of the week homesick undergrads who'd been steered there by sentimental parents or older siblings. By Kevin's time it was cluttered and dark, the entryway heaped with boxes, the counter lined with dusty jars of mummified candy. The owner, an enormous, bald old man, bloodless as a slug, his trousers pulled up to his armpits, slumped immovably on a stool at the end of the counter, doing God knows what; Kevin never saw him stir or speak. And the portions were small: a Coke came in an eight-ounce glass, more crushed ice than cola, and a sandwich was a flavorless scoop of something pink in mayonnaise on wilted lettuce and dry white bread, cut into fussy little triangles skewered with toothpicks. Worst of all, you had to fill out your own order ticket with a blunt pencil stub and then try to catch the attention of one of the sullen girls behind the counter.

The first time Kevin laid eyes on Beth, he vainly waved his ticket at her as she whispered with another haughty Drake's girl, the two of them casually ignoring him. He hadn't been in Drake's since he'd graduated, despite working only a block away at Big Star for years, but this was his first week at the Asia Center, and he figured, if you work at the U, you might as well eat at Drake's at least once. Plus the girls behind the counter were usually cute, despite the shapeless green tunics they wore, and looking back at that first exchange of glances now, as he steps up out of the crosswalk at Sixth and Congress in Austin, Texas, it comes to him as a much-belated revelation that it was probably her Drakette hauteur that drew him to Beth in the first place. At last she pried herself away from her conversation with the other girl—Debra, Kevin learned later, shorter but equally cute; how different would his life have been if *she*'d come to take his order?—and carried herself down the narrow aisle behind the counter as imperiously as a runway model, tall, clear-skinned, wide-eyed. She fixed him with her gaze and, without a word, plucked the ticket from Kevin's hand with two fingers and pivoted away, her hair swinging. Kevin, who fell easily and hard, felt a tingle that started in his balls and reverberated all the way up his spine and down his arms to the tips of his fingers. And she knew it, too. When she called him back to pick up his sandwich, she thrust her lower lip at him and slid the plate across the counter with a surly clatter, fixing him with her gaze again as if daring him to say something. He started back to his booth, heart pounding, then turned and carried it back to the counter, where he lifted his finger to get the tall girl's attention. She exchanged a look with Debra—what does this idiot want?—and carried herself down the aisle to Kevin again. She placed her long, pale fingers on the countertop, canted her hip, and lifted an eyebrow.

Kevin leaned on the counter, extracted a toothpick, and peeled back the top of one quarter of his sandwich. He frowned sheepishly. "Is this tuna?" he said.

For a long, thrilling moment she locked eyes with him, then

deigned to drop her gaze to the pink clot of chunky paste he'd laid bare. They both regarded it for a moment, then looked at each other again. "What do you think it is?" she said.

"I'm not sure."

She angled her head, as if to regard the sandwich in a slightly better light. "Why don't you try it and see?"

"Well," said Kevin, keenly aware, in his peripheral vision, of the lovely Debra trying not to laugh, "if I'm not sure what it is, I don't think I want to put it in my mouth."

"I see," said the tall girl, speaking with faux gravity. She pinned him once more with her gaze, and Kevin thought he might never breathe again. Then he felt the sandwich moving under his hands as the girl slid her hand across the counter and hooked one long, pale finger over the lip of the plate. She never took her eyes off Kevin's as she pulled it toward her. The little flap of bread Kevin had lifted curled slowly back down.

"Only one way to find out," she said, and she picked up the triangle of sandwich and bit it in two. Kevin gasped and stood up straight. Debra turned sharply away, lips pinched bloodlessly shut, while the enormous old man on his stool at the end of the counter sat as immobile as the Buddha. Meanwhile the tall girl deliberately masticated one-eighth of Kevin's lunch, gazing pensively upward.

"Well," she said, and paused to push a loose fleck of whatever back into the corner of her lips with her pinky, "it tastes like tuna to me."

Kevin watched the girl in astonishment. His blood was singing. Finally she swallowed and replaced the uneaten half of the triangle with a little pat and nudged the plate back toward Kevin. Who picked it up, fastidiously turned her teethmarks toward him, and put the rest of the section in his mouth. As he swallowed it whole, nearly choking on tuna and his own laughter, the girl smiled and turned a dark shade of red.

"You're right," he said, tapping his sternum lightly. "It is tuna."

Thus began a battle of wills that lasted thirteen years. God knows it was her Drakette hauteur on display that day in the bath when she told him she was leaving. Several years ago now, and it still stings as if it had happened this morning. It stings right now, in fact, along with the sudden, unbidden taste of tuna in the vault of his palate. Beth, what hath thou wrought? If it weren't for her, he probably wouldn't be sweltering outside Starbucks on a street corner in subtropical Austin. He touches the taste of tuna with the tip of his tongue, the taste of Beth. The men in khakis are walking toward the capitol, still laughing, while the camisole girls sway fetchingly in the other direction, as hearty as Minoan dancing girls. On a bus stop bench a couple of Hispanic girls hunch together in matching fast-food uniforms and consult a sheet of paper. One girl runs her blunt finger along a line, syllable by syllable, while the other girl reads haltingly, "Heh, hel-lo. Wel-come. To. Pancho's Taco. Ex, express. Hah, how. May I. Heh, heh, *help* you?"

"*Bueno.*" The first girl nods and moves her finger down a line. "*El siguiente,*" she says. Next.

Kevin veers to the steps of Starbucks, which are guarded by a street musician—dirty gray beard, sleeveless T-shirt, pale upper arms—standing against the wall, aimlessly but vigorously strumming a guitar. Is he in his forties, Kevin wonders, or his fifties? He's so frayed by bad luck it's hard to tell, but even in the heat Kevin feels the cold breath of time brush them both. The guy's eyes shift mournfully from side to side, following passersby, and Kevin wonders, what memory is *he* trying to erase? Is he another McNulty, hitting rock bottom? The man's scuffed guitar case is closed at his feet. Perhaps he's forgotten to open it, or maybe it's a rare example of *ars gratia artis*. Kevin steps past him up into the coffee shop.

The morning rush is nearly over, and the place is disheveled — napkins on the floor, crumbs underfoot, a plastic stirrer in a little pool of coffee on the countertop. Behind the counter a black girl with dreadlocks hangs on a lever at the espresso machine, and a golden-haired white girl with a stain on the breast of her company tunic slouches at the register. They each have that end-of-shift, thousand-yard stare that Kevin recognizes from his own days in retail. Meanwhile a rotund young woman with a buzz cut works up a sweat changing out the trash bins; she yanks a bulging bag of cups into the air and twists it sharply, as if snapping its neck. The only person ahead of Kevin is a businesswoman in her late thirties — no, thinks Kevin, looking closer through her makeup at the crinkled corners of her eyes, mid forties. She steps aside and smiles at him. "I'm waiting," she says.

Kevin needs to wash the taste of Beth out of his mouth, so he orders an iced tea.

"With legs?" says the golden blond, absently pressing a key on the register.

"Pardon?" Starbucks is like its own country, you have to know the silly argot.

"To go?" says the fortysomething woman, in a rising, Texas singsong. "'With legs' means 'to go.'"

Cheerleader, thinks Kevin. Sorority girl, marketing major, party girl once upon a time. A Republican, maybe, but a fun Republican, a *sexy* Republican. He smiles and she purses her lips — nicely red, but not too red, sort of business sensual — which Kevin finds mildly flirty, and instinctively, in spite of himself, before his forebrain can get a word in edgewise, he looks her up and down. She's pretty, formerly pert, now softening around the edges. Brown hair pulled back with a ribbon the same color as her lipstick. Wide eyes, cornflower blue, a little too made-up for close range, but just right (Kevin's guessing) for a presentation in front of a boardroom. Snug jacket, but not too snug, knee-length skirt. Matching nail polish, no wedding ring. A little wide in the hips, but nice calves. Kevin's appraising gaze glides back up to her face, and she blushes and looks away, over the counter, at nothing in particular.

"Yes," says Kevin, his forebrain at last wresting the controls away. "I mean, *no*."

"What?" says the barista. The middle-aged are *so* boring.

"It's for here," says Kevin. "No legs."

The girl slouches away for his legless tea, and Kevin smiles sidelong at the woman and says, " 'With legs,' huh?"

She smiles warily.

"What am I," says Kevin, "Damon Runyon?"

Her eyebrows lift, her smile widens ever so slightly, and Kevin can see his joke sailing deep into the cornflower blue yonder, without striking a goddamn thing. She doesn't get it, she's just being polite—guess they never did *Guys and Dolls* at Texas A&M—and the embarrassment pulls tight as a wire between them until it's blessedly snapped by the dreadlocked girl reaching over the counter with the woman's steaming paper cup of venti double cap something, and Kevin and the woman turn from each other with relief. Kevin pretends to study the baked goods under glass next to the register while the woman taps across the floor in her sensible heels. One of the pastries, he notices, is a madeleine. Good thing he didn't make a joke about *that*.

Kevin watches the rotund barista swipe at tables with a damp cloth until the blond barista returns and money and iced tea are exchanged across the retail membrane of the countertop. Kevin hesitates, buys a muffin, and then juggles cup, muffin, and change past the love seat where the businesswoman, legs crossed, displays her excellent calves and swings her toe as she consults a very thin, very stylish silver laptop. A little wheeled suitcase waits at her feet like a faithful dog. She glances up, he glances back, they look away, and Kevin makes for a small round table in the corner, still gleaming from the stout barista's damp cloth. He sets his tea and muffin before him and takes a bentwood chair where the businesswoman is at the corner of his eye. The windows look up both Sixth and Congress, offering a wide, 270-degree vista of the street corner, like Captain Nemo's observation bubble in the *Nautilus,* only instead of flashing schools of fish and lumbering manta rays, he sees just beyond the glass a gangly man in a sleeveless, gold lamé minidress teetering on platform heels, his calves and thighs ropy, his arms veined and hairy. He wears badly applied lipstick and a crooked wig, a Bizarro Mary Tyler Moore circa *The Dick Van Dyke Show.* A frayed evening bag that doesn't quite match the minidress dangles from the guy's knotty forearm.

Kevin sips at his tea. For the first time he notices the rhythmic world music over the speakers—women singing wordlessly over drums—and he hears the padded tapping of the businesswoman at her keyboard. Out of the corner of his eye he notes her pretty pout as she concentrates on her e-mail or whatever. He nibbles the muffin; it's sweet, but still Beth troubles Kevin like indigestion, a sour backwash that his snack can't extinguish. Bitch, he thinks, without saying it out loud. Thirteen years they were together, until he was forty-six and she was thirty-eight, and the day Beth told Kevin she was leaving him, he had been lying in the bath in four inches of warm water, a little square of sodden gauze on the loose flesh around his belly button. Somehow, during a walk out at Silver Lake the weekend before, he'd gotten poison ivy. Not on his arms or ankles where he usually got it, but on this little patch of belly. How it got there, under the elastic of his shorts, he had no idea, but now he had a reddened cordillera around the crater of his navel, a little archipelago of pustules that oozed clear liquid, and he was lying in warm water with a coffee cup full of warm Domeboro's solution on the edge of the tub. It was a black promotional cup, the logo for *The Sopranos* with its semi-automatic *R* printed in red on the side. He was reading an old Martin Amis novel with a black cover as he soaked, and every couple of pages he carefully balanced the split-spined paperback on the edge of the tub and ladled another teaspoon or two of warm, grainy solution onto his belly, little white flecks of powder catching in the soaking weave of the gauze. When Beth came in, Kevin looked up cluelessly, thinking she'd just come for a leisurely chat, and for a moment he contemplated lunging out of the tub, damn the cup and the book, and dragging her in, jeans and T-shirt and all. He'd done it before, though not for years, but why not? She looked good, and, if he did say so himself, he didn't look too bad for forty-six, even stretched out pale and hairy in lukewarm bathwater. His arms and chest were firm and his legs strong, though he'd got this little pouch just below his belly button that he couldn't make go away, no matter how many crunches he did. But Beth perched on the lid of the toilet, the toes of her Birkenstocks pressed to the tile and her heels lifted, her knees primly together. She leaned forward with her forearms together and her long fingers tightly laced and looked intently at him for a moment before she reached over the edge of the tub and lifted the book out of his hand. Then, without preface, she said, "I'm pregnant and it's not yours."

He lay there with the water cooling all around him, the gauze turning chill on his slack belly. As he listened to her—"I'm in love with him, and I want to have a child with him"—he reached for the cup. Instead of ladling out more solution, he put the wet spoon on the open book, where a wet patch instantly soaked into the page, and he poured the rest of the cup slowly over his belly, watching the milky water pool in his navel and overflow through the thicket of hair into the bath.

Then he set the cup back on the edge of the tub, very carefully so that it didn't make a sound, and he turned it around so that he was reading the *Sopranos* tagline on the other side, in fat red letters against the black ceramic: FAMILY. REDEFINED. Beth said she wouldn't make a fuss, she didn't want his money or his house, and she hoped he wouldn't make a fuss either. "I want a child," she said, squeezing her fingers bloodless, "and you won't give me one." Now the urge to grab her and haul her into the tub was almost overwhelming. Not out of rage, Kevin thought—though he couldn't be sure—but for some reason he felt an overpowering lust for her that he hadn't felt in a couple of years. He really wanted to fuck her right there in the tub, the way they used to, in a rubbery tangle of limbs and bumping elbows and splashing water. There was probably some evolutionary reading of his desire—she'd been with another man and now his genes needed to reassert their dominance over the guy who'd knocked her up, or some Dawkins shit like that. But even knowing that, Kevin thought there was something irreducible and elemental about the emotion. It was what it was: she'd been with another man, and it made him hot. In the tub he'd been aware of his penis lolling, the black nimbus of hair at its root shifting like seaweed in the sloshing bathwater. God help me if it gets hard, thought Kevin, because he knew that what would have been friskiness a few years before would be something close to assault now. Plus, even he could read her body language: toes and knees together, hands clenched into a single white-knuckled fist. His lust cooled like the water lapping his flanks and thighs, and he was filled with sorrow at the thought that he'd already made love to this woman, whom he used to love and maybe still did, sorta, kinda, for the last time.

Now, in Starbucks, slumped over his muffin, he's not the least bit aroused, just really, really sad. The morning sunlight pours through the window and across the table before him, warming his iced tea. The muffin has a scallop in it, though he doesn't remember taking a bite, couldn't even say exactly what kind of muffin it is. He's almost nauseous with melancholy now, and he pushes the dead muffin across the tabletop. He's angry, too, for letting this get to him, today of all days. It's been four years, for chrissakes, going on five, he has a new lover, a striking, high-maintenance woman even younger than Beth. And Beth—boy, has *she* moved on, she has a *kid* who's almost as old as their breakup. Even so, he's always pissed off when he stumbles over another hidden trip wire of regret. The insipid moaning of the women over the stereo only makes it worse, and the rattle of the businesswoman's keyboard behind him makes him want to snap at her. Still, he's sorry he ever called Beth a bitch, even silently. Then he sits up a little straighter in the chair because he's got nothing to be sorry for, goddammit, it's not his fault that sorrow overwhelms him, that's just middle-age, buddy, *everybody* regrets *something*. He and Beth were together for thirteen years, and that's a lot of emotional momentum, a runaway freight train rolling downhill, nothing but tanker cars full of toxic waste and high explosives, and sometimes he feels like he's tied to the fucking track.

"Excuse me?" trills a voice with a rising, singsong inflection. Kevin turns; the businesswoman is smiling at him. At this distance her makeup is just right, and his heart fibrillates with unexpected pleasure that this yellow rose of Texas is beaming at him over the screen of her silvery laptop.

"Do you know another word for 'regret'?" she says.

Wow, thinks Kevin, that's a little on the nose. Can former Texas cheerleaders read minds? Do they teach telepathy at Baylor? Outside the window, a school of colorful fish enters the crosswalk from each direction, sifting neatly through each other. Another couple of girls in tank tops stride away from him—do they travel only in pairs?—and Kevin turns back to the beaming woman.

"Regret, huh?" he says. "Sounds serious."

"That's just it," says the Yellow Rose of Starbucks. "It sounds *too* serious." She tilts her head. "I want to say, 'I regret the misunderstanding,' but on the other hand" — she tilts her head the other way — "I don't really think it was my fault."

"Huh." Kevin looks down at his muffin, sneaks a glance at the sunlit girls, but someone carrying a big green duffel bag is blocking his view. *Move,* he thinks.

"Business or personal?" He takes a nip of his muffin. Cranberry, that's what it is.

"Wellll," drawls the Yellow Rose, "*mostly* business." She really does have a rather fetching, crooked smile.

This should be easy, thinks Kevin, I'm an editor. A professional. This is my job, helping folks find the right word. He furrows his brow to show he's mulling it over, but what flashes across his eyeballs is *big green duffel bag.*

"I mean, I'm sorry he misunderstood?" says the woman, crinkling her nose, which is going a little too far. "But I'm not really *sorry?*"

The big green duffel bag is balanced on the shoulder of a tall, swaying Asian girl threading her unsmiling way through the knot of homeless and day laborers on the corner, neatly sidestepping the woozy stagger of Mr. Mary Tyler Moore. She sails by Kevin's window, just beyond the glass, and all the pagan priestesses on the stereo sing *alleluia!* Kevin nearly chokes on his muffin. O frabjous day! Callooh, callay! It's Joy Luck!

Kevin chases the chunk of muffin with a gulp of tea. The Yellow Rose is still talking but he's not listening; instead he's rising from his chair and shuffling like a zombie to the window.

"Uh huh," he says, splaying a hand against the warm glass and peering sideways up Sixth Street after Joy Luck. Her arm curls around the duffel, her head is neatly obscured, so that she looks like a hybrid creature, a land-bound hammerhead shark with a very sexy walk. But she keeps close to the building and after a moment all he can see is the butt end of the duffel before it too disappears. "Sorry," he says, pushing back from the window, leaving his palm print on the glass. "What was the question?"

The businesswoman has stopped talking, her bright red nails hooked over the upright screen of her laptop. Kevin's heart sinks at the sight: a frost has touched the Yellow Rose. She's seen what he was looking at; she's watched him levitate from his chair and stumble to the window, all the blood rushing from his head. Her bright mouth has crumpled, her eyes have hardened, and all at once she looks ten years older. It breaks his heart to see, and inwardly he lacerates himself even as his tongue stumbles uselessly in every direction at once.

"She's, uh..." He gestures at the window. "I know her from..."

The Yellow Rose's petals turn brittle in the chill. She spreads her fingers as if to say, *whatever*, none of *my* damn business.

"I know her father." Kevin's face burns as he sidles toward the door. But the businesswoman has withdrawn within her suit as if behind a rampart, so Kevin snatches his iced tea. Then turns back and grabs the muffin—at these prices, he's not leaving it behind.

"I'm sorry you misunderstood," Kevin says as he slips past the Yellow Rose, and she snaps her head back as if he's slapped her. "Just say that," he adds, gesturing at the laptop before he plunges out the door into the heat.

He hustles around the corner onto Sixth Street. Half a block ahead, without breaking stride, Joy Luck swivels the duffel from her left shoulder to her right, jogging a little like a sailor to hike the load up higher. The muscles in her arm, the glide of her shoulder blades, the little apple in the dimple of her back—all are nicely picked out by the sunlight pouring down Sixth from behind. Kevin feels a little surge of, well, joy.

"Nice," someone says next to him. Kevin pulls up short and instantly dances away from the wavelet of tea sloshing from his cup. He's still standing outside Starbucks, and from the window above the chunky barista glowers at him and rubs away the palm print he's left on the glass. It's not her speaking, but another shaggy homeless guy hunkered against the building, smoking a cigarette. No, not a cigarette—Kevin recognizes the sweet, resinous smell. The homeless man—cadaverous in T-shirt and jeans and an ancient tweed sport coat—watches Joy Luck walk away. He draws deep on the joint, then turns his dilated gaze to Kevin.

"Friend of yours?" he rasps.

"I know her father." He has no idea why he keeps repeating this lie, especially to strangers.

The guy cocks a bird-bright eye at Kevin and says, "O-kay. What's her name?"

Kevin laughs. In cannabis veritas. He weighs the cup in one hand and the half-eaten muffin in the other, and impulsively, as if propitiating some local deity, he offers them to the homeless man, who peers at them warily, then slowly takes the muffin and stuffs it in the pocket of his jacket. He waves away the cup. Up ahead, Joy Luck pauses at the next cross street, stoops to look right under her duffel, then sways into the intersection. Meanwhile, with grave hippie generosity, the homeless man offers the joint to Kevin with a smooth, palm-down gesture, the smoke pooling under his hand and rising through his fingers. He lifts his scraggy eyebrows and holds his own toke as he waits. For the tiniest increment of time Kevin considers it—in Ann Arbor, under the right circumstances, he wouldn't hesitate—and then a train of considerations rumbles by—strange city, Texas drug laws, job interview in a few hours—and he shakes his head subtly, as cool as the homeless guy making the offer. The international brotherhood of dopers. No thanks, bro. The homeless guy shrugs and gasps out a puff of smoke. Kevin starts up the street after Joy Luck.

"Go get her, dude," rasps the homeless guy.

What am I doing? thinks Kevin, treading on his own shadow. Who am I kidding? What am I going to do, strike up a conversation with her like some drunken Shriner? Hey honey, I'm only in town for the day, what's a fella do for fun in this burg, har har har? The very thought shrivels him, but he keeps walking. Cars pour west down Sixth toward the bright, hazy hills in the distance, but there's no other foot traffic, only Joy Luck and him. Get a grip, he thinks, she's twenty-five years younger, maybe even thirty. But so what? The first day he met Stella, in Expresso Royale, she told him she was twenty-nine. The fact that she lied about her age—he knows because after she moved into his rental apartment downstairs and started spending most of her nights upstairs with him, he snuck a peek at her driver's license and found out she was actually thirty-five—is sort of beside the point. Fact is, the look on Beth's face when he told her how old his new lover was—it was worth all the grief he knew she'd give him. Who cares if Stella's actually five, six years older? Whatever the actual difference, the gap in their ages is the running gag of their relationship, it's the grain around which their relationship formed.

"The Black Crowes" was the first thing she'd ever said to him, as they both waited in line at the Royale one bright spring morning. They'd been taking turns glancing at each other for the past minute or so, and at last she'd turned and caught him admiring her firm calves and the way she dangled her slim briefcase before her, her slender fingers linked through the leather handle. And what she said was "The Black Crowes."

"Sorry?"

She dipped her broad forehead toward him. It was a calculated effect, he knew it the moment she did it, but even so it worked and he leaned closer.

"The Black Crowes?" She shimmied a little in place. "On the stereo?"

Kevin lifted his chin and put on his listening face. One of the harried undergrads on the morning shift at the Royale was feeling retro this morning; the speakers were broadcasting "Brown Sugar," the first song Kevin had ever danced to, back in the Pleistocene. Before he could stop himself, Kevin laughed.

The young woman pursed her lips and narrowed her eyes. She had a mane of kinky, dirty-blond hair, barely restrained in a shaggy ponytail; clear skin pulled tight across a flawless forehead; a strong jaw. She was very slightly bandy-legged, accentuated by the boxy heels of her pumps. A black-and-white polka-dot skirt, wasp-waisted blazer.

"Can't a girl like the old bands?" she growled, and in spite of himself, in spite of her lovely narrow waist and strong-looking legs, Kevin laughed again.

"How old are you?" he asked her, before he had time to think.

"Twenty-nine?" she said, blushing. "What's that got to do with anything?"

"Sorry." Kevin brushed her elbow with the tips of his fingers. "It's the music. It's just…" He smiled. "You made me feel old is all."

She looked puzzled, but turned a little more in his direction. Kevin was aware without looking that the twenty-year-olds ahead of and behind them were rolling their eyes and exchanging smirks at this elderly flirtation, but fuck 'em. The young \'yeη\ n, pl: those on whom youth is wasted.

"The band's older than you think." Kevin lowered his voice

and gestured with his eyebrows into the aural space above their heads, where the song had reached the climactic moment when Mick and the lads chanted, "Yeah...yeah...yeah...*whoooo!*" The very point at which, in the sweaty, paneled, suburban basements of his youth, Kevin and his tube- or halter-topped partner, shaking their hip-huggers to the *thumpa-thumpa* Watts and Wyman beat, would chant along and waggle their hands in the air. "How come ya, how come ya *dance so good?*"

"It's not the Black Crowes," he murmured, inclining his head toward hers. "It's the Rolling Stones." Then he added, "The Black Crowes of their day," never sure how much a young person would know of the popular music of the Pleistocene. "Sort of."

"*I* know that," said the young woman, and she unlaced the long fingers of one hand from the grip of her briefcase, her nails a deep but not unprofessional shade of red, and playfully rapped his arm with her knuckles. "How old are *you?*"

Good question, thinks Kevin, trotting through the Texas heat after a girl who's even younger than Stella, a girl whose father he is old enough to be. Up ahead Joy Luck dashes on tiptoe across Sixth Street, the duffel bouncing heavily on her shoulder, her arm thrown out for balance, her sandals flapping loose of her heels. A block behind her Kevin crosses, too. She turns left down a side street, and when he reaches the corner, Kevin pauses to slug down the rest of his tea in one long, wobbling gulp. By now it's as warm as his sweating palm, it's like drinking some bodily fluid of his own, and as Joy Luck sways downhill toward the river, he tosses the empty cup in a trash can and plods after her. His shirt's wilting under his jacket, sweat courses along his sideburns and down the groove of his spine.

What will he say if he catches her? Will he say anything at all, or just watch her longingly from a distance, some cow-eyed, sweaty loser in a wilted suit? What if she recognizes him and asks him, point-blank, why he's following her? Does he even *know* why? Say he tells her it's because she walks like a girl he slept with for three months back in the eighties—Christ, that's even more ridiculous than simple, middle-aged lust. What would a young woman say to such an avowal? What *could* she say? Would she find it poignant or touching, or just pathetic? *Is* it pathetic? It makes him feel old just to think about it. This is way out of the ordinary for Kevin, he doesn't follow young women in strange cities as a general rule, but still he keeps walking. Certainly he expects nothing to happen. In Ann Arbor he knows the ground, has a clearer sense of where he has a shot and where he doesn't. Indeed, his flirtations in Ann Arbor, like that first morning in Expresso Royale, have paid off occasionally, though rarely as precipitately as they did with Stella.

"Let an old man buy you coffee," he'd said when they reached the counter, and "Brown Sugar" had segued into "Sway." Half an hour later, they had a dinner date, and that evening, during a pleasantly anticipatory meal at the Mongolian Barbecue downtown, where he took all his first dates, he got the Stella backstory: sales rep for a textbook company, just moved here from St. Louis, didn't know a soul, did he know of any apartments for rent? Funny you should ask, he said, not really thinking it through. Forty-five minutes later he was showing her the empty apartment on the ground floor of his house on Fifth Avenue. Where, up against a bare wall, in the dark, and against his better judgment, he agreed on the spot to rent her the apartment—"French doors!" she'd exclaimed. "Oh God, a fireplace!"—and then uttered not a word of demurral as she dropped to her knees on the newly revarnished hardwood floor and fellated him. Well, maybe it was the other way around, she blew him first and *then* he offered her the apartment—he's hazy on the details, he was a little drunk at the time—but either way it was an epic fellation. She took her time, she acted as if she enjoyed it, she had *technique*. Whatever warnings the Jiminy Cricket in his forebrain might have had about a young woman who was willing to blow her potential landlord on the first date were sluiced away in the patella-rattling rush of pleasure, and by his relief, considering where she was putting her mouth, that she hadn't ordered the bird peppers with her stir-fry.

The street before him descends toward the river between low, old, brick warehouses converted into bars and restaurants. A half-built condo tower looms over the end of the street, the giant crane above it sweeping as slow as a second hand. Joy Luck crosses an alley and sails up a raised sidewalk under an awning. Kevin jogs to close the gap, and suddenly a battered white van pulls out of the alley right in front of him, and a young driver with a jigging Adam's apple cranes over the steering wheel, looking both ways. Kevin dodges left to go round the back of the van, but it's too close to a telephone pole, and he finds himself nose-to-nose with an old red flyer, now faded to pink, stapled to the splintered wood—DOES MARX MATTER? Sponsored, Kevin notes, by the Intercontinental Socialist Alliance, six months ago, on the University of Texas campus. He sees flyers like this every day of his life in Ann Arbor, and over thirty years he's gone from a mildly guilty, dilettantish interest through grumpiness to eye-rolling bemusement. He can see the sparse crowd, most of them coreligionists of the speaker, and most of them, men and women both, fatally uncool: humorless, pedantic, puritanical little narcissists with burning eyes and a Talmudic grasp of infinitesimal ideological details. During Kevin's undergraduate years, people like this seemed like the vanguard of something, but now, after the Fall of the Wall and the Fall of the Two Towers and the Fall of Kevin's Fiftieth Birthday, a meeting like this seems as quaint as college boys in raccoon coats strumming ukuleles. Nowadays disaffected young men like the Other Kevin—slave of the Prophet, blessings be upon him—turn to actual religions for their ideology. Same sort of cheerless meetings, Kevin suspects, in the same sort of cheerless, overlit meeting rooms, only with fewer girls. Or probably no girls at all.

The van's driver guns the engine and lurches forward, all of six inches. Kevin bounces on his toes. "Come *on*." Somewhere the Intercontinental Socialists are laughing mirthlessly at his middle-aged longing—another instance, no doubt, of the cultural alienation of late monopoly capitalism. Or maybe some dark-eyed mullah is cursing Kevin's corrupt Crusader lust, quoting chapter and verse from the Koran. If only the Other Kevin had been luckier with girls, thinks Kevin, maybe he wouldn't have taken his frustration and rage out on the defenseless commuters of Buchanan Street. The only reason to go to meetings like that, in Kevin's day, was to meet girls, and if there aren't any girls, what's the point? In fact, the last time he went to a meeting like that was with none other than Lynda herself—Lynda *à la plage!* Lynda on the railing! He was still working at Big Star that summer, and she'd been a fairly regular customer, so he began flirting with her one afternoon as she diffidently flipped through the jazz section, clearly with no intention of buying anything, but slouching in her jeans and tank top over the record bin, bending back the toe of her sandal, pushing aside her strawberry blond hair with the tips of her fingers as she smiled sidelong at him. After some desultory conversation—"Are you into Sun Ra?" "Sort of"—she said she was going to a meeting that night, and would he like to come?

"What kind of meeting?" he'd said, as his Jiminy Cricket started jumping up and down in his brain, shouting, "Watch out! Danger! She's a Moonie! A Maranatha! A Young Spartacist! All she wants is your soul!"

"Oh, I dunno," she sighed. "Some nuclear freeze, pro-Sandinista, fuck Reagan kind of thing." With one hand she lifted her hair at the nape of her neck, exposing to Kevin the pale, expertly shaved scallop of her underarm. "I promised some boy I'd go, but I don't want to show up, you know, alone?"

"Sure," said Kevin, throttling Jiminy. "Cool."

Indeed, it was that same afternoon, shortly after she left, that Mick McNulty had told him of the Battle of Bertrand Russell, and he told Kevin he should definitely go with Lynda to her meeting.

"You ever see the usual guys who show up at those things?" McNulty said in his hipster mumble, politely expelling his cigarette smoke out the side of his mouth away from Kevin. "Scrawny vegetarians, man. Guys who bathe once a week, if that. Guys who wouldn't know what to do with a girl if one dropped in their lap." He squinted across the store through his haze of smoke, at something only he could see. "Tom Courtenay," he said.

"Tom Courtenay?"

"In *Zhivago,* man. You ever see that flick?"

"Sure," said Kevin.

"Yeah, *Dr. Zhivago,*" McNulty continued, slowly remembering. "Julie Christie's his girlfriend—Julie Christie, man!—but he has a hard-on for Trotsky."

"What are you saying?"

"I'm saying *you,* you're Omar Sharif, okay?" McNulty gestured with his cigarette, dragging tendrils of smoke through the air. "Take it from me, man, these political chicks are desperate for some red meat." He tapped Kevin meaningfully on his sternum. "So you go be Yuri Zhivago."

Kevin laughed, and McNulty shrugged and dragged the last out of his Marlboro. "You'll have to listen to some political shit," he gasped, "but so what? At least you don't have to tell her you love her."

And so, after hearing balalaika music in his head all

afternoon, Kevin went. He can't remember now what the meeting was about, except that it rapidly devolved into an argument about the number of women of color on the organizing committee. He vividly remembers the venue, though, a windowless, subterranean classroom in the Modern Languages Building—he can picture it down to the subliminal strobing of the fluorescents, the unswept candy wrappers in the corners, the useless fragments of chalk in the chalkboard tray. Christ, he can *smell* it even now, the dank air-conditioning of MLB, the years of floor polish and disinfectant. And he remembers Lynda introducing him to the boy who'd invited her, a rodent-faced little guy in a leather vest who looked more like Ratso Rizzo than Tom Courtenay, who limply shook Kevin's hand and said to Lynda, with barely disguised anger, "I think it's *cool* that you brought somebody."

Most of all, though, Kevin remembers sitting in the back of the room with Lynda, the two of them slumped in classroom desks like a couple of bored sixteen-year-olds. Lynda had brought a pint of Jack Daniels in a little paper sack, and they passed it back and forth, sneaking swigs and stifling their laughter. Poor, luckless Ratso Rizzo would have murdered them with his gaze, but as luck would have it, he ended up as one of the chief combatants in the climactic contretemps, violently shaking his miniature forefinger at a plump black girl with cornrows, who waved her more substantial forefinger back at him and shouted, "Motherfucker, don't you *shake* that finger at me!" At which point, Lynda grabbed Kevin by the wrist with her cool fingers and dragged him out of the room, where they ran doubled over with laughter down the hall. Ten minutes later, they were seated halfway up the steps of the grad library, looking over the Diag in the long midwestern twilight, the top of Burton Tower golden in the last of the day's light, and they finished the Jack swig by swig, turn and turn about, getting a nice, mutual buzz on. Kevin sat on the step above her and Lynda sat between his thighs, drumming her fingers on his knees, the bottle on the step between her legs. He lightly pulled at the hair at the nape of her neck, and she tilted her head back and handed up the last of the whiskey, pursing her lips when she caught him enjoying the view down the front of her tank top.

"What are *you* looking at?" she said. And half an hour after that, in Lynda's summer sublet, a steamy attic room at the top of a cooperative house on Jefferson Avenue, they were happily balling on her sketchy mattress—yes, balling, Kevin thought, that's *exactly* the word—and he laughed out loud, right in the saddle as it were, thrusting away in that lovely, loose-hipped way the girls loved. The two of them slick as seals in the heat, the window wide open, their grunts and moans wafting into the treetops just under the eaves, *eine kleine nachtmusik* for an Ann Arbor summer evening.

"Why were you laughing?" she asked him afterward, pursing her lips at him again as they sprawled together, hot and panting and reeking of sweat and semen and pussy.

"I'm just really . . . happy!" Kevin laughed, just drunk enough to be telling the truth.

"*Move,*" he shouts now, rapping on the side of the van with his knuckles, filling it with a hollow rumble. The driver guns it into the street, wheels smoking against the pavement. Kevin hears a muffled, diminishing, "Fuck you, asshole!" from the driver, and feels, without actually seeing it, the guy's middle finger thrust in his direction. But he doesn't care, because right there, up ahead, silhouetted against the blazing Texas sky, lifting her hair away from the sweaty nape of her neck in a gesture he hasn't seen in a quarter of a century, a gesture that makes his heart tumble like a gymnast, is *Lynda herself,* swaying round the corner out of sight, the ends of her duffel bounding slowly with every step.

Okay, not Lynda, actually, but close enough. He rounds the corner and finds another, funkier coffeehouse called Empyrean, with a hand-painted sign, purple letters across a starry sky between a grinning sun and a sultry moon. Through a side window he sees swaybacked sofas, blowsy easy chairs, a vintage floor lamp with a fringed shade. In the shade of an awning, he tiptoes between the empty tables of a patio—formerly a loading dock—and plays peekaboo behind the flyers taped in the front window, watching Joy Luck prop her duffel on end against a couch at the back of the shop. As Kevin pretends to read flyers for a poetry slam and a band called Titty Bingo, Joy Luck smiles at someone he can't see and tugs at a zipper at the bulging end of the duffel. He watches her yank *The Joy Luck Club* free and with a backhand snap of the wrist sail it toward her unseen interlocutor. Then she gives the duffel a proprietorial little pat and disappears down a dim hallway into the back.

And before Kevin has a chance to think, he's pulled the door open and entered. Empyrean is self-consciously contra-Starbucks, aggressively laid-back, an echoing old warehouse with a high ceiling and bare rafters, a scuffed hardwood floor in need of a sweeping, mismatched tables and chairs. Earnest and slightly amateurish paintings in black and red line the bare brick wall along one side, each with a little card announcing its asking price with calligraphic self-importance. Even the air-conditioning is laid-back, a dank, shadowy breeze instead of the industrial, fluorescent deep freeze of Starbucks. The counter is an old wooden bar top, and the boy behind it is slender to the point of gauntness, with sharp cheekbones and a pointed chin and a high forehead. His narrow sideburns hang as low as the tips of his earlobes, his black T-shirt hangs from his collarbone, his jeans from the points of his pelvis. He's puckering his lips and thumbing through *The Joy Luck Club,* as if trying to figure out what's wrong with it. As Kevin crosses the creaking floor, the boy stows the paperback out of sight and lifts his eyebrows.

"Iced tea," Kevin says. The boy carries Kevin's glass in knuckly fingers; Kevin drops his change in the tip jar. The boy nods, then stoops to retrieve the paperback from under the counter. Sweating tea in hand, Kevin plucks a disheveled newspaper out of a rack and sinks into a worn corduroy sofa the color of oatmeal, just inside the door, facing toward the back. Knees higher than his lap, he grunts to set his tea on the scruffy little table before the sofa. Then he spreads the paper in front of his face, watching for Joy Luck over the top of the page.

The only other customer is a guy with a shaved head, who is slightly older than the barista, though not by much, and who slumps in his chair at another table, nodding slowly to himself as he peers into a laptop. His clothes seem to have just barely survived some apocalyptic blast—his short-sleeved shirt is faded blue plaid, and the knees of his jeans have simply vanished. He's crossed an ankle over the other leg, exposing his entire knee and a long reach of white, hairless thigh. He extends his long arm to the laptop and gives the keyboard a sharp tap.

Just then Joy Luck reemerges from the hallway at the back, and Kevin ducks behind his paper. Without thinking, he's picked up a section of the *Wall Street Journal,* and his leathery middle-aged pupils laboriously refocus on the close-ranked print, his heart racing at the sight of Joy Luck, at the memory of Lynda, at the mild thrill of his own shamelessness.

"So." It's Joy Luck's voice, he recognizes it from the plane: flat, midwestern, uninflected. "Any more sentimental crap you want me to read?"

Maybe not midwestern, thinks Kevin. Midwesterners aren't that tart, usually. Maybe she's a Texan, maybe he got the accent all wrong. Kevin risks another peek. The gaunt barista is shrugging. The book is out of sight.

"Thought you'd like," he says. "Sorry," he adds, though he doesn't really mean it.

"Whatever," says Joy Luck, waving her fingers. It might almost be an apology. Then, "Where's Ian?"

"Ian," says the barista. "Oh."

"Tall guy?" says Joy Luck. "Kind of funny-looking? Claims to be my boyfriend?" She's standing at the counter now, hip canted, fingertips just touching the countertop.

"Didn't he tell you?"

"Didn't he tell me what?" She's doing it again, that Lynda thing she does, twisting her hair one-handed away from her neck, her long arm bent at the elbow in a perfect triangle, a taut triceps displayed.

"I *so* don't want to be in the middle of this." The barista backs away from his side of the counter, as if he expects her to reach across like Lee Marvin grabbing the barkeep by the lapels.

"He knew I was coming back today, right?" She looks like she might do it, too. She's certainly got the upper-body strength for it. "He had the flight number and all?"

The barista glances away toward Kevin, who ducks behind his paper.

"He started at Gaia last week," Kevin hears him say. "Didn't he tell you?"

There's a long, tense silence.

"Gaia?" she says at last. "Since when?"

"Since last week?"

"Is that where he is now?" For the first time she sounds not just angry, but hurt.

"Sweetie, I don't know his schedule."

The *Wall Street Journal* swims before Kevin. Joy Luck and the barista lower their voices, their exact words lost in the rafters, under the hum of the AC and the music on the sound system. Kevin's surprised to realize that this self-consciously hip little coffeehouse is playing an oldies station—some ironic whim of the gaunt barista, no doubt—and the song that's drowning out the conversation he'd like to hear is, of all things, "Snoopy vs. the Red Baron." Jesus Christ, when was the last time he heard *that?* He peeks around the left edge of the paper. Barista and Joy Luck are leaning toward each other over the counter. Barista's eyes are wide in sympathy. He nods slowly as he speaks. Joy Luck's kneading the edge of the counter with her fingers. She looks stricken.

Whatever she says next is drowned out by the rat-a-tat beat of the idiotic song, and Kevin thinks, these two weren't even *born* yet when this song was on the charts. I'm the oldest guy in here. I'm the oldest guy for blocks in any direction.

Kevin turns the page and sees his tea, untouched, sweating on the table beyond his knee, but he doesn't want to draw attention to himself by reaching for it, doesn't want to reveal his face. The sweat along his hairline is evaporating in the AC; the smell of his armpits rises from between the lapels of his jacket. Tucking his chin, he leans slowly to the right to peek around the paper.

"Can I leave this here?" Joy Luck has pushed away from the counter, but she sways on her long legs, almost as if she's going to fall over. Almost as if someone has hit her. She gestures wanly to her duffel. There's a tremor in her voice.

"Bring it around," the gaunt barista says. "I'll keep an eye on it."

With a thump like a body hitting the floorboards and a long, gritty scrape, Joy Luck drags her duffel one-handed around the far end of the counter. Kevin dips guiltily to the paper again.

"That's fine, sweetie. It'll be fine with me."

Now she's sailing down the length of the coffeehouse, and Kevin can hear the creak of the floorboards, the rhythmic slap of her sandals.

"You good?" the barista calls after her.

"*No,*" she says.

He peeks, not a good idea because she's headed in his direction, but it doesn't matter. He could be right in her path and she'd never see him. Her eyes glisten, her gaze is fixed straight ahead. Behind her the barista blows out a sigh. The other customer, the laptop guy with the shaved head, is watching her sidelong as his bony fingers tremble over his keyboard.

"Hey," he says, with the ghost of a smile.

Joy Luck pauses, glances, then says, "Hey!" and breaks into a sad, heartfelt smile and pivots on the toe of her sandal. She coos at the laptop guy, who murmurs something back, and Kevin's heart tumbles again in his chest. Joy Luck is smiling down at the guy, and he's beaming shyly up at her as if he can't believe his good luck. She's holding his hand by the thumb and waggling his long arm playfully back and forth. Laptop grins sheepishly, baring his pink gums. Even at this distance, in the crepuscular cool of the café, Kevin can see the guy blush. Joy Luck's eyes have brightened and she's laughing—a musical laugh, a charming laugh, a laugh that makes Kevin's balls tingle—and the laughter and the carefree grasp of the man's hand pierce Kevin right through to his spine, because it's a gesture that reminds him of another old flame—not Lynda this time, but the Philosopher's Daughter, his great unrequited crush, the girl that got away. She had a laugh like that, mocking and affectionate all at once, and an effortlessly flirtatious manner. Kevin never made a bigger fool of himself over anyone than he did over her.

Across the room Joy Luck drops the guy's hand, and the poor guy almost involuntarily reaches for her again. Then he catches himself, as spastic as Dr. Strangelove, and jerks his hand back over the sheen of his head, rubbing so hard he furrows the back of his scalp. That was the other side of the Philosopher's Daughter, of course—jolt you awake like a nine-volt battery, then cut you off at the knees. Not to mix a metaphor or anything, thinks Kevin, but she could cut you dead in an instant, stick a shiv between your ribs, yank your heart out of your chest, and drop-kick it into the next county. Even after all these years, Kevin can feel the little blood pressure gauge in his head throb into the red zone. Half a moment more and he'll be as red-faced as a cartoon character, veins bulging and steam shooting out of his ears.

"Do you want to know why I don't think I could love you, Kevin?" said the Philosopher's Daughter, in that voice at once sensible and pixieish.

"Not really," said Kevin, and then she told him anyway.

"Curses, foiled again!" goes the singer on the radio, and Kevin's another victim of the Red Baroness of Washtenaw County: he's shrieking toward earth, his legs shot off at the knees, his guns jammed, his craft in flames and trailing a winding spiral of bitter black smoke. Many men died trying to end that spree, and he's just another stencil on her fuselage. Mere moments to live, he should be making peace with the Almighty, but all he can see is her porcelain face and the cool, appraising light in her eye as she watches him bleed slowly to death.

"Shit," Kevin says aloud, and too late he realizes he's gripped the paper so hard that the section has doubled over as if in pain. I can't believe, he almost says aloud, I can't *believe* that I still let this get to me after twenty-five years. It's not like he still loves her—he's seen her a couple, three times since then, he even went to her wedding with no ill effect—but he still experiences that one moment, when she told him what she told him, as if it happened ten minutes ago. Love fades, but rage and humiliation endure forever.

And so it's now, while Kevin's glowering like a serial killer, that Joy Luck turns away from the laptop guy with a final, flirty wag of her fingertips, and walks straight toward him. Kevin's right in her eye line, and as his eyes refocus from the memory of the Philosopher's Daughter's cold victory to the midmorning twilight of Empyrean, he finds himself looking straight at Joy Luck. Her eyes were fixed and glistening before, now they're hard. She's angry again, and Kevin's breath catches in his throat, his heart thumps like an animal trying to burst out of his chest. She's knows who I am! He cannot look away—but Joy Luck does. Her glare glides right over him as she sails past his sofa and pushes out the door. A little gust of warmth from the hot morning outside brushes Kevin's knees.

Kevin sags into the cushions, relieved, but also disappointed. She doesn't recognize me, he thinks. She sat next to me for three hours on the plane, six inches apart for *three hours,* and she doesn't *fucking recognize me.* I'm wearing my magic ring of middle-aged invisibility, a dog-faced old burgher like Bilbo Baggins, only taller.

He starts to laugh, and the two other men in Empyrean look up from behind the counter and a dimly glowing laptop screen. Kevin discovers that he's standing, clutching the crumpled newspaper in one hand. The laptop guy sighs (over what, Kevin wonders, over whom?) and raps at his keyboard. The gaunt barista, *The Joy Luck Club* in his hands once again, watches Kevin with professional wariness. His eyes slide to the untouched glass of tea and back to Kevin. Kevin forces a smile and drops the paper on the couch behind him.

"Bad news," he says. The barista says nothing, doesn't even nod, just watches, and Kevin slides around the coffee table and pushes out the door, after Joy Luck.

Walking into the heat again is like wading fully clothed into warm water, and the air itself drags Kevin to a halt just beyond the shadow of Empyrean's awning. Across the empty street the low old buildings have been divvied up into trendy bars and restaurants, nighttime facades of dark brick and tinted glass like the bars along Liberty and Washington in Ann Arbor, only here, on a Texas morning, they have a hungover squint against the unblinking sunlight. The street is empty. Where's Joy Luck?

There she is! Empyrean's patio, the old loading dock, pushes out into the intersection like a prow, and he can see the top of her head as she descends the steps and pauses for the wall of oncoming traffic to pass. He sidles between the little round tables, wondering what he'll do if he gets to the corner before she crosses. How can she not recognize him from the plane? And how can she not wonder what the hell he's doing right next to her on an Austin street corner, radiating longing and strenuously acting like *he* doesn't recognize *her*?

But then she crosses the street against the light, not slinking now, but marching, because she's out for blood. At the corner Kevin waits for another shoal of cars, their tires making a hollow rumble against the pavement. Up ahead Joy Luck marches past a bar, the Ginger Man, and the little green apple in the small of her back winks at him over the martial but still sensual switch of her jeans. I wouldn't want to be Ian right now, Kevin thinks. Ian's in for it, Ian has no idea what's coming.

Kevin keeps his distance, passing the Ginger Man and another bar, The Fox and Hound. What's up with this, two English pubs on the same block — these royal thrones of kings, these sceptered isles, these earths of majesty, desiccating in the unforgiving Texas heat. Joy Luck and Kevin, girl and man, are the only pedestrians in sight. From the blank, tinted gaze of the square windows of the office building across the street, is some bored middle manager watching her with the same longing Kevin is? And is he watching Kevin following her? Give it up, bud, says Mr. Middle Manager, you haven't got a prayer. Or is he the Noel Coward of central Texas, watching in fey bemusement as Kevin—pale, sweating, overdressed—follows the silken-skinned Oriental in a fever of lust and longing past this corner of a foreign land that is forever England. A fox and a hound, indeed, dear boy, how wonderfully droll! Kevin's dad used to sing Noel Coward in the car, to the mutual embarrassment of Kevin and his sister: *Only mad dogs and Englishmen go out in the noonday, out in the noonday, out in the noonday sun.*

But if he stops now, he'll never know how Joy Luck *does* that, how she manages to embody not one, but two old flames from Kevin's Summer of Love, the summer he fell harder for a woman than he ever had before, and the summer he had the most wanton and least guilty sex of his life—but not with the same woman. And Joy Luck reminds him vividly and unmistakably of both. Is she some kind of succubus? Or is it incubus?

At the next corner, cars rushing past her heels, she crosses against the light again into a little park. Keeping well back, Kevin trots after her past a tall, verdigris green sculpture, two elongated, abstract, but sensual figures, one broad in the shoulders, the other broad in the hips, who look like they're just about to kiss. Succubus, Kevin suddenly concludes, that's the female version, though he's not sure why he thinks so. Perhaps it's because it sounds like "suck." God, laughs Kevin, am I still that much of an adolescent? She said "suck," heh heh heh heh. He's got Stella to thank, he supposes, trudging past the canoodling sculptures. Stella's epic fellation on the first evening of their acquaintance, the one that emptied his brain of all common sense, is still a high point of their relationship. Beth never was particularly enthusiastic or skillful at going down—*"Teeth,"* he always had to warn her—and she did it only when she was really excited for some reason, nodding furiously over his cock with her eyes squeezed shut. Stella, God bless her, tickles and teases and takes her time, she knows tricks as if she's actually thought about it. And she keeps her eyes open, watching him wide-eyed over his heaving rib cage. When he reciprocates—a specialty of his, another American practice McNulty told him that the girls all love—he keeps his own eyes shut, nose buried in wiry pubic hair, glancing up only occasionally past her flattened breasts at the straining muscles in her throat. Beth always seemed distracted when he went down on her, as if her own pleasure irritated her somehow, though she always climaxed convincingly enough. There's a lot of theater in Stella's ecstasy, though: she arches her back, she claws the sheets, she thrashes her head from side to side. Her voice cracks as she calls his name; a blue vein pounds in her neck. Kevin's never entirely convinced he's actually gotten her off, her response is too self-consciously intense, too pornographically hysterical. God knows, though, she takes him in gratefully afterward, when, in another one of his signature moves, he launches himself up between her legs and enters her in one smooth thrust, without looking or guiding himself with his hand. At that moment Beth always turned her face away with a grimace and swiped his lips with the palm of her hand, an exasperated mother wiping her messy brat. But Stella, praise Jesus, mashes her mouth against his and sucks her own juices greedily off his lips.

Now Lynda, Kevin recalls, watching Joy Luck's angry strut at the far corner of the park—the legendary Lynda, the Lynda of song and story, Lynda *à la plage,* etc., etc.—Lynda was good at it, too, but she never took him all the way, not once in three months. She'd lower her lips to his cock, gathering her hair one-handed away from her face, baring her lovely throat, and she'd dip, once, twice, three times, until he was straight and hard and taut, and then she'd pull away and give him a filthy grin. "Oh, God, don't *stop*," Kevin moaned, his cock chilled by her saliva, but she swung her long, freckled thigh over him and slid slickly onto him, doubling over him with her hair pooling coolly on his chest, nuzzling him and laughing in his ear.

Jesus, Kevin thinks, if Joy Luck knew what I'm thinking back here, she'd scream bloody murder, or call a cop, or — more likely, he thinks, focusing on the glide of her back muscles beneath her flawless skin — she'd go all Michelle Yeoh on his melancholy middle-aged ass, leaping straight up into the air and slapping the side of his face in slow motion with the hot sole of her sandal, quivering his flesh like Jell-O, spinning his head a spine-splintering 180 degrees.

Kevin stops to peel off his jacket as if readying himself for single combat. The street ahead is a garden of new condo towers, some completed, some still under construction with tall T square cranes affixed to their sides, like the stalks from which they grew. One finished tower is wide and flat like the monolith in *2001*, another rises in the same proportions as a Zippo lighter, the farthest one, still skeletal on top, sheathed halfway up in green panels that throw the sun back in Kevin's eyes, is tall and narrow like a Pez dispenser without the head. He fishes inside his jacket for his sunglasses and looks back toward downtown Austin's foreshortened skyline, like a three-quarters-scale Manhattan in some imperial Las Vegas casino. What looked like a great big urban canyon when he was coming up it in the cab is now, he realizes, just an arroyo. He sees the sleek, narrow, ice-blue tower, Barad-dûr, much taller than all the other buildings, too tall, really, for this theme-park skyline. It's only three or four blocks away, its glassy spires bleached a little paler in the sun. He puts on his sunglasses and it dims a little more.

Then something moves behind the translucent panes of the spires, something dark and quick and massive, and Kevin is chilled all over. The hell is that? he wonders, his pulse racing. The hand holding his jacket seizes up, and a wave passes down the coat like a shiver. Something sleek is issuing now from between the spires, as if the tower really is the lair of Sauron, the Dark Lord. It's a snake...it's a dragon...holy shit, it's a winged Nazgûl! Kevin's heart thumps in his chest, and even behind the amber tint of his glasses the glare of sunlight off the spires is magnified into an enormous, burning eye...

No, it's a jet, coming out from behind the tower, climbing from Austin's airport over the city so steeply and slowly it looks as if it's winching itself into the sky. Kevin breathes again and folds his jacket over his elbow as he rolls his shirt cuffs back. The aircraft is gray with a long, white underbelly, its wings swept back, its long throat bared, a migrating goose straining for altitude. And though Kevin's pulse has slowed, the still surprising and indelible conjunction of two formerly unrelated compound nouns—airplane, skyscraper—makes his stomach drop. What's worse is that he can't even hear the jet yet, and its silence as it crawls glittering against the bleached sky makes the sight even creepier. And he can't help thinking again of shoulder-fired missiles; from where he's standing at the center of the park he could bring down this plane. Or maybe it'll be brought down by Another Kevin, sweatily mixing liquid explosives in the lavatory and urgently murmuring *"Allahu akbar"* over and over again. Stinger or no Stinger, jihadist or no jihadist, the plane looks as if it's barely going to make it, and Kevin expects it any moment to stall and slide sickeningly backward, then tumble wing over wing straight down into the city below, hitting the earth with an echoing boom and a roiling cloud of black smoke.

Then at last he hears the hollow, throbbing roar of the jet, trailing like a banner just behind the plane. Wow, thinks Kevin, his pulse still racing a little. It's weird how much the climbing jet has freaked him out, and he only saw the two towers fall on television like most people. What if he'd actually been there? What if he'd actually seen the planes hit the towers, seen the falling bodies, watched the towers flower hideously into dust, run for his life through the midmorning darkness, breathed the choking air, felt the acrid sting of burning plastic and jet fuel and God knows what else at the back of his sinuses? All he'd seen — sheer repetition has graven the image permanently into his lizard brain — was a toy plane colliding with a scale model of a skyscraper and a little silent orange bloom against the blue September sky. It looked like a special effect and a mediocre one at that — a blurry, trembling, telephoto image with none of the digital polish and Dolby rumble of an A-list production. If something he'd seen on TV could take him by the throat like that years later, imagine if he'd actually been there.

He turns, his jacket still draped over his arm. The chill is fading, the heat folds around him again. He really should go back, sit in goddamn Starbucks for three hours, but it's too late, he's already walking, damp all over with sweat, his shirt stuck to his spine. The broiling sky opens high and wide before him. By the time he gets to the curb — the corner of Fifth and San Antonio, says the street sign — Joy Luck is halfway up San Antonio, turning left on Sixth Street, heading west, so Kevin turns left on Fifth, walking parallel to her on a covered walkway underneath one of the half-built condo towers. His feet thump on the flooring, and through the plywood overhead he can hear the ricocheting ring of mallets, the insistent beeping of a vehicle backing up, some guy yelling in Spanish. The traffic rushes up Fifth Street toward him, springing from light to light in quantum bursts, enormous, candy-colored trucks with bulbous curves, spotlessly clean, piloted by pink-cheeked, freshly barbered young evangelicals in crisp shirts talking on cell phones.

Across the stream of traffic, between buildings and up side streets, Kevin watches Joy Luck on Sixth Street, but at the next cross street he's lost her, and he dithers for a moment, not sure whether to go forward or back. His heart beginning to race, he walks the next block more quickly. Under a big condo block bristling with balconies, he crosses Fifth, trotting north past the snouts of a row of SUVs. He's already halfway across before he realizes that the traffic was already moving, but he doesn't stop, and four lanes of SUVs lurch forward on their toes as he wards them off with his palm. He hardly notices, because Joy Luck should be crossing the intersection ahead of him, but he still can't see her, and he's thinking she's gotten away, he's lost her, but suddenly, when he's ten paces from the corner, she appears from behind the building and stops for the light. Kevin's heart soars, but his relief is cut short by the fact that in another three seconds he'll be right next to her on the curb. Kevin pivots on the toe of his shoe, grinding the fat black tread into the hot pavement, slapping his trouser pockets like he's forgotten his keys or something, swinging the jacket off his shoulder and rummaging in every pocket, lifting his eyes to the sky like he's concentrating. Doesn't matter, though, he's already caught, busted, blown; he expects a tap on the shoulder any moment now, or even something way less demure, way more Michelle Yeoh, an iron grip spinning him around, grinding another millimeter of shoe sole into the pavement, and an angry, beautiful young woman nose to nose with him, her eyes blazing, demanding to know, "Why are you following me? *What the hell do you think you're doing?*"

When he finally peeks over his shoulder, her swaying backside is disappearing behind the liquor store across the street, and he sags with relief. At the corner, he sits on a ledge outside a bar called Molotov to catch his breath and let her get ahead of him. In the shade for the first time since he left Empyrean, he clutches his limp jacket to his chest with both arms, watching Joy Luck stride up Sixth toward a massive redbrick building like a fortress. He peers through the tinted window into Molotov, taking off his sunglasses and shading his eyes against the warm glass. The place is empty at this hour: an unpainted concrete floor; a long, featureless curve of space-age banquette; a pair of thirty-year-old, piss-yellow La-Z-Boys. There's a mock social-ist realist painting along the back wall, an idiotically smiling rocket scientist holding up an ICBM like it was a banana. Six months from now — if he's offered the job and he takes it — he could be on the other side of this window listening to music he doesn't recognize, chatting up women much too young for him, and paying extortionate prices for some cocktail they'd seen on *The Hills* or whatever they're watching now. Not like his days at the Central Café back in Ann Arbor, when just after closing he and the rest of the immortally young waitstaff used to do a line each right off the prep table — hello, Mr. Health Inspec-tor! — and then swagger en masse to the Rubiyat, where they would do more blow in the bathroom and dance to "It's Rain-ing Men" or "Atomic Dog" until three or four in the morning, and where one memorable dawn — a dawn he has never spo-ken of to another living soul and never will, a dawn that both mortifies and titillates him until this very moment — he woke up in Ypsilanti in the bed of a man he didn't recognize and never saw again, and walked all the way up Washtenaw back to Ann Arbor in the freezing rain even before the buses were run-ning, with a crippling headache and a taste in his mouth that he hoped never to identify. Bow-wow-wow, yippie-yo, yippie-yay!

Or — as he turned away from the gloom of Molotov's win-dow — there were his less cringe-worthy Big Star days, when he had an arrangement with the bouncer of Second Chance across the street—he gave Danny advance copies of reggae records and Danny comped him into shows—and he saw the Ramones for free. Those were the days when he took the Philosopher's Daughter to see R.E.M. not once, but twice—once at the Blind Pig and again at Joe's Star Lounge—and she spurned his advances both times. Once because he wasn't tender enough, and the other because he wasn't sufficiently passionate. Stop! he nearly says aloud, and reminds himself that most nights at the Pig or Joe's, he could buy a girl three or four beers in a plastic cup and at least count on making out with her later on, sometimes even right outside the club in the narrow back seat of his yellow Pinto. "A Pinto?" she'd say, half-drunk. "Aren't you afraid it'll, like, blow up?" And Kevin, tugging at the strap of her tank top and clumsily trying to find her nipple with the tip of his tongue, would pause to say, "Kinda adds to the thrill, doesn't it?"

But the thing is, standing here now in the heat, twenty-five years later and fifteen hundred miles from Michigan, he knows he couldn't say a word about any of this to any of the girls he'd meet in a lounge like Molotov; they wouldn't give a shit that he'd seen the Police at Bookie's on their first American tour. Or that he once drunkenly yelled, "I wanna have your child!" to Patti Smith in Second Chance and that Patti gave him the finger. Or that once, in the Fleetwood Diner at two in the morning, he sat next to James Osterberg, aka Iggy Pop—a tiny little guy in eyeliner, Ypsilanti's favorite son—and that Iggy accepted a steak fry from Kevin's plate. Hell, apart from their first conversation vis-à-vis the Rolling Stones and the Black Crowes, he couldn't even have this conversation with Stella, even though she isn't quite as young as she said she was. The thing is, Kevin thinks, still sitting in the shadow of the lounge's awning, Stella would like Molotov, just like she likes watching reruns of *Sex and the City* over and over again. They usually watch from his bed, Stella clinging to him like a limpet, tapping his chest with her red nails, asking him, what does he think of the shoes Carrie's wearing? Or does he ever wonder if Miranda is too much of a bitch? Or is Samantha empowered, or just a slut? She asks him like it matters what he thinks, but then shushes him when he tries to answer. So he has no doubt she'd love this pretentious little lounge in Austin: she'd want to live in a hideously expensive condominium in one of the new blocks, right up at the top, and she'd doll herself up every night and come down here and drink too much and laugh too loud, her eyes swimming in Absolut, and she'd wriggle her delightful ass in that awful La-Z-Boy like a happy little girl in the teacup ride at Disneyland, because to her a La-Z-Boy is *funny,* wonderfully retro, not a stomach-churning reminder (as it is to Kevin) of the suburban anomie of the hideous paneled basements of his youth. That's what a twenty-year difference in age (okay, fifteen, if we're going by Stella's driver's license) does to a relationship: artifacts that make Kevin suicidally despondent—a recliner, his mother's cocktail glasses, his father's golf trophies, his sister's Partridge Family 45s—are exotic objets d'art to Stella, like African masks or Indonesian batik. Kevin's depressing *Ice Storm* boyhood is Stella's theme park.

He sighs. In the bright sunlight ahead, Joy Luck has crossed a bridge and started up a hill toward the redbrick fortress. She's dwindled in the sunlight from a flesh-and-blood girl, with muscles gliding beneath her skin, her apple tattoo winking over her jeans, to an incorporeal, impressionist squiggle that means Girl, a couple of charcoal lines narrow in the middle and wide at the hips. He stands and steps out into the sunlight again and starts after her. Stella, Stella, Stella, he's thinking, how'd *that* happen? She's even met his mother, once, through no fault of Kevin's, the day his mother asked him and his sister to come sort through the junk in the basement in Royal Oak. At last she was selling the old house and moving into a condo—"If you want any of this stuff," she warned him over the phone, "it's speak now or forever hold your peace"—and Stella invited herself along, as pert as Sarah Jessica herself in white tennis shorts and a ball cap with her bushy pony tail tugged through the back. She and Mom yakked it up in the kitchen, drinking highballs at one on a Saturday afternoon while Kevin and Kathleen sweated and sneezed in the basement, going through mold-spotted cardboard boxes full of nameless crap that Kevin, honest to God, had hoped never to see again.

"Ohmi*god!*" he heard Stella cry as he stumbled up out of the basement. "You're not getting rid of this, are you?" Through the archway he saw Mom in the living room, swinging her leg in the rocking chair, dangling her second or third highball from her bent wrist. He got himself a glass of water at the kitchen sink, then came in and saw Stella bent over the back of the sofa, running her palms sensuously over the nubbly fabric. It used to be white, but now it was dirty white like an old dog, kind of gray, really, with cigarette burns and other unidentifiable stains that no combination of flipping the cushions could disguise.

"If you want to haul it out of here, hon," Kevin's mother said, "it's all yours."

Stella characteristically overdid her gratitude, dropping her jaw and widening her eyes at Mom. "No *way*," she said, stamping her foot. "You are *not*."

Mom shrugged and swiveled the tall glass up to her lips. Even backlit, with the afternoon light pouring in the picture window behind her, Kevin could see the lipstick print on the glass. "Take it," she said.

Stella pivoted to Kevin and theatrically batted her eyes, a little girl who wants a pony. But before she actually said a word, Kevin slumped in the archway—God, he hated that fucking couch—and said, "Where you gonna put it?"

Not "Where are *we* going to put it?" He was careful never to say "we" with Stella, not like Stella ever noticed. But Mom did.

"Well." Stella actually shifted her hip and cupped her elbow and put a forefinger to her cheek—just like Jack Benny, though she wouldn't have had the slightest idea who Jack Benny was. "We could put it in my place," she said, watching him, "until you get rid of that awful futon, slash sofa, slash whatever in your living room."

Kevin's mom gave him a look, and they each drank from their respective glasses, like a salute.

A little later, as Stella was squealing with delight over God knows what in the basement with Kathleen, Kevin's mother asked him, "So how old is this one." Very flat, more a statement than a question.

Kevin hesitated, because he didn't know what Stella had told her. "Early thirties?" he said, like he wasn't sure himself. He knew better than to try to lie to his mother. "Never kid a kidder" was her motto.

"How do you do it?" she said.

"Do what?" This was an old routine, Mom sounding more like an ex-wife than his mother.

"You don't make that much money," she said. "You're not the best-looking guy in the world."

"Thanks, Mom."

"Well, you're not bad," she said. "For your age."

Kevin drained his water and set the glass on an end table, pointedly missing the coaster.

"And how did you meet her?"

"I told you, Mom."

"Tell me again."

Kevin crossed his arms. "She's my tenant."

"Your tenant! You mean, she pays rent?"

"That's what a tenant does, Mom."

"What do you charge her?"

Now she's just messing with me, Kevin thought. "She's on commission, Mom. She makes more money than I do." He wasn't actually sure about that, but it sounded good, and it made Mom pause for a moment.

"So she's in sales."

"Yup. She's a saleswoman."

"What's she sell?"

"Books," he said. "Textbooks."

"Hm." Mom held her glass up to the light and regarded the level. He knew what she was thinking. She doesn't seem like a reader to me. Never kid a kidder, bub. But instead, turning the glass in the light, admiring the stream of bubbles and the swirl of Dewar's amidst the melting ice cubes, she said, "Now that Beth, she was a neat lady."

"A little louder, Mom, I don't think Stella heard you."

"I'm just saying," his mother said. "You shouldn't have let that one go so easily."

"She let me go, Mom, remember? She moved out."

Things were about to get uglier when they were interrupted — rescued, really — by Stella herself, thumping quickly up the basement stairs. She had erupted into the kitchen beaming like a kid at Christmas, bearing in both hands his father's old ice bucket, the silvery round one with the embossed penguins on it.

"*Look* at this!" she'd cried. "Isn't it *gorgeous?*"

Joy Luck is nearly at the redbrick fortress. Kevin crosses a bridge over a creek bed of bleached stones and a stagnant trickle of water, unwholesomely green, the banks overgrown with untrimmed bushes and trees and clotted with weeds full of sun-bleached trash. The walls of the fortress up ahead turn out not to be redbrick at all, but some sort of reddish panels. The sun stings the back of Kevin's neck; his shortening shadow glides ahead of him up the sidewalk. Joy Luck has crossed a little street that runs between a vacant lot and the building, and she's passing under the lee of the building itself, which rises seven stories above Sixth Street. But by the time Kevin gets to the corner, Joy Luck has vanished. Kevin stops dead in his wilted shirt and hot, heavy shoes, dangling his limp suit coat over his shoulder. She's vanished into thin air, squirted from the universe (as McNulty used to say) like a watermelon seed. He could swear he feels the thick soles of his shoes melting into the pavement, and he knows it's only a matter of time before he's a mere puddle himself, running back down into the dry creek bed behind him. He turns, looking wildly around him, but he's the only pedestrian in sight. He looks up at the big block of building looming over him, where a sign says GAIA MARKET, and it slowly dawns on him where Joy Luck is going. Up ahead an SUV turns left off Sixth and disappears into the building itself, and Kevin breaks into a run despite the heat. A moment later, pouring sweat, a little light-headed, he's in the echoing, exhaust-scented parking garage under Gaia Market, and there she is again, crossing the garage toward a bank of sliding doors.

Of course there was going to be a Gaia Market here. Hadn't Kevin heard that Austin was just like Ann Arbor, only bigger, hipper, hotter? His eyes adjust to the shadowless fluorescent light of the garage, and his ears to the starship hum of ventilators and the echoing percussion of car doors. Kevin weaves between Beemers and Mercedes and high-end SUVs, zigzagging toward the sliding doors where Joy Luck is just now slipping through. In Ann Arbor every car from junker to luxury auto is marked by the stigmata of a Michigan winter—patches of rust, a rime of road salt—but here even a lowly Corolla has a gleaming finish and tinted windows, like a B-list actress with perfect skin and impenetrable sunglasses. Just as in the Gaia lot in Ann Arbor, many of the vehicles display Obama bumper stickers.

Just as Kevin gets to the glass doors, they slide shut, breathing a puff of cool air into his sweating face. Even though he craves the arctic AC, even though he sees Joy Luck gliding up the escalator within, even though she's doing the thing with her hair again that pierces his heart like a blade, he hesitates. She's nearly at the top of the escalator, her head rising between the twin ramparts of a massive floor display of red wine. But Kevin stands just out of range of the photocell, warded off like a vampire by a sign on the door that commands

Love
Where You Shop

Or what? thinks Kevin. His stomach clenches. The peevish professional in him wants to put a period at the end of that sentence, but his inner suburbanite—the guy who goes to Gaia Market in Ann Arbor only when his girlfriend drags him there, the defensively proud patron of *real* grocery stores like Kroger and the late, great Farmer Jack's—that guy immediately resents the poster's imperative voice, its implicit superiority, its barely disguised snob appeal. You're not just shopping for groceries at Gaia, you're making a political statement, a moral choice—no artificial colors, flavors, or sweeteners, say the signs, no exploited farmworkers—and you're also proving that you're not one of the lumpen, morbidly obese proles in synthetic fibers waddling under unflattering lights up the aisle of Meijer's, filling your vast cart with family-sized packages of chicken, five-pound bags of frozen french fries, big plastic tubs of chunky peanut butter. Does your lumbering prole, stuffed into jeans and a gaudy sports jacket like a sausage in its casing, love where he shops? Because if you don't love where you shop, then where you're shopping isn't good enough. In fact, if loving where you shop doesn't matter to you, then maybe you shouldn't shop here. That's right, the sign's telling Kevin, I'm talking to you, Mr. Royal Oak, Mr. Bachelor of General Studies, Mr. Non-Tenured Staffer, Mr. Maybe You'd Be Happier at Sam's Club. It's the same thing Kevin hears in his head every time he parks his five-year-old Accord among the Volvos and Subarus at the Gaia in Ann Arbor out on Washtenaw, where there used to be cheap motels and discount carpet emporia and the Ponderosa Steak House where his mother always took him to dinner when she came to visit him in college. It's the voice that's telling him that he's an underachiever in every way he can imagine, professionally, personally, financially.

But it's not just the snobbery that gets to him. He grew up with snobbery, he spent his teens hanging out at Somerset Mall and making time with rich, smart-mouthed Jewish girls from Franklin or Huntington Woods, or even richer Kingswood School girls, spooky-intense WASP princesses from Bloomfield Hills and Grosse Pointe, and by age sixteen he was used to being cut dead for his store-brand jeans or his haircut or his shitty Pinto. Hell, he wasn't just used to it—he wore their condescension like a badge, he thought it was *funny*. (And it's even funnier in retrospect, because in the years since, he has gone to work in academia, which means that on a daily basis he's condescended to by *experts*.) It's just that once upon a time, Ann Arbor was different, Ann Arbor was above all that suburban class-warfare bullshit. Okay, maybe it never was, not really, maybe it's the soft-focus blur of mid-life nostalgia, maybe he's been soaking for too long in Ann Arbor's marinade of pretension and infinite self-regard—but he remembers his college days and a few years after as a time of great leveling, when even the mouthy daughters of

Southfield furriers and the guilty-rich daughters of GM executives found the lanky son of a middle manager from Royal Oak exotic; when everybody he knew voted for the Rainbow People's Party candidate for mayor, a sexy manager from Borders; when the owner of Big Star Records used to hold parties in the basement of his house in Burns Park and supply the weed himself; when the term "politically correct" was a joke that lefties told on themselves. Sure we were smug, thinks Kevin, sure we were superior, but I was part of something then, I belonged in Ann Arbor in a way that I never belonged at Somerset Mall or in Bloomfield Hills or even Royal Oak for that matter. I was one of them.

Of course, even if you were one of them, Ann Arbor's righteousness could be a pain in the ass. Kevin can still hear the humorless whine of some grim little rich girl whose painter's pants he tried to get into one summer evening, the painter's pants that she wore just tight enough to make her unattainable ass perfectly round. They were toking up on the battered couch on the porch of her communal house on Greenwood Street, and she told him that the personal is political, that a woman needs a man like a fish needs a bicycle, that she's sure he's a nice guy and all, but has he read Shulamith Firestone on love? (He had, and it depressed him for a month, not because he believed a word of it, but because every girl he had a crush on did.) And besides, she continued, sadistically pressing herself closer to him on the ancient sofa, she was thinking maybe it was time for her take a woman for a lover.

"I'm just not that into penetration anymore," she said, calibrating to the fucking millimeter *exactly* what effect that kind of talk has on a guy. But Kevin knew the drill, he knew the speech by heart by now, so he said, "I hear you. That's cool." And they each took another hit off the joint, thigh to thigh on the swaybacked couch during the long midwestern twilight, the girl weighing her lust against her ideological purity, and Kevin wondering—as the weed tugged at his dick with little silk strings—what would happen if he put his hand on her breast.

Without realizing it, he's already floated through the doors of the Gaia Market in Austin as if on a little cannabis cloud, as if he's tapped into some long dormant reserve of THC stored deep in his body fat. Frosty air smelling of produce curls around him like a big mitt, reeling him in, chilling the sweat all over his body, and he glides past three more iterations of the sign: LOVE WHERE YOU SHOP, LOVE WHERE YOU SHOP, LOVE WHERE YOU SHOP. The repetition is intended to plant the slogan deep in his medulla oblongata, making it instinctive like fear or hunger, while at the same time rendering it functionally meaningless to his conscious mind, like saying "cat" over and over again. That's exactly what bothers him the most, in fact, and he wants to dig his heels in, but his feet aren't even touching the ground, he's floating up the escalator now under the big posterboard banners that proclaim Gaia's brand identity with Newspeak directness: ORGANIC, PURE FOOD, QUALITY, WELLNESS. At the top Joy Luck is talking to one of Gaia's whole-food jihadists, an überfoodie, a lean boy with biceps and a wispy beard, wearing a green Gaia T-shirt and matching ball cap. Maybe it's Ian, about to have his ass handed to him, and Kevin thinks, you tell him, sister, because when you're done, I want a piece of him, too. Kevin wants to dig his fingers into that smug green T-shirt and rock that grinning, gentle, clueless boy back on his heels and tell him what the problem is with Gaia: that they've taken everything that was both special and obnoxious about the Ann Arbor Kevin used to love—the food, the politics, *and* the attitude—and they've packaged it, art-directed it, and marketed it to Kevin at three times the price he used to pay at the Packard Food Co-op. It's just like Wal-Mart crushing small-town pharmacies and hardware stores, only it's worse, because the stores that Gaia is exterminating weren't like the mom-and-pop grocery stores that never knew what hit them, no, Gaia's victims actually had a political analysis of consumer culture, and now here's this national, centralized, corporate simulacrum of everything co-opers held dear and it's successfully wooing away the co-op's clientele on the same principle as Office Max or Home Depot. And *because* the brainy Chomsky readers who run the co-ops have a political analysis, they know *exactly* what's happening to them: it's the last reenactment of the Battle of Bertrand Russell — first time as farce, second time as tragedy — as the gentle vegans and pacifists who thought they could wear down corporate hegemony like water on a rock find instead that corporate hegemony has opened wide and is eating them alive, and they get to watch their own death, kicking and screaming like Robert Shaw in *Jaws*.

Whoa, thinks Kevin, who am I kidding? Who the hell do I think I am? Let's be honest here, he reminds himself, I was just another suburban counterculture dilettante. Doing blow at the Rubiyat and going to nuclear freeze rallies to meet girls didn't exactly make him Walter Benjamin. Because it's not like he was ever actually a *member* of the Food Co-op, basically he only ever shopped there to get close to the girl in the painter's pants, who stood out mainly by virtue of being surrounded by squat lesbians in overalls. With a knowing, karmic nudge, Gaia's escalator deposits him abruptly at the top and he nearly stumbles to his knees. Luckily Joy Luck's looking the other way, as she and the Gaian gesture in the same direction. Kevin turns his back and shrugs on his jacket again, glancing back at them. So this isn't Ian, she obviously doesn't know the guy, she's just asking for directions. Kevin hangs back a bit, pretending to read the label of a bottle of wine as he watches Joy Luck stride away in the mellow light up the wide aisle behind the checkout lanes, past giant stacks of organic popcorn and pesticide-free apple juice and jars of chipotle ketchup.

"Are you a fan of Chilean wine?"

"Sorry?"

"That's a really nice Merlot." It's the kid Joy Luck was just talking to. "From Curicó province?"

But Kevin's not even looking at the bottle in his hands, but gazing dumbstruck across the vast interior of Gaia Market, from the high ceiling like a forest canopy where every conduit and AC duct is painted the same sylvan green, to the woody labyrinth of custom shelving below. In between are bright constellations of track lights as far as he can see, which makes the store look like a lavish modernist set for the fairy wood in *A Midsummer Night's Dream,* a faux forest full of mysterious, twinkling lights, and beautiful and slightly alien creatures. (Almost an English major, was Kevin.) And music—not pan pipes, exactly, but something light and airy and subtly engineered to appeal to the better instincts of the boomer clientele. It's the high, elven voice of Joni Mitchell, the Canadian Galadriel, singing in harmony with herself, "Hellllp me, I think I'm falling...in love with you..."

"It's got subtle highlights of black pepper and sour cherries and beeswax," says the Gaian, clasping his hands before him like a New Age sommelier. "It has a good attack with a roundish body, and a hint of tannin."

Kevin rolls his eyes: this is why he'd rather shop at Wal-Mart, where none of the harried minimum wagers is likely to treat him like a rude mechanical, where the only question they ever ask him is "Paper or plastic?"

"Thanks anyway," he says, and replaces the bottle with a glassy clank. The boy shrugs, and Kevin edges past him, deeper into the magic forest, after Joy Luck. He sees her swaying up the aisle, which isn't as crowded as it would be on a Friday evening or a Sunday afternoon. One thing you have to say about Gaia is just how good-looking its clientele is. Even in Ann Arbor, in the gloomiest months of winter, when every-body's swaddled in bulky parkas and padded boots and ugly woolen caps, the women and men Kevin sees at Gaia are clearly an order of magnitude more attractive than the wide loads he walks behind at Kroger. And here in sultry Austin, where every-body dresses year round like they're at the gym, Kevin passes a svelte young woman with a midriff like a gymnast; a guy his own age with the bulging calves of a bicycle racer; and a couple of fantastically fit women, anywhere from thirty-five to fifty, in capri pants and tank tops, whose upper arms are better defined than Kevin's—and Kevin works out twice a week with the free weights at CCRB. With a guilty pang he realizes that Stella would love it here. She drags him to Gaia once a week at least, dressing for the occasion like he's taking her to a restaurant. At Kroger she wears sweatpants and wraparound sunglasses like a movie star hoping to go unrecognized, but to Gaia she wears her work blouse and skirt, her earrings, her heels. Stella loves where she shops. When he launches involuntarily into his I Hate Gaia rant, she rolls her eyes like an impatient teenager.

"Yadda yadda yadda," she says, waggling her fingers. "Who cares, if everything here is so *yummy?*"

But it's not just Gaia, she'd love Austin, too. She'd settle into the subtropical heat like a sauna, she'd shed her Midwestern pelt and show off her own firm midriff and muscular calves, she'd drag him every Friday to happy hour at Molotov. She'd be in Gaia two or three times a week asking for samples from every flirty young Gaian at every specialty counter. Suddenly Kevin's wondering if he'd even be able to hang onto Stella in a town like this, full of fit, yummy guys her own age or younger who make ten times more money than he does, who drive the high-performance automobiles in the garage below, and who could chat knowledgeably for hours on end about Chilean fucking wine. Of course, if he gets the job he's interviewing for today, he's planning on leaving Stella. Though he hasn't said it out loud to a soul, hasn't even formulated it in so many words in the privacy of his own head, leaving Stella is half the reason he wants to move from Ann Arbor. But still, the frisson of guilt he feels sparks into a little flare of righteous anger, that she would dare follow him here, even if only in his imagination, and then dump him for a younger, richer, fitter guy! The nerve! That bitch! No way that's happening to me twice, Kevin thinks, and just for an instant, the mellow sylvan light of Gaia turns a little red at the edges. It doesn't help, of course, that the last time he saw Beth was in the Gaia in Ann Arbor, when he was with Stella.

It was the only time Stella and Beth have ever met—after work one frigid February evening. Gaia's lot was nearly full, and everything glittered under the halogen lights: the luxury cars and SUVs where they weren't streaked with slush; the gouts of exhaust from salt-rimed tailpipes; the heaps of plowed snow; the twinkling motes of new flakes; the air itself. Even their streamers of breath glittered as Kevin and Stella crunched across ridges of refrozen slush. They held hands like school-kids, her trim leather glove in his vast Gore-Tex mitten. Stella's woolen cap was jammed like a helmet over her hair, and Kevin breathed from within the hood of his parka, the opening cinched so tight that Stella said he looked like Kenny from *South Park*. But inside the hood Kevin felt like Darth Vader, seeing only through the narrow aperture of his helmet, hearing only the rhythmic rasp of his own breath. On the sidewalk in front of the store the crunch of their steps became the Styrofoam squeak of packed snow, and inside the Gaia airlock they performed the Michigan clog dance, stamping the snow off their boots on the squishy entry mat.

As always, Kevin pushed the cart while Stella tapped up and down each aisle in her high-heeled boots, her quilted coat billowing after her like a cape. By now he had learned to keep his mouth shut — "Would it kill them to sell a little Diet Coke? Some fucking Ruffles?" — and to admire instead Stella's consumer ruthlessness. He had no doubt that if civilization collapsed and they were reduced to living like australopithecines, it would be Stella who'd pluck up her spear and go out hunting, while Kevin tended the fire and sewed together the skins of the animals that she dragged back to their cave. Leaning wearily on the handle of the shopping cart, he had to admire the way Stella rocked on one sharp heel and briskly peeled off her leather gloves a finger at a time, the better to squeeze a kiwi fruit or an avocado, or spear a sample ball of marinated mozzarella. She'd offer him one first, putting it right in his mouth, then expertly spear another for herself with the same toothpick, watching for his reaction with a raised eyebrow. If he nodded, she'd brighten at the kid behind the counter and order a pound of the stuff, and if he didn't, she'd crinkle her nose and waggle her fingers *ta-ta* and they would march on to the next counter. And even when she raced ahead of him and he ended up stranded with the cart, feeling simultaneously like an abandoned child and old enough to be Stella's father, she often surprised him by coming up from behind and slipping her hand through his elbow, nuzzling him, ruffling the hair at the back of his neck. Right there in the condiments aisle, she'd kiss him on the ear.

"Love you," she'd whisper, and then, "Oh! Capers! I love capers!"

That night, though, the bitter cold had chilled her effervescence somewhat, and she left her gloves on in the store. She moved a little more quickly than usual, and Kevin found himself hustling to keep up with her. Finally, at the prepared foods counter, she squeezed his wrist and said, "Wait here, okay? Don't move," and then marched away. Luckily the young woman behind the counter was busy with other customers, so Kevin propped himself on his cart, sweating in his parka, and surveyed the astonishing heaps of glossy foods under the glass: Grilled chicken breasts marinated in lemon. Mushrooms stuffed with spinach and feta. Smoked salmon crostini. Squares of pecan-encrusted tofu like Rice Krispie treats. Turkey meatloaf with hatch chilies, sliced crosswise for easy service. And none of it for under twelve bucks a pound. In his head he writhed with mixed emotions like a gaffed fish: Who can afford to eat like this? *and* I could make my own salmon crostini for half that — assuming I knew what salmon crostini was *and* Don't they know there's a war on? *and* And a recession? *and* I'd kill for a Blimpy burger right now *and* Okay, the salmon really does look yummy. He thought of McNulty, laughing his ass off at the sight of Kevin, middle-aged, middle-class, docile as a neutered spaniel, waiting to pay $15.99 a pound for salmon on behalf of his much younger girlfriend. He saw his mother, dipping her pinky into her highball glass and licking it, then looking at him over her half-glasses. *Pecan-encrusted tofu?*

"So, what looks good to you?" a woman said to him.

Kevin looked up, but the girl behind the counter was scooping curried chicken salad into a plastic takeout shell. He turned to see a mother in a parka, holding a bundle in a snowsuit in the crook of one arm and a small wire basket full of groceries hanging from the other. She was watching him wryly, like she knew him, but out of context he couldn't place her at first — her hair was longer than she'd ever worn it for him, and she'd put on a little weight. The smile she was suppressing crinkled the corners of her eyes. God help me, thought Kevin, my younger ex-girlfriend is middle-aged.

"Beth," he said.

The crow's feet crinkled deeper. "You had to think about it, didn't you?" Still she didn't smile.

"Sorry." He pushed himself erect behind his cart.

Now she did smile—mostly friendly, with a hint of I've-got-your-number. "How are you?"

"Good!" A little high-pitched, a little too loud. "Great! How are you?"

She mimed a shudder. "Cold."

"Me too." His heart was hammering, which surprised him. It wasn't like he hadn't already run into her several times the last couple of years, in Shaman Drum or Zingerman's Roadhouse, or on line at the Michigan Theater. There had even been some stilted e-mails back and forth. When her son was born he had sent her flowers. "You look good," he said.

"Really?" He could tell she didn't believe him, but she wanted to. And he was being mostly honest. She was all bundled up in her parka and sweater and scarf, so he couldn't really check her out, but the way her face had filled out suited her. He even felt a stab of guilt, remembering how gaunt she'd looked in those last months they lived together. Was that my fault, he wondered—her hollow cheeks, the dark skin under her eyes? After all this time he still went back and forth: was he a selfish bastard, or was there no making that woman happy? After all, Kevin thought, Beth couldn't blame him for her own scary combination of intensity and indecision. But now, flushed in the heat of her winter clothes, she did look good, really, truly. She used to crop her hair boyishly short, but now it fell to her shoulders. Her cheekbones weren't as sharp as they used to be, but neither were her nerves right on the surface anymore, radiating every tremor of emotion. Her eyes were brighter, warmer.

"Really," he said. "You look...calmer."

This he regretted immediately, but she only smiled and hefted the snowsuit bundle. Kevin glimpsed a little spheric section of pink forehead; Beth's son appeared to be fast asleep inside the cinched hood of his suit.

"You hear that?" she said. "Mommy's perfectly calm."

He nearly repeated Stella's joke about Kenny from *South Park*, but in the nick of time he remembered that Kenny dies at the end of each episode.

"How's he doing?" he said instead. What do you say about the four-year-old kid of your ex, who left you to have him after thirteen years together? Especially if you can't remember the kid's name?

"It's a she," Beth said.

"A she?" Kevin's brain ground to a halt. He was certain Beth had had a son. Dear God, he thought, how could I misremember that? Okay, so I spaced on his name, but I'm too young to have forgotten the kid's sex.

"Naomi," she said, enjoying Kevin's confusion way too much. "My second child."

"Whoa." He couldn't disguise his surprise. "I didn't know."

She shrugged. "No reason you should."

"How old ... ?"

"Eighteen months."

"Huh." Kevin's geriatric brain sparked and sizzled uselessly. "Well, she looks very relaxed."

"She's like her father that way." She was looking at the child when she said this, but then she glanced at Kevin.

"Huh." That name he did know: Noah. A junior professor in ... something. A much younger guy than Kevin, younger even by a couple years than Beth. And already the father of two children. Huh.

"Not to bring the conversation to a screeching halt or anything," Beth said, smiling.

I mean, who's the injured party here? Kevin wondered. As miserable as I may have made her, in the end she left *me*. I'm the one who got the push.

"How is he?" he said, slipping about on the high ground. "Noah," he added. She wasn't going to do *that* to him again.

"Busy," said Beth, still watching him closely. He knew that look, and even now, when it shouldn't matter anymore what she thought of him, he hated it and feared it. It was the look she gave him when she was measuring him against some private standard in her head. It was a look that already held the expectation that he would disappoint her. The problem was that he never knew what the standard was, and she wouldn't tell him. It was a look that still made him angry—not the implied judgment itself, but the fact that he still let it get to him.

"I'll bet," said Kevin. He had no idea what he meant by that.

"Sir?" The girl behind the counter was speaking to him.

He and Beth nodded at each other, a couple of sparring partners separated for a moment by the ref, catching their breath, gauging each other's stamina.

"Sir? What can I get you?"

"I think she's next," he said, gesturing to Beth, who stepped right up to the counter. "I'd like a couple of slices of the turkey loaf," she said, lifting her chin at the girl. The bundle on her arm shifted, and through the deep-sea diver porthole of her hood, Kevin could see that young Naomi, daughter of Noah and not-as-young-as-she-used-to-be Beth, younger sister of whathisname, was awake and watching Kevin with cool, blue, unblinking eyes.

Kevin looked quickly away, then back into the kid's gaze. You don't know me, Kevin thought, but for a while there, I was supposed to be your father. The child just stared at him, and Kevin thought, Jesus, even the kid's judging me. He started inching away, without saying goodbye, but then something rattled into his cart—a box of couscous—and he felt a squeeze in the crook of his elbow.

"What looks good to you, sweetie?" Stella twined her arm through his and looked up at him calmly, then let her gaze drift slowly across the platters of chicken, salmon, and tofu. Nothing, he wanted to say, not a goddamn thing. Waiting for you, I'm a stationary target, a sitting duck, a great big bull's-eye for any ex-girlfriend and her *second* kid who happens by. But before he could edit this for actual conversation, Beth turned away from the case, where the girl was lifting slices of turkey loaf with a pair of tongs, and Kevin's ex narrowed her eyes at the young woman who had appeared beside him. She shot Kevin a look that made him blanch, a look that said (and Kevin ought to know) *I want you dead,* and not just dead, but crusted with pecans, stuffed with feta and spinach, and mounted on a platter with an organic apple in his mouth, sliced crosswise for easy service. Then she smiled and caught Stella's eye.

"Hi," she said.

Stella blinked, and said, "Hi" in her professional voice.

Beth looked at Kevin. By now Kevin had recovered enough to give Beth a look that said, *You dumped me, remember?* When Stella noticed the two of them looking at each other, she looked at Kevin, too.

"Um," said Kevin.

"He's too embarrassed to speak," Beth said, hefting her child to show that she couldn't shake hands, "but I'm Beth."

There should have been a little rising inflection at the end of that, thought Kevin, at least the implication of a question mark. What made Beth think Stella should recognize the name? What made her think he'd ever uttered her name to his new lover? But he had, of course, and instantly Stella opened her eyes as wide as they would go.

"Oh, *hi!*" And still clutching Kevin with one hand, she squeezed Beth on the sleeve with her leather glove. Naomi twisted in her mother's arm, swiveling her porthole toward Stella.

"Oh my God!" cried Stella, a whole octave higher. "Who's this little cutie?" Her gloved hand floated in the air, and Beth swung the kid a little closer to Stella, who tugged on one of her blunt appendages.

"That's Naomi," Kevin said, before Beth could. My archenemy. My judge. My replacement.

"She's *so* adorable." For some reason Stella was clutching Kevin even tighter. "How old is she?"

"Eighteen months." Beth let her eyes slide toward the counter, where the girl was holding her turkey loaf.

"Oh, let me!" Stella lunged for the container and slid it into Beth's basket, all without letting go of Kevin.

"Thanks," said Beth.

"Kev," Stella said, tugging on Kevin, "don't you think Naomi looks just like Kenny?"

Beth looked at him, and he could tell she was thinking, *Kev?*

But Stella just beamed at Beth. "I was just telling Kevin how much he looked like Kenny from *South Park* in his hood." She tugged again at Naomi's foot or whatever it was. "But *you* look *just* like him, don't you, munchkin?"

Beth looked skeptically at Stella. "Isn't Kenny the one who dies every episode?"

God help me, thought Kevin, but her crow's feet are sexy.

Stella gasped and pressed her leather fingers to her mouth. She blushed. "Oh my God!" She gasped again and reached across Kevin and squeezed Beth's arm. "I didn't mean...oh, I'm *so* sorry!"

Even through her gloves and the stuffing of his parka, Kevin could feel Stella's nails digging into his flesh.

"I didn't mean *that!*" she was saying.

"I know," Beth smiled. "It's okay."

Still, Kevin thought, she's enjoying this. Point, Beth.

"I feel just awful!" Stella looked up at Kevin, as if to say, *do* something. She was squeezing his arm so hard he was losing the feeling in his fingers.

"Well," he said, "Kenny always comes back in the next episode."

"That's right!" said Stella. In a minute she was going to drag him to his knees.

"The eternal return," said Kevin, almost a philosophy major. "The phoenix rising from the ashes."

Beth pursed her lips at him. Point, Kev.

"The *ouroboros,*" he said.

"The Euro-what?" said Stella.

"You asshole," says Joy Luck.

She's stopped short, and Kevin nearly blunders into her, swiveling away on the ball of his foot at the last moment. Without realizing it, he's followed her out of the forest of shelves and into the archipelago of specialty islands, where shoppers carrying baskets are grazing at buffet tables and edging up to rounded counters with signs over them that say SPECIALTY ARTISAN CHEESES and CHARCUTERIE. Jesus Christ, thinks Kevin, insinuating himself between two young women at a buffet table, *Charcuterie?* Can't they just say "deli meats" like a normal grocery store? Even the buffet he's stepped up to can't just be a buffet—GOURMET FLAVORS says the sign. He swipes his hand over his hair—damp with sweat—and blows out a sigh, as if he's trying to decide between the heirloom tomato gazpacho or the ancho honey glazed pineapple. Under his elbow he glances back at Joy Luck, to make sure she's not talking to him.

"You *asshole,*" she says again, even louder.

She's radiating anger like a tuning fork, but her back, thank God, is to Kevin. Her fists are balled and her shoulders are hunched, like she's ready to start swinging. The muscles in her long neck are pulled tight. She's attracting the glances of other shoppers, who are oh-so-subtly veering around her. Her rage is being beamed—though Kevin can't see her eyes—at a tall boy in a white, double-breasted smock and chef's cap standing behind yet another curved counter, under a sign that says, in silver letters, TRATTORIA. It's a little Italian café right in the middle of the store, with a blond wood counter and high, blond wood chairs. The tall guy is tending to some pots on a small stove behind the counter; he has a long nose and a narrow jaw and a frozen smile, and his eyes are dodging from side to side under Joy Luck's murderous gaze. The muffin top of his cap is only a foot below the lower edge of the sign, which hangs over him at the moment like the blade of a guillotine. He's holding a large wooden spoon stained with red, but even so he looks utterly defenseless against the focused rage of Joy Luck, who seems, even from behind, all sinew, claws, and teeth. Even the sexy little apple at the small of her back looks poisonous.

"Kelly!" says the boy, his eyes bouncing side to side like a doll's. *Kelly?*

"Ian, what are you doing here?" says the girl, with a disbelieving shake of her head.

What kind of name is Kelly for an Asian girl? She's the least Irish-looking young woman he's ever seen in his life. But then, of course, there's the late Kevin MacDonald, the world's only freckled, ginger-headed Islamic terrorist.

"You're back," says Ian.

"You took a new *job* while I was gone?" She's edging forward, but she's not lowering her voice. Poor Ian glances to either side, but he can't back up, and there's only a dripping wooden spoon between him and the wrath of Kelly. Kevin ducks his head and moves slowly around the end of the buffet to the other side. He still can't get over this Kelly business, though he supposes it could be worse. They could have named her Colleen. Or Bridget. Or Sinead.

"They called me on Tuesday," says Ian, "and said they needed me to start right away."

"Oh really," says the girl formerly known as Joy Luck. "So...what? They picked your name out of the phone book?"

Ian sighs. Another trattorian has appeared behind the counter, a short, dark young woman in a stained smock, her black hair coiled tightly under a hairnet except for a sweaty strand pasted to her forehead. With obvious effort she's holding a large, heavy, steaming stockpot by both handles, and she's glancing anxiously from Ian to Kelly and back again.

"Kelly," says Ian, gesturing with the wooden spoon.

"Ian," gasps the short, dark girl. Her wrists are trembling as she holds the pot.

"Maria!" says Ian, startled, and he casts about for someplace to put the spoon, thrusts it under his arm, and takes the pot from her, hefting it onto a burner behind him.

"Golly," says Kelly, "did I come at a bad time?"

The short girl glances at Kelly, then more meaningfully at Ian, and she scoots away. Ian lights the burner, raising an even rim of blue flame under the pot.

"We're setting up for lunch, Kell." Ian's looking for his spoon, can't find it anywhere. "Can we talk later?"

Aha! The spoon's under his arm, and he plunges it into the pot.

"Ian!" She stamps her foot. "What the *fuck?*"

On the safe side of the buffet a couple of guys stand to either side of Kevin, another man in a business suit and a young guy in cargo shorts and T-shirt. The suit is loading up a takeout box with marinated teriyaki tofu with ponzu sauce, while Cargo Shorts is heaping his with smokey cavatappi pasta salad. All three men exchange glances with each other: Glad it's not me!

Without looking at Kelly, Ian stirs his pot and gestures at

her with his other hand. "It's a great job, Kell. I couldn't turn it down."

"Then what the fuck was I doing in Ann Arbor, looking for an apartment?"

Ann Arbor! Kevin stands a little straighter. Huh!

"I was going to talk to you about it when you got back." Ian's stirring so hard that little spatters of red are appearing on his smock, like blood.

"This is how you tell me?" She stamps her foot again, and Kevin can almost feel the floor shake, as if from the approaching stomp of an angry T. rex. Behind the buffet, all three men lower their noses a little closer to the sneeze guard.

"I signed a lease, you *asshole*, I put down a *deposit*."

Kelly's rage has cleared a space around her in the middle of Gaia. She's like a neutron bomb — there's no blast damage, but no people left alive on the other side of the buffet table. Only Kelly shooting gamma rays in every direction, and poor Ian at the epicenter with his wooden spoon. Any second now he's going to burst into flames, his skeleton turning to dust like a particularly slow-witted vampire on *Buffy the Vampire Slayer*. But he doesn't, he only scowls at the sauce he's stirring as if he expects to find a turd in it. The front of his smock is beginning to look like a butcher's apron. Sweeney Todd, the Asshole Boyfriend of Sixth Street.

Kelly sighs. She droops. "We talked about this." She's near tears now, and Kevin feels like he personally let her down. "We *decided*."

Ian sighs and stops stirring and drops his broad chin to his chest. Then he looks up and Kevin can see Kelly's rage reflected back at her. Ian's eyes are focused and hard. He gestures toward her with his free hand, all five fingertips splayed at her, like Harry Potter casting a spell. Or warding one off.

"*You* decided," he says. "I'm not so sure I want to go to Ann Arbor."

Kelly's body tightens again. "Fine," she says, all the hurt burned out of her voice. She and Ian glare across the trattoria counter at each other. The entire store seems to have gone utterly silent, like a forest holding its breath as two snarling jungle cats circle each other. The two men on either side of Kevin slink away with their gourmet flavors, leaving Kevin paralyzed like a rabbit.

Kelly turns abruptly away from the trattoria, and Kevin flinches. Furiously impassive, Ian watches her go, and he slowly starts stirring. Then Kelly stops and turns halfway back, and Kevin flinches again. Her body's turned toward him, her legs slightly apart, but she's looking along her handsome shoulder back at Ian. It's like a dance position, or a martial arts stance, and she jerks her spectacularly firm right arm up at the elbow, and then lets it spring out to its full length, her middle finger cocked like a switchblade at Ian.

"Fuck you, *asshole*." Every muscle in that magnificent arm is taut. You could hang a cinderblock off it. "*Fuck. You.*"

Then she's gone. Kevin realizes he's been holding his breath for so long he's lightheaded, and he touches his fingertips to the edge of the buffet table to keep from toppling over. The murmur of voices flows into the silence, and the store's music reasserts itself — another boomer anthem, "Stuck in the Middle with You." Kevin turns as if in a daze, and sees Kelly parting the crowd, twisting her torso like a wide receiver. Folk feigning interest in the contents of their own baskets scurry out of her path, clowns to the left of her, jokers to the right. Kevin glances back once more at Ian, who is frowning at the splashes of red sauce on his jacket, then he draws a breath and starts after Kelly, giddily riding the eddies in her wake.

*   *   *

Outside the sliding glass doors, the air clings to his skin like cotton, but he just brushes it aside like cobwebs. He doesn't even take off his jacket. His feet aren't even touching the ground. All he's thinking is, she's moving to Ann Arbor!

Up ahead Kelly glides between the gleaming cars in the Gaia parking lot; the glitter makes Kevin fumble for his sunglasses. His inner Jiminy Cricket is hauling on the reins, pounding his little fists on the inside of Kevin's skull, screaming in Kevin's inner ear, "You're *leaving* Ann Arbor! You're moving *here!* You've *got* a girlfriend! What do you think is going to *happen?*"

"Shut up," says Kevin out loud, threading between the cars. Heat radiates off the hot metal, off the pavement at his feet. Kelly waits impatiently at the busy corner of (say the signs) Fifth and Lamar, a phalanx of vehicles streaming down Fifth while a perpendicular phalanx on Lamar idles at the light. But before the light even changes, she sprints across on her toes. In the middle of Fifth her sandal comes off. Kevin's heart stops as she staggers, turns, and hops on one foot back across the hot asphalt. Cars swerve, horns blare, and Kevin nearly dashes forward, gallant as Sir Walter Raleigh, to sweep her in his arms and carry her to safety. But then she jams her foot into the flip-flop, grips it with her toes, and marches to the curb, while angry vehicles pass only inches behind her. By time Kevin gets to the corner, cars are streaming before him, and Kelly is marching south, toward the river, down into an underpass beneath a railroad bridge. As Kevin jigs on the lee shore, frantic as a five-year-old with a full bladder, she disappears down the hill. Now he sees her only from the waist up, now only the top of her head. And now she's dropped below the horizon, out of his life, forever.

"Wait!" Kevin says, and steps into the street. Kelly's his last chance, his escape route from Stella, the last younger woman he'll ever need! And she's available! A turning car jams on its brakes, its driver leans on the horn, but it's a Lexus, so fuck you, asshole, and your forty-thousand-dollar car. Kevin nearly gives him the finger, but by time he's thought of it, he's on the other side, jogging through the viscous heat into the underpass. He should stop and take off his jacket again, he should stop and think about what he's doing—in Kevin's control room a klaxon is rhythmically blaring and red lights are flashing and a central mainframe's calm voice (a woman's, like in *Star Trek* or *Alien*) is counting down *t-minus 30, t-minus 29,* and Jiminy Cricket's clutching, what, a strut or something for dear life and kicking back desperately with his little spats at a control stick jammed all the way forward to full speed ahead. But Kevin's not slowing down, he's walking a narrow, gritty sidewalk in his fat-soled shoes, only inches from the hot cars backed up down the hill, waiting for the light behind him, because up ahead, striding toward the river, is his last chance—Kelly, Joy Luck, the Girl Formerly Known as the Girl Who Walks Like Lynda. He's not kidding himself, he knows she's not Lynda, and that's okay, because she's *better* than Lynda—Lynda was always too diffident, she fucked like a man, selfishly, taking what she wanted and not really giving a damn about him—which, don't get him wrong, was lots and lots of fun for the three months they were lovers, because nine times out of ten, Kevin totally got what he wanted, too. Up ahead Kelly skirts the plastic fencing of another construction site, nothing but concrete piers and rebar so far, as she makes her way toward a gleam of water through the trees along the river. The last time he followed that same stride toward the water, it was the afternoon of Lynda *à la plage,* only a week or so after his first night with her, when he took her to the beach at Silver Lake in his deathtrap Pinto. Well, okay, the

beach at Silver Lake isn't really a beach, only a strip of gravelly
sand a foot wide where the lawn crumbles away, so maybe he
should think of her as Lynda *du lac*. Either way she'd worn a
not-very-sexy Speedo one-piece, black, that went all the way up
to her neck and flattened her breasts, but there was no way to
unflatter her delicious backside, or her flat belly, or the fetching
points of her pelvis. When it was wet, the suit glimmered in the
bright July sunlight, and despite the mobs of splashing children
and raucous teens and the speedboats foaming just beyond the
floats marking off the swimming area, Kevin saw nothing but
the glitter of the water and the sheen of the suit as Lynda waded
into the lake, the waterline swallowing her thighs, her swaying
ass, the small of her back, creeping toward the wings of her
shoulder blades. Then she plunged in and Kevin's heart stopped
where he lay with his hands folded behind his head on a beach
towel on the grass, wearing a raggedy pair of cutoffs and trying
unsuccessfully not to have an erection. A moment later Lynda
surfaced, her strawberry hair slicked back from her freckled
forehead, and she stood in shoulder-deep water and squeezed
the water out of her hair with both hands, and Kevin, losing
the battle with his erection, launched himself from the blanket
and down the bank and splashed into the cool water with crazy,
high steps, and then dived, gliding slick as a seal, his eyes open
in the grainy, greenish water, his hard-on like a homing tracker,
until he shot up right in front of her, gasping. She gave him a
slow, heavy-lidded smile and draped her hands over his shoulders and kissed him, and he slid his hands up her Speedo'd back
and lifted her and she wrapped her legs around his waist under-
water. And then, right there, wordlessly, nose to nose with each
other, in front of the families lunching at picnic tables on the
shore and the dripping kids crowded around the snack bar, in
full sight of the screened-in porches across the lake and the
slow-paddling canoeists and the speedboats buzzing by only

twenty yards away, Lynda rocked herself against Kevin under the surface of the lake. You could hardly call it dry humping under the circumstances, and even through the thick, sodden denim of his shorts, the slick glide of the crotch of her suit was exquisite. It wasn't even that so much that made Kevin's pulse pound, made him pinch his lips bloodless to keep from moaning out loud, but rather the warmth of her under the water, both firm and weightless all at once, her flattened breasts pressing rhythmically against his bare chest, her warm thighs clenched around his waist. Looking between them at her foreshortened, refracted body, he glimpsed her sheathed belly flexing with each thrust; looking up, she was so close she seemed to have a third eye in the middle of her face, and he focused instead on the shining droplets caught in the fine blond hairs before her ear. She said nothing, but only breathed a little harder and smiled without losing that look of being half-asleep. Apart from the rhythmic rings of ripples radiating from their shoulders, you'd never know what was going on, or at least that's what Kevin told himself, and when he came his choked groan was smothered by a series of waves from a passing speedboat that slapped over his and Lynda's faces, making them both gasp and sputter. He staggered back in slow motion through the water, and she pushed off and glided away on her back, while he let the speedboat's wake and his pleasure lift him off his feet and float him toward shore.

But he never loved her. So that when she dumped him — or rather when he walked in on her fucking one of her housemates in her bare little room up under the eaves on Jefferson Avenue and she sat up on the mattress without even bothering to pull the covers up, she smiled and just kind of shrugged at him, and he just kind of shrugged back. Because that was the same summer he was in love with the Philosopher's Daughter, and what he sees now in Kelly/Joy Luck/TGWWLL is the best of both worlds—both Lynda's effortless sensuality and the imperious passion of the Philosopher's Daughter, or at least the passion the Philosopher's Daughter said she was looking for—and now this is his last chance, while he's still young enough, fit enough, good-looking and charming enough to persuade a girl possibly half his age that, despite what Ian did to her—that feckless asshole—and despite what the Philosopher's Daughter told him—that vain, heartless bitch—he *is* capable of tenderness and passion.

Kelly's veering from Lamar Avenue now, away from the water-fall rumble of traffic crossing a bridge over the river, toward a pedestrian bridge running parallel to it. Under the shadows of the exhausted, drooping trees along the riverbank, Kevin can see figures improbably jogging along a dirt trail. Kelly pauses at a crosswalk to slam a lamppost button with the heel of her hand, then sprints across without waiting for the light. Kevin jogs to catch up, sweat pouring off him, his own scent rising like steam from the open collar of his wilted shirt, and this time he reaches the crosswalk just as the signal flashes WALK. Kelly disappears under a wide spiral ramp that descends from the end of the pedestrian bridge, and Kevin hangs back at the edge of the running trail, his heart pounding from the heat, his exertion, his excitement. In the shadow of the bridge and the trees it's just as hot as it is in the sun, like being stuck in a win-dowless, airless room. Two runners in opposite directions labor past each other on the trail, dust puffing behind their shoes: a bare-chested young man in skimpy shorts, his calves and thighs bulging, and a firm-limbed young woman in a sweat-splotched sports bra, her taut muscles gliding under her skin, her blond ponytail swinging metronomically, the hem of her shorts—the Texas state flag—swaying like a bell. Kevin notes the rictus of effort on their faces, the knotted foreheads, the tightened mouths; it's almost like they're having sex with each other, but they pass without a glance. Beyond them, even the river looks exhausted—a dull, unmoving sheen of olive green. These people, Kevin thinks, these jogging Texans, they're like a whole other race of creatures, subtropical *übermenschen* genetically engineered to run in the heat, killer androids from the future walking through flame. It makes him even hotter to watch them; he can feel his shirt clinging to him like wet tissue. He glances at his watch; it's nearly twelve o'clock, but then he remembers that he didn't set his watch back, which means it's only eleven here, but even so, his interview is at two. What does he think is going to happen if he actually catches up to Kelly? For an instant Jiminy Cricket nearly gets the upper hand—she just broke up with her boyfriend, you idiot, like, ten minutes ago, so go back the way you came, scuttle from coffee shop to air-conditioned coffee shop, drink lots of iced tea, let your shirt air out, and *act your age*—but then he sees Kelly again, on a flight of stairs that rises to the pedestrian bridge under the winding ramp. Her back is erect with rage and hurt, but her walk is still as feral as a cat's, a stain of sweat plastering the back of her camisole to her spine.

He's tugged forward by the sight, he can't help himself. He's never felt this excited about Stella, not even at the beginning. Stella was an accident, a mistake, and now she's practically living with him. She's even talking about *children,* for God's sake. In the car on the way home from Gaia, the same frigid February night they'd run into Beth, Stella was quieter than usual as they crawled through the dark toward home. She held their dinner—two fat slices of turkey loaf—on her lap, under the roaring heat vent to keep it warm. Normally she'd have been talking a mile a minute, restlessly dipping into their takeout and eating crumbling pieces of turkey loaf with her fingers, but instead she sat with her cap pulled down to her eyebrows and watched the blurred lights of oncoming cars and the snow gliding in long streaks toward the windshield, all the while making those abrupt little gestures that meant she was having a conversation with herself in the Stella Continuum. At last she sighed and turned to him, and he thought: this won't be good.

"What?" He shifted in his seat, his parka hissing.

"We haven't talked about kids," she said.

Wherever Beth was at the moment—Kevin realized with a pang that he had no idea anymore where she and Noah lived—she was picking up the vibe of this conversation, hearing it in real time over whatever jungle telegraph women are hooked into and, of course, laughing her ass off. Joining her from wherever he was, was McNulty, though his laughter was less sarcastic and triumphant and I-told-you-so, and more rueful and world-weary and I-been-there-buddy. Back when they were both working at Big Star, McNulty had somehow managed to score a younger girlfriend for a time, a tall, spooky redhead, and he'd gotten her pregnant. He told Kevin about it late one soporific weekday afternoon when they were both at the cash register. McNulty wreathed his head in a cloud of cigarette smoke as if he was trying to hide behind it.

"Is she going to have it?" Kevin dropped his voice, even though there were no customers in the store. He could only wonder what that would be like, to be a father at McNulty's advanced age of forty.

"No," said McNulty, wearily rubbing his face. "I'm paying for an abortion." He breathed smoke. "Least I could do." He sucked the smoke back in. "But she doesn't want to see me after that."

Kevin stammered something, but McNulty only shook his head and stared through the swirling smoke as if at something on the horizon. "The thing is," he said, "at my age, if you want to hang onto a younger woman, you have to be willing to give her children."

Only now did he focus on Kevin through the blue haze.

"I don't expect you to understand this now," McNulty said, in his diffident stoner drone. "But someday, you will."

And now, Kevin did. In the stifling silence of the car, the tires of his Accord crunching over packed snow and the chains of the cars in the opposite lane rattling like maracas, Kevin thought of all the things he could say. *We haven't talked about kids? I'll say we haven't! And we're not going to! Not now, not ever.* It was one of those heart-freezing moments, when they wait to let you have it until you're in an enclosed space, with no place to run. (When Beth cornered him in the bath, for example.) *What are you talking about—kids? Are you crazy? We're not like that, Stella.* Their relationship was predicated on a cute meet and a blow job, and maintained on the basis of a lot of semisincerely enthusiastic sex. But of course he couldn't say that, so he said nothing, listening to the chains of the oncoming cars clinking at him like Marley's ghost.

"So what do you think?" she said.

His mouth was so dry, he wasn't sure he could speak, even if he wanted to.

"I'm almost fifty," he said at last.

"So?"

"So, figure it out. Say we start tonight, I'd be fifty-one by time the kid would be born. That means I'd be"—God help him, was this true?—"nearly seventy before he graduates from high school."

This would have silenced Beth, because it would have made her furious, leading to an explosion later on. But give Stella credit, he's thinking now, in the heat under the pedestrian bridge in Austin, Stella's not an idiot, Stella can read subtext like a Kremlinologist. And Stella's wily, she's not a slugger like Beth was. Stella would never ask him point-blank, "Don't you want to be with me for the next eighteen years?" No, Stella's got footwork, Stella floats like a butterfly and stings like a bee. Stella knows how to not take no for an answer.

"You'd be so *cute*," she'd said, reaching across the car. His hood was pushed back around his earlobes, and her glove rasped along the fabric as she stroked the side of his head. "You'll have graying sides at her graduation, like that guy on *The Sopranos*."

"Paulie Walnuts?" Kevin said. "That's your role model for fatherhood?"

Stella laughed and said, in her best HBO Jersey accent, "He's a good earner!"

Then she cracked open the plastic shell and filled the car with the warm scent of turkey loaf, popping a piece between her lips. Leaving Kevin's head ringing with the idea of children, just like she meant to.

But who would bring children into the world, now? The pillars under the ramp of the pedestrian bridge are spattered with stickers and stenciled slogans, which Kevin recognizes from the kiosks and sidewalks around the Diag back home. HAPPY OILDE-PENDENCE DAY says one sticker. 100,000 DEAD IRAQIS—HAD ENOUGH WAR YET? says another. That's the pitch he needs to try on Stella, to discourage her from childbearing. New York, Madrid, London, Mumbai—it's only a matter of time before it happens again: not if, but when—and next time it'll be a car bomb on State Street, a suicide bomber at Briarwood Mall, an airliner dropped from the sky over Metro by a Stinger. Plague virus in a reservoir, nerve gas in the subway, a nuke in a cargo container. Everybody knows it, even Stella. Buchanan Street Station freaked her out, too.

"When I'm in Chicago next week?" she told him that night, standing behind the couch, watching CNN over his shoulder, clutching her elbows. "I may have to ride the El. I mean, God!"

Maybe that's why she clings to him at night, why she wakes

up wild-eyed and trembling like a child. He passes another stenciled slogan that reads

ISLAM IS
NOT THE ENEMY,

and instinctively Kevin hears the dismissive grunt of his late Uncle Stan, his mother's oldest brother. Stan was a jowly, gin-blossomed veteran of World War II, owner of a Polish bakery on Joseph Campau Street in Hamtramck, and a habitué of the VFW hall, where he drank silently with his buddies and sometimes let eight-year-old Kevin have a sip of his Schlitz. "Tell it to the Marines, buddy boy," that's what Uncle Stan would've said if he'd lived to see the "war on terror." Some of the other guys would've found some colorful way to mispronounce Osama Bin Laden or Saddam Hussein, and one in particular, Uncle Stan's best friend, a wiry, ginger-haired little guy everybody called Rooster, would have launched into a cheerfully racist rant about the goddamn Ay-rabs in goddamn Dearborn. He'd've called them sand niggers, camel jockeys, towel heads, goat fuckers, boy lovers—"You ever see that guy, Omar whatshisname, in *Lawrence of Arabia?* Fairy son-of-a-bitch was wearing eyeliner the whole goddamn movie, like some two-dollar whore out on Eight Mile." Then he'd conclude, as he often did about the jigaboos, jungle bunnies, and spear chuckers who had ruined Detroit, "Ah hell, at least they're not Jews." Throughout all of this, Uncle Stan never joined in, but he never objected, either. He just shook his head and smiled. The closest he ever came to a demurral was when he'd noisily swallow a mouthful of beer, clear his throat, and roll his rheumy eyes toward the impressionable young Kevin. "C'mon, Rooster. My sister's kid, for chrissakes."

All that—Stan's boozing, his passive racism—was on the

one hand. On the other, Uncle Stan had provided Kevin's entrée into the middle class. That's what Stella probably didn't understand. Perhaps she assumed that because he owned a rental property two blocks from the Michigan campus, Kevin had money he wasn't telling her about, but the house was a fluke, a one-time deal. Stan had never married — he knew a thing or two, Kevin supposes, about two-dollar whores on Eight Mile — and never had any kids of his own — "That he knows about, har har har," said Rooster — and he left all his money to his nieces and nephews when he died. Who knew that fifty years of making pierogi could be so lucrative? Kevin had used his share to make the down payment on his house on Fifth Street, a purchase he'd never have been able to swing on his salary as a university staffer, and which enables him to say to Kelly — if he ever catches up to her, if he ever works up the nerve — come to Ann Arbor anyway! Forget that loser Ian! Don't worry about your deposit! I have a place where you can stay, rent free! Thank you, Uncle Stan!

That's assuming he does catch up to her. Kelly's disappeared around the turn at the landing, and all Kevin sees above him is a wedge of bleached blue sky. He can smell the river under the bridge, sour and organic, not especially unpleasant. The water is seamlessly green, soaking up the light and giving little back. Just below the surface floats a turtle, its snout thrust up for air; even it seems exhausted, its flippers barely moving.

Kevin quickens his pace up the stairs. So what if Kelly is thirty years younger? I could be Warren Beatty to her Annette Bening, I could be Michael Douglas to her Catherine Zeta-Jones. Hey, thinks Kevin, rounding the landing and starting up the next flight, I could be Sinatra to her Mia Farrow! Even if she insisted on kids — he's dimly remembering now that Mia Farrow has, what, fifteen or twenty children — Kelly would never get heavy after childbirth, she'd never lose her feral strut, never thicken around the middle, never become distracted and demanding like Beth has. He thinks of his own hollow-eyed, high-strung mother swirling a scotch on the rocks, tinkling the ice cubes, her gaze on something a million miles away. He thinks of his father, who—even more than Kevin does right now—wanted to be Frank Sinatra, wanted to be the Irish chairman of the board. An engineer for Ford, he rose without much ambition to middle management and no further, bumping along the ceiling like a half-deflated helium balloon the morning after a party. But Kevin's dad had the same first name as Ol' Blue Eyes, didn't he? And didn't Kevin's mother like to say, even affectionately sometimes, "It's Frank's world, we just live in it"? What wouldn't his father have given to have Angie or Mia hanging on his arm as he walked into the Sands? What wouldn't he have given to have some meaty goon in a cheap suit precede him into the London Chop House and say, "That's Mr. Quinn's seat you're sitting in"? Climbing the steps, Kevin remembers how his father used to sing Sinatra in the bathroom—oddly enough, never the cocky, up-tempo, ring-a-ding tunes, but always the slow, melancholy, I-had-Ava-Gardner-and-I-lost-her ones—until he was usually interrupted by his wife's sardonic rap on the bathroom door. *Two minutes, Mr. Sinatra.*

Kevin pauses on the top step, back in the sunlight. He's looking north, back the way he's come, over the trees along the riverbank toward the imperial bulk of Gaia, toward the garden of half-built condominium blocks, the toy dome of the state capitol, and the white smokestacks of the City of Austin power plant. Something overhead is buzzing, and Kevin realizes that when he heard his father singing those sad songs all alone in the bathroom, it never occurred to him to wonder—youthful narcissist that he was—what makes my father so sad? Because now, right this moment, he totally gets where his father's melancholy came from, and the realization presses down on him with all the force of central Texas's brutal sunshine. His jacket drags at him like chain mail, his shoes weigh like bricks, he's not sure if he could move even if he wanted to. And what's that buzzing, anyway? He swats at the air around his ear.

A jogger is coming toward him up the spiral ramp, another Latina Amazon like the soldier in the airport, or the bustling woman in the tight skirt on Congress. Only this one is older than the soldier and younger than the businesswoman, a no-nonsense woman in her thirties, glossy hair pulled scalp-tight, powerful thighs pistoning as she charges up the ramp, black eyes fierce on either side of her sharp Aztec nose. Her fists clench and unclench as she runs, her shoes slap the pavement, her breath comes in sharp bursts, *huh-huh-huh-huh*. She pounds by him without a glance, close enough for him to smell the ammoniac tang of her sweat, her ponytail whipping like a lash.

And there's Kelly halfway across the bridge, tightly gripping the railing with both hands, gazing back along the river at Austin's boomtown skyline. He can't see her face from here, can't read her expression, but her hair is pushed back behind her ear, the ends of it plastered to the long, lovely curve of her neck. If he gets a little closer, maybe he can read her mood, guess what she's thinking, figure out what to say to her. He moves along the bridge, which is wide and sinuous and paved with cream and pink lanes of concrete, with square planters and green benches along the sides. Kelly is standing at a buffed steel railing next to a short lamppost with a flat steel shade like a monsignor's hat, and now she's gazing up at a little single-engine plane buzzing high over the river, dragging behind it a limp orange banner that Kevin can't quite read. *HOT*something. Or is it *OTT*? As the plane banks back toward the skyline in the breathless heat, the banner only folds a different way instead of straightening, and Kevin sees the letters *ERS*. Can that be right? Is someone paying to advertise *OTTERS* over Austin, Texas?

Well, there's your opening line, thinks Kevin, edging forward. His feet are burning, and he's pretty sure the sour odor he smells now is not the sluggish river, but the steam from his own armpits, under his jacket. Despite the utter lack of wind, the buzzing of the little plane comes and goes; maybe the heat dampens the sound. He's hoping Kelly is as puzzled by the banner as he is.

" 'Otters'?" he'll say.

But won't she freak when she sees it's the guy from the seat next to her on the airplane? Or what if it's worse — what if she doesn't recognize him at all? She hasn't yet; she walked right past him in the coffeehouse and the grocery store, and somehow she hasn't noticed him treading after her like a faithful mutt for the last hour. Could it be that he's that anonymous, that middle-aged? Now he knows why his father sang melancholy Sinatra in the shower, and the memory of his father's bass-baritone — too low for Sinatra, he strained for the high notes — unexpectedly tightens his throat. It kills Kevin to think he never put it together, the difference between what his father sang when he was alone and thought no one could hear, and what he sang when he was harmonizing with his SPEBSQSA buddies two Saturdays a month, one hideous old chestnut after another: *By the liiiight...(by the light, by the light)...of the silvery mooooon...(that silv'ry moon!).*

"Oh God," Kevin used to moan, slouching into the family room where Mom watched TV with the sound way up, while Dad and his florid friends preserved and encouraged barbershop quartet singing in America from the paneled basement below, "make it *stop.*"

"Shh." His mother cradled her drink in one hand and with the other aimed the huge remote at the Zenith, clicking *M*A*S*H* up even louder.

"He can't hear me," Kevin whined.

"I don't care if he can hear you," said his mother. "I'm trying to watch Alan Alda."

"Fuck Alan Alda," muttered Kevin.

"What's that?" She heard that, even over the tinny laughter from the Zenith.

"Nothing." Slouching away again, down the hall toward his room.

"What did you say, young man?"

"*Nothing*, okay? *Jee*-zus." Rolling his eyes as the idiot laugh track swelled and the blowhards in the basement swung with terrifying enthusiasm into some awful tune from *The Music Man*. *Oh Lida Rose, oh, Lida Rose, oh, you put the sun back in the skyyyyy* ... God! Another Saturday night in Royal fucking Oak, the armpit of the fucking universe. Another fucking Saturday night in hell. He slammed his bedroom door and switched on the stereo, twirling the volume as high as it would go, to WRIF. The fucking turntable was broken and he'd spent all his money last week on weed — weak shit, too, fucking worthless — and the thought of *that* stalled him in the middle of his littered bedroom floor while Arthur Penhallow breathed heavily out of the speakers. If only Mom'd have another highball, he could tiptoe past her snoring on the sectional couch and ride his ten-speed up Twelve Mile to the mall, where he was pretty sure he could score some better weed off a guy who worked at Spencer Gifts. Worse yet, 'RIF was bumming him out; it's always fucking "Stairway to Heaven" or fucking Bob Seger or J. fucking Geils — and tonight it's fucking "Aqualung," he fucking *hates* that song. So he switched the stereo off and flung himself onto his bed and piled both pillows over his face and screamed as loud as he could, "I wish I was an ORPHAN!"

And later that evening, he was halfway there. Cruising home at eleven with no light on his bike, standing on the pedals, his pupils dilated wide as dimes, he found an ambulance in the driveway and a police car at the curb, and the Murrays and the Nowakowskis on his front lawn. Mrs. Murray and Mrs. Nowakowski each struck the same pose, one arm pressed across her midriff, one hand pressed to her mouth. Mr. Murray stood with his arms crossed talking in low tones to Mr. Nowakowski, who had his hands thrust in his pockets. Nancy Nowakowski, with whom Kevin had almost lost his virginity another Saturday night not long before—"Aren't we naughty?" he'd said to her before she peeled his hand off her warm breast—Nancy gave him a look of wide-eyed pity, brushing his arm in passing with her fingertips as he dropped his bike on the grass and went up the steps. Inside, in the living room, his gawky sister, Kathleen, all knees and elbows, was doubled over on the sofa, sobbing, while Mom's priest, Father Vince, perched on the cushion next to her and patted her awkwardly on the back. Kevin floated through the room toward the hallway, at the end of which he could see his mother standing just outside the master bedroom in the same pose as Mesdames Murray and Nowakoski, arm over midriff as if she'd been punched, hand to her mouth. Kevin's growing alarm sparked uselessly through the fog of his high like a flint that wouldn't light, and a cop like a middle linebacker stopped Kevin by putting his beefy hands on Kevin's shoulders and looked knowingly into the boy's dilated pupils.

"Are you Kevin?" he said with surprising tenderness.

Wow, thinks Kevin on the bridge. He turns his back on Kelly and palms the tears out of the corners of his eyes. I don't need this now, I really, really don't, but there's no stopping it: thirty-five years later, the night of his father's death can still sneak up on him. Sitting on the end of the bed after his barbershop buddies went home, Kevin's father died as he bent over to untie his shoes, a pair of Hush Puppies that he wore around the house. Mom was talking to him through their open bathroom door. She saw him puff out his cheeks and pat his stomach as if he had indigestion, then she turned away. When she turned back, he was already dead, in a heap on the carpet. It was that quick. Unlike Grandpa Quinn's death later in a morphine fog from colon cancer, which was slow and unpleasant and as well-attended as an English king's, half a dozen people crowded into the bedroom watching each whispery breath from his blue lips, Kevin's father vanished when no one was looking. No one ever talked to Kevin about it, so everything he knows about what a heart attack is like is from that old Richard Pryor routine, and the older he gets, the more he thinks about it, not just because it might foreshadow what will happen to him, but because he can't help but wonder what his father thought in that last moment. Was it painful? Did he feel a blow to the chest? A seam of fire up his left arm? Did he hear the voice of God, *pace* Pryor, telling him to *stay down, motherfucker?* Was it a good way to go, not seeing it coming, not having to think about it, blindsided by death? Did his life fast-forward before his eyes? Was he scared? Was he resigned? Was he relieved? Annoyed? Angry? Did he think it was funny to die like that, bending over to untie your Hush Puppies, with your wife ignoring you from across the room? Did he even know it was happening, or was it, now you see me, now you don't? Going, going, gone. Did he snuff out like a candle, like a spark floating away from a fire? Or did he just bend over into oblivion, like someone diving into dark water?

Is it the heat that's making Kevin breathless? Or is he having a heart attack right now, just like his dad? He steadies himself on the railing, which is warm to the touch, on the other side of the bridge from Kelly, facing west. Directly before him is the Lamar Avenue Bridge, a gray, weather-stained, WPA-era span that springs wearily across the river on five low arches. Kevin can hear the clack of tires over expansion joints as cars charge too fast onto the bridge, and then the squeal of tires as one impatient SUV lurches to a stop where the snake of traffic has kinked up at the light at the south end of the bridge. Beyond it tiny, glittering cars flash along a highway bridge over a distant bend in the river, and on the hills beyond that the mansions Kevin saw from Congress Avenue rise more clearly now, cream-walled and red-roofed.

He glances sideways. The Amazon runner has stopped to stretch, folding herself in two and grabbing her ankles from behind, a sight that is alternately painful and thrilling to see. Nearer to Kevin, a portly young guy with an unkempt black beard and a distended black T-shirt sits on a bench smoking, while a plump, liver and white springer spaniel pants at his feet, the two of them connected by a long, red canvas leash that winds around the fat guy's wrist. Kevin turns a little more, and there's Kelly still gazing east up the river where the plane is still weaving a weary figure eight over the skyline, still unsuccessfully trying to make that stupid banner unfurl. An old, rust-red railroad trestle supported by cement pylons comes out of the treetops of one bank and disappears into the treetops on the other, and over each pylon graffiti writers have left a fat-lettered slogan like a tangle of yellow pythons, completely unreadable, except for one, SCOPE LORIC, whatever that means, right in the middle of the trestle, in bold white letters. Beyond the trestle, more bridges, with cars shuttling silently back and forth, and on the north bank the coppery pyramids and pale deco skyscrapers and the thicket of cranes. The ice-blue tower of Barad-dûr rises out of the sunlit haze, improbably tall and narrow. Meanwhile another jet climbs steeply over Austin's skyline, baring its long neck. Kevin can hear its hollow roar trailing behind it, a bass note to the annoying treble buzz of the little plane, and he wonders, which one is Snoopy and which the Red Baron? Is it wise these days to let either plane fly so close to a city skyline? Thinks Kevin, am I the only one who worries about stuff like this? Or does everybody, these days?

Kelly steps back from the railing, and pushes her hair back with both hands, arching her back. Kevin flinches and looks over his side of the bridge at a moiré of ripples on the water below. Closer to the shore, five startlingly white swans, two big ones and three baby ones, paddle idly among the reeds along the bank. On the jogging trail above them a single file of jogging mothers push fabulously engineered strollers like little Formula One racers, and when the mother in the lead turns and starts galloping sideways, her legs scissoring, all the other mothers do the same. Out of the deep bucket seat of the last stroller flies a petulantly flung stuffed animal, which rolls in the dust, and the last mother stops and stoops to retrieve the toy. Some of the jogging mothers are a bit broad in the beam yet, still losing their baby weight, but as the last woman returns the stuffed animal to her invisible little tyrant in the stroller, Kevin admires the long, lean line of her leg as she bends over. She's a MILF, thinks Kevin, an acronym he never knew until he heard it on *The Daily Show,* which he watches in bed with Stella. Oh God, he thinks, is Stella already a Mother I'd Like to Fuck? A year from now, is that going to be Stella, in Gallup Park or the Arb, pushing her expensive, high-tech jogging stroller along the river with her child? With *my* child?

Now Kevin's heart is racing. He's feeling breathless again. Maybe he is having a heart attack. Or at least heatstroke. He grips the warm railing with both hands and takes a couple of deep breaths, but the air is so hot he can't draw it deeply enough. It's like drowning in warm water, and he squeezes the railing to steady himself. There's a bench nearby, and he wonders if it's better to hang onto the railing before his dizziness passes, or risk the few paces and have a seat. The fat guy with the hefty spaniel is standing and stubbing his cigarette out on the side of a planter, and his dog is on its feet, too, looking up at its master with a goofy, gummy grin, his long tongue draped sideways over his teeth like a big pink necktie. Beyond him the Amazon runner stands with her legs apart and her hands clasped under her ponytail, elbows in the air, and she's bending slowly from side to side. Kevin starts slowly toward the bench; he's feeling a little less lightheaded, but he trails one hand along the railing. From the Lamar Avenue Bridge he hears another squeal of brakes and the sharp blare of a horn. The fat guy looks up and loosens his grip on the leash, which unloops from his fat wrist, and the goofy spaniel trots toward Kevin. Nearly to the bench now, Kevin sees that Kelly has turned away from the railing on her side of the bridge and she's looking at him, as if trying to remember where she's seen him. Kevin's not sure where to look. The wet nose of the spaniel brushes his left hand, and Kevin hears the fat guy say, "It's cool, he's friendly." But Kevin ignores the dog, which circles round him to the railing, trailing the slack leash. Instead Kevin looks past Kelly, past the railing, past the railroad trestle to see the single-engined plane climbing like mad, whining like an angry lawnmower. The orange banner has at last snapped straight behind the plane. HOOTERS, it says.

In spite of himself, in spite of the heat, in spite of his racing heart, Kevin starts to laugh. In spite of his lightheadedness, in spite of his fear of incipient fatherhood, in spite of the prospect of Kelly recognizing him, in spite of the prospect of her *not* recognizing him, he laughs. Kelly's expression turns quizzical. Their eyes have met, it's too late to turn back now, so he just grins like the sad, middle-aged loser that he is, and points at the banner in the sky. She turns to see what he is pointing at. The dog is nuzzling Kevin's leg; the fat guy is saying, "Barney, not your party, buddy, *not your party*," and reeling in the leash. Then just as another long squeal of brakes peals from the traffic bridge, Kelly sees the banner and her spine stiffens. A horn blares, the squeal of tires goes on and on, Kelly turns back toward Kevin, and before their eyes even meet, he can see the withering, soul-shriveling look of disdain on her lovely face. Oh boy, thinks Kevin, but still, he laughs.

And then — the squeal of brakes ends in a loud, metallic bang. Kelly starts at the sound. The spaniel flinches and darts between Kevin and the railing. And the leash tightens around Kevin's calves and jerks him off his feet.

Kevin knows he's falling, but at the same time he knows there's nothing he can do about it. Events seem to slow and to become more inevitable all at once. It's a moment of perfect, blissful contradiction: it feels like it could last forever, as if Kevin falling is something that has always happened and always will, but he also knows it's only an instant, and will be over almost before it's started. A moment like this is the closest Kevin has ever come or ever will come to a spiritual experience, when he is perfectly aware of everything around him even as he loses all control. He's thrilled by the vastness and infinite complexity of the world, even as he's aware of its utter indifference to him. And so he's calm, in spite of the pain he knows is coming and doesn't have time to brace for, and yet it's not as if he's watching someone else. He's fully present in himself and in the moment, and yet he, too, feels a sublime indifference, because the outcome is inevitable, so why worry about it? There's nothing you can do, so just enjoy this vivid clarity, this glimpse of eternity, this momentary lifting of the veil. He wonders, is this what my father felt — bending over, falling into darkness — did he feel this peeling back of the senses, this simultaneous stillness and tumult of sound and light? As the ground rushes up to meet him, Kevin wonders, is this what it's like to die?

PART TWO

Can't You
Hear Me
Knocking?

"DON'T SIT UP."

Kevin has no intention of sitting up. Sitting up is the furthest thing from his mind. He's aware of someone near him—more than one person, in fact—but all he can see is faded blue sky, a spiderweb in an angle of railing, and the blurred silhouettes of dead bugs in the frosted dome of one of the flat-topped lights along the bridge. The sight is startlingly clear and strange all at once; the sunlight seems to be brighter than it was before. He feels like he does when he wakes up disoriented from a long nap on a Sunday afternoon, or after snoozing for an hour or two after dinner on a weeknight—unsure of where he is or what time it is, but everything around him vivid and bright. He's aware that his fall represents a caesura, and it doesn't really matter whether he's been out for hours or minutes or only seconds: the break somehow stands for infinity, and now, on the other side of it, everything is strange and as sharply defined as a cartoon.

"Did you hit your head?" says the same voice, a woman's.

Kevin blinks and tries to focus his attention on the back of his head. What just happened? Why is he flat on his back? The numbers 666 float before him, which jolts him a little further alert. Is this a Buchanan Street Station situation? He didn't hear a bang, but then he wouldn't have, would he? Or at least he wouldn't remember it. His ears are ringing a little but then they always are, from all that loud music he heard years ago in Second Chance and Joe's Star Lounge. Are there other people around him, flat on their backs as well? Or worse, pieces of other people? Is he all there himself, or is he bleeding to death from a severed leg? Maybe that's why his head doesn't hurt, because all his blood is draining out his femoral artery. He lifts his head to look.

"Barney, *no*," somebody else says, and suddenly, in monstrous close-up, Kevin sees gummy, drooling jaws, yellowed incisors, bloodshot eyes. There's a hoarse panting in his ear, a wet nose against his cheek, sour doggy breath all over his face.

"Could you please keep your dog back, please?" says the woman.

The dog recedes with a yelp and a scrabbling of claws.

"Sorry, sorry," says the second voice, a man. Then, louder, "Dude, I'm sorry. Are you okay?"

"No," says Kevin.

"Lie still," says the woman, and at last Kevin sees a face — Aztec nose, dark eyes, glossy, scalp-tight black hair — between him and the sky. She holds her hand over his face. "How many fingers am I holding up?"

Now Kevin's Admiral Adama in the CIC of the *Galactica*, which is full of smoke and sparking wires, and he's waiting for a damage control report. All decks are checking in: the bulkheads held, the hull's intact, nobody was vented into space. He can wriggle his toes and fingers, his head feels fine. The pavement under his back is very warm. Meanwhile the Amazon runner is splaying her thumb and two fingers just beyond his nose, so close that they're out of focus.

"Three," says Kevin, and he lifts his own hand to push them away. "Let me up."

She presses his chest with the tips of her fingers to keep him down, but he levers up onto his elbows anyway. Only now is he beginning to worry about his suit. Just beyond the toes of his shoes, the spaniel Barney reposes like the Sphinx, panting, while the fat guy holds the leash tight and bounces awkwardly on his toes as if he's about to run away. The Amazon is squatting next to Kevin on her powerful thighs, peering at him intently. She's close enough that he can smell her sweat.

"Easy." She grips him firmly under one arm as he pushes himself up off the warm pavement. On his feet he feels light-headed, and he's aware of his heart hammering. He brushes the grit off his palms.

"Sit." The Amazon's warrior grip guides wobbly Kevin to a bench.

"Man, I'm so sorry," says the fat guy. "Barney," he snaps, "bad dog. *Bad* dog." The dog only looks up at its master mournfully, his big pink tongue lolling out of his mouth.

"Here." The Amazon offers Kevin his sunglasses, and he turns them over in his hands as if he's never seen anything like them before. Then he notices that his hands are trembling a little, so he folds the glasses and slides them into his jacket to cover it up. Then he remembers what the glasses are for and takes them out again and puts them on. In their autumnal glaze the Amazon stands with her hands on her hips, watching him.

"Just let me catch my breath." Kevin puts his hands on his thighs. It isn't until then that he notices the rip in his right trouser leg, and the blood oozing through the grit embedded in the skin of his knee.

"Oh, *man*," says Kevin, with a petulant, rising inflection. "Son of a *bitch*."

And it isn't until he actually looks at the scrape, at the blood running down his shin and into his sock, that he realizes how much it hurts. He lifts his foot to flex the knee; he can move the joint without any trouble, but the scrape burns.

"Ow!" he says, his hands twitching over the torn fabric of his trousers. He wants to brush away the grit embedded in his kneecap, but he's afraid to touch it. He looks up at the sheepishly grinning fat guy, and now, along with the pain, Kevin's aware that he's angry.

"Goddammit, I have a job interview in a couple of hours." He gestures at the irreparable rip in his suit trousers, at the blood trailing down his leg.

"Oh, man," says the fat guy. "I'm really sorry. You should've—"

"I should've *what*? Kicked your fucking dog?"

The guy cringes and hauls on the leash, forcing the spaniel to his feet and out of range. Now Kevin feels bad. It's not Barney's fault, he was just being a dog. Kevin slumps back against the bench, wondering if he's torn his jacket, too. In frustration he flops his hands into his lap.

"I mean, *fuck*. I have a job interview. In three *hours*."

"Easy." The Amazon has perched on one buttock on the bench next to Kevin. "Right now, we should do something about that scrape. Think you can walk on it?"

Kevin's knee is really beginning to sting, and the sun is pressing down on him again. Even if the jacket isn't torn, his whole suit is wilted now in the heat, wrinkled and dusty and marinated in his sweat.

"Yeah." He flexes the knee again; the pain doesn't seem to go any deeper than his lacerated skin. "I think so."

The woman stands. "My vehicle's right over there." She nods toward the south end of the pedestrian bridge, where it empties into some drooping trees. "I've got a first aid kit." Her hand hovers over his arm.

"I can make it." Kevin waves her away. His hands are still shaking, though. He doesn't even look at the fat guy as he pushes up off the bench and limps after the woman. The pain's not so bad after the first couple of steps, and he's aware again of the oppressive heat and the enervating sunlight and the angry buzzing of the little airplane overhead. Which is getting louder now, not so much a buzz as a deep, throbbing grind. He looks up to see the plane crawling straight overhead, hauling the HOOTERS sign at a steep, unreadable angle west, up the river. The plane's so low he can see the cables that lead from the fuselage to the banner. He stops, and the woman stops, too, her hand discreetly poised at his elbow, but Kevin's only scanning the sky for the jet as a gauge of how long he's been out. Except for the dwindling dopplered drone of the Hooters plane, the sky is empty and silent, but Kevin looks around him for a moment longer. The fat guy has been following, and he stops, too, yanking the dog painfully tight on the shortened leash. "You lose something?" he says.

Kevin's not sure. On the Lamar Avenue Bridge, the southbound traffic is backed all the way up the hill toward Gaia; halfway across the bridge, the front end of a small white car is accordioned under the rear bumper of an SUV, and two figures stand gesticulating in the heat. Kevin recognizes neither of them, but then he's got it, what's gone missing, what he's lost: Kelly, Joy Luck, the Girl Who Walks Like Lynda, Kevin's once and future lover. *La belle dame sans merci,* his last chance. He's been flat on his back and bleeding from the leg long enough for her to vanish completely, as if she never existed in the first place. Her absence stings even worse than the scrape on his knee. He hasn't just lost her, he's lost the original Lynda, Lynda 1.0, Lynda Classic. Lynda on the dance floor, Lynda *à la plage,* Lynda on the railing.

"No," says Kevin, and he starts walking again. As the three of them—four, if you count the dog—approach the end of the bridge, the fat guy blurts out a further apology.

"I'd offer to pay for the pants, sir?" he says. "But I'm sort of between jobs right now? But what I *could* do, I have a really nice pair of pants in my apartment—it's not far from here?—and I could let you borrow them? Actually, you could *have* them, they're a really nice pair of pants..."

Beyond the trees at the end of the bridge Kevin can see the flash of a passing car. He stops and sighs and looks the guy up and down. Kevin's not particularly proud of much, but he is proud of the fact that at age fifty, he's still wearing a 34-inch waist. This guy will never see the inside of 40 inches again. The kid notices Kevin looking, but Kevin doesn't care.

"I've had them for a while." Even in the heat, the guy is blushing. "I can't get into them anymore—"

"It's okay." Kevin waves him away. "Don't worry about it."

The kid, Kevin can see, wants nothing more than to be let off the hook, and Kevin, even though he's hot, angry, and frustrated, can't for the life of him see any reason to make this boy more uncomfortable than he already is. Kevin's a midwestern college-town liberal not just by accident of birth, but by temperament. It's in his bones to see both sides of a question, and even now he knows just how this boy is feeling—simultaneously guilty and resentful, wanting to do the right thing but afraid he'll have to pay for something that he doesn't really think is his fault. Times like this, Kevin wishes he were a Republican, full of absolute certainty and righteous, tribal wrath: he'd yell at the guy, threaten to sue him, offer to visit some Old Testament shock and awe on the kid's fat ass. He could even have the dog impounded—and then the very thought pierces Kevin's congenitally bleeding heart, because the spaniel is looking up at his plump master with a goofy, endearing look of pure devotion. At the very least he should dress the kid down, tell him (like Kevin's mother would) that *some people* shouldn't be allowed to *have dogs* if they can't *keep them under control*. But Kevin can't even muster enough righteous anger to do that. Not to mention the Amazon is watching them both: if he loses his cool in front of her, she might leave him here, bleeding and limping, to fend for himself in a strange city. Suddenly I'm Blanche Dubois, thinks Kevin, depending on the kindness of strangers.

"Seriously," Kevin says, softening his tone, "I'm not mad. I got a couple hours, I'll just go buy another pair of pants. Don't worry about it."

He turns away, but the kid, God bless him, says, "I could give you my address, so when I get a job I could pay you back..."

Twenty years or so ago, Kevin stood with a weeping Rooster on the sticky roof of Uncle Stan's bakery in Hamtramck and watched the popemobile glide between mobbed sidewalks under listless Polish flags along Joseph Campau Avenue, and he saw John Paul II in his bulletproof cube like an action figure in its original packaging, gently slicing the air from side to side before him. Now Kevin makes the same benedictory gesture.

"*Ego te absolvo,*" he says to the boy with the dog. "Go and sin no more." Before the boy can say anything else, Kevin limps away alongside the Amazon.

"That was nice of you," she says.

Kevin shrugs. His nerves are still jangling from his fall, his emotions are right at the surface, and the last thing he wants to do is lose it in front of this rather intense woman. He exaggerates his limp a bit so that he can hang back and get a grip on himself. And also, though this wasn't his first thought, so that he can check her out from behind. She's certainly powerful-looking. He likes leanness in a woman, but actual muscles, like this woman's got, don't do much for him. The fact that he's not automatically attracted to her worries him a bit—is it possible that he's not turned on by a woman that he doesn't think he could overpower? Sometimes with Beth sex used to be a kind of wrestling match, and he'd enjoyed grappling with her as much as (so far as he knew) she'd enjoyed grappling with him, until he'd pinned her, breathless, to the bed. It wasn't always like this, of course, but often enough, right to the end of their time together. What does that say about him? All these years later, does it turn out that Shulamith Firestone was right all along, that all men are rapists deep down? This woman is certainly solid, almost brawny, with a formidable gravitas; her military bearing tells him that she doesn't suffer fools gladly. If he tried to pin this woman to a bed, no matter how playfully, she'd break his neck. As he follows her off the pedestrian bridge and along the street toward a narrow parking lot under the looming, rusting span of the railroad trestle, Kevin gratefully leaps at the possibility that it's her humorlessness, not her strength, that turns him off. That's it, that's the problem: it's not who would win two out of three takedowns, it's that he's never known how to deal with a woman if he couldn't make her laugh.

"How you doing?" she says without looking at him, and from a pocket of her running shorts she pulls a key remote and clicks it. The lights of an enormous, shiny red pickup truck blink and chirp.

"I'm hot." Limping up to the truck, Kevin takes off his jacket and splays his fingers under the collar so he can slap the dust off the back of it. No rips, thank God, no permanent scrapes. If he'd had to replace the jacket, then he really would be angry.

"You're a little overdressed for the trail, don't you think?" Now the Amazon smiles back at him. It's a knowing smile, showing some bright teeth. Okay, thinks Kevin, she's capable of irony, that's a start. She opens the driver's door and pats the seat, and he climbs up into the baking heat of the cab and sits sideways in the bucket seat with his jacket folded across his lap and his knees sticking out the door. Meanwhile she leans over the side of the truck bed and rattles around in a big plastic storage box. His scrape is really burning now, and his sock is sticky and warm where the blood has soaked into it. New trousers, new socks—he draws the line at a new pair of shoes, no matter how much blood soaks into one of them. A hundred and fifty dollar shoes, he reminds himself, his anger flaring again. He slumps sideways in the seat, his temple against the padded headrest, the heat at his back even worse than the heat outside, the glitter from the traffic at the end of the Lamar bridge getting to him even through his sunglasses. Maybe I should just pack it in, he thinks, call a cab, go back to the airport, fly home. I can't live in this wretched heat, in this merciless sunlight, surrounded by upscale Gaians and mouthy homeless guys and fat slackers with clumsy spaniels. Not to mention brawny, imperious women who could break me in two. I can't take it. I'm not engineered for it.

"What's that?" The Amazon is standing in front of Kevin again, twisting the cap off a bottle of water; there's a red plastic first aid kit wedged under her arm. Now that he's marginally less distracted by everything that's happened in the last few minutes—falling, bleeding, sweating—Kevin takes a good look at her. She's a little older than he thought—she has laugh lines, improbably enough, and a few more lines in her neck than he noticed before—but she truly is amazingly fit. Even when all she's doing is twisting the cap off the bottle, her biceps flex under her glistening bronze skin. Sweat beads across her tight forehead and along the struts of her collarbone, and she peers at him with some sort of professional gaze, like she's sizing him up.

"Sorry?" Kevin says.

"You said something about engineering." She hands him the bottle. "Are you an engineer?"

"No." Kevin's alarmed that he spoke without realizing it. The bottle is blessedly cold in his hand, and he puts it to his lips and chugs a third of it. The shock of the cold water against his palate almost blinds him. Meanwhile the woman reaches into the truck bed again, and Kevin hears the hollow thump of a cooler lid and the liquid rattle of ice. She comes back with a bottle of orange Gatorade, which she twists open just as briskly.

"Editor," gasps Kevin, the cold water freezing all the bones around his sinuses.

"Mm." The woman nods with her mouth full, recaps the Gatorade, and sets it on the pavement.

"I'm an editor." Kevin presses the cool lower half of the water bottle to his forehead.

"Okay," she says. "Hold this." She lays the first aid kit on top of Kevin's jacket on his lap; it's like the grade-school lunchboxes of his youth, only without gaudy pictures of the Monkees or the Man from UNCLE. She stands so close to him now that he can see the fine texture of her skin, but she doesn't meet his eye; Kevin can't tell if she's being wary or demure. Of course, it has to be wariness—who's demure anymore? She pops open the kit with her thumbs, reaches in, and snaps on a pair of surgical gloves.

"Wow," says Kevin. "Is it that bad?"

"No." She stoops to pry apart the rip in his pant leg with her latex fingers. The whitish gloves stand out on her dusky skin like she's dipped her hands in paint. Kevin notes the Euclidean straightness of the part in her tight, glossy hair, admires its military precision.

"But I don't know where your blood's been, do I?" She says this abstractedly; it's a line she's used before. Then she looks up, fixes his gaze with her dark eyes, and smiles. "These pants are goners. Mind if I tear them a little wider to get at your knee?"

"Usually I'd expect dinner and a movie first," Kevin says, "but go ahead."

She smiles, but it's a professional smile. She's heard *that* one before, too. Kevin's lizard brain begins to race. Who needs Kelly? Who needs the shopworn memory of Lynda on the railing? This moment right here, as the Amazon in latex tears his pant leg down to the middle of his shin with one sharp jerk, *this* is his official Austin Cute Meet. Yes, she's formidable, and certainly fitter than Kevin—those biceps, those quads—but didn't he used to fantasize about Sigourney Weaver in *Aliens?* And buff Linda Hamilton in the second *Terminator?* And, more recently, tough little Starbuck on *Battlestar Galactica?* Not to mention that the Amazon is more age-appropriate for him than Kelly or Stella or even Beth. Linda Hamilton, yeah, sort of crossed with that Latina actress he likes—not Jennifer Lopez, but the one who used to be in those John Sayles movies. She didn't get those muscles and her brisk, no-nonsense manner from working in an office, thinks Kevin, and he remembers the first Amazon he saw today, the fierce National Guardswoman at the airport, and he wonders if this warrior priestess, dabbing the blood and grit away from his knee with a piece of gauze, might also be in the military. Wouldn't that freak out his friends in Ann Arbor, if he ended up with a Texan, a Chicana, and a soldier!

"Am I hurting you?" She lifts the bloody gauze away from his knee.

"No," Kevin says, so she presses a little harder. It does hurt, a little, but he'd never admit it to a woman like this. Obviously she's some sort of health care professional—she snapped those gloves on without hesitation, and she's probing expertly at his knee. Oh my God, she's a nurse, concludes Kevin, this *is* my lucky day, not just because he's getting his minor injury treated for free by a professional, but because she's a *nurse.* Mick McNulty used to rhapsodize about nurses: among all the crummy jobs he'd held before his crummy job at Big Star Records, he'd been an orderly in a couple of nursing homes, and he used to tell Kevin that nurses made the best lovers, that they weren't squeamish or sentimental about bodies, that they saw blood and shit and puckered flesh all day long, that fucking was just another natural function as far as they were concerned. In the years since, Kevin has realized that McNulty's enthusiasm about the sexual sangfroid of nurses was just a variant of the male erotic mythology that celebrates the innate lubricity of cheerleaders, flight attendants, and waitresses. But on the other hand, McNulty claimed to be speaking from a deep and intimate experience of his subject.

"Get yourself a nurse, young man," said McNulty, the Horace Greeley of guilt-free balling, and now Kevin can't help but smile, because his inner nineteen-year-old is telling him that he's hit pay dirt. Meanwhile Nurse Amazon is shaking up a little plastic bottle.

"Now *this* is going to sting," she says, soaking a fresh piece of gauze.

But it doesn't sting at first, it only stains his knee a rusty orange, and Kevin is relieved. It wouldn't do to squeal like a girl in front of Nurse Amazon, but then of course his knee begins to sting like the slow burn of a hot sauce, and Kevin gasps in spite of himself.

"Told you," she says.

"What is that," Kevin says, as the burn creeps all the way through to his kneecap, "some sort of jalapeño marinade?"

"Actually," says the woman as she rips the backing off a large, square bandage, "capsaicin, which is what makes jalapeños hot, is the active ingredient in some topical pain ointments."

"It's not working, then," says Kevin, wincing as she presses the bandage across his scrape.

"Not *this*." She smoothes the adhesive edges down with her thumbs. "This is an antiseptic, and it's citrus-based. It's supposed to burn." She smiles at him again, and her laugh lines crinkle fetchingly. "That's how we know it's working."

"Mission accomplished." The sting of the antiseptic actually seems to be making Kevin sweat more, if that's even possible. "Plus," he says, "my wound will be lemony fresh."

She laughs, this time for real. Suddenly Kevin's tumble on the bridge, his embarrassment, the citric acid burning through his patella—now it all seems worth it. He's gotten Nurse Amazon, the Priestess of Minor Injuries, to laugh.

She snaps off the gloves as briskly as she snapped them on—no wedding ring, notes Kevin—and pitches them into the truck bed. "You'll want to keep that clean and dry. And here." She hands him another, clean bandage from the first aid kit. "Just in case."

She has to stand close to him again to shut the kit on his lap. This time he catches her eye, and she purses her lips and ducks her gaze—can it be?—demurely.

"Thanks. You've been really great." Kevin tucks the bandage into the breast pocket of his shirt, while she returns the first aid kit to the storage box. "You take Blue Cross?"

Nurse Amazon has stepped back from the truck to swig some more Gatorade. It's almost as if she wants Kevin to get a better look at her, but then he considers how he must look to her—pale, sweaty, rumpled—and thinks, I should be so lucky. But of course he takes a good long look anyway, admiring her solid, fat-free thighs, the definition of her biceps, the muscles in her throat as she tips her head back and swallows. Then she lowers the bottle, swipes her lips with the back of her hand, and says, "No charge."

"Must be my lucky day, then," Kevin says, pausing to swig the last of his water, which is noticeably warmer already. "Getting nursing care for free."

Immediately Kevin realizes he's said something he shouldn't have. She stiffens; there's a slight catch in her breathing, not quite a gasp. For a moment Kevin thought he'd seen a brightness in her gaze, not necessarily flirtatious, but the gleam of a good-looking, fit, fortysomething woman appreciating a man's regard, even if she wasn't particularly interested in return. But now that's gone, as if a curtain has fallen.

"Nursing care?" Her voice, too, has noticeably cooled.

"It's just you seemed to know your way around a bandage." Kevin knows he ought to shut up, but that's never stopped him before. "The way you snapped on those gloves..."

The Amazon slugs the last of her Gatorade and twists the top back on the empty bottle like she's twisting Kevin's neck. He's trying to put it all together—the military bearing, the sculpted physique, the pickup truck—of course! She's a lesbian—a weight-lifting, Latina, ex-military lesbian—and she thinks he's coming on to her.

"I didn't...," Kevin starts to say, with no idea how he's going to finish the sentence.

"Thoracic surgeon," says the woman, tossing the empty bottle into the truck bed. "And I'm afraid I'm running a little late."

"Ah," says Kevin. "Of course." Idiot, he thinks. Idiot, idiot, idiot.

"You're going to need a department store to replace those trousers." She holds her palm out for his empty water bottle. "Do you have a car?" She drills him with her gaze, daring him to apologize.

"No," he says, his mouth suddenly dry again. "I'm just here for the day." He gingerly hands her the bottle, and she practically flings it into the back. "I have a job interview."

"Yes, you said." She steps back and gestures to the side like a maitre d', and it takes a moment for Kevin to realize she wants him to get out of the truck. Clutching his coat, he scrambles down to the pavement and turns awkwardly, his torn trouser leg flapping, his knee still smarting from the antiseptic. Meanwhile

Dr. Amazon grips the side of the driver's doorway and yanks herself in one go up into the seat.

"There's a Nordstrom's out at the mall." She looks down at him from the truck. "Do you have a cell, to call a cab?"

"No, actually." He deliberately left his cell in Ann Arbor, so that if Stella calls him from Chicago, he won't have to lie.

The good doctor slams the door and starts her truck, and the well-tuned roar of the engine startles Kevin a few paces back. I guess a ride's out of the question, he thinks. Then her darkly tinted window whirs down, and she drapes her elbow out the window. He moistens his lips and says, "I don't suppose you have a cell I could borrow." He has to raise his voice to be heard over the confident rumble of the truck.

"My cell's for emergencies only." She points past him toward the bridge. "You can catch a bus right over there, far side of Lamar." She looks him up and down. "There's a Target a couple miles south, at Ben White."

Her truck jerks into gear, the engine roars. Did she just say Target?

"Hey, thank you!" Kevin cries over the rumble, minding his manners, hating the way his voice rises an octave. "You've been very kind, Miz..."

"*Doctor* Barrientos." She guns her engine to drown out any further bleatings from Kevin. He steps back as her glossy truck reverses out of its space, screeches to a stop, then heaves forward, past the toes of Kevin's shoes and out of the lot onto the street.

Kevin limps past the end of the pedestrian bridge, toward Lamar. He drapes his jacket over his arm, careful not to empty his inside pocket. His knee stings, his sock is sticky with blood, and his nerves are still jangling. He feels old and slow and a good deal more fragile than he felt just fifteen minutes ago, all because of his little accident, and it doesn't help that he's been insulted by his good Samaritan, through no fault of his own. His misunderstanding about her had been wholly inadvertent, and let's face it, not all that much of an insult. What the hell's wrong with being a nurse?

He sees her truck idling angrily at the intersection. Target, he thinks. She said that just to piss me off. I'll have you know, *Doctor,* these trousers were picked out by my very *stylish* and much *younger* girlfriend at the Abercrombie & Fitch in Briarwood Mall, thank you *very much.* Say what you want about Stella, she has an eye for quality; she'd never take him to fucking Target. Say what you want about Stella, but she knows what she wants, and goes for it without hesitation. Her single-mindedness, her ferocity, is what still thrills him about her after three years, even though he's certain that he doesn't love her. Well, pretty certain: he's a little surprised at the moment at the depth of his anger at the doctor's implied insult of his girlfriend's sartorial judgment. It's one thing for him to roll his eyes at his girlfriend's joy at the gaudiest artifacts of pop culture — *American Idol,* anyone? *Project Runway?* — and her guilt-free uninterest in the books and movies and music Kevin loves, but it's another for some humorless bitch in a pickup truck to do it. Don't say nothin' bad about my baby, *Doctor.*

He hobbles a little faster toward the corner, almost as if he means to come alongside the surgeon's truck and catch her eye and give her a piece of his mind. But the intersection where the bridge meets the cross street is crowded with vehicles, radiating heat and impatience; the fender bender on the bridge has reduced traffic to a single lane each way, and cars are backed up along Lamar. As Kevin comes to the corner, a motorcycle cop in a tight, dark uniform — now *that* guy must be hot — is weaving his massive bike through the gridlock toward the center of the bridge, his flasher bright even in the midday glare. By the time

Kevin turns back to the doctor's truck, she's rounded the corner and accelerated south down Lamar, shifting up with a stuttering, guttural roar.

The motorcycle cop glides to a stop at the corner, right in front of Kevin. His helmet dips toward Kevin's leg and then his mouth speaks loudly from under his tinted visor.

"You hurt?" he shouts. His idling bike makes his whole body vibrate, as if he's just a little out of focus. He points at Kevin's leg, and Kevin, like an idiot, looks down at his own injury as if he's surprised to see it.

"No," Kevin shouts back. "I just fell down. It's got nothing to do with that." He lifts his chin up the bridge toward the accident, and the cop gives him a brisk cop nod and rumbles away. Actually, Kevin feels a little wobbly, a little lightheaded, as if his brain is floating free of his head. Perhaps that's why he doesn't wait for the walk sign and hobbles out into the clotted traffic across Lamar, his surgically incised trouser leg flapping. The heat reverberates off the backed-up vehicles, and the air stinks of exhaust. He turns left across the street and limps alongside an exhausted little park of underachieving trees and yellowed grass. Southbound cars rev up Lamar as they escape from the jam on the bridge, and over their rumble Kevin hears birds creaking and cawing from the drooping trees.

I should've rented a car, Kevin thinks. Even if all he'd done was drive it from the airport and back again, at the very least it would have kept him off the streets, where he has been lured by nostalgia and middle-aged lust into the labyrinth of a strange city, accosted by homeless men, tripped by a dog, condescended to by a surgeon. Right now, though, he'd settle for a place to sit down. The wide-open sky hammers the cartoon colors of the fast food franchises up ahead—Schlotzsky's, Taco Bell, Jack in the Box—their bright colors simultaneously blanched by the sun and deepened by the tint of Kevin's glasses. A low, stucco restaurant with a big pink sign that says TACO CABANA wafts a spicy, greasy aroma across all six lanes of Lamar, but Kevin's still too hot, shaky, and pissed off to think about food. The racket of the birds taunts him. What he needs more than a meal right now is a bench, but along the sidewalk up ahead all he sees is a NO PARKING sign and the great big red and green Schlotzsky's sign — but no bus stop, and no bench.

"Goddammit," he says out loud, slapping the soles of his shoes against the pavement, as flat-footed as Willie Loman. "Mother*fucker*," he adds for good measure, aware that he's trudging even further away from where he's supposed to be in a few hours. There's a hill up ahead covered with trees, which means that thanks to Dr. Barrientos's bum directions, he's heading into residential Austin and away from downtown. He's off the map, into terra incognita. Here there be Schlotzsky's.

Where, it occurs to him, at least I can sit and cool off and collect myself, have a glass of iced tea. Where maybe I can lock myself in the restroom and wash my face, maybe even take off my shirt and sponge-bathe myself in the sink with paper towels. He hobbles toward the Schlotzsky's sign, the angry rush of traffic on his left, the inhuman rattle of the birds on his right. Then up ahead he sees a bus stop sign and a bench. Kevin stops at the edge of Schlotzsky's parking lot, trying to decide whether to go into the restaurant or wait for the bus. The vast, heatstruck Texas sky throbbing overhead, birds screaming in his ear, Kevin feels like he's slowly melting into a puddle on the concrete. But before he can make his move one way or the other — bus stop or Schlotzsky's — a glossy red wall of vehicle heaves to a stop right in front of him. Kevin's too tired and lightheaded to jump back, so he just sways on his feet and blinks in alarm at the long, thin, red reflection of himself in the vast passenger door of the truck. He sees his own round, Irish-Polish peasant face in the tinted window, with the dark lenses of his sunglasses where his eyes ought to be. He looks like a ghost from a Japanese horror film. Then his image is decapitated as the window whirs down.

Saints preserve us, thinks Kevin, it's Dr. Barrientos!

"Hey." She gestures at him out of the tinted dusk of the truck's cab. "I think you dropped this."

She's holding something pale in his direction, pinched between her fingers. Kevin blinks, sways, then steps forward, lifting his glasses onto his forehead to peer into the gloom of the cab. She's holding his invitation letter for the job interview. He reaches slowly into the cool air blowing out the window, hears the sibilant roar of the AC ducts, and takes the letter from her gingerly, as if she might snatch it back at any moment.

"Thanks." He roughly folds the letter into quarters and wedges it with some difficulty into the breast pocket of his shirt, crumpling the bandage she gave him.

"Would you like a ride?" says the doctor, but Kevin has suddenly swung his jacket off his arm and thrust his fingers into the inside pocket. What else has he dropped along the way? His fingers find his notebook, his boarding pass, but where are his sunglasses?

"Would you like a ride?" she says again, raising her voice. Her truck idles, a big, purring cat. "I can drop you off on South Lamar somewhere."

Kevin just gawps at her, so she enunciates more slowly. "There are a couple of department stores I can take you to."

But he's not listening, he's digging fruitlessly in every pocket of his jacket. He looks up at her. "You didn't happen to find my sunglasses?"

Out of the gloom of her truck she says, "They're on your head."

Kevin pats his hot forehead, fingers the lenses like a blind man.

"Get in," says Dr. Barrientos. "Out of the heat."

Kevin doesn't remember climbing into the truck, but next thing he knows he's sitting in a padded leather bucket seat while the truck idles in Schlotzsky's parking lot. The AC blasts in his face. Beyond the little park with the limp trees he sees the glitter of cars backed up on the bridge. Even through the closed windows and the rush of the AC, he can still hear the birds chattering in the trees. The sun shines at a steep angle through the windshield, a sharp line of light falling across his wrists. His jacket is folded on his lap, he's holding another cold bottle of water, and Dr. Barrientos's warm palm is pressed against his sweating forehead.

"Drink it slowly," she says. "Just a sip at a time."

He drinks. The water freezes his sinuses.

"How's your blood pressure?" She turns his left arm palm up and presses two fingers firmly against his wrist.

"My blood pressure? How would I know?" You're the doctor, he almost says.

"I mean generally, not right this minute."

He drinks again. The cold is blinding. "Good," he gasps.

She presses her knuckles lightly against his temple again. "Were you dizzy or nauseous before you passed out on the bridge?"

"No."

"Good." She rests her hand on his upper arm.

"And I didn't pass out," Kevin says, slightly annoyed now. "That guy's dog tripped me."

"So you didn't feel lightheaded or . . ."

"No." He lifts the bottle. "I'm fine. Really."

The doctor cocks her head as if she's considering his truthfulness. He can smell sweat, though he can't tell if it's hers or his or some commingling of both.

"Aren't I?"

She nods. "I think you're probably okay."

"Probably?"

Her hand shifts on his arm. "I was a little worried when I saw you just now, but your pulse isn't racing, and you're still sweating freely, so you're not presenting with heatstroke."

"Glad to hear it." Some bedside manner she's got, Dr. Barrientos. But then she's a surgeon: most of her patients are probably unconscious when she sees them, so she doesn't really need a bedside manner.

"Look, I shouldn't have left you so quickly back there," she says. "I'm sorry if I was abrupt." The way she's composed her face tells Kevin that apologies don't come easy to her, but that she has disciplined herself to make them when necessary. He is appropriately appeased that she's taking the trouble for him.

"I'm sorry, too," he says, ever the midwesterner.

"For what?"

"For assuming you were a nurse. I mean, this day and age, I should know better."

She gestures dismissively and looks out the windshield. She has made up her mind to be nice, and nothing, evidently, will deter Dr. Barrientos after she's made up her mind. She has that in common with Stella.

"That wasn't about you," she says. "That was about something else." She gives him another surprising, sidelong smile, only instead of knowing, now she looks rueful.

"Well, I'm sorry anyway."

She nods and puts the truck in gear. "You're not heatstroked," she says, checking her mirrors, "but I'd feel better if you'd just sit and drink your water and let me drop you off someplace where you can buy another pair of trousers. Okay?"

Kevin salutes her with his bottle. "How can I say no?"

"Buckle up," she says.

*   *   *

Rehydrated, air-conditioned, buckled in, Kevin rides comfortably up South Lamar in the well-padded cab of Dr. Barrientos's powerful red pickup.

"I'm Kevin." He reaches across the cab to offer her his hand.

"Claudia." Her handshake is not particularly firm, which surprises him, because you'd think a surgeon, not to mention someone with her obvious upper-body strength, would have a grip like a C-clamp. But he reminds himself that he's through making assumptions, for now, anyway. Inside the cab the guttural roar of the engine is a vibrationless purr; it's like riding in a recording booth. Beyond the tinted windows smaller cars and the fast food joints fall quickly behind. Up ahead some blocky brown condos rise out of the green mass of trees, atop a low cliff of crumbling yellow stone. Across a brownish lawn below the cliff is a line of stout palm trees, with squat pineapple trunks and spiky crowns. An hour or so ago the sight of palm trees startled him, but now Kevin's too lightheaded to feel amazement.

"So you exercise in this heat?" he says.

"That surprises you?"

Dr. Barrientos is a confident driver, to say the least, accelerating through a big intersection, crowding a yellow light that turns red as they pass under it. She guns the truck up the hill and under the lee of the bluff.

"Well, my experience in Texas so far pretty clearly shows that I can't even walk around in it," Kevin says. "And here you are, running."

A glance from the doctor. "Where are you from exactly?"

"Michigan."

"And you're here for an interview, no?"

"Yeah," drawls Kevin, like he's not so sure any longer.

"Is the job a good one?"

"It had better be, if I have to get used to this heat."

The doctor laughs, not much more than a snort. "This is nothing."

Kevin watches her sidelong, past the edge of his sunglasses. She drives like a man, her legs spread casually, her right hand loose on the top of the steering wheel, the way his dad used to settle in on long drives. At the same time she's reaching behind her with her left hand, elbow in the air, squeezing the headrest and flexing her biceps. The smell of her sweat is powerful, even in the arctic AC, but it's not unpleasant. It even reminds Kevin of sex, and he lets his sidelong gaze linger on her sweat-glistening thigh. He wonders if what McNulty assumed about nurses goes for doctors as well.

"I grew up in the Valley," she says, "where it gets even hotter than here."

"The Valley?"

"Brownsville? McAllen?" She glances at him. "Down along the Rio Grande."

She says "Rio Grande" like a Spanish speaker, with flowing R's and the E on the end. *Rrrio Grrran-day.*

"Laredo," she says. "You've heard of Laredo, right?" Saying "Laredo" her tongue does something with the R that Kevin could never imitate.

"Sure."

"Well, we never lived in Laredo. But it's in the Valley."

They sail effortlessly past an Austin city bus grinding up the hill. Lamar is five lanes wide here, but the canopy of trees hanging over either side of the street makes it feel narrow. Even the regular trees here look strange to Kevin, not just the palms. It's the leaves, he decides, they're smaller and sharper than the broad deciduous leaves of Michigan trees. Shinier, too, like green leather.

"So you were never out walking the streets of Laredo," he says.

"Excuse me?" She looks at him as sharply as she did when he implied she was a nurse. Now she's gripping the wheel with both hands. Oh hell, thinks Kevin, now she thinks I just called her a streetwalker. Maybe she noticed him checking her out and has decided she doesn't like it. Keep Your Mouth Shut, he reminds himself. I should just get out and walk. But instead he starts singing.

"'As I walked out on the streets of Laredo,'"—thank God for Grampa Quinn and his Sons of the Pioneers LPs—"'as I walked out in Laredo one day...'" Kevin's quavering rendition has none of his grandfather's confident tenor—like his dad, Kevin's more of a baritone, and he's reaching for the high notes—and the padded upholstery of the truck muffles the music. But even so, it seems to have soothed Dr. Barrientos's savage breast.

"Ah," she says.

Kevin takes another gulp of water. With this woman, it's always two steps forward, one step back. At the top of the hill ahead, a crowded strip-mall sign rises against the whitish sky. HEART OF TEXAS MUSIC says the top of the sign, with an electric guitar outlined in red neon. Phone and power lines cross and recross above the street like laces, slung between wooden telephone poles silhouetted against the glare. A haze blurs the signs and power lines and telephone poles ever so slightly, but it's not humidity, it's the light ricocheting off itself, glittering, fracturing. Even behind his sunglasses, even through the twilight tint of the doctor's windows, it makes him squint. No wonder everybody here's so testy.

"'Beat the drum slowly,' right?" she says, not quite smiling. She lifts her other hand to the headrest and starts squeezing and flexing. Kevin glimpses the blued shadow of stubble under her arm. He's pierced with desire for her; he'd like to bury his nose in that armpit.

"My grandfather used to sing it." He smiles at her. "Back where I come from, it's all anyone knows of Texas."

"'The Streets of Laredo'? Really?" Her fingers press so deep into the leather of the headrest Kevin's sure she's going to puncture it. Her biceps throbs like a heart. He's thinking that in bed she could clamp a man between her powerful thighs like a predator, and he's wondering—in the vernacular of his old-school Polish uncle and his VFW buddies—if he's even man enough for a woman like Dr. Barrientos.

"Well, you know. Cowboys. Cattle. Oil." Lawless border towns, he nearly says. The Alamo, *The Searchers*. Docile, flat-faced Mexican peasants. Mariachi bands. Fiery, finger-snapping, hat-dancing señoritas.

"Chips and salsa," he says instead.

"Chips and salsa." She gives her little snorting laugh again and drapes both hands loosely over the wheel, just like his dad used to. That cools his ardor a bit. He can live with the idea that he might fall for a woman like his mother, but would he really fall for one like his dad?

"And Dubya," Kevin says. "We blame Texans for that."

Of course he shouldn't have said that—what if she's a Republican? A lot of them are, he knows—Bush-voting Hispanics, conservative Catholic Chicanos, who voted for Obama only because the rest of the Republican Party got so squirrelly about immigration. But to his relief, she gives him a heartfelt laugh, if a little grudging and melancholy. They sail under another yellow light, weaving between slower cars to the top of the hill, out from under the trees and into the glare again. Ahead is a little foreshortened forest of plainspoken signs—COLOR COPIES 69¢, SELF-STORAGE, SAXON PUB—punctuated by telephone poles.

"You can't blame us for that," she says. "He's from Connecticut."

"Ah, a Yankee. So it's our fault."

"A *Norte Americano*." She lifts one finger off the wheel. "You don't get more *norte* than Connecticut."

"Hey, I'm from Michigan, remember?" says Kevin. "I'm practically a Canadian."

She smiles, still attractively melancholy. "Oh, Canadians are all right." Her eyes seem distracted again.

Now they're passing the slightly scruffy sort of local businesses that he'd find on the down-market end of Stadium Boulevard back home, out toward Ypsilanti: a Mexican restaurant in bright orange stucco; a Goodwill shop; another Mexican restaurant; a gas station and convenience store where unleaded regular is twenty cents cheaper than in Ann Arbor. The very pavement of Lamar looks scruffy, as leached of color as a faded pair of jeans. Behind these roadside establishments rise masses of trees, their leaves glittering in the nearly vertical sunlight, deep green in the mutually reinforcing tints of Kevin's glasses and the windows of the truck. Who knew Austin was so leafy? But even at a distance the treetops still look strange, more like the bristling feathers of some prehistoric bird than leaves, and all this archaeopteryx foliage unsettles him even more. Strange trees; strange car; strange, distracted woman—Kevin feels the mild but distinct queasiness of being a passenger in a stranger's vehicle. And not just a strange vehicle, but a fastidiously antiseptic one—even the cab he caught at the airport had more character than Dr. Barrientos's truck. There's no yin-yang medallion spinning from her rearview, no CDs in the pockets between the seats, no crumbs in the upholstery, not even any dust on the padded dash. Apart from her sweat, it doesn't even have a smell apart from the clammy chill of the AC. But then she's a surgeon. Perhaps she maintains a sterile environment even in her car.

"You get used to it," she says.

"Sorry?"

"The heat."

A silence descends, like an awkward pause on a first date. There's something about the furrowing of her forehead, about her headrest-squeezing and her gunning of the accelerator, that tells him her mind's on something other than her passenger and his tolerance for the Texas climate. He recognizes distraction, because Stella is always carrying on a conversation with herself in her head. Sometimes in the car, when they're riding without talking, she gestures suddenly; sometimes her lips move silently. Or she'll say quietly to herself, "Uh huh" or "That's right," with a sharp little nod. Times like this Kevin thinks of her as wandering in the Stella Continuum, and early on he learned not to disturb her, because when he has, she's started with a wild look in her eye, as frightened, and frightening, as a sleepwalker jolted awake. (Actually waking her up at night, in fact, from one of her feverish nightmares, is even scarier.) So he knows better than to say anything to this intense woman he's only just met. Instead, instinctively, he does what he usually does when Stella's lost in the Stella Continuum.

"Cartridge World," he says absently, reading the first sign he sees, a big, square yellow one.

"Sorry?"

"That sign." Kevin gestures, Claudia glances. Cartridge World glides by, a narrow storefront with tinted windows.

"I think I'm having a Texas moment," he says.

"Right." She nods slowly. "Everybody in Texas drives a pickup and carries a gun."

Kevin gestures palms up to encompass the cab of the truck.

"Pickup," he says. Tips his head back toward the shop, dwindling in the rear window. "Cartridge World."

"They sell toner," she says. "Printer cartridges."

"Ah." Repeat after me: KYMS, KYMS, KYMS.

"You'll pardon my saying so," says Claudia, "but you seem to be a man who jumps to conclusions."

"Actually," he says, "I'm not. I mean, I don't. Jump to conclusions. Not usually. It's just..."

He's not even sure what he means to say. Lamar winds through a series of slow curves, still climbing slightly. Trees with bristling little leaves crowd close to the road again, and now there are actual houses along the street, little one-story bungalows, decades old. Most of them are small, funky businesses now: a hair and nail salon, a chiropractor, a pawnshop that advertises PAYDAY LOANS. A colorfully hip vintage shop, an immigration lawyer named Gonzalez. A psychic palm reader—as opposed to what, Kevin wonders, a nonpsychic palm reader?—whose hand-painted sign declares that she can HABLA ESPAÑOL. Just beyond that he sees a billboard in Español—*La nueva AT&T*—and an exterminator's sign that features a giant, brown, neon cockroach, all legs and antennae, unlit and unwriggling at midday. And then he sees another Mexican restaurant, an unlit neon sign with a stepped Mayan pyramid and the name MEXICO LINDO in red tubing. The phrase rings in his head in Dolby surround sound—it's a line from *The Wild Bunch,* but he can't remember who says it. Not William Holden or Ernest Borgnine, certainly not Warren Oates or Ben Johnson. No, it was the fifth guy, the Mexican member of the gang. The first time Kevin saw the film, he watched a bootleg print of the director's cut on the Michigan campus during his Big Star days. Saw it with McNulty, in fact, who slumped in his seat next to Kevin in the back row and laughed quietly to himself all the way through the orgy of carnage at the end.

Kevin's seen it half a dozen times since on VHS and DVD, but he still remembers that raucous, grainy, badly focused first viewing, a film co-op screening attended mainly by whooping, drunken engineering students, who cheered at the end when Holden shot the beautiful señorita who'd just shot him, and called her, "*Bitch*." What *was* that character's name, the Mexican guy? The one whose cut throat was the incitement for all that subsequent bloodshed, the wholesale slaughter of peasants, little boys, and women? The whole situation made him uncomfortable at the time, and makes him uncomfortable still, and the best he can do in defense of it is to put it in the context of when he saw it and who he saw it with. And where he saw it: Auditorium A, Angell Hall. That's it! *That* was the guy's name! Angel! The Mexican in the bunch, the guy they went back to rescue from the bandit warlord at the end. Angel says "*Mexico lindo*" near the beginning of the film, as they leave Texas and cross the Rio Grande. The Rrrio Grrran-day. "*Meh-hee-co leen-do*," Angel says. Lovely Mexico.

But Kevin can't point that out, because he doesn't want to be seen jumping to conclusions again, doesn't want to tell this touchy Latina who grew up on the border that everything he knows about Mexican culture comes from the films of Sam Peckinpah. He might as well invoke Speedy Gonzales or the Taco Bell Chihuahua, might as well tell her, "We don' need no steenking badges." His default liberal guilt and his native midwestern decency jerk him short like a leash. But he can't help what he's thinking, and right now he feels like he's riding into another country—a hot, dusty, sun-blanched place with immigration lawyers and bilingual palm readers and corporate billboards in Spanish and leaves that bristle like blades and giant neon cockroaches and *palm trees*. Sweaty, dehydrated, and enervated, his torn trousers flapping wide over his bandaged knee, Kevin feels like Humphrey Bogart as Fred C. Dobbs in either the first twenty minutes or the last twenty minutes of *The Treasure of Sierra Madre;* all he needs is two days of stubble and the shakes. But he can't tell Claudia any of this, either. Oh Christ, thinks Kevin, his liberal guilt cinching tighter, she's right. I do jump to conclusions.

"It's just what?" says Claudia.

"You know how it is when you're in a strange city?" His voice shoots up an octave, which he hates, but he can't stop himself. "It's like you're fourteen years old again, big and gawky and clueless. You know? Everything you normally take for granted, in fact everything that everybody around you is taking for granted, you have to stop and think about. You know what I mean?"

"Hm," she says.

Of course, Claudia—Dr. Barrientos, that is—has probably never felt defenseless or clueless in her entire life. Or if she has, she'd never admit to it.

"It's just that here I am, in Texas, where I never thought I'd be, and I'm seeing all this stuff I just don't see at home—Cartridge World and palm trees and that neon cockroach we just passed and all these Mexican restaurants..."

Shouldn't have said that, of course, but just then he points excitedly through the windshield at yet another Mexican restaurant, this one with a line of fraying palms around the edge of its parking lot.

"And Mexican restaurants *with* palm trees!" He's laughing now, he knows he sounds like an idiot, but she's laughing, too, at his excitement, if nothing else. "And I try to link it all with what I bring with me from Michigan, and what little I know about Texas. Which is, of course, mostly clichés and stereotypes." He's gesturing with both hands now, which makes him even more self-conscious. "So of course I get everything wrong, and not only that, I get it wrong in front of a native Texan. Who's been very kind to me. Which only makes me feel more like a fish out of water. Like I'm fourteen years old all over again."

Breathlessly he stops and lets his hands drop. At least he didn't mention *The Wild Bunch*. He's almost afraid to look at her, but when he does, he sees that she's still smiling.

"Good thing we didn't drive up South Congress," she says. "There's a store there called Just Guns."

Kevin's laughter doesn't lessen the ache of his alienation. Moving here would mean that he'd feel fourteen years old for months, maybe even years, before he became acclimated to Texas. All along the street for the last few minutes, between the bungalows and under the trees, he's seen several one- and two-bay specialty garages of cinderblock, where, repair by repair, you can remake your aging auto until it's been rebuilt from the treads up — replace your muffler, rebuild your transmission, reline your brakes, rotate your tires. Change the oil in fifteen minutes, precision tune the engine in thirty, tint the windows, customize the audio. A collision shop, a paint-and-body shop, reconditioned auto parts. And the funky little businesses in the bungalows in between offer to rebuild and customize Kevin himself: he could get his hair and nails done; he could be tanned, tattooed, and pierced; he could lose weight under the supervision of a physician. He could bulk up or slim down; he could have his teeth whitened and his vision laser-sharpened; he could have his bones chiropractically manipulated; he could have his aura read and his fortune told in two languages. He and his Honda Accord could start at one end of Lamar, and shop by shop, repair by repair, treatment by treatment, they could weave helically past each other from one side of the street to the other, until, at the far end — wherever and whenever that was — they would be remade as Texans, like the ship of Theseus, plank by plank and oar by oar, until the question becomes, is it the same ship any longer? Remade as a Texan, would Kevin be the same man any more? Does he even want to be? And is it even possible to remake a fifty-year-old man? Or has he been remade once too often already?

Kevin's still laughing, though.

"I'm sorry," he says. "Is ranting a sign of heatstroke?"

"Not usually," says Dr. Barrientos. "Fear of palm trees, though..." She wobbles her hand in the air between them. "And Mexican restaurants," she adds. "What have you got against Mexicans?"

She says "Mexican" now with the hard X like a Norte Americano. He can't tell if she's being polite or condescending or both.

"Tell you what," Kevin says, full of surprises, "you pick the place and I'll buy you lunch." He peeks at his watch; there's two and a half hours yet until his interview.

Another silence, but not so awkward. Or at least awkward in a different way. Watching her sidelong he's pretty sure she's thinking it over.

"I'm not really dressed for it," she says. "And I need a shower."

"Look at me." Kevin plucks at his wilted shirt, the knee of his torn trousers. "I look like I just survived a terrorist attack."

Their gazes cross obliquely across the cab of the truck, neither quite looking at the other. Even here, light years from Glasgow, there's a little Buchanan Street frisson between them.

"I appeal to your Hippocratic oath, Doctor," Kevin says. "I'm still kinda wobbly. I may need a medicinal burrito."

For the first time since Kevin got into the truck Dr. Barrientos has been stopped by a traffic light. It's as if she's been brought up short by his question, and the sudden lack of forward momentum seems to heighten the padded quiet of the cab. Her eyes look distracted again, and watching her past the edge of his sunglasses, Kevin's not sure that what's distracting her is his invitation, or even his presence. The silence stretches on as the vehicles waiting for the light on the far side of the intersection glitter and sizzle in the heat. Beyond them Lamar curves up and to the left, where he sees more colorful signs, more bilingual billboards, more power lines against the whitish sky. The cross street of the intersection cuts into Lamar at a bias, and on the arrowhead corner sits a scruffy little used car lot packed with five- and ten-year-old automobiles, mostly compacts and subcompacts, all a little the worse for wear. The dealer's office is an old, flat-roofed, whitewashed, cinderblock service station with a sign in bright red letters that reads (with wholly unnecessary quotation marks and heavy-handed punctuation, thinks Kevin the professional editor), "IF YOU HAVE A CAR YOU CAN GET A JOB!!!"

I have a car, thinks Kevin. I have a job. I have a house, a mortgage, job security, a retirement plan, friends, a history, a *life,* all in Ann Arbor, Michigan. I have a girlfriend, even, more or less—a live-in lover, at any rate, who, from the outside, from the point of view of his middle-aged, married male friends with children, looks like an improbable piece of guilt-free midlife arm candy, wholly undeserved, and the incitement for a fair amount of jealousy and disbelief, thinly disguised as salacious joshing. They slap his arm and say, "You lucky bastard," or they laugh harshly and say, "What does she see in *you?*" Sometimes their rage is even undisguised, as when his friend Dale, at a Labor Day cookout in his suburban backyard, only half an hour after Kevin had introduced him to Stella, had shoved Kevin in the chest with both hands and said, "You mother*fucker.*" Of course, none of them have seen Stella when she wakes up sweating and shaking at three in the morning, recoiling from Kevin's touch, no recognition of him in her wild eyes; none of them have seen the faint white scars along the insides of her forearms and her thighs, which she covers with makeup and *will not* talk about, will not even acknowledge the existence of. And none of them (at least not recently, at least not in the last month) has discovered the used plastic wand of a pregnancy test stuffed at the bottom of the kitchen trash, under coffee grounds and egg-shells and rusty apple cores, wrapped in three layers of paper towels.

Yeah, thinks Kevin, I have a girlfriend, and he looks at the doctor again, not so sidelong this time, and wonders if it's too late to...what? Leave Stella? Leave Ann Arbor? Start his life over in sun-bleached Austin? Live happily ever after with Clau-dia Barrientos, MD? Just as Kevin is thinking he should change the subject, let his luncheon invitation die unanswered, pretend he never said it, Claudia's eyes refocus and she speaks.

"All right," she says.

Almost before the light changes her pickup has surged through the intersection and glided into the left-turn lane — where, after an instant of hesitation, it roars in front of oncoming traffic and into a parking lot that rides like it's unpaved, though Kevin can see ancient, bleached asphalt. The truck lurches to a stop in front of a low, makeshift building with a latticed awning and a faded redbrick front papered with faded flyers. On the flat roof above the door, a large plaster woman with unnaturally pink skin and black, Betty Page bangs spreads her bare arms wide like an invocation. The figure's six-foot wingspan and fixed, upward gaze makes Kevin think it's Wonder Woman, then Eva Peron, then Madonna playing Eva Peron. But it's none of these women, for across her bosom where a Stars and Stripes bust-ier or a spangled ball gown should be, instead there's a hand-painted sign that reads ANNA'S TACO RAPIDO. Don't cry for me, Austin, Texas.

Kevin's still hanging against his shoulder belt as Claudia opens her door and steps down to the pavement.

"Leave your jacket, why don't you?" she says, and slams the door.

In the time it takes him to catch his breath, unharness himself, and climb gingerly down from the truck—his scraped knee throbbing, the heat enfolding him—Claudia has already passed through the narrow door. In the patterned shadow of the awning, Kevin limps across the wooden porch, hauls open the glass door, and steps into a clammy gust of AC heavily scented with grease and grilling onions. It's cooler inside, but smoky and humid and so dim that Kevin can hardly see a thing until he remembers to take off his sunglasses, thrusting them absently toward his jacket pocket. But his jacket's in the truck, so he slides them instead into his trouser pocket. The long, dusky room has a smooth concrete floor and a low ceiling of crumbling particleboard, lit only by a couple of thin, purple fluorescent tubes and some tiny red Christmas lights. Even with his glasses off he's still adjusting to the gloom, and yet there's a strong feeling of déjà vu. The room is bisected lengthwise by a wide wooden counter—on the left are high, narrow tables and stools, and behind the counter on the right, a couple of sweaty figures in stained aprons and baseball caps jostle each other in the narrow aisle before the sizzling grill. Behind a cash register at the end of the counter a figure is silhouetted against a grimy window, talking to another silhouette across from him. Just as Kevin recognizes her broad shoulders and powerful thighs, the second silhouette speaks to him.

"Sorry?" He can't hear her over the clatter of the spatula against the grill and the *wh-wh-whirl* of the ceiling fans and the thumping dance beat of a Latin pop song, but still he seems to know this place instinctively. The wholly satisfying smell of frying meat, the insistent music, the narrow layout with high tables on one side and the grill on the other, the grease-laminated workers jostling each other—he's been here before.

Claudia beckons him to the register, where a sad-eyed man in a white guayabera and crisp khakis turns his melancholy gaze to Kevin.

"He's paying," she says to the man, then, to Kevin, "right?"

"Absolutely!" Kevin jerks his wallet from his hip pocket. Only then does he see the big hand-lettered menu board behind Claudia, four columns of tight little letters, yellow and blue against black, listing tacos in all their infinite variety.

"You don't even want to look at that," Claudia says. "We'll be here all day. I already ordered for both of us."

"Great!" But as Kevin pops his wallet open, Claudia touches his wrist.

"Unless you're a vegetarian. I should have asked."

"Me? No," says Kevin, and as he hands the guayabera a twenty a veil falls from his eyes and the déjà vu resolves; he almost hears a heavenly choir. It's the menu board that's put him over: all it needs is a couple of cartoon bears and the slogan "2,147,483,648 Combinations!" He starts laughing, causing Claudia and the cashier to exchange a glance.

"Blimpy Burger!" Kevin exclaims. "You've taken me to Austin's Blimpy Burger!"

The guayabera frowns and hands Kevin his change and a receipt. "You're number fifty-eight." He hands a couple of plastic glasses over the counter to Claudia.

"Why don't you find us a seat outside." She nods toward an open door where the midday glare leaches in. "And I'll get us some tea."

Kevin stops to pee in a tiny toilet, no bigger than a broom closet. Then, with the greasy gust of AC at his back like a gentle shove, he steps down into a courtyard of packed dirt, surrounded by a wooden fence and overhung with an enormous, leafy tree. His torn trouser leg flapping, he limps under unlit strings of party lights and settles gratefully into a plastic chair at a rough, unsteady wooden table. A couple of lean young guys in shorts and T-shirts slouch at another table, talking quietly, while a pair of black birds looking for scraps strut in the dirt like little T. rexes. One of them boldly flaps up onto a nearby table and insolently fixes Kevin with one fathomless black eye. Kevin waves his hand until the bird flaps into the dirt again, then he settles back into the flexible grip of the chair.

The mottled shadow of the tree trembles in a breeze Kevin can't feel, but it *is* cooler than in the direct sunlight, and the rumble of traffic on Lamar is muffled by the fence. An old Mobil sign with a faded Pegasus hangs on the fence, while across the side of the building is a colorful and very un-Texan mural of two clumsily drawn sheep in an alpine meadow full of freakishly large dandelions. Nailed to the whitish bark of the tree are three desiccated old cowboy boots, shriveled and colorless, with broken toes. The décor is accretive and eclectic, but authentically so (though as a scholarly editor Kevin knows better than to take "authenticity" at face value), not like the fastidiously art-directed eclecticism of the yuppie bars in Ann Arbor — the kind Stella likes — or the Disneyfied hominess of a chain family restaurant — the kind his mother frequents for lunch with her gal pals. Still, there's something self-conscious about it — it's a hip place that knows it's hip — but then, what isn't self-conscious anymore?

Indeed, Kevin's experiencing a very self-conscious sort of metahappiness at the moment: relieved that Claudia has brought him to an unexpectedly familiar place, while at the same time surprised by his own relief. The strangeness and alienation of the morning, the uncharacteristic behavior he's indulged in, the awkwardness of every exchange so far — all of it is temporarily eased by the familiar feel and smell of a place where he's never been in his life. It's like a little bit of Ann Arbor, and not just any bit, but Krazy Jim's Blimpy Burger — "Cheaper Than Food!" — one of the few constants of his last thirty years. Ann Arbor has grown a thick crust like barnacles all around it, of strip malls and big box stores, which is surrounded in turn by vast plantations of McMansions, all the way out to Saline and Dexter. Most of the funky little bars and clubs and restaurants of his younger days are long gone. But Blimpy's, God bless it, Blimpy's endures. It's been his unofficial polestar — for most of his adult life he's lived within a five-minute walk of the place, at Packard and South Division, from his freshman year in the hive of South Quad to his middle age as a homeowner on Fifth Avenue. Sometimes he even wonders if the real reason he bought his house was just to stay in walking distance of his regular burger — a triple with provolone, grilled onions, and mushrooms on an onion roll. Beth objected to Blimpy's at first, until he shrewdly made the buy-local, at-least-it's-not-McDonald's argument, after which she beat a tactical retreat and stopped giving him a hard time about it. Stella, however, won't eat there at all anymore after their one disastrous visit together. She wrinkled her nose at the smell the moment they walked in, then tried to order a single patty, extra lean, on a whole wheat bun.

"Extra *lean?*" said the gloriously mouthy black woman at the grill. "Girl, you know where you are?" Part of the charm of the place, Kevin tried to explain later, was the surliness of the help.

Stella settled for a double without cheese on a regular roll, then sat with Kevin at his favorite spot in the wide front window — with its Cinemascope view of the old redbrick Perry School across the street and the leafy ridge of the Old West Side beyond — pinching her knees together and tucking in her elbows as if afraid to touch anything. With undisguised distaste she lifted the top of her bun between two sharp red fingernails.

Kevin almost pointed out that at Zingermann's Deli she regularly ordered the most enormous, and enormously calorific, sandwiches; what you're objecting to, he almost said, is that the food here is cheap. But instead he repeated what the woman at the grill had said, which turned out to be another mistake.

"Have you ever seen a picture," she said, wide-eyed with schadenfreude, "of a human heart encased in fat?"

"My heart's fine," he said, though his glorious mouthful of beef, provolone, mushroom, onion, and mayo had suddenly turned to offal in his mouth. "I'm a runner, remember?"

"A friend of my father?" she whispered. "A runner? For twenty years? Keeled over dead with a massive coronary. During a marathon."

"Huh," said Kevin, swallowing hard.

Since then they don't talk about it, and Kevin's visits are clandestine and guilty, as if he's cheating on her instead of merely indulging in the occasional greasy cheeseburger. Luckily, her job takes her out of town for two or three days at a time, and in fact, Kevin ate at Blimpy's just last night, indulging himself in a quad and a large order of rings, knowing that for once it didn't matter if his breath smelled of onions afterward.

With a little electric crackle, the amplified voice of the guayabera issues from a loudspeaker bolted to the tree. "Number fifty-six, your order's ready," says the voice, and one of the young guys at the other table glances at his receipt, rises, and crosses the courtyard, scattering the black birds strutting at his feet. At the door he stands aside for Claudia, who is bearing a glass of iced tea in each hand. Without smiling, she fixes Kevin in her dark-eyed gaze like a raptor zeroing in on a rabbit, and Kevin, thrilled and terrified, sits up straighter in his wobbly chair. She switches her hips between the tables, never taking her gaze off him, and sets the sweating glasses on their table. She lifts her plastic chair back one-handed.

"I didn't think to ask," she says. "Do you take lemon? Sugar?"

Kevin would love some sweetener, but he says, "This is great," lifting the glass. The tea is refreshing, but mostly what he tastes is ice.

"Good." Claudia leans back in her seat, lifting both hands to loosen her ponytail. She shakes her hair back and sighs, as if she's willing herself to relax. Kevin watches her over his glass. He hadn't noticed it when her hair was pulled back, but she has a Susan Sontag streak of white. She isn't looking at him now, but gazing distractedly across the courtyard. Then, having shaken out her hair, lank with sweat, she pulls it tightly back again and nimbly slips the elastic over her ponytail. Somehow she's figured out how to make the streak of white disappear when she pulls her hair back, and now he's not even sure he saw it. He wonders why she let her hair down if she was just going to tie it back up again.

"How are you feeling?" she says.

"Fine," he says. "Thanks again, for everything."

She lifts her own tea, scowling as she swallows. She looks across the table, sighs, and carefully sets her glass to one side.

"May I impose upon you a little?" She leans forward on her crossed arms, making the table wobble. "I have a favor to ask."

Kevin wonders if Dr. Barrientos is able to do anything at all without you being able to see the wheels turning. That could be a kind of curse, especially if she's aware of it, leading to an infinite regression of self-consciousness. He worries he's about to hear a pitch for Amway, or testimony of the doctor's personal relationship with Christ, or—oh hell—both, simultaneously.

"Sure," he says warily.

"I want to talk to you about something important." She's hunched forward, watching him, gauging his reaction.

Oh fuck, thinks Kevin, here it comes. Have you thought

about how you're going to spend eternity? And are you familiar with distributed sales? But then her eyes slide away from him, and Kevin thinks, if she were about to pitch him Christ and/or laundry detergent, she'd be less nervous.

"Well, it's important to me, anyway," she says, staring across the courtyard at nothing in particular. "It may not mean that much to you. But I want to tell somebody."

"Okay." Kevin's still wary, but now he's also curious.

She looks down at the table, tightening her grip on her own biceps.

"It's just that we don't really know each other," she says, "and the odds are we'll never see each other after today."

Kevin's surprised at his own sharp dismay. Oh no! he almost says aloud. Don't say that!

"It's just that makes you the perfect person to tell this to." She looks up at him. "Does that make any sense?"

Now he really is curious, but a little disappointed as well: is she about to come out to him? Just his luck, the day he meets a really attractive woman in a city where he might be moving, that's the same day she decides to announce to the world, or at least to him, that she's a lesbian.

"I guess that depends." He leans forward and rests his own arms on the table. Now they're only a couple feet apart, like two lovers gazing into each other's eyes in some dimly lit bistro, over a little bowl of candlelight. "On what you want to tell me."

He regrets having put it so bluntly, regrets having sat forward like this. Is that alarm in her gaze? He should've just stayed where he was, slumped in his chair, looking blasé. Now he's afraid she won't go on.

"Though whatever it is," he adds, trying to inch back from this intimate proximity without being too obvious about it, "I'm sure it's okay with me."

She lets her gaze drift again, and as she opens her mouth, probably to tell him to forget the whole thing, the loudspeaker crackles and says, in the melancholy voice of the guayabera, "Number fifty-eight, your order's ready."

"Is that us?" Kevin slaps his pockets for the receipt.

"I'll get it," says Claudia, suddenly upright. "Don't get up." Halfway to the door, she looks back. "Salsa?"

"Not too hot." Kevin leans back in his chair, and she disappears into the greasy gloom.

Kevin sighs. The moment's gone, she'll never tell him now, and he'll wonder for the rest of the day what it was she wanted say to him, some random guy she never plans on seeing again. Then his Jiminy Cricket chirps up, saying, this is your chance, leave now while she's gone. Whatever she wants to tell you, trust me, you don't want to know. You'll regret it. This is your last chance, chump, get up and go. Vamoose. Scram. Skedaddle. Maybe Jiminy's talking sense, thinks Kevin, God knows I should've listened to him earlier today. He sits up straight in the unsteady chair, puts his hands on the arms. He twists to look behind him, and sees a doorway in the courtyard fence that leads straight to the parking lot. If he gets up right now, without hesitating, he could be half a block up Lamar before she comes back. And no harm done, really; he's already paid for her lunch. Of course, he'd have to do it *right now . . .*

Too late. He faces forward to see her in the doorway holding a plastic tray in both hands. She's just standing there, watching him, which means that she caught him just now contemplating his escape. He shifts in his seat and ventures a smile, and she steps down out into the courtyard, carefully balancing the two paper cartons on the tray. As she sets it on the table between them, she smiles to herself, then directs the smile at him.

"You're still here." She lifts one carton to his side of the table and the other to hers. Each contains a fat, steaming soft taco, bulging with chunks of brown meat, grilled onions, and a liberal sprinkling of what looks like fresh cilantro. She also sets aside a small stack of paper napkins. "I haven't scared you off," she adds, setting a little plastic cup of lumpy red salsa before him. Her own cup of salsa is green and thick with what looks like stems and seeds.

"You don't know me," he says. "I'm not like that." Not to mention he just remembered that his jacket's still in her truck. He looks up at her. "Claudia," he adds. It's the first time he's called her by name.

She's standing with all her weight on one solid, glorious leg, her hand lightly on the back of her chair, as if she's contemplating fleeing, too. Then she nods briskly, jerks the chair back, and sits. She squares her taco in front of her and opens it to coat the filling with salsa verde. Kevin moves aside the warm flap of his own taco and pours salsa over the meat and onions and green leaves. It smells wonderful. Lifting it with both hands, Kevin's pleasantly surprised by his first bite. The taco's spices, whatever they are, hit places on his palate that he didn't know existed. His usual Mexican place in Ann Arbor, a little dive near campus, basically serves up ground beef and cheese with jalapeños. This is richer and much more subtle. "Wonderful," he mumbles with his mouth full. "What is it?"

"*Al pastor.*" She picks up her own taco with the tips of her fingers. "Pork."

"Wonderful." Kevin takes another big bite, grease and salsa rojo sliding down his fingers. Then he swallows and says, "So. The doctor is in. I'm listening."

Claudia chews for a moment, still making up her mind. She takes one more bite, lifts her tea. Then she sets the glass and the taco to one side and puts her forearms on the table.

"Okay," she says. "I think I told you, I'm a surgeon."

Kevin nods.

"Well," she says, with steely calm, "I'm being sued for malpractice."

She says "malpractice" with the emphasis on the first syllable. *Mal*practice. He's glad his mouth is full. He can't say anything, so he just nods again.

"Someone died during an operation, and now a lawsuit has been filed."

Kevin the professional editor can't help but notice the mistakes-were-made form of her disclosure, the lack of a pronoun, first-person or otherwise. He also notices that his heart has begun to race. This isn't at all what he thought he was going to hear.

"Against me," adds Dr. Barrientos.

Kevin plucks a napkin off the stack and wipes his lips and fingertips. She picks up her taco and sets it down again without taking a bite.

"And you haven't told anybody this?" he says. "I don't understand."

"Oh no, everyone knows," she says. "It's a matter of public record."

"Ah." He's not sure if he should continue eating, but as the silence stretches again he picks up his taco and takes another bite just for something to do.

"When I said no one else knows," she says, "that's not what I meant."

"Okay."

"I don't want to get into what happened." She pushes her unfinished taco away from her. "That's not really a mealtime conversation."

"Mmph," says Kevin.

By now their gazes are sort of feinting at each other, not really making eye contact, but just checking to see if the other is watching.

"What it is," she's saying, "it's about my family. My father, specifically. He never finished high school, but he's worked like a bull his whole life, taught himself everything he knows. Never put himself first, but never gave an inch." She pauses, nodding slightly as if at something only she can see or hear. "He put everything he had into making sure his kids had the chances he never did. Pretty typical story, where I come from."

"The Valley," offers Kevin.

"The Valley." She rewards him with a quick smile, to show that she appreciates that he's been paying attention. "But the thing about my father is," she continues, looking away, "the thing you need to know is, he wanted me to be a nurse."

Their eyes meet for a moment.

"Ah," says Kevin.

"You see what I mean."

"I think so." Though he doesn't, really.

"Don't get me wrong," says Dr. Barrientos. "It's not that he's not proud of me. He is. And he's not shy about saying it. He loves to introduce me as his daughter, *la cirujana*." Adding, "The surgeon."

"Of course."

"It's just that..." She lifts her hand, her fingers parted as if she means to pluck the right words out of the air. "Where I come from, or maybe I should say, where my father comes from, a man has to be, well, *tough* is what people usually say, but a better word is, *decisive*." She glances at Kevin. "You have to judge how things really are, how *people* really are, take their measure very quickly, and then act accordingly. A man like that, once he decides what you are, and what you can and cannot do, he doesn't change his mind very easily."

Which is a trait, Kevin suspects, that Dr. Barrientos shares with her father.

"On top of that, a man like my father, coming from that

place and time, he saw people defeated more often than he saw them succeed. You see what I'm saying?"

Kevin does, surprisingly. What he sees, in fact, just for an instant, is his own father at the dinner table, looking older than his age, his face sagging in a mask of fatigue and resignation. What his sister Kathleen has called, in retrospect, long after their father died, "one of his Willie Loman moments."

"What he decided about me, was that I was good enough to be a nurse, but no more than that. So when I told him I was studying pre-med at A&M, we had some...difficulties. They went away somewhat when I got into med school, and I really thought he'd come around by time I graduated and finished my internship and residency."

Claudia shifts in her chair as if she's uncomfortable, and Kevin is struck by how vulnerable this makes her seem. He's never met a woman as physically self-possessed as Dr. Barrientos—not comfortable in her own body, exactly, but in complete command of every inch of it at all times—and there's something about this restless movement that seems as shocking as if she'd burst into tears.

"It's just that even now," she's saying, "after all this time, after twelve years of being a surgeon, I can still detect a...hesitation in him. Like he doesn't really believe it. Like he thinks it's some sort of clerical error. Like I'm not telling him the whole truth."

"We all think that sometimes," Kevin says. "About ourselves, anyway." In fact, he thinks, it's the story of my life.

"Not me," says Dr. Barrientos definitively. "I've earned everything I have. I've worked damn hard for everything I've got."

Just like her father, Kevin thinks, and this time he almost says it out loud. But Claudia has lifted her hand again, and caught her breath.

"I'm sorry," she says. "I don't mean to..."

"It's okay." Kevin's mouth is dry suddenly, and he wonders if he should reach for his tea.

"It's just that when I told him," she says, and stops. "About the lawsuit," and stops. Her gaze is fixed in his direction, but she isn't really looking at him. It's an uncanny look, creepy, even, like meeting the inward gaze of a sleepwalker. It's what he sees sometimes when he looks at Stella, even when she's awake. He feels a rush of pity and tenderness for Dr. Barrientos, because he realizes she'd rather die than show vulnerability, and yet she's showing it to him, a man she hardly knows.

"He didn't say anything for a long time." Her voice is taut as a wire. "Not a word. Just looked at me, drilled me with his eyes all the way down to my spine." She breathes slowly in and out. "Then all he said was, 'If you'd only gone to nursing school...'"

She's nodding slightly, her gaze directed entirely within. Over the muffled rumble of traffic beyond the fence and the faint beat of Mexican pop through the courtyard door, Kevin can hear her breath hissing through her nose. Then, like a sleeper waking, she shudders, her gaze softens, and she looks at Kevin, sad but utterly dry-eyed.

"That look he gave me," she says evenly, "that was my father making up his mind. He didn't have to finish the sentence. I knew what he meant. If I'd only gone to nursing school, I wouldn't be in this situation." She breathes in, out. "If I'd only gone to nursing school, that woman would still be alive."

Kevin says nothing. What can he say? He can hardly bear to look at her, but he can hardly look away. He can feel his heart pounding. What's more, he's flooded again with a strong feeling of déjà vu, which only adds to his anxiety, because he has no idea why this moment should feel so familiar. This place, this woman, this situation—she killed somebody, if inadvertently, and an admission like that, only an hour after he's met her, is sort of new in Kevin's experience.

She manages a rueful smile. "Have I freaked you out?"

Kevin blows out a sigh. "That's serious stuff."

"You don't have to say anything." She leans back in her seat. "I'm sorry to burden you with it."

"And of course I said just the wrong thing, didn't I," Kevin continues, just to be saying something, "back by the river."

"Oh, no no no." Claudia lifts her hand from the table. "That's not it. That's not why I…"

"I know, I just meant…"

"Oh, no no no. It's fine."

"But what I said made you think of it."

Claudia laughs sharply and looks away. "Trust me, I was thinking of it anyway. It's pretty much all I think about lately."

Kevin sits back and says nothing. A little of his anger comes back, just an echo. It wasn't unreasonable to assume she was a nurse. Can I help it, he thinks, if her father's a judgmental SOB? But now the déjà vu is stronger than ever, and mainly Kevin's still puzzled. Why *does* this moment feel so familiar?

"That's hard," he says. "A thing like that. Somebody you love says the last thing you want to hear."

"Yes." Her gaze is withdrawing again. Another moment, and they'll both be casting about for something to do with their hands, looking everywhere but at each other, like a first date gone bad. Gosh, look at the time. Suddenly he's certain he's disappointed her somehow — she's just told him this story that she hasn't told anyone else, thinking he might understand in a way that the men she usually deals with might not, and the best he can do is offer bromides. No doubt she's just made up her mind about him as peremptorily as her father would have, and the last thing he wants to know is what she thinks of him, some soft-handed, sweaty, heatstruck, middle-aged white guy from up north. In fact, he suddenly has an unreasonable fear that that's precisely what she's about to do, fix him with her gaze across the table, drill him down to his spine, and tell him exactly what he doesn't want to hear.

"Listen." Kevin sits sharply forward, rocking the rickety table, sloshing tea over the lip of his glass. Both of them react instinctively, steadying the table with their palms, reaching for their respective glasses.

"Listen," says Kevin again, and their eyes lock across the table. "I was in love with this girl once. This is, like...twenty-five years ago."

Now that he says it out loud—twenty-five years!—it feels more like a century. It's half his lifetime ago, but at the same time it feels like it was yesterday.

"She was the daughter of a professor of mine, a philosophy professor, in the town where I went to college. In the town where I still live, in fact."

Where did this come from? He can't believe he's telling her this. He never told Beth, and certainly not Stella. He's started speaking, in fact, before he's even realized that this was what he was going to say. But it was on his mind earlier, in Empyrean, and now he's sitting up straight in his chair, keenly aware of the muffled rumble of traffic beyond the fence, the tinny throb of amplified music, the tremor of leaves overhead, the black-eyed birds strutting in the dirt, the pressure of the heat all around their table. He's aware of Claudia's startled gaze over their never-to-be-finished lunch.

"I didn't know her when I was in school," he's saying, "when her father was my professor. I only met her a few years after I graduated, when she was still in college and she used to share a house with a friend of mine."

Who also loved her, though Kevin doesn't say that. Half the guys Kevin knew in Ann Arbor in the mid-eighties were in love with the Philosopher's Daughter.

"And even then, I didn't really get to know her until a year or two later, one summer after she graduated from Michigan, and she was living in her parents' attic, in this big old farmhouse halfway to Saline." He pauses. "That's a little town outside of Ann Arbor." Then he adds, "Michigan."

Claudia gestures, go on.

"Anyway, this girl, she always had a cloud of guys circling around her, waiting for whoever she was seeing at the moment to go away or be dumped, so they could take their shot. You know what I mean?"

Kevin's dimly aware of the potential awkwardness of telling a middle-aged woman what a babe another, younger woman used to be—though, actually, she'd be older now than Claudia—but Dr. Barrientos seems to be taking it in stride. She nods, at any rate.

"I don't know where her parents were that particular summer, but she always seemed to have the house to herself, and she used to have people out there all the time, for cook-outs or parties or whatever."

One party in particular, thinks Kevin, but that's not the half of this story that he's telling right now.

"One night that spring, early May maybe, she had five or six of us out, just her and five or six guys, and we stayed up late watching movies on TV. And these five or six guys, all of us had crushes on her to varying degrees, though only one of us was her actual, official boyfriend at the time. And the thing was, he was leaving in a couple weeks to go to Europe or something, and the rest of us were, you know, *circling*, angling to take his slot. So you get the idea—five guys and this irresistible girl, all of us in our twenties, more or less, and we all kind of know why we're there. It's like a casting call, and she's playing it very cool, but enjoying every minute of it."

"Do you blame her?" says Claudia.

"Wait and see," Kevin says. "So we ordered pizza or grilled

hot dogs or something, and we stayed up really late watching whatever we could pull in on her parents' shitty little black-and-white TV. This was before VCRs, understand. You'd think a full professor at Michigan would have a decent television, and cable, and a color TV, but no, it was a little Zenith black-and-white portable, yay big, with rabbit ears and one of those loops for UHF." Kevin laughs. "Christ, they didn't even have a roof antenna!"

Claudia smiles, if only at his enthusiasm.

"So we're watching Channel 50 out of Detroit, this low-rent station that showed movies all the time, and I can still remember the movies we saw that night, in order." He ticks them off on his fingers. "*Trilogy of Terror, The Snakepit,* and *The Big Country.*" He laughs again. "*Trilogy of Terror?* Karen Black versus the devil doll?" He crosses his eyes, mimes stabbing with a carving knife, cries, "Ai yi yi yi yi!" loud enough to startle a bird and attract the attention of the two lean guys across the courtyard. Claudia shakes her head—she has probably never wasted her time watching horror movies—but she smiles slightly.

"Never mind. Point is, halfway through *The Snakepit,* which was this old forties melodrama, I realize I'm not watching the movie. I'm lying on the floor with my head on a throw pillow and instead I'm watching the Philosopher's Daughter with her boyfriend, Tom or Bill or Gary or whatever his name was, the two of them draped over each other on the couch. I can see the TV light flickering over them, I can even see the little black-and-white reflection of the screen in her eyes. He's behind her with one hand on her hip, and she's curled against him with her head on his arm, and he's, like, half-asleep, bored out of his mind, but she's absolutely rapt, okay, she's watching this dopey old picture like it's, I dunno, *Citizen Kane.* And I'm watching her, I can't take my eyes off her, and I'm thinking: I want to be *that* guy. I want to be the guy with her on the couch with my hand on her hip and her head on my arm. Only, believe me, I wouldn't look so fucking bored."

Kevin stares at nothing, reliving the moment.

"Anyway," he starts up again, abruptly, "one by one, everybody else crawled off to find places to sleep, and it was just me and the Philosopher's Daughter and her sleeping boyfriend. By now we're watching *The Big Country,* which has got to be one of the most overblown, overproduced, *boring* Westerns I've ever seen. Nothing happens for, like, hours. Gregory Peck plays this sea captain who's engaged to a rancher's daughter, only he ends up in love with a schoolteacher played by Audrey Hepburn. Or maybe not Audrey Hepburn, but somebody just like her. Point is, for most of the movie, Peck gets insulted, beaten, and abused by all the cowboys, especially Charlton Heston, who all think he's just the most pathetic" — almost says "pussy," but says instead — "sissy imaginable. He's got some sort of Quaker thing going, won't talk back, won't fight, unless he's absolutely forced into it."

Kevin inches forward.

"Lousy, frustrating, *infuriating* movie, because you want Gregory Peck to deck somebody, or shoot somebody, or at least take the girl he loves away from that bonehead Charlton Heston. Instead, he's doing Atticus Finch, only with less balls." Easy, thinks Kevin. "Meantime, I'm half-watching this goddamn movie, and half-watching the Philosopher's Daughter nestled in the arms of this asshole who has *no idea* how lucky he is. And the thing is, she knows I'm watching her. She catches me at it, and she doesn't look away. She doesn't say anything, doesn't smile, doesn't frown, just watches me back until I can't stand it anymore, and I have to look back at the screen. And that's the moment I knew I was in love with her, and it's also the moment when I knew that I was as big a pussy as Gregory Peck in that movie, because I was afraid to *do* anything about it."

"So do something," says Claudia unexpectedly. "Tell her."

He's surprised she spoke up, he's half-certain he's boring her senseless, but she's leaning across the table, watching him intently.

"I did!" he says. "Eventually. I mean, even Gregory Peck rode off in the sunset with the schoolteacher. So after her boyfriend left for Europe, I ended up taking her out to see bands two, three times a week. I was working at a record store that summer and I used to get comp tickets, so I took her to see some pretty amazing stuff—U2, before they were really big, okay? But the thing is, these weren't like dates, per se, it was more like, hey, I've got tickets to this thing, you want to go? And she always said yes. We used to go dancing all the time, too, sometimes at clubs, sometimes at parties at people's houses we knew, and sometimes," Kevin laughs, "sometimes we'd walk the streets near campus on a Friday or Saturday night until we found a big party, and just walk in. I mean, nobody cared, everybody was usually pretty drunk already, it was..." He's lost in the memory for a moment.

"God, she was a great dancer!" He sighs. "This is going to sound really stupid, but she danced like Molly Ringwald in *The Breakfast Club,* back when Molly Ringwald was really something. Do you remember how she danced? She used to toss herself back and forth, like that."

He almost demonstrates from his chair, but to his surprise, the thoracic surgeon nods.

"And one night we were at a party, dancing, drinking beer, and we went out on the porch of this house." He pauses. "I don't remember the address, but I could find it for you again, it's still there, out on West Liberty, in the Old West Side. Won't mean anything to you." He waves his hand, clearing the air before him. "But that was the night I...That was the night we were...That was the night I decided to..." Pause. "Well, I didn't decide anything, it just happened, because we were both really relaxed and happy, we'd both been drinking but we weren't really drunk, we were just dancing without thinking about anything, brushing up against each other and touching and..."

Kevin can feel the mild midwestern heat of that summer, not like the stifling heat here in Austin. He can hear the crickets, the throb of the bass from the stereo inside the house, the cries of the dancers inside, the thump of their feet. He can see the Philosopher's Daughter leaning against the porch railing in the dark, irresistibly silhouetted against the glow of a streetlight. He can see the red spark of her cigarette.

"We went out to take a break, to cool off, and she asked me, 'Do you think I dance like a geek? Am I totally embarrassing myself?' And I couldn't help myself, so before I had a chance to think about it I said, 'I *love* the way you dance. You're *adorable.*' God, I just..."

Twenty-five years after the fact, even in the Texas heat, Kevin's blushing.

"Thing is, she had this way of watching you like she thought you were really funny, or really stupid, or stupid in a really funny way, and she'd laugh at you, but I didn't care, because she had the loveliest laugh. I can't explain it, but she was always watching you like she was right on the cusp of derision. But in a nice way, if that makes sense. And even in the dark on the porch, even when I couldn't see her face, I knew she was watching me like that."

Somehow in the heat, Kevin's face feels cool again.

"So of course that's when I told her I loved her. Just blurted it out." Pause. "Dead silence." The thump of the bass. The crickets. The Philosopher's Daughter in exquisite silhouette, saying nothing. "They were playing the B-52s inside the house, 'Rock Lobster,' and everyone was chanting, 'Down, down,' and sinking slowly to the floor in a big tangle. Meantime, me, on the porch, having just handed my beating heart to this girl, I just stood there like an asshole, listening to dead silence from the girl I just said I loved." Kevin stops.

"What happened?" says Claudia after a moment.

"Here's the thing," says Kevin hoarsely. "This is why I thought of this right now. This was my moment like the one with your father. This is why I brought this up. You know what she said to me?"

Claudia waits.

"She said to me, 'Kevin,' she said to me, 'I don't think I could love you.' Bad enough, right? Under the circumstances."

Claudia says nothing.

"Bear in mind, we're in the dark, I can't see her face, I can't see her eyes. But she can see through me like a fucking x-ray. And if she laughs right now?" Kevin shakes his head. "But I'll give her this much, she knew better than to laugh. Even she wasn't that cruel."

"What did she say?" Claudia says quietly.

"She asked me a question," says Kevin. "She said, 'Do you want to know why I don't think I could love you?'"

Claudia gasps slightly.

"Exactly," Kevin laughs. "Loaded question, right? I'm not as dumb as I look, so naturally I said, 'No, not really. I'd actually rather you didn't tell me that.'"

Claudia waits.

"And then she told me anyway."

Claudia breathes out.

"She said, 'I don't think you're capable of tenderness and passion.'"

Claudia winces.

"Yeah. Ouch, huh?"

"You just should have kissed her," says Claudia.

"Thought of that," says Kevin briskly. "Not right then, of course, not till it was too late. At the moment I was too busy bleeding to death. And anyway, if I was going to kiss her, it should have been *before* she told me that I had no soul, not after."

"She shouldn't have said that to you."

"Maybe not," says Kevin. "Unless it was true."

"Was it?"

Kevin gasps, turns it into a weak laugh. I asked for that, he realizes, I left myself wide open. He feels a little spike of anger, but then he gave her the opportunity. And anyway, it's just like him wanting to know what she did or didn't do to that patient who died on her operating table.

"I'm sorry," she says. "I shouldn't have asked that."

"It's a fair question," says Kevin. "And it's not like I haven't asked it myself, every day of my life for the last, oh, quarter of a century."

"Maybe you give her too much power."

"I could say the same thing to you."

Claudia gives him a sharp look. "That's different. That was my father."

"You're right. I'm sorry."

"You ever tell her?"

"Tell her what?"

"How she made you feel."

Kevin shrugs. "I haven't seen her in years. I don't even know where she is anymore. And by now, what's the point? I'm going to call her up all these years later, and say, hey, remember stabbing me in the heart and twisting the knife that night back in the eighties?" Kevin laughs. "She must be, what, forty-five now?

Whatever she did to me, whether she meant to hurt me or not, by now she's no doubt had the same or worse done to her." He smiles ruefully. "Bombardier, it's your karma."

"Pardon?"

"Firesign Theatre." Kevin waves it away. "Forget it."

They sit for a moment in silence, and Kevin feels the Texas heat closing in around him again, hears the traffic beyond the fence. "Rock Lobster" is replaced in his head by another rhythmic pop song in Spanish from the tinny loudspeaker.

"So what happened after that?" says Claudia.

"Oh," says Kevin, "I started seeing this other girl that summer, someone I didn't actually, you know, love. And who didn't love me, either, but that was okay."

Lynda *à la plage,* Lynda on the railing. No way he's telling Dr. Barrientos the second half of the story. He's told her what the Philosopher's Daughter said, how it set up a vibration in him that he still feels a quarter-century later, but no way he's telling her about Lynda on the Philosopher's Daughter's front porch.

"No," says Dr. Claudia. "I mean right then, at the party, on the porch. What happened next?"

"Oh." In the flexing embrace of the flimsy plastic chair, Kevin runs his palm over his sweaty forehead and hair. "I really don't remember. We probably went back inside and danced some more, I don't know. It was kind of like the moment right after an explosion, my ears were ringing, I couldn't really hear or see anything. I honestly don't remember."

He's feeling calm now, calmer than he's felt all day, actually. Calmer than he's felt in weeks, even, since before he found Stella's pregnancy test in the kitchen trash. You put a moment like that in the context of a lifetime, and it's not such a big deal. Makes him wonder why he's been so fretful about it. Makes him wonder why he's in Texas at all.

"Why'd she tell me that, though," he hears himself say, "when I asked her not to? That's what I still don't get. That's what I still can't get my mind around after all this time. Maybe she was just being cruel to be kind, telling me what she thought I needed to know so that I wouldn't embarrass her again. A girl like that, I'm sure she had guys throwing themselves at her all the time. In fact, I know she did. Like I say, half the guys I knew..."

He thinks of her name, even as her face fades into the glare leaking through the leaves of the tree over the courtyard.

"I mean, she must have felt constantly besieged, and I'm sure she did her best to deflect all that uninvited interest as nicely as possible, because she wasn't a bad person, or mean, or bitchy. It's just that she must have gotten tired of all that... *longing* coming at her, all the time. So she learned to cut to the chase, say just the right thing that would stop the latest lovesick bastard in his tracks."

Now he just feels tired. He wishes he could go somewhere and lie down. Even Lynda's face is hard to recall now.

"But you know," Kevin says, "that thing she said? What she told me about myself? It wasn't exactly helpful. In fact, if you want to know the truth, it feels like a curse. I've never forgotten it, and it's always there, at the back of my mind. Especially when I'm with a woman I love, or think I love. Or think I want to love. It's like a leash, with the Philosopher's Daughter at the other end. If I try too hard with a woman, if I make the effort, then I feel this little tug, like, not so fast, buster, who do you think you're kidding?"

"Ah," says Claudia.

"Because here's the thing." Kevin leans forward, rocking the table again. "Even it wasn't true when she told me, it's been true ever since *because* she told me."

In the time they've been sitting there, a few more people have settled at tables in the courtyard. Some of them are already eating, so somewhere along the way the loudspeaker has announced more numbers, and Kevin just hasn't heard them. A black bird is goose-stepping to and fro on a tabletop close to Kevin and Claudia's, eyeing their half-finished tacos, first with one unblinking eye and then the other. In the heat under the tree Kevin and Claudia look at each other across the table as if they have each only just realized the other person is there. Their silence is no longer like a first date, but like the silence at the end of a break-up, when there's nothing more left to say. Kevin doesn't feel embarrassed or exposed or angry, just spent. Now what? he thinks. What's next?

"Shall we go?" says Dr. Barrientos.

Out on Lamar again, in the hot cab of the truck, Claudia lowers the side windows a few inches, which lets out the heat and lets in a wedge of midday glare from either side.

"Just till the AC blows cold," she says, though Kevin can already feel the difference from a vent as it plays over the rip in his trouser leg. His jacket folded again on his lap, Kevin gazes dully through the windshield at South Lamar finishing its slow, sinuous climb up from the river. As the glaring sky opens out above the street, Kevin sees a large church with a vast yellow lawn and a diner with a big neon coffee cup and more scruffy garages and bottom-rung car dealers, but he barely registers them. He feels numb and hollowed out by his exchange of intimacies with Dr. Barrientos, as if he's just survived a loud explosion and is struggling to form a coherent thought in the reverberating silence. But all he can hear is *tenderness and passion, tenderness and passion*—oddly enough, though, not in the Philosopher's Daughter's own midwestern pixie's intonation, but in the slightly nasal drawl of her lanky father, the professor himself, from whom Kevin took a class in ethics and who reminded Kevin of Jimmy Stewart. In fact, over the course of the semester, the professor managed to embody not one, but several avatars of Jimmy Stewart: narrating the death of Socrates as if it were the last reel of *Mr. Smith Goes to Washington;* explaining utilitarianism as if he were the flinty, selfless technician of *Strategic Air Command;* and throughout the semester eyeing with barely repressed longing, as if he were the embittered sexual obsessive of *Vertigo,* a pair of ripe and stylish Southfield girls who always sat together in cashmere sweaters in the front row. So much did the professor remind Kevin of the actor, down to stammering and widening his eyes and waving his big-fingered hands when he was excited, that now, as the professor lectures Kevin about tenderness and passion—which he never did in real life—Kevin can't really picture the Philosopher's Daughter's father at all, but sees instead the graying, middle-aged, parentally befuddled Stewart of the late-career comedies, flying off to Paris to rescue his teenaged daughter from some dreamy French boy, or his teenaged son from Brigitte Bardot, or even the professor's own, real, vixenish daughter from some passionless son of Royal Oak.

"Duh, duh, de*fine* your terms, son," stammers Professor Stewart. "Wha, wha, what do you *mean* by tenderness and passion?"

I have no idea! Kevin wants to shout. I *can't* define them. To define them would be to pin them like butterflies to a corkboard. And anyway, professor, according to your own daughter, my problem isn't that I can't *define* them, it's that I can't *express* them. Besides, what do tenderness and/or passion get you? When Stella wakes up crying in the middle of the night, he holds her tightly until she stops shuddering. Neither of them says a word, they just clutch each other in the dark until she's breathing evenly again. Then he loosens his grip but doesn't let go of her completely. In the morning they never speak of it. What has his tenderness accomplished?

And passion, what of it? The Other Kevin, the Jihadist Kevin, the Freckled Suicide Bomber, he was passionate, wasn't he? How many people died because of his passion? The Other Kevin's blurry martyrdom video has been running nonstop on CNN and Fox all weekend, perhaps because it's one of the rare examples performed in English. And even then they've been running it with subtitles, because Kevin/Abdul—posing in a green headband before a grainy blow-up of Osama bin Laden—speaks of jihad in an incomprehensibly thick Glaswegian monotone. Without the subtitles Kevin—Quinn, not MacDonald—would understand only every third or fourth word. Yeah, young Kevin was one confused, inarticulate young bastard, but at least he believed in something, didn't he? At least he was willing to die for something. What would I be willing to die for, wonders Kevin—the decent Kevin, not the murderous Kevin—anything? *Who* would I be willing to die for? The Philosopher's Daughter? That would have been a waste, she didn't want me anyway. Lynda? Don't be stupid, that wasn't passion. Beth? Would he have died for her? Would he have died for her when she was pregnant with another man's child? Say they were in a public place—the aisles of Gaia, say—and say Kevin saw some nervous-looking young guy suddenly open his overcoat to reveal a canvas vest bulging with plastic explosives, and say the guy started yelling *Allahu akbar* or whatever—would Kevin throw himself between Beth and her unborn child and the bomber? Probably, but that might just be good manners. In that last instant before everything went black, Kevin would feel like a chump. He'd be thinking, it's not even my kid. And what if Stella's life were in danger? Would he die for her if she was carrying *his* child? Would he sacrifice himself then more willingly, the way the Other Kevin did? That's what passion does, thinks

Michigan Kev (not Glasgow Kev)—passion makes you stupid, passion uses you and then throws you away.

He glances at Claudia, afraid he might have said some of this out loud, but if he has, she either didn't hear it or chooses to ignore it. She's driving distractedly again, one-handed, while with her other hand she pinches and unpinches a crease in her lower lip. Kevin's not sure conversation is even possible now, as if the padded upholstery of the cab would soak up every sound. He's not sure he would make any sense if he did speak, he's not even sure if he would make sense to himself. For all he knows she's feeling the same numbness, preoccupied with her father's disappointment, her own uncertainty, the face of the woman she killed. Way to go, Dr. Barrientos, with the bedside manner! Just what he needs on the day of a job interview, the doctor passing her lacerating self-doubt along to him like Typhoid Mary. He's still tongue-tied, but somebody better say something quick, because at last Lamar has widened and straightened out, lying as broad as the Champs-Élysées between strip malls and garages and down-market apartment complexes, and instead of the Arc de Triomphe at the far end, South Lamar's vanishing point is obscured by a freeway overpass where the glittering roofs of cars and SUVs glide in the midday sun.

"How far are these stores?" Kevin says abruptly, at the same moment as Claudia says, "What sort of store are you looking for?"

They glance at each other.

"Sorry?" says Kevin.

"You first," says Claudia.

Up ahead, freeway signs hang over the road like big green guillotine blades, blunt white arrows pointing the way to Johnson City, Llano, Bastrop. Kevin shifts in his seat, afraid that if they survive the steel blades and enter the tangle of overpasses, Claudia's truck will get snagged and slotted in and shot like a pellet further south than Kevin wants to go, all the way to San Antonio, all the way to *Mexico lindo*.

"I don't want to get too far from downtown," he says. "I still have to find my way back to, ah..." He nearly says Barad-dûr, catches himself. He can't remember the actual name of the building, which only makes him feel worse. Bad enough he bared his soul uselessly to this woman, dredging up an ancient hurt for no particular reason and with no particular result other than to embarrass her and make himself feel awful. Now on top of it, he's having a senior moment, and all at once he thinks of the growing hair in his ears, his enlarging prostate, his receding gums, and how the location of his job interview has become yet another alarming pothole in his memory.

He's still saying "Ah..." when Claudia cuts to the right and they glide across two lanes into a driveway with a grassy median and a brick sign that says LAMAR OAKS.

Kevin closes his mouth. Her briskness annoys him, makes him feel even frailer, just like Stella does when she brings in his mail and sorts it for him. Technically they have separate mailboxes, she's still paying rent on the downstairs apartment, but if she's home before he is, she empties both boxes and brings the mail up to his kitchen table and sorts it into piles, his and hers, junk and not-junk. She especially likes to fish out envelopes from the AARP, the first one of which appeared just before his fiftieth birthday as ominously as a crack in a levee, which has since widened into an irreparable breach, flooding his kitchen table with offers for life insurance, prescription drug delivery, low-interest credit cards, and Mediterranean cruises, not to mention anodyne and unconvincing reassurances that the best of life is yet to come. Stella loves to eat an apple and slice the envelope open and read the letter aloud while he pretends to be a good sport.

"They'll help you choose a Medicare plan," she says, chomping with her mouth open. "You'll get discounts at Applebee's."

She thinks she's coming across as pertly as Sarah Jessica teasing Mr. Big, but she's being more bitchy Miranda than flirty Carrie. It's all he can do to keep from telling her, you're closer to this than you admit, baby, I've seen your driver's license, but he hasn't yet. And to be fair, she always ends her dramatic reading with a little slap and tickle. "Chicks dig a guy with a senior discount," she likes to whisper in his hairy ear.

"There's a Neiman Marcus," Claudia is saying as she creeps the truck over speed bumps through a labyrinthine parking lot sectioned with bristling waist-high hedges and little trees with purple flowers.

"Whoa," Kevin says. "Neiman Marcus? Didn't you say something about Target?"

"It's Neiman's Last Call store." She glances at him. "Everything's marked way down."

"Huh."

"There's a Wohl's, too," she says. "They're less expensive."

"Ah." He relaxes a bit—Wohl's he knows, there's a Wohl's out near Briarwood, on the far side of 94. It's not much further up the retail evolutionary tree than Target or Sears, but it's all he needs. Stella would drag him into Neiman Marcus, but then Stella's not here, is she?

"Wohl's is good," he says as the truck rounds a corner into a wide-open, sun-hammered, nearly empty parking lot. A few cars are clustered at the far end where the bleached yellow façade of Wohl's is taking the sun full in its face, and a few more are parked along the bland redbrick storefronts on the right: postal store, Christian books, big and tall menswear. The rest of the lot, with its faded chevrons of empty parking spaces and minimalist light poles staring down like surveillance devices, seems as desolate as a salt flat. All it needs are the bleached ribs and eyeless skulls of dead cattle. Even through the window tint and the icy blast of AC in his lap, Kevin can feel the blinding glare and the baking heat, and suddenly his stomach knots up so tight he nearly winces.

Don't leave me here, he almost says aloud. This wasteland is indistinguishable from any strip mall parking lot in North America, but suddenly it seems like the most alien landscape Kevin's ever seen. He'll get out of the truck as Kevin Quinn, but by the time he stumbles across to Wohl's, he'll be Fred C. Dobbs for sure, all alone and thousands of miles from anybody who loves him—assuming anybody does—hollow-eyed, stubbled, footsore, and lip-blistered, muttering to the first person he sees, "Can ya stake a fellow American down on his luck?" His stomach only clenches tighter when Claudia's truck rolls to a stop in the emptiest portion of the lot, equidistant from Wohl's and the shops on the right.

"Last Call's just around the corner," she says, and he realizes she's being polite, leaving the choice to him, but it feels as if she's leaving him to die. He's afraid he's going to beg her not to abandon him, that she's going to have to get out of the truck herself and drag him out into the heat as he clings to the headrest for dear life, leaving long, desperate fingernail scratches in the upholstery. He turns to her, his mouth dry again.

"He's wrong," he says, and when she looks at him quizzically, he adds, "Your father. I'll bet you're a fantastic surgeon."

She blinks at him, momentarily speechless. He shrugs, but makes no effort to get out of the truck.

"Who needs another nurse?" he says. "World's lousy with nurses."

She gives a harsh bark of a laugh. "Not really, but thank you."

"Thank *you*. For everything." He hugs the jacket to his chest, gestures weakly at his knee. "I feel better already."

"Good."

As he watches her sidelong, desperately trying to think of

something else to say, she shifts her focus rather meaningfully toward the department store. No doubt she's wondering what he's doing, why he's postponing their parting, and he can't decide if he wants her to misunderstand—wants her, in other words, to think it has something to do with her and what passed between them—or if he wants her to understand the truth, that he simply doesn't want to be left to fend for himself in this empty parking lot under a semiforeign sun, semisunstroked and wearing semitattered clothes, not knowing a soul for miles in any direction, left alone to think only of all the frustrations and disappointments that have led him here, to this barren place. Either way, he realizes, he's going to seem pathetic to a woman like Dr. Barrientos, and at last, like a dying prospector accepting his fate in that last euphoric moment before the sun kills him, he starts fumbling—for the seat belt release, for the door handle, for something to say that will leave a better impression than he has so far. He's got the belt unlatched somehow and is disentangling his right arm, and then he cracks the door and lets in the heat, and as he nudges the panel with his injured knee, pushing the door wider, he hears her say, "Everybody."

He's got one foot on the running board, his jacket clutched to his chest. She's not looking at him, but staring through the windshield, not at Wohl's, but at something infinitely far away.

"Well, listen." He edges down into the heat. As he plants both shoes on the gritty pavement and puts his hand on the door to swing it shut, she shifts her gaze to him slowly, eerily.

"Everybody is tender and passionate." It's almost as if she's not talking to him, it's more like she's talking in her sleep, an utterance out of a dream.

"Everybody," she says again, her gaze sharpening in his direction.

"I know," says Kevin.

She gives him the barest of smiles, one lonely prospector passing another in a trackless waste.

"Good luck to you." She puts her truck in gear.

"And to you," he says, and bangs the door shut. With a throaty roar the truck glides away in a wide curve across the empty lot, and Kevin lifts his eyes to the freeway interchange, which is close now, ramps swooping over and under each other, lines of cars gliding as if pulled by strings, high above sunburned yellow grass. When he can't hear the grumble of Claudia's truck anymore, only the windy rush of traffic, he turns and limps through the heat toward the department store, pulling his sunglasses out of his pocket.

Stepping up on the curb in front of Wohl's, he meets his reflection in the tinted glass of the doors, and it's the first time he's seen himself full-length since the men's room at the airport—his shirt is half-untucked, the rip in his trouser leg bares the white square of his bandage and an alarming reach of pale shin. Around the bug eyes of his sunglasses, his head seems swollen. That's just a flaw in the glass, he tells himself, my head's not that big, but then his image trembles and he has the awful feeling he's about to evaporate into the overheated air. The door opens as he reaches for it, startling him again, and out comes an elderly woman unflatteringly packed into white capri pants and a red striped top. Kevin holds the door as she teeters past on hot pink heels, her tight coiffure dyed an unconvincing blond, her bright mouth, the same shade of pink as her shoes, puckered under wraparound sunglasses. He nods, but she sails by as if she hasn't seen him, stepping heavily down off the curb and mincing toward her car. And who am I to call her elderly? he wonders, as earnest as Jimmy Stewart. She gets the same mail from the AARP that I do. Twenty years ago, he might have thought of her as a sexy older woman. And twenty-five years from now, that could be Stella, dyeing her hair and risking her ankles and packing herself into pants two sizes too small. He folds his sunglasses into his jacket pocket and passes through the second set of doors into the mellow fluorescence and cool, dry, floral air of the store, thinking of the once and future Stella. In the three years they've been together, this is the first time he's been shopping for clothes without her and he feels the same mildly illicit, slightly queasy thrill he felt last night when he sat in the big picture window of Blimpy's and greedily ate a cheeseburger and onion rings. But this is even riskier, because by the time he sees her again — tomorrow night, when she gets back from Chicago — he will no longer smell of onions, but he will have a new pair of trousers, and Stella, who could star in her own production of *CSI: Ann Arbor,* will eventually come across them in his closet or in the laundry and she'll say, oh my God, not Wohl's! Because she'll know. What on earth were you doing in *Wohl's?*

None of your business, Kevin thinks, not any more, but as he limps up the wide entrance aisle, he knows it doesn't matter what he thinks, because Stella's going to kibitz whether he likes it or not, in spirit at least. There doesn't seem to be anybody behind the glittering jewelry counter, but it's a measure of his anxiety — at shopping without her, at sneaking away for a job interview without telling her, at thinking he could leave her and start over in Texas — that he feels a blinding, guilt-inducing beam from the engagement rings under glass, as if the ranked zirconia are focused in his direction like a navy searchlight. Though, to be fair, Stella would never shine that light on him here. Who would marry the oaf who bought a ring at *Wohl's?* Puh-leeze.

He limps past the counter and up the wide aisle, his thick-soled shoes squeaking on the spotless white tile. The tiles and white suspended ceiling recede in mirror-image toward a vanishing point behind the pastel folded towels in the bath shop at the far end. Kevin still doesn't see any employees, doesn't even see another customer, just receding ranks of breastbone-high racks, pink and burgundy lingerie to his right, trousers to his left. He angles onto the silent gray carpeting of the labyrinth of slacks, and someone moves directly into his path, startling him, but it's only himself in a mirrored column, still disheveled and pale. The store seems to be sailing on mysteriously unmanned like the *Marie Celeste,* with tantalizing indications of recent activity—the AC still humming, the Muzak still playing. Standing directly under a little round ceiling grille, Kevin can hear Tina Turner singing "What's Love Got to Do With It?"

Kevin sighs. The AC's cold enough that he slips on his jacket over his wilted shirt, inventorying each pocket by touch. He finds his tie rolled in a side pocket and shakes it out to check it for creases, but it seems to have survived the heat and his fall on the bridge, so he rolls it up and puts it back. He moves the folded letter and spare bandage from his breast pocket into his jacket, fingers his boarding pass for the return flight. In the dry refrigeration of the store he can smell himself, and he lifts the lapels of his jacket to see sweat stains under his arms. Now he'll have to buy a new shirt, too.

To the beat of the Tina Turner song, Kevin walks his fingers through one rack of trousers after another. He avoids the worsted dress pants—he's not spending $75.00, no matter what Stella would say. But then Stella's shade scares him away from the $45.00 trousers, because they're microfiber. "That's just itsy bitsy polyester," she whispers in his ear. Kevin moves to the Dockers, which are only $29.99, and starts to dicker with Stella's spirit. Didn't I tell you, protests Stella, I wouldn't be caught dead with a man in pleated khakis? But they're 100 percent cotton, replies Kevin, not a trace of microfiber. And they're only thirty bucks. I'm not even sure I want this job, I'm not dropping another seventy-five bucks on a pair of trousers just to impress a bunch of strangers I'll probably never see again. Reaching a compromise with his inner Stella, Kevin pulls out a dark blue pair of flat-front khakis in his size, 34/36.

Clutching the trousers, he winds through the slacks toward a display of shirts. Who is Stella to lecture him, anyway? Even during their worst moments, at least he and Beth *got* each other. He could carry on a conversation with her and not feel like he was speaking to a bratty younger cousin. She may not have liked Martin Amis's books (she hated them, in fact) but at least she knew who he was and could tell you why she hated him (she called him a motormouthed misogynist). But Stella, on the other hand, Stella reads featherweight novels with pastel covers, when she reads at all. And the first thing she does is turn to the back of the book and read the last few pages, to see how it turns out. "I need to know," she says. "I can't stand the suspense."

"What suspense?" Kevin said. "They all have the same ending: Reader, I married him."

"Well, *yeah*," she said. "Which is why I look: if she doesn't get the guy, then I know I don't want to read the book."

Beth used to drag him to operas and gamelan performances and concerts by Tuvan throat singers. They worked out a compromise about live music, by which she would consent to go see Richard Thompson at the Ark, and he would accompany her to hear some jazz performer he'd never heard of at the Firefly. One of their ancient arguments was over a Betty Carter album that Beth loved, called *It's Not About the Melody*.

"Actually, it *is* about the melody," protested Kevin, a second-generation Sinatra fan.

But with Stella, the roles were reversed. She agreed to go see a Royal Shakespeare Company production of *Antony and Cleopatra* at the Power Center only after Kevin told her that Captain Picard from *Star Trek* was playing Antony—and then Stella's chief reaction was awe at Patrick Stewart's abs, which you could see from the second balcony.

"I'd jump him in a heartbeat," she'd said on the walk home.

"He's in his sixties," Kevin had said.

"I like older men," she'd said, linking arms with him. "You know that."

Stella's idea of high culture is one those gaudy, fascistic shows in which some formerly charming folk genre—Irish step-dancing or Japanese drummers or Chinese acrobats—is blown all out of proportion into the sort of spectacle that would have fit right in at the Nuremburg rallies. Or a show that takes something vaguely "street" or mildly avant-garde—hip-hop dancers banging trash-can lids, men painted blue whacking each other with plastic tubing—and turns it into Vegas spectacle. Don't even get him started about Cirque de Soleil. She dragged him all the way to Chicago on his fiftieth birthday—and, to be fair, paid for the whole trip—to surprise him with a bewildering, assaultive show full of faux mysticism and pointless virtuosity. When she asked him if he didn't just *love* it, he stifled his gut response: that this was what entertainment would have been like if the Soviet Union had won the Cold War, fantastically fit but facelessly interchangeable performers in revealing outfits doing spectacular but meaningless stunts for a mindlessly bedazzled audience. Even the show's title wasn't really a word, he was convinced—vaguely Italian- or French-sounding, but signifying nothing, in the manner of some expensively concocted corporate brand name.

"It was great" is what he actually said, after which she took him back to their room at the Drake—"Don't worry," she'd said, "I'm expensing it"—and engaged him in some elaborately silly sex involving feathers, restraints, and a pair of Cirque-style masks. All of which, he had to admit, put the show retrospectively in a much more favorable light, as a kind of public foreplay. She also insisted on playing a CD of Cirque music she'd bought at the show—a rhythmic hash of ethnic music, like the folk tunes of Benetton—and Kevin started to laugh halfway through. But Stella just took his laughter as pleasure—which it mostly was—and redoubled her efforts.

He's startled again by the sight of himself in another mirrored column, and he wonders if Stella would be caught dead with a man in torn trousers and sweaty, wilted shirt and one blood-soaked sock. He zeroes in on a poly/cotton dress shirt—fuck it, it's marked down to twenty bucks. He pulls the tie from his pocket and makes sure the shirt matches. Then he pivots on his injured leg and lurches toward the socks. The gray carpet has no give to it, it's like walking on the green of a minigolf course. From a wall of socks he plucks off a pair for ten bucks—it's a lot for socks, but they're antimicrobial, so his sweaty feet won't smell. Note that, Stella? You can't go all *Queer Eye* on me when I buy antimicrobial socks. And even I know you don't buy a woman an engagement ring at a department store. Who said anything about a ring, anyway? I know how to read a home pregnancy test, too, and I know when I'm off the hook. What's love got to do, got to do with it?

He finds a cash register where the only apparent survivor of whatever plague cleared out the store, a pudgy, round-faced, lank-haired salesgirl, is flipping through a ring binder. She pushes it to one side as he lays his purchases on the counter.

"Find everything you need?" she says robotically, without making eye contact. "Do you have a Wohl's charge card?" She flips the trousers to find the tag.

"No." He should have tried the trousers on first, but fuck it.

"Are you interested in opening a Wohl's account?" the girl says in her retail zombie monotone, scanning the tags.

"No thanks," says Kevin. "Do you have a public restroom?"

For the first time, the girl's bovine gaze flickers at Kevin, and her fingers hesitate over the register. What must he look like? He wonders if she can smell him.

"Up front, by the service desk." She looks him up and down and says, "Sixty-six fifty-one."

Kevin fishes for his wallet, plucks out his Visa, and the salesgirl swipes the card with two fingers as if it's infectious, then holds it out to him at arm's length, watching him warily. As she scoops his purchases toward a plastic bag, Kevin startles them both by pressing his hand next to hers on top of the clothes, not quite touching. He tugs the trousers out from under her palm. "Where'd you say the men's room is?"

She lifts her chin over the labyrinth of racks toward the front. Kevin tucks his receipt inside his jacket and cradles his purchases in the crook of his arm. Her eyes slide down to his shoes and all the way up to his face again. "You okay?" she says.

"Never better," he says, limping away.

Customer Service is off to one side of the store — CUSTOMER CONVENIENCE says the sign, CONVENIENCIA PARA EL CLIENTE — and it's even more brightly lit than the sales floor. This desk, too, seems to be unstaffed, and as he passes the counter toward the restrooms Kevin feels vaguely guilty, as if he's stealing the clothes. The men's room is just as brightly lit as the rest of the store, and it's aggressively clean, smelling of urinal cakes and floral air freshener. Just inside the door there's even a framed print of orchids. There are four sinks on the wide counter, with boxes of tissue between them. The Muzak is louder in here, some contemporary pop hit he doesn't recognize, a young woman with a sharpish voice telling him to "Breathe, just breathe."

If you say so, thinks Kevin. Avoiding his image in the wide mirror, he casts about for someplace to put his purchases, wishing now he'd let the girl put them in a bag. The counter looks spotless, making him wonder again if anybody ever actually comes into this store, but instead he tilts the baby-changing table down from the wall, inspects it carefully, even sniffs it, and lays down his new clothes. He takes off his jacket, spreads his fingers under the collar, and brushes off any remaining dust. A little rumpled, he thinks, but presentable, and he hangs it on the hook behind the door of the handicapped stall. Then, at last, he confronts himself in the mirror.

In the pastel glitter of the reflected restroom, he sees an admirably slender but pale, round-faced, and baggy-eyed middle-aged man, his formerly crisp shirt wilted and stained under his arms, his forehead damp with sweat, his sandy hair matted along his sideburns and against the back of his neck. The shirt is half-untucked all around his waist, and his ruined trousers hang low like oversized jeans on some teenager. He resists the instinct to tuck in the shirt and tug up his pants, leaning over the sink instead and pushing the button on a faucet, waiting with his hands under the water for it to run hot. Nose to nose with the mirror he sees melancholy eyes and the unsubtle features of a peasant, son of an Irish father and a Polish mother—a Mick and a Polack, Uncle Stan used to say—good-looking enough, he supposes, to hang onto his younger girlfriend, at least for now. But he can already see where his cheeks are going to sag, and the bags under his eyes aren't entirely the result of heat and fatigue; they are becoming a more or less permanent feature. Face to face with himself, he realizes he looks like somebody's dad. Not like my dad, though, he thinks. He's already four years older than his father was when he died.

The water stops running before it gets hot, so Kevin mashes the button again with the heel of his palm. He dips his head, cups lukewarm water in both hands, and splashes his face. He knows how to read a pregnancy test—he knows he's nobody's dad yet—but he still doesn't know what the discarded test really means. He found the stick five weeks ago, and Stella hasn't said a word about it. She must have missed a period, but did she take the test because she hoped she was pregnant or because she hoped she wasn't? He's seen her little clamshell birth-control dispenser in the medicine cabinet, but it's not like he keeps track, it's not like he counts the pills to make sure she's taking one each day. Kevin wears a condom most of the time, too, but sometimes he doesn't. He didn't that night in Chicago, when Stella, her eyes shining behind that goofy mask, plucked the little foil square out of his fingers and flipped it across the room, murmuring wetly in his ear, "I want it to be just us, Kevin, skin to skin."

Where does she get this stuff? he wondered at the time, but even now, his cock stirs at the memory. He'd thought the masks were silly, he'd hated the music, but he remembers that night vividly: the shudder of her thighs around his waist, the rabbit pulse of the vein in her neck, the tremble of her lower lip under the gaudy mask. He splashes his face again and presses the soap dispenser. The milky goo in his palm looks like semen and smells like coconut, and he starts to laugh as he lathers his face, pushing his fingers up into his hairline and along his sideburns and around the back of his neck. He squeezes his eyes shut and scrubs with his fingertips, and in the reddened blackness behind his eyelids he can see Stella's wrists straining against the leather cuffs—well, vinyl really, she isn't as snobbish about sex gear as she is with trousers—and he can hear the rhythmic chirp of her excitement. He opens his eyes to peer through soapy eyelashes at the lather dripping off his nose and eyebrows and into the collar of his shirt, then presses the faucet again and splashes double handfuls of lukewarm water against his face, spattering the mirror and the countertop. Blinking at his reflection, he yanks a fistful of paper towels out of the dispenser and scrubs himself dry, vigorously rubbing his hair.

Chicago was eight months ago, so the pregnancy test wasn't the result of their own Cirque de Drake, but they've gone bareback since. More frequently since then, in fact, with Stella assuring him that it's okay, she's got it taken care of, or that she's just had her period, or that she's just about to have it. He unbuckles his belt, slides it out, and coils it on the changing table, and he unbuttons his shirt slowly, pausing only to glance up at the ceiling for a security camera. Fuck it, he's a customer, he's dropped nearly seventy bucks here today, and anyway, there can't be a law against changing clothes in a public restroom, not even in Texas. There's always the possibility, of course that Stella took the test because she wanted to make sure she *wasn't* pregnant. And she wasn't, this time, anyway, which was probably just as well, because Kevin had just read of some study in the *New York Times* that said older men were more likely to father autistic children or kids with birth defects. Just like men, spermatozoa don't stay young forever—they age, they break down, they decay. He didn't actually say anything to her about the article, but he left the newspaper on the kitchen table with the article prominently displayed, and it was gone when he came home from work.

He strips off the shirt and with a twinge of midwestern guilt—what a waste, all it needs is laundering—he wads it into a ball and stuffs it in the trash. Who is he kidding? Stella's announcement in the car coming home from Gaia, her spinning of condoms across the room like little Frisbees, supposedly in the heat of the moment—there's only one thing on Stella's mind. No matter how geriatric his seed is, Stella wants a child.

He takes off his pricey shoes and puts the left one on the counter. He sniffs the right one and runs a dry paper towel through it, which comes out a little damp, smelling of his foot, but showing no blood. It's all soaked into his sticky sock, which he peels off with two fingers and flings into the trash. Then he peels off the other one and tosses it, too, and then, right there in the overlit, over-air-conditioned, Muzaked men's room, miles from home, surrounded by strangers in all directions, Kevin feels the shock of the icy tile against his bare soles like the opening of an abyss at his feet. It's like the time he was hiking the coast of Donegal—back when he was responsible for no one but himself and could do things like that—and the red-faced warden of the slovenly youth hostel told him not to go up on the cliffs, the fog had rolled in and it wasn't safe, and Kevin went anyway, figuring as long as he couldn't hear the surf booming against the rocks, he probably wasn't close to the cliff edge, and he strode happily through the mist beading on his anorak like diamonds, until a sudden shift in the wind simultaneously carried the thunder of the surf to him and blew the mist away like a veil to reveal that he was inches, *inches,* from a sheer, thousand-foot drop into roiling black water. His whole body convulsed in shock, nearly tipping him over the edge, and he saved himself only by dropping to his ass and scuttling crabwise back away from the edge.

Just as he scuttles crabwise now back away from the very thought of fatherhood, because he knows fatherhood would upend his life. For starters, it would cost him lots and lots of money—not just the prenatal care and the birth, but food, clothing, shelter, medicine, fees, tuition, toys—twenty years of it at least, without the kid contributing one thin dime. Thousands of dollars right off the bat, because Stella would want nothing but the best baby paraphernalia, wireless baby monitors and Baby Einstein DVDs and handcrafted wooden toys and some Swedish-engineered stroller with more safety features than a Volvo. Not to mention Kevin's house would have to be babyproofed top to bottom: every socket capped, every cabinet latched, every blade locked away, the chemicals under Kevin's sinks sealed up like a Superfund site. And never mind the expense—what perks of his semibachelor life would he have to give up? He has friends with kids, he knows that for *years* he'd have to forego movies, concerts, going to clubs. No more eating out. No more spur of the moment weekend trips. No more reading Martin Amis for hours in the bath. No more performances by the Royal Shakespeare Company. No more devoting an entire weekend to watching a whole season and all the extras of *Galactica* straight through on DVD. And no more HBO, if there's a chance that little Kevin or Stella Jr. could wander into the room and glimpse a bloody murder or a pole dance, and he'd have to answer the question, "What's that, Daddy?"

And, again, how old would he be when the kid's graduating from high school? Kevin would never have a real retirement, he'd be working to pay for the kid's college till he keeled over dead. He wouldn't live long enough for the kid to take care of him. And what if he gets sick or dies when the kid's still young? Could Stella raise a child on her own? High-strung, tense, impatient, capricious—not the most maternal qualities, if he does say so himself. Not to mention those scars on her arms and inside her thighs—old and pale, but unmistakable—and her nightmares and her periodic daylight sojourns in the Stella Continuum. What happens when little Kevin or Stella Jr. is sticking his or her finger into an electrical socket or choking on strained peas or squeezing through the railing of Kevin's second-story deck, and Mommy's just staring into space, gesturing and murmuring to herself? If I'm not around, the kid's dead, and if I am around, I'm the alpha parent by default, picking up the slack while Stella freaks or zones out, with me telling the screaming kid, "Mommy needs a little time out, kiddo. Mommy loves you, but Mommy needs her space."

He empties his trouser pockets onto the counter—wallet, keys, a handful of change—and panics for a moment when he can't find his Swiss Army knife, until he remembers he left it on the dresser at home, knowing he couldn't take it on the plane. He's feeling a little naked without it—and in fact, now that he's stripping off his ruined trousers and stuffing them in the trash, he *is* nearly naked in the mirror, wearing nothing but black boxer briefs that have gone saggy in the heat. The semi-erection that stirred when he was thinking about Stella in Chicago has gone saggy, too, drooping down one leg of his shorts. He sniffs his armpits and hits the faucet and pulls out another fistful of paper towels. He soaks them, squeezes them out, and runs the makeshift sponge over his bare chest and down his arms and into his armpits. The water is barely lukewarm, and the AC chills his wet skin. He arches his spine and reaches as far as he can behind his back. In the mirror he's happy to see his ribs and not to see a gut, but while he's got a flat belly—mostly—it's no Patrick Stewart six-pack, never was and never will be. And he can already see where his pecs and his upper arms are going to slacken and droop in the not-distant future, no matter how many bench presses he does. I'm not going to have another shot at a younger woman, he thinks. Stella's my last chance.

He lathers up more milky soap between his palms and rubs coconut scent across his chest and under his arms and down his back. So that's the choice, he thinks as soapy water dampens the waistband of his saggy shorts. Lose Stella and find a woman his own age who's already had her kids. Learn to love, or at least live with, wrinkles, wattles, a thickening waist, spreading hips. Or hang on to Stella and lose his life, basically. With a kid there'd be less sleep, less sex, less time to exercise. Fatherhood would mean he'd lose what muscle tone he still has. No more hour-long runs in Gallup Park, no more lifting free weights after work, no more brisk hikes around Silver Lake, because every waking moment would be devoted to, or at least planned around, the kid, the kid, the kid. What's the kid doing, where'd she get to, is she okay, is she safe? I thought *you* were watching her. Where did she *go?* Did somebody take her? Because it's not like when Kevin was a child, when he could disappear with his friends for hours—playing with matches, frying ants with a magnifying glass, setting off firecrackers—or take off on his own—wandering up alleys, breaking bottles in vacant lots, gliding on his Stingray through traffic—no, these days you can't leave them alone for an instant, every moment has to be accounted for, every contingency foreseen, which is why they carry cell phones like tracking devices, why they have to be fingerprinted and microchipped like cats, why they have to be padded and helmeted like middle linebackers just to ride a bicycle. Because the world's full of crazed, childless women who will murder you and steal your kid for their own; pedophiles lurking on the Internet pretending to be twelve-year-olds; angry working-class white guys taking whole schoolrooms of little girls hostage. And that's not even taking into account the kid's *peers:* the distracted teenaged girl behind the wheel of daddy's SUV with a learner's permit and a cell phone and your daughter in the passenger seat, not buckled in; the hulking guy dropping Rohypnol in her punch at a party; the sullen little Columbine wannabe striding up a school hallway with a Mac-10 under his long black overcoat like Keanu Reeves in *The Matrix*. And terrorists—oh my God, they watch cable news, they're not stupid, they know an opportunity when they see it. Forget Al Qaeda, there's no central planning anymore, it's all eager beaver freelancers now, or so Kevin understands from *Frontline*. It's only a matter of time before some nasty, self-pitying little fuck takes a whole school hostage, decapitating children one by one, live on CNN. It could happen; it's already happened elsewhere in the world. There was that massacre not so long ago in Russia, a whole cell of terrorists storming a school and killing kids; he's forgotten the name but he remembers the video: desperate parents running under fire with limp, bloodied children in their arms. The guys who did that were Muslims, weren't they? He's not actually sure, but what does Kevin's instinctive racial profiling mean anymore when some round-faced white guy like the Other Kevin could memorize a few verses of the Koran and carry out his own jerry-rigged jihad under the streets of Glasgow? It's the worst of both worlds, adolescent rage meets religious fanaticism, Dylan Klebold meets Mohammed Atta. That's what fatherhood gets you—your kid's either a monster or a victim. A father is either guilty or grieving.

He rinses with another damp handful of towels, then wipes himself with some dry ones, chafing his skin. The trash bin is filling up with wadded paper; he can't even see his discarded clothes anymore. He props his bare right foot on the rounded edge of the counter and scrubs the sticky blood away with soap and water. Coconut between his toes, behind his ears, in his armpits—he's going to smell like a Piña Colada. With his knee bent and the stained bandage pulled tight, he feels the ache of his scrape, and he yanks the bandage painfully off and tosses it. Pinpricks of fresh blood ooze through the orange stain on his patella, so he puts his foot down on the cool floor, steps into the handicapped stall—only now does it occur to him that maybe he shouldn't be walking around barefoot in a public restroom—and fishes the clean bandage out of his jacket pocket. He peels off the backing, props his foot back up on the counter, and pastes the new bandage against the scrape, smoothing down the edges.

Then Kevin tugs his new trousers out from under the shirt and socks on the changing table, tearing off the tag and picking out the threads with his teeth and fingernails, missing his Swiss Army knife again. He balances for a moment like a stork on one bare foot, the other foot poised over the empty waist of his new trousers, and surveys one more time his own pale, slackening, coconut-scented flesh. He hasn't washed and changed his clothes in public since he used to go swimming at Silver Lake, and he hasn't done that in years. Kevin doesn't even like to take his shirt off in public anymore. He thinks of the Other Kevin, ritually bathing himself in the dank bathroom of some gloomy Glaswegian tower block, just before he strapped on his suicide vest and blew himself and a lot of other people to smithereens, and Kevin thinks, maybe if the Other Kevin'd had a girl, maybe if he'd gotten laid once in a while, he wouldn't have felt that loathing for his own flesh, wouldn't have felt the need to express his rage through plastic explosives.

Wobbling, Kevin thrusts one leg and then the other into the pants and zips them up. A little snug, but not too bad. He's aware that he's squaring his shoulders and sticking his chest out, even though he's alone in the restroom with the Muzak. He's been tuning it out until now, perhaps because it's been playing songs he doesn't know. But now it's a song he recognizes, "Tempted" by Squeeze, more boomer comfort food, and now Kevin just feels tired. He doesn't want to think about fatherhood anymore. He wishes the interview were over with, he wishes he were on his way to the airport, he wishes he were already on the plane. No, it's more than that: he wishes he'd never come to Austin in the first place, wishes he'd never applied for the job, wishes he were back at his desk in Willoughby Hall, editing some deadly dull manuscript, reading his e-mail, mollifying some paranoid junior academic on the phone. He wishes he were on his deck drinking a Molson's, waiting for Stella to come home from Chicago.

I said to my reflection, let's get out of this play-ee-ace, goes the song, and he manages to unpin the new shirt without sticking himself and discovers that it's short-sleeved, which ticks him off—at himself, mainly, for not checking in the first place—but he puts it on anyway, because if he wants to return it, he'd have to dig his old, soiled shirt out of the trash or go back into the store bare-chested. At least the new shirt buttons all the way to the top without choking him, so he just tucks it in and snakes his belt through the loops of his new trousers. He tugs on the new socks, hopping one-footed on the cold floor. Drops his shoes *smack* on the tile, steps into them, props each on the counter to tie the laces. Then he retrieves his jacket from the stall and watches himself in the mirror as he shrugs it on, shooting the cuffs. Did some bored security guard watch Kevin's entire striptease on CCTV? Is he even now calling the Austin police, to report some pasty, Celtic suicide bomber in the men's room, ritually preparing himself for an atrocity? Kevin wonders if he'll be arrested before he even leaves the store.

"Relax," Kevin says out loud, smiling insincerely at himself in the mirror. "I'm harmless." He replaces his wallet and keys in the pockets of his new trousers, scoops the change off the damp counter into his palm. He steps to the urinal and empties his bladder of all the iced tea he's been drinking, his stream spattering the little plastic filter that says JUST SAY NO TO DRUGS. Then he returns to the sinks and washes his hands, turning his newly scrubbed face this way and that in the mirror. He stands, squares his shoulders, plucks the tie out of his pocket, and ties it quickly in the mirror, cinching it until he's happy, then loosening it a bit and undoing his top shirt button for the trip back downtown. He flips the changing table up against the wall—for the last time or the first?—and hits the door just as the singer gives a final, soulful grunt—*Unhhh, tempted by the fruit of another, tempted but the truth is discovered...*

...what's been going on, thinks Kevin. At last there's someone

behind the Customer Service counter, a short, buxom, black-haired young woman in a fitted shirt, also flipping through a ring binder, and Kevin, cooled and cleaned and smelling of coconut and new clothes, steps up with a smile and puts both hands on the counter.

"Excuse me," he says. "I'm afraid I've left my cell phone at home. Could you call me a cab?"

Feeling refreshed and dapper, Kevin waits in the vestibule between the two banks of doors at the front of store. Gazing out the tinted doors at a yellow minivan coasting toward him through the dusty glare of the nearly empty parking lot, he's thinking he should just tell the cabbie to take him straight to the airport, adding like some wiseguy in a snap-brim fedora, "And make it snappy, chief." Might as well just go home, he thinks. He still can't make up his mind about Stella, but what he'll probably do is let things drift until she presents him with a positive pregnancy test, and by then it'll be too late to abandon her. He will back into fatherhood the way he's backed into everything else in his life. He's already certain that he's not going to take the job here, whatever it is, even if they offer it to him. Move to Texas? What the hell was he thinking?

The cab stops at the curb, and the cabbie's silhouette peers toward the store. Kevin puts on his sunglasses and pushes out the door into the midday sun. Through the viscous air he hears the grumble of the cab's engine and the waterfall rush of the nearby freeway. Only mad dogs and Englishmen, thinks Kevin, gripping the hot door handle and sliding open the minivan's rear door. He climbs up onto the stiff seat, then heaves the door shut with a satisfying chunk. Enfolded in the cab's pine-scented AC, he hauls the seat belt across and clicks it. The cabbie, a skeletally lean young black man, tilts his close-cropped head slightly, so that Kevin can only see his sharp, ebony cheekbone.

"Downtown," Kevin says, tugging his jacket straight, shooting his cuffs like some high roller. Without a word, the cabbie puts the minivan in gear. Wohl's glides backwards in Kevin's window.

Well, why not? He's spent all this money to come all this way, he might as well go through with the interview, even if he doesn't really want the job. Five hundred for the plane ticket—though they're going to reimburse him—another forty bucks on two cab rides, wait, make that sixty for three cab rides, because it'll cost him another twenty to get back to the airport from downtown. Not to mention seventy bucks on new clothes. Cruising down the parking lot, the cabbie taps on the brake for an attractive thirtysomething in khaki shorts and a tight sleeveless blouse who is carrying a bag from Neiman Marcus. The cab passes behind her as she approaches a parked SUV, and Kevin turns to watch her open the hatchback, her heels lifted from her flip-flops, her calves taut, her firm arm extended, her blouse lifting to bare the small of her back. No tattoo like Kelly had, alas, but an admirably round ass, and dirty blond hair brushing her freckled shoulders. Kevin faces front again, simultaneously reminded of Stella's toned upper arms and of the freckled shoulders of long-lost Lynda, and he smiles to realize that *that's* why he just dropped seventy dollars on new clothes—the money isn't an index of his professional ambition, it's the price of his foolish middle-aged longing, his geriatric priapism. If he'd kept his mind on the interview to begin with, he'd still be downtown in Starbucks. It wasn't ambition, but lust and nostalgia that wilted his shirt and tore his trousers and bloodied his socks, and it wasn't even really lust for Kelly, fine as she was, it was lust for a woman he hasn't even seen in twenty-five years. Lynda would be forty-five now, at least. Probably thicker around the middle, broader in the hips, her slinky walk buried under the sediment of middle age, her sleekness blunted, her pale skin a little less springy than it was. And what happens to freckled girls as they age? What do freckles look like on a forty-five-year-old? Do they fade away or do they become age spots? Do women at midlife pay cosmetic surgeons to save their freckles or erase them? Is it cruel to think this way? Having lived in Ann Arbor for thirty years, he regularly runs into old lovers or college classmates — the way he ran into Beth at Gaia Market — but he's watched them age in small increments. What takes him by surprise is running into some old high school crush when he's visiting his mom in Royal Oak, someone he hasn't seen since the seventies. Usually she recognizes him before he recognizes her, and he has to fake it for a moment, pretending at first that he knows who she is, and then pretending he isn't taken aback at how she's changed since her days of hip-hugging bell bottoms and halter tops and ironed hair. He doesn't always succeed, and no matter how enthusiastically he says, "You look great!" or "Of course I knew it was you!" he can see her gauge his response. It's the same when he's channel-surfing and he comes across some formerly dewy sitcom actress he fantasized about in his teens and twenties, and the sight of her playing a gruff lesbian mom on Lifetime or a gorgon of a defense attorney on *Law and Order* depresses him like nothing else. But Lynda, Lynda, whatever happened to Lynda? From that steamy summer until now, as often as he's retrospectively fantasized about that one night on the porch, it has rarely occurred to him to wonder where she is now. Would he even recognize her if he passed her on the street?

The cab negotiates the maze of hedges, and the little bushes with purple flowers bristle at Kevin from beyond his window. Without his intending it to happen, the faces of the women he's known are stuttering now before him like a mis-sprocketed film. Beth, Stella, the Philosopher's Daughter, Lynda—there are others, but those are the four who are popping up most often in his sexual highlight reel. The minivan rocks over a speed bump, and Kevin feels a tingling in his balls. He and Beth sometimes made love as if they were struggling for mastery, grappling like a pair of sweaty high school wrestlers, each trying for a more lethal grip, muscles taut as guy lines as they grunted and strained against each other, racing to see who could make the other finish first. In this battle of wills, making the other climax wasn't tenderness but one-upmanship: it was getting the other to cry uncle, it was earning a victory by which the other was stripped bare. He grinned fiercely in her face as he pinned her by the wrists and pounded her, grunting, "Give it up, give it up." And sometimes she'd pinned him, straddling him like a playground bully and grinding against him, pressing him down by the wrists and baring her teeth and laughing like a frat-boy date rapist: "You know you want it." In these ruthless contests, if he came first he sobbed aloud as if he were ashamed and turned his face away. And if she came first, she groaned as if in pain and then fended him off with a forearm and rolled out from under him, curled on the edge of the bed with her chest heaving as if she'd just pulled herself out of dark, cold water. It wasn't like this all the time or even most of the time—they had sentimental sex and sleepy sex and conversational sex and make-up sex like any other long-term couple—but what he remembers now are those desperate grapplings.

There's passion for you, Kevin thinks, his cock semihard in his boxer briefs. He wonders if he could adjust himself without the cabbie noticing, but just as he glances at the glossy back of the cabbie's head—trapezius muscles like a weightlifter's, a shiny scalp under stubbled hair—the driver looks right as he changes lanes. The radio is muttering now, the cabbie's turned it up. More talk radio; Kevin can hear the shrillness of the announcer, though he can't make out what he's saying. Don't the cabbies here ever listen to music? Isn't Austin supposed to be the live music capital of the world? Kevin grips his knees and shifts his legs, which relieves the pressure on his hard-on. He's surprised to see that they've left the shopping center and are already cruising north up Lamar, back the way he came with Claudia Barrientos, the street wide and flat and laced over with wires, under a whitish sky. Kevin sees things he hadn't noticed coming the other way: a Wendy's in a grove of gnarled trees; a scruffy used-car lot flying both American and Mexican flags; a low, ancient, ramshackle wooden dance hall with an unlit neon sign reading THE BROKEN SPOKE. Another place I'll never go, thinks Kevin, coasting downhill back toward downtown, then back to the airport, back to Ann Arbor, back to Stella.

Whom he doesn't love, or so he keeps telling himself. Yet their lovemaking can be surprisingly tender. Part of that's the difference in their ages: no matter how many bench presses he does or how far he runs, he's still fifty, so no more three vigorous copulations a night — it's two if he's lucky, once or twice a week, and the second time is an uphill climb. Like a general fighting the previous war, a couple of times early on he tried to grapple with Stella the way he'd grappled with Beth, pinning her wrists to the sheets, but she stiffened as if in pain and gasped, "Please don't."

"I'm sorry," he'd said, instantly releasing her. "Sorry, sorry, sorry." Stella may like her faux-leather handcuffs from time to time, but that's about performance and make-believe and a kind of adolescent role-playing that Kevin has learned to go along with and even enjoy. Instead, what he can offer Stella in bed is midlife courtliness. What he feels toward her, in fact, is a kind of protectiveness, and on those rare occasions when he tries to plumb the mystery of Stella — who made the scars on her inner thighs and why, who she's talking to in the Stella Continuum and what they're talking about, why she wakes up sweating and shuddering in the middle of the night, what she's looking at when she doesn't seem to be looking at anything—he wonders what could have happened to her before he met her that makes her respond so gratefully to simple kindness. Mutual gratitude may even be the foundation of their relationship, because he knows that at his age he's lucky to be having any sex at all with a fit and energetic younger woman.

"...in St. Paul, Minnesota," says the minivan's radio, suddenly even louder. "Reports are still sketchy at this time..."

Kevin watches the cabbie's long arm, all muscle and bone, withdrawing from the radio dial. Their gazes meet in the rearview. The cabbie has wide, deep-set, mournful eyes, and the instant he sees Kevin looking back, he reaches for the radio again and turns down the volume.

"We goin' where downtown, exactly?" the cabbie says to Kevin in the mirror. He has a musical accent, which Kevin guesses is African.

Up ahead, framed by telephone poles and power lines, broad Lamar descends into a gentle curve lined with trees and billboards and low buildings. Against the bleached sky rises a new condo tower like something made of Legos, and the narrow dome of the Texas capitol. Kevin can't see the pronged tower, and he still can't remember its name, nearly calling it Barad-dûr out loud.

"Sixth and Congress," he says, shifting in his seat, picturing the view from Starbucks: the homeless guy in the lamé dress and Laura Petrie wig; the flat-bellied, sweat-free guys in khakis; the swaying, bare-midriffed nymphets; Kelly, with her duffel over her shoulder, swinging her hips like a sailor on shore leave. Kelly, who led him astray and wilted his suit and tore his trousers and lacerated his knee, who lured him off the map to his fall. Only it wasn't really Kelly who's to blame, it was Lynda, and it wasn't even really Lynda, but his nostalgia for the only truly uncomplicated and regret-free fucking he's ever done in his life. Not even in retrospect does he feel any tenderness for Lynda, which is probably why he hardly ever wonders what happened to her. Even when they were lovers, she provoked no other emotion in him but desire, and for that reason, probably, twenty-five years later she looms larger in his fantasy life than all the other women he's known put together. Even more than the Philosopher's Daughter—about whom, it sometimes amazes him to realize, he has never fantasized sexually.

Whoa, thinks Kevin, nearly saying it out loud. Riding semi-aroused in an air-conditioned minivan in sweltering Austin, the glare outside cut by the window tint and his own amber sunglasses, Kevin is breathless suddenly, his heart racing. The tapestry of trees and bungalows on either side scrolls past the windows, while up ahead the sun-hazed backdrop of the capitol dome and condo towers and skeletal construction cranes slides from side to side with each curve of Lamar. At last Barad-dûr is visible, and it seems to glide back and forth like it's being trundled about by unseen stagehands. Not once over the years has he ever daydreamed about the Philosopher's Daughter, who at the time he thought he would love until he died, and yet his three month's worth of couplings with Lynda, whose last name he doesn't even remember, are his go-to memories—*à la plage,* on the dance floor, on the railing—whenever he needs to arouse himself. She is his default fantasy, his shortcut to a quick ecstasy.

And now, in a little bubble of freezing air drifting down a wide commercial street in Austin, Texas, he realizes once again that the primacy of Lynda in his imagination is *because* of the Philosopher's Daughter. He's not proud of it, and it's not something that he likes to contemplate, but it's true. The reason he has never sullied his memory of the Philosopher's Daughter with self-abuse is because of that night at her parent's house, the night of one of her impromptu parties, when their mutual friend Wayne carted his whole stereo out to the house because her parents' ancient hi-fi wasn't up to the job. Wayne set up the system in her parents' living room and blasted his painstakingly composed party tapes into the warm summer night while everyone danced on the creaking floorboards of the Philosopher's farmhouse. Kevin had been out dancing with Lynda already on a number of occasions — he loved to watch her wave her arms in the air, like Anna's arms on the roof of Taco Rapido, raised to the sky (as Kevin now passes) in invocation of . . . what? Perhaps she overheard Kevin's story on the packed dirt patio below and like some local, tutelary deity, the Tex-Mex goddess of desire, she has lifted her hands to bless his nostalgic erection, or at least to bless his memory of that one particular night, because that's the night he best remembers Lynda on the dance floor, with the Philosopher's surprisingly shabby Persian rug rolled up and the sofa pushed back, the coffee table jammed against the wall and littered with flakes of weed and grains of cocaine. On the sofa sprawled Wayne, a plump Asian guy, smoking cigarette after cigarette and nodding behind the screen of his long black hair to the music, watching the dancers and only occasionally dancing himself. The Philosopher's Daughter herself danced to every song, often bolting from the dance floor midsong, laughing, to abandon one partner and pull another onto the floor, working her way with a teasing evenhandedness through her entire roster of suitors. But this wasn't like the TV party, when she had been a queen bee surrounded only by wistful wannabees — no, tonight there were actually other girls at this party, lots of them. This was only a month or two after the Philosopher's Daughter had rejected him, and Kevin made a point of introducing Lynda to the Daughter during the ringing silence between dance tapes, while Wayne squatted at the tape deck picking the next one with exquisite judgment and the sweaty dancers wandered out to the back porch for beer and a breeze.

"This is Lynda," Kevin had said, his arm curled around her narrow waist, his hand cupped over her hip. The room was lit only by a couple of red bulbs plugged into a floor lamp in the corner. The sash windows were open to the whirring crickets outside, but even so the room was fifteen degrees hotter than the summer night, humid with sweat and spilled beer and the sweet reek of reefer. Even in the resinous gloom, Kevin could see that the Philosopher's Daughter was flushed and excited, her hair pasted with sweat to her forehead.

"Oh, hi!" she shouted, rocking back on her heels and laughing, piercing Kevin's heart even as he stood with his arm around another warm girl. "Hi!" she chirped again, as high-pitched as a chipmunk, but Lynda gave her just a slow, sleepy smile, stroking Kevin's back as she let her heavy-lidded gaze stray around the room. The Daughter, her pupils dilated, just blinked at Kevin and laughed again, and Kevin, to fill the silence, was about to say "Great party" when the music erupted once more and Wayne jumped up and started one of his infrequent boogies, throwing his bulk around and flinging his black hair about like a go-go dancer's. Without a word Lynda tugged Kevin away by the hand as the Philosopher's Daughter blinked dopily after them in the dim cathouse light. He turned away from her and instead watched Lynda kick her flip-flops to the wall, then start snapping her fingers over her head, slouching and swaying and closing her eyes behind the screen of her disheveled hair.

Kevin's dimly aware of the metallic insinuation of the radio—"Early indications," in the measured tones of an NPR announcer, "significant casualties"—and above the trees along a stretch of Lamar Kevin doesn't remember, all he sees is the faded bedsheet of Texas sky. His hand on the radio, the cabbie is watching Kevin in the rearview, but Kevin's trying to remember that first song he danced to at the party with Lynda, and he can't. Despite his record store job, he was just enough older than the other dancers that the music wasn't instantly familiar to him, a throbbing, quasidisco beat he identified as something from Manchester, England, though he couldn't name the band. In fact, he remembers only the one song from that night, but he still remembers the way Lynda danced mostly on her toes in that steamy living room, pivoting and twirling so that her hair lashed across her face, the old farmhouse floor bouncing under their feet. At first Kevin simply chugged in place, closing his eyes as if he were really caught up in the music, which he wasn't, not to begin with, still experiencing the thunderous, pounding bass as an assault, still self-consciously sober among all these swaying, drunken dancers, hoping the Philosopher's Daughter was watching him, hoping she was wondering who this new girl was. But he kept his eyes on Lynda, who danced with her eyes closed, swaying her hips and her long, freckled arms in a complex, sinuous, but precise relationship to the beat. She wore a loose sundress that swung with every movement of her hips and flared to reveal her calves. The dress had no back to speak of, so that when she spun Kevin saw, under her flying hair, a single, smooth curve of skin, stained red by the lamplight. As the cab glides down the long slope of Lamar toward the river, the busy skyline out of sight behind the heatstruck trees, Kevin remembers hoping the Philosopher's Daughter was noticing what a good dancer Lynda was, how effortless and sensual and unself-conscious, with not a hint of the Daughter's spastic Molly Ringwaldisms. In the breaks between tapes he and Lynda visited the keg out back, and soon he was drunk enough so that it wasn't even an effort not to glance around the dance floor, soon he was drunk enough to dance like Lynda, swaying his own hips and snapping his fingers over his head.

During another break he stood breathless to one side as Lynda did a line off the coffee table, lifting her hair back with one hand, baring her slender neck, and he felt an electric surge from his medulla down his spine to the tip of his cock as if he'd done the line himself. He feels it now, in fact.

"Somethin' bad happen," says the cabbie. He's fiddling with the radio, which hisses and spits from station to station.

"I'm sorry?" Kevin shifts on the backseat. A moment after she did the line, he and Lynda were dancing again, and now she was watching him with half-lidded eyes through her wild screen of hair, now she spun closer and ran the tips of her fingers down his arms. He grinned stupidly back at her, woozy and aroused, almost touching her but not quite, close enough to feel the lash of her hair across his cheek, close enough to smell her sweat.

"On the radio," says the cabbie, searching the dial without pausing. "Somethin' bad in Minnesota."

The cab is already crawling across the Lamar Avenue Bridge, though Kevin can't remember descending that last mile, curve after curve, to the river. He's disoriented by the view out his window, where he sees a line of boxcars crawling across the rust-red trestle, the inverted reflections of the railcars crawling through the glassy green water of the river below. On the pedestrian bridge where he fell an hour or two ago, sweaty joggers trudge past a cluster of busy young men in polo shirts and khakis, some sort of film crew, it seems, working within a rough rampart of metal boxes, setting up a couple of tripods and aiming them at Austin's dynamic skyline. Kevin feels as if his own film is being rewound, as if his lust has reeled him out to the end of the line, and is now reeling him back in, all the way down Lamar back to the center of town where he started. His disarticulation and reconstruction as a Texan as he traveled south down Lamar has been reversed, and now he's being returned to his former state, the original Kevin, Michigan Kev.

The cabbie's watching him in the rearview, his gaze more mournful than before, but Kevin can't remember what the guy just said. He cranes around the headrest in front of him and sees traffic kinking and unkinking up the hill toward Gaia Market. Perhaps there's been another accident; it can't be the same one. Kevin, restless and rattled, notes the glowing red numbers of the fare; this is going to be another expensive cab ride.

"I got a brother up there." The cabbie has given up on the radio; he's feeling for something on the front seat. "He drive a cab, too, in the Twin Cities. I gettin' worried."

"I'm sorry," Kevin says. "I didn't hear what you said."

The cabbie's cradling a glossy red cell phone in his broad palm and thumbing the tiny keypad, shifting his gaze back and forth between the traffic ahead and the cell's display as the cab glides and stops, glides and stops.

"What's this about Minnesota?" Kevin leans forward against his seat belt, but the cabbie raises his finger for silence as he cups the tiny phone to his ear. The man's other hand grips the wheel tightly, even though they're crawling at only fifteen miles per hour off the end of the bridge and under the railway underpass.

"Fine," mutters Kevin, settling back against the seat. Over the rush of the AC vents Kevin hears the tiny ring of the cabbie's phone and then the ringing silence on the dance floor when the tape cuts off in midsong and everybody sags in place and groans in the heat and humidity. "Waaayyyne!" sings out the Philosopher's Daughter, laughing, mocking. Wayne vaults from the couch, the old floor shuddering under his weight, and pushes his way through the breathless dancers to the stereo. Kevin and Lynda sink back on their heels, and Lynda pushes her hair away from her face with both hands and fixes Kevin with her cocaine eyes. All around them people are shouting over the music that isn't playing, and Wayne and the Philosopher's

Daughter are loudly haggling over which tape to play next. Lynda sways against Kevin and catches his T-shirt with one hand and tugs him toward the door. They pinball off other dancers who don't seem to notice and stumble out onto the empty farmhouse porch, the screen door slapping shut behind them. The red light within tints the windows but casts no glow on the porch, and Kevin isn't sure if the shrilling all around him is the absence of amplified music ringing in his ears or the crickets under the shadowy trees on the farmhouse lawn. Lynda backs up to a porch upright and pulls Kevin up against her, and she drapes her arms over his shoulder and kisses him. She tastes salty from sweat. Kevin slips his hands inside the loose arm-holes of her dress and slides his palms up her warm, slippery rib cage, stiffens her nipples under his thumbs, feels her blood pulsing through the tips of his fingers. She kisses him deeper in the ringing, buzzing silence, her fingers through the sweaty hair at the back of his head. Kevin's cock was already stirring on the dance floor, and now he's hard. He frees a hand and slides it up under her skirt. "That's the one!" he hears their hostess cry over the chatter inside the house, and now he's aware of the Philosopher's Daughter somewhere behind him like a source of heat, and he sends a thought in her direction, *watch this,* his thumb sliding up the inside of Lynda's slick thigh, *I'll show you passion.* Lynda flinches, catching her breath.

(The cabbie is speaking rapid-fire into his phone in a foreign language. He's repeating the same word—a name?—over and over again. Nobody seems to be answering him.)

Then the stereo erupts again to shouts and cheers, a ragged electric guitar in a sharp, insinuating figure that Kevin recognizes instantly. In the clinch, Kevin and Lynda gaze through the dark at each other as the drums kick in, Charlie Watts playing a slow, sensual, urgent beat. On the sloping old porch they can feel the trembling of the farmhouse floor under the dancer's feet, and Kevin starts to laugh.

"What's so funny?" murmurs Lynda.

"Nothing," he breathes as the bass comes in, Bill Wyman playing a balling rhythm. He kisses Lynda and slides his sweaty palm farther up under her skirt, and she grips his wrist and holds him back. They part slightly, their mutual humidity rising between them, and he tries to catch her gaze, *why not?* But she's looking past him, blinking through her scrim of hair as if listening carefully for something. Then Jagger starts singing, *Yeah, you got . . . satin shoes,* and she eases from under him and sways her hips to Watts and Wyman down the porch, away from the windows. She doesn't look back, but he follows her past one dim red window and then the other, brushing the porch swing and making it twist slowly, end by end. Dim red figures bob and sway in the farmhouse windows, and Kevin can't make out anyone in particular, but he knows the Philosopher's Daughter is there, he can feel her radiating through the wall of the house.

(Cupping the cell, the cabbie makes the turn by Gaia Market one-handed, accelerating east down Fifth into the canyon of construction sites. He presses Dial again and lifts the phone to his ear.)

At the end of the porch Lynda lifts her chin and pushes her hair back again with both hands, saying nothing. Jagger growls through the window screens, *Y'all got . . . cocaine eyes,* and she grips Kevin by the forearms and wheels him around and settles him on the wooden railing, never taking her half-lidded eyes off his. His feet flat on the floorboards, the bass pounds through the soles of his sneakers. Lynda glances back at the windows, tosses her hair, then squats barefoot before him, pushing Kevin's knees apart. "Oh," he breathes, so quietly that no one could possibly hear him over the music, not even himself. In the windows crimsoned bodies churn while at his feet Lynda tugs the zipper of his jeans and pries his cock free with the tips of her fingers. He lays his trembling hand on the crown of her head as she takes the tip of it in her mouth and strokes him three times, up and down, like she's nodding at something he said. One long-fingered hand rests on his thigh, the other curled under her skirt, between her legs. His cock aches it's so hard, but Lynda lifts her mouth away and pushes herself to her feet with her hands on his knees. Even in the humid summer air her saliva chills his hard-on. "Don't stop," he says, still not loud enough to be heard over the music, but Lynda lifts her skirt to thumb her panties down into a knot on the porch. Her face is in shadow, her eyes hooded. She slips the straps of her dress off her shoulders, baring her breasts, and leans into him and kisses him, her hair falling across their faces. He slides his hands up under her dress and digs his fingers into her slippery ass. She pushes down on his shoulders, he lifts, and somehow she's straddling his lap with her knees on the railing, her thighs taut, her moist cunt sliding exquisitely onto his cock.

(The cab dashes from light to light toward Austin's downtown as the cabbie mutters into the phone, then presses Quit and tosses it in frustration on the seat beside him.)

The porch railing creaks under their weight, and even drunk and excited Kevin wonders about the farmhouse's craftsmanship and hopes the Philosopher's Daughter's father is as good a handyman as he is a philosopher. He worries about toppling backward into the bushes, he worries about splinters, but the beer and the anxiety are making him last longer, otherwise he might have come the instant he was inside her. Then Lynda murmurs "Wait" right in his ear, and as he clutches her waist under her dress she unbends first one leg and then the other over the railing, settling tightly against him, taking him in even deeper. She tightens her calves against the railing and squeezes with her thighs, and he groans, because he's deeper inside this girl than he's ever been inside any girl before, and he presses his open mouth against the long, salty curve of her neck. He's inhaling her humidity, she's panting like an animal just above the top of his head. They can't move much—if she thrusts too hard against him she'll topple them into the bushes—but the song has finished with words and now it's just a driving sax, and they rock together to the beat, her sweat dripping into the dress bunched at her waist, her hands kneading his back, his face pressed between her salty breasts, her heart thumping against his lips. He can't move much, he can hardly breathe, but he can't stop now, and he hooks his chin over her shoulder, her hair scratching his nose and filling his mouth, and through it he can see the red window where the music's pouring out, he can see pumping limbs and torsos in the red light, hair swinging, heads shaking. There's someone in the window, he can't make out who in the darkness, just a silhouette against the red glow, catching a breeze through the screen, breathing in something other than sweat and beer and marijuana. Kevin wants it to be her, and he thinks, *look at me,* but he can't be sure, it's just a shape in the window, it might not be her, it might be someone else. Now the music is circling and building, just the rhythm section and an insinuating solo guitar, and as Lynda rocks against him, he surges with each bar of the solo, almost cresting but not quite, and he thinks, *I want you to see me.* He hopes this lasts forever, he hopes that it doesn't and that he comes like a waterfall, but either way he wants her to know, he wants her to see him. His heart hammers, his breath rasps through Lynda's hair. *Turn around,* he wills the silhouette in the window, *this could have been us.*

(The cab idles impatiently at the corner of Fifth and Congress. The cabbie breathes heavily through his nose; he has the phone in hand again, and he's staring at the little screen, as if willing it to ring.)

Now the guitar and the saxophone are trading off, leading each other on, and Lynda starts thrusting harder against him, faster than the beat, gasping like a runner. Kevin tries to grip her tighter, but she's so slippery under her dress and she's moving so urgently it's all he can do to keep them both on the railing. His thighs ache and his back hurts, and under his hands he can feel every muscle in her body pulling tighter. All he can do is hold on tight and flex his buttocks. Now her gasps are high-pitched and squeaky and he hopes they finish before the song does because he doesn't want her to come out loud in the gap between the songs when everybody could hear them. *Only her,* he thinks, hanging on to Lynda for dear life, *I only want her to know.* Lynda digs her nails into the back of his neck, and he sinks his teeth into the taut curve of her throat to keep from groaning aloud. Her sweat pours over his fingers, and now she's whimpering rhythmically, chirping like a bird, and through the window the guitar and the saxophone are winding tightly round and round each other, and Kevin thinks, *Turn around,* just about to come himself, *look this way.*

(As the cab turns onto Congress, the cell phone sings, and the cabbie exclaims aloud, inclining his head toward the red phone like a tiny heart in his palm. There's a torrent of speech, both ends of the conversation talking excitedly over each other. The cabbie sounds like he's about to cry.)

Lynda sucks in her breath and her cunt seizes tightly around Kevin's cock and Kevin feels it all the way up his spine and down to his toes, blood pounding in his temples, his heart squeezing tighter than a fist, as if it will never relax again. He clenches his arms around her back, digging his fingers into her; he groans wordlessly into the salty flesh of her shoulder. He can feel his balls pumping into her. Then Lynda goes slack, her head drooping over his shoulder, her ass sagging back against his knees. His own limbs turn rubbery and he can barely hold her up, her sweat pooling under his palms. Through her tangled hair he sees bodies thumping in the living room, limned in red light. Nobody's in the window anymore. It's another song now, they fucked right past the end of the last one. Lynda's pulse is still pounding, she's panting against his cheek. His own heart is beating again, slow and hard, and he feels postcoital lassitude spreading through him like a barbiturate. Lynda sighs and rocks back, counting on him to keep her from sliding off his lap to the porch. Her breasts gleam in dark, and she lifts her elbows one more time and brushes back her sweat-stringy strands of hair and gives him the slowest, dirtiest smile he's ever seen, before or since, the same smile she'll give him a month or so later, when he finds her in bed with another guy.

"Hey, mister." The cabbie is looking right at Kevin through the gap between the minivan's bucket seats.

So what if I didn't love her—she didn't love me, no big deal. That night on the porch wasn't even the best sex he ever had, but it's the moment he always comes back to, and after fingering this memory threadbare for all these years, he knows it's only because of where it happened and who might have been watching. Did he really love the Philosopher's Daughter? Has he ever really loved any of the women he's known? Has any of them ever really loved him? He's pretty sure he loved Beth, but they fought all the time. The worst he can say about Stella is that she irritates him, frustrates him, bores him, but Beth, holy shit, Beth used to send him into a rage. There were shouting matches and tears and slammed doors and a couple of times the flinging of substantial objects, capable of inflicting injury. She threw a plate at him once, and he just laughed and said, "A *plate?* Really? You couldn't find the rolling pin?" and then she threw another one at him. And once he threw a book at her, a hardcover copy of *Rabbit Is Rich,* which is a pretty big book, bruising her backside and making him feel guilty for weeks afterward. But that's what proves he loved her—at least that's what he tells himself—the fact that they stayed together for so long despite driving each other crazy. It was the longest relationship he's ever had, it went on for years, but in all that time together he never shook the feeling that she was still making up her mind about him, and in the end, when she did make up her mind, she left. When Beth decided at long last to have a child, she found somebody else to have it with. She didn't want it to be his, not any more. Stella, on the other hand, tells him all the time she loves him, but always in passing—in the aisle at Gaia, or squeezing him from behind at the kitchen counter, or at the end of a phone call, saying "Love you" in the same singsong way she'd say "Keep in touch" or "Take care." Never face to face, never in some tender moment, never in bed. She never even meets his eye when she says it. Maybe she thinks she's wearing him down, like drops of water on a stone. But who's he to complain? He's never told her *at all* he loves her, not once, not even just to be polite, the way he has upon occasion with other women. Yet Stella, thinks Kevin, whom I don't love, and who may not really love me—maybe *she's* just being polite—Stella not only wants to have a child, she wants to have a child with *me*. She wants *us* to have a child. She wants to have *my* child.

"Mister, you're here." The cabbie's glaring at him, tears welling out of the corner of his eyes. "You gotta get out now."

"I'm sorry," Kevin says, shifting in his seat, detumescent at last. He glances out the window, where he's surprised to see the ice-blue doors of One Longhorn Place, Barad-dûr. He's even more surprised to see the cabbie sniffling in the driver's seat. "Are you okay?" Kevin says.

The cabbie shakes the cell phone like a rattle or a talisman, knuckling tears away with his other hand. "Sixth and Congress, mister, you gotta get out now. I gotta go."

"Okay, sure, yeah." Kevin fumbles for the seat belt release. "What do I owe you?" He looks at the meter and yanks out his wallet, hoping he still has enough after the last cab ride and lunch with Dr. Barrientos.

"Just go, man. No charge."

"Sorry?" Kevin freezes with his fingers in his wallet.

The cabbie's facing forward again, scraping the heel of his hand over his sharp cheekbones, wiping away tears.

"Just be gettin' out of my cab, okay?" He draws a sharp breath and lets it out. "My brother's alive and I gotta go, so it's free, okay?"

"Okay," Kevin says warily, wondering if the guy's trying to pull some sort of scam. "You're sure?"

"Man, will you *go?*" cries the cabbie, nearly sobbing, and Kevin flinches and stuffs his wallet away and fumbles for the door. "Listen, thanks," he says, untangling the seat belt, yanking on the door. "I appreciate it, I hope everything's okay with your, with your..."

The cabbie's hammering the steering wheel with his wrist, already checking his mirrors so he can pull away as soon as this stammering idiot is out of his cab. "Gonna be a bad day for everybody today." He glances back at Kevin one last time. "You need to pay attention, man."

Kevin's out in the heat again, patting his pockets, making sure he hasn't left anything behind. The cab starts to pull away before he's even shut the door, and he yells, "Wait! Lemme get the door!" But without stopping the cabbie reaches back with his long arm and hauls it shut, then guns the cab through the intersection as the light turns yellow, leaving Kevin curbside by the rush of downtown traffic, with the unforgiving sun beating straight down on the top of his head.

Kevin's a little disoriented, and he looks up and down the street to situate himself — south down the canyon of Congress toward the two squashed ziggurats by the river, then up at the capitol squatting under the steep sun of midafternoon. The sidewalk is crowded with lunchtime pedestrians, businessmen and women traveling in packs, or alone and chatting on cell phones, all of them sifting through the scruffy homeless orbiting a bus stop. The clock on the corner of Sixth and Congress tells him his interview is still forty-five minutes away, but it's time to quit screwing around, so he cuts across the stream of pedestrians to the tower, hauls at the glass door—*pongggg*—and steps into the arctic AC. Time to get this over with so he can go back to the airport, get on the plane, and go home.

As he squeaks across the lobby floor toward the elevator alcoves, he buttons the top button of his shirt and tightens the knot of his tie. He's a little queasy with adolescent test anxiety—instead of wandering and woolgathering he should have been thinking all this time about the interview, he should have brought with him the Web pages he printed off from the Hemphill Associates site and reviewed them on the plane—but he quashes the feeling, reminds himself he doesn't even want the job. He loosens the tie again. The tower's lobby reverberates with indistinct voices, like a museum. The black woman in the blazer is standing behind the rampart of the security desk, and she's been joined by another blazered colleague, a tall, rangy white guy with a bushy Josef Stalin moustache, and together they're watching the big, silent flatscreen on the lobby wall. In fact, a loose group of people has gathered under the screen just beyond the security desk, faces all tilted up at the unnaturally vivid image. Kevin notes only the aggressive red, white, and blue of Fox as he turns to the touch screen in the prow of the desk, where the Texas flag waves on its endless loop. He thumbs the cool glass, the video keyboard flickers up, and he touches *H* for Hemphill Associates.

"Can you turn it up?" says a man standing under the flatscreen.

"Ain't supposed to," says the black security guard.

"I tell you what," murmurs the white guard, in a deep, confidential drawl, "I'd like to hear it, too."

"At least put on the captions," says another one of the flatscreeners.

Kevin notes the floor of Hemphill Associates—52—and looks up at the two guards.

"Excuse me," he says, but the black woman is fussing through the clutter on her desktop. Without taking his eyes off the screen, the white guard says, "Can't you find it?"

"No." She's sliding stuff around.

"Well, how'd you turn it on this morning?" His eyes still on the cable news.

"I *didn't*," she says, peeved at him, at the missing remote, at herself. "We don't never turn it off."

"Excuse me," Kevin says again, and the white guard slowly lowers his gaze.

"Sir."

"Which elevator goes to Hemphill Associates?" Kevin jerks his thumb toward the alcoves.

The black woman looks up wide-eyed at Kevin; he's not sure if she recognizes him from a few hours before. "What floor they on?" she says.

Kevin consults the screen. "Fifty-two?" he says.

The white guard sighs and looks back at the television. The black woman widens her eyes a fraction. She points over Kevin's head. "Can you read?"

Kevin turns and sees big black numbers over the entrance to each elevator alcove, *11–26* over one, *26–52* over the other. He feels his face get hot. Suddenly the black woman stands up straight, clutching the remote. "Found it!" she cries.

"Fine." Kevin lifts both his palms; now he's peeved, too. "That's all I wanted to know." He swivels away from the desk, and his gaze glides away from the distracted guards, over the knot of people straining like sunflowers toward the television, and past the cluttered graphics of the flatscreen itself—the speeding crawl, the bright red tab reading BREAKING NEWS, the helmet-haired anchor centered against the out-of-focus newsroom. As he enters the alcove for floors 26 through 52, he performs an involuntary little stutter step—did he just see the caption ATTACK IN ST. PAUL in bold white sans serif against a livid red?—but under the momentum of his own impatience Kevin presses the elevator button. Immediately one of the elevators pings, the doors slide open, Kevin enters. As he presses the button for 52, an amplified voice swells out of the museum reverb of the lobby, saying, "We're getting reports of what seems to be *another* missile attack, in *another* American city," and Kevin involuntarily glances through the closing doors. But he can't see the TV, can't even see the security desk.

"A building appears to be burning in downtown Baltimore," says the flatscreen as the doors slide shut and the elevator accelerates at an absurd speed, nearly buckling Kevin's knees. His stomach drops, his balls tighten, and in the burnished door of the car Kevin glimpses his own blurred incredulity. Did I just hear, he wonders, what I thought I heard? It's like the time in high school when a girl a couple grades ahead of him cut school to go to the Hash Bash in Ann Arbor, and she came back with a copy of the April 1 edition of the Michigan student paper, with the giant headline NIXON DECLARES MARTIAL LAW. In the cafeteria at lunchtime she sat with the headline ostentatiously displayed, and Kevin fell for it, leaping from his seat and stalking across the dining room and yanking the paper from her hands, all the while saying loudly, over and over again, "I don't fucking believe it, I do *not* fucking believe it," until she pointed out the date on the paper. "April Fool's," she said, laughing. As the entire cafeteria rose as one to applaud Kevin's righteous if unnecessary outrage, he blushed and carefully refolded the paper and handed it back to the girl—he still remembers that she had pretty green eyes—and he said to her, "Really. I didn't believe it." Then walked the long mile back to his own table where his buddies gagged with laughter on their sloppy joes.

But this is different, because it's not April 1, because the whole world is jumpier than it was in 1974, and because he's thirty-five years older and resigned to the fact that sometimes the worst thing that you can imagine happening, actually does. Of course, arguably he understood that earlier in life than most people, with the death of his father. He sighs and tightens the knot of his tie again. He lifts his chin and runs his finger under his collar. The car wobbles ever so slightly in its breathless ascent, and the glowing red floor indicator, which has remained on 1 ever since he left the ground, suddenly starts to beep through the floors—26, 27, 28—and he realizes that, these days, hearing of simultaneous attacks in Minnesota and Maryland is not much more shocking than hearing "Your father is dead" or "Your mother drinks too much" or "Your sister's a lesbian." Or "Stella used to cut herself." Or "Stella's pregnant."

Now his heart is racing, but he's not sure why. Is it because of what he just heard on the television, or is it because Stella's trying to trap him into fatherhood, or is it because he has a sudden case of nerves over this interview for a job that he doesn't even want any longer? Or is it just the g-forces of his rapid ascent up the gullet of Barad-dûr? The red numbers are flicking as fast as his pulse—47, 48, 49—but even as the elevator slows, relieving the pressure on Kevin's knees, his heart keeps racing. Kevin leans against the back wall of the car, bracing his feet. Compared to its jackrabbit start, the car crawls the last couple of floors—fiiiiffty, fiiiiiifffty-onnnnne—and Kevin feels a pressure in his ears that he's surprised to realize is because of the altitude. He's yawning to make them pop when the elevator comes to a stop so slow, so gentle, that Kevin's surprised again when the doors slide open.

He steps tentatively into the elevator alcove of the fifty-second floor, which flows uninterrupted into a severe black and gray reception area. Beyond the glass wall of an empty conference room the chairs are all awry around the table as if everyone just left in a hurry, and beyond the table a floor-to-ceiling glass wall gives a jaw-dropping vista of Austin. Even as Kevin stops dead, he knows he looks like a rubbernecking rube, but under the bleached sky beyond the window he can see the flat green river between leafy parkland, tiny glittering cars streaming both ways over a freeway bridge in the distance, and beyond that, the rampart of hills, their dull green foliage studded with red tile roofs. He's viewing it all through the tint of two windows, which lends it the slightly dark, digitally graded grandeur of a glossy film: *Austin, Texas,* directed by Ridley Scott. The condo towers under construction look even grander somehow when seen from slightly above — heroic, even. The tall, T square crane above the nearest one rises almost as high as the floor where Kevin is standing, and he can see a little man in an orange vest and hardhat climbing slowly up a ladder up the center of the crane's framework near the top, just under the cab. Kevin nearly gasps at the idea of simultaneously being that high up and that exposed.

"May I help you?"

Kevin starts and, embarrassed, turns to a very pretty dark-haired young woman seated behind a low reception desk, an artful sweep of dark wood with a black marble top. She's lean and sharp-featured, and she wears a tight black knit top over form-fitting gray slacks; her top is sleeveless, showing off her impeccably toned arms. She sits with perfect posture in her chair, watching him with professional brightness, and maybe even a little bemusement at his reaction to the view out the window.

"Hi!" says Kevin, a little too chipper.

"Hi," she says back, squaring her office chair with both hands on the desktop below the marble counter. Her response is slightly firmer this time, as if she's bracing herself to deal with an idiot.

"Is this, uh, Hemphill Associates?" He cringes inside, realizing he ought to be projecting confidence, not asking dumb questions that he should already know the answer to.

"Yes, it is," she says, lifting her fastidiously maintained eyebrows like a kindergarten teacher with a dull student who unexpectedly gave the right answer.

God, she's pretty, Kevin's thinking, and stepping up to the counter he draws a breath and gathers his threadbare professionalism about him. The thing to do now, he's telling himself, is to empty his mind of all the sturm and drang of the last few hours—his seminostalgic, semihorndog stalking of Joy Luck; his fateful fall on the bridge; his emotionally tumultuous lunch with Dr. Barrientos; his epiphanic sponge bath in the men's room in Wohl's; his erotic reverie in the cab; his apocalyptic aural fantasy in the elevator just now—and just calm the fuck down. But as he lays his hands lightly on the frosty countertop, he finds himself wondering how this girl in her thin sleeveless blouse stays warm in the icy AC. It's all he can do not to say, "Aren't you freezing?" and offer her his jacket.

"I'm Kevin Quinn," he manages to say instead. "I'm here for an interview."

The girl's face brightens, almost as if she's genuinely happy to see him, and Kevin's heart brightens, too, even though he knows her smile is purely professional. How many more smiles like that, he wonders, smiling back, can a man my age expect to see in his lifetime? So what if it's not personal. He'll take what he can get.

"You're early!" She widens her eyes at a computer screen under the counter. Then she rises, and Kevin's even more thrilled to see that she's nearly as tall as he is. Kevin's always been an easy touch for tall women. "But I'll go let Patsy know you're here." She steps away from the desk, her perfect shoulders squared, the hollow of her back perfectly erect, and disappears up a hallway that runs parallel to the dazzling view.

Stop it! thinks Kevin, resisting the temptation to edge around the end of the reception desk to watch her walk away. Enough already! Haven't you already made enough of a fool of yourself for one day? He pinches his lips together to keep from laughing out loud. He's not normally like this, at least he doesn't think he is. Certainly he has no problem admiring a good-looking young woman, he's a standard-issue middle-aged man, but he normally doesn't walk around like a cartoon wolf, his eyes bugging out of his head, his tongue unscrolling to the floor. He doesn't usually erupt into a full-blown reverie within the first seconds of meeting someone, or at least he doesn't go from zero to ninety quite so quickly. What's going on with me today, he wonders—is it the change of scene, or the slightly exotic, subtropical women he's met here, or is it just the heat? Or, now that he's fifty-two stories up, is it the altitude? Or is it because he's actually contemplating going back to Ann Arbor as if this whole episode in Austin never happened? Is it because he's thinking he might actually go back and be a father to Stella's child? Is this the death of the old Kevin or the birth pangs of the new, and how can he tell the difference?

In spite of himself, he's stepped far enough into the lobby to peer down the hall where the receptionist went. But it's empty, a long row of glass-walled offices that he can't see into.

He walks to the wall of the empty conference room and looks through it at the view again. Over the leaden river he can see the two bridges at Lamar Avenue, the old traffic bridge and the pedestrian bridge where he fell down. Even now, in the ungodly midday heat, there are joggers crossing the pedestrian bridge, simultaneously vivid and featureless at this distance, like Sims. In fact, the whole scene below has the aspect of a fantastically detailed computer animation, from the bustling film crew of clean-cut young men with their three tripods—wow, how many cameras do they need?—down to the tiny white sliver of a rowing scull dragging a miniature V across the green surface of the river, its tiny oars dimpling the water on either side. It's Austin by Pixar Studios, with their characteristic eye for busy detail.

"Mr. Quinn?"

Kevin's startled again by the dazzling receptionist, who's giving him a spokesmodel smile from only a couple of feet away.

"Quite a view, isn't it," she says in a way that implies that Kevin's not really entitled to it. She swivels her gaze out the window and then fixes on Kevin again, lowering her voice a register. "Patsy's just finishing up a phone call, but she'll be with you in a few minutes."

Kevin gives her a halfhearted smile, but he's distracted by a bright flash from the pedestrian bridge. Wow, thinks Kevin, what's that? Even a movie light wouldn't be that bright in this sunlight, but instead of zeroing in on the bustling little group on the bridge, his gaze instinctively follows an equally dazzling streak trailing a tight spiral of smoke in a long smooth curve that stops abruptly at one of the new, finished condo towers. Kevin's gaze automatically keeps tracking beyond the tower, so that he has to correct himself and jerk his head back to see a black flower of smoke threaded with flame bursting from an upper floor.

"Sir?" The receptionist is tilting her head. "Perhaps you'd like to have a seat."

Kevin turns to the girl, but he's speechless and his mouth is suddenly dry and his pulse is racing. He hears a sharp, hollow boom, and he jerks his gaze out the window again, where he sees not one, but two dazzling streaks rising from the bridge, brightening as they come, gushing smoke as they rise in a fatal arc, straight for him. The beautiful young receptionist has flinched slightly at the sound of the boom, but instead of following his gaze out the window at the furious missiles miraculously threading the construction cranes and ziggurats and condominiums — now only an inch away, now half an inch, now a quarter-inch — she has placed one hand near Kevin's elbow without quite touching him, gesturing spokesmodelishly with her other hand to a pair of square, black leather chairs angled toward each other at the center of the severe lobby.

"Please sit down," she says.

PART THREE   Next

KEVIN IS AIRBORNE, but unlike his moment of caesura on the bridge, he's not falling, he's rising straight up into the air. The lovely receptionist is rising, too, her eyes wide, her hair flying, her mouth a startled O, her sweater rucked up to bare her firm midriff. In this alarming and vivid moment of super slo-mo, Kevin recalls a picture he saw years ago, by a famous photographer of his youth, that showed a young Richard Nixon with his jacket buttoned and his legs together, jumping straight up off the floor of some government office or hotel suite. His hands were spread beatifically and there were two or three inches of air between the pointed toes of his Oxfords and the nap of the carpet. He wore a bemused smile. Imagine that, thinks Kevin — Nixon, beatific, bemused — as the interior window of the conference room disintegrates into infinite points of light. Beyond the glittering scrim of splintering glass, the conference table hangs in the air, the chairs orbiting it six inches off the floor, their little wheels spinning. Meanwhile the outer window bursts out into the void, fifty-two stories up. Kevin's ears fill with the disintegrating hiss of glass and a cracking rumble like rocks tumbling in a drum.

Then he's bouncing painfully on the hard, cold floor of the reception area. He hasn't landed on his feet (the way Nixon did, presumably), but on his hip, bruisingly, his shoes over his head, the heel of his hand skidding across the floor. Everything around him is also bouncing—the two stylish black leather chairs, a large potted fern, the receptionist—and from behind the reception desk all sorts of things that were airborne a moment ago—pens, pencils, a legal pad, a stapler, a cell phone, a ring binder—are tumbling end over end. Marble from the desktop shatters against the floor, and atomized glass skitters like popcorn, surging across the floor like incoming surf. Kevin tumbles through all this chaos, just another bouncing thing, until he hits his shoulder blade against the floor, whacks his knee on something, and lands finally on his back with his arms curled over his head and his fists clenched. Directly above him the suspended ceiling is rippling, panels cracking, cables and wiring jigging like snakes. Grit streams toward the floor. Dust trembles in the air all around him.

Kevin is shaking all over, though whether that's just him or the floor is still moving, it's too early to tell. All around him he hears cracking and clattering and rumbling, and from a more specific direction, somewhere out of sight, the sharp, percussive spitting of something electrical. He lifts his head but he can't see sparks anywhere. He does see that he's lying with his feet splayed and the right leg of his new trousers pushed up past his knee, baring his bandage with its pink stain in the center. From his left foot he's missing his shoe, and beyond the reinforced toe of his brand-new sock he sees that the conference room has been nearly emptied out. The long table is gone and only three chairs remain, two of them lying on their sides coated in dust and glass and shredded drywall. The third chair has landed on its wheels, its seat slowly turning on its axis as if somebody has just gotten up out of it. Harsh sunlight streams through the swirling dust where the outer window used to be, and Kevin can already feel the blush on his face as the heat from outside swells into the room.

Now his trembling has become rhythmic and rapid, synchronous with the thunder of his own pulse. The air is dusty and acrid, something chemical stinging the back of his nostrils. Oh God, does he smell smoke? He can't tell, he can't place the odor, and he tells himself desperately that it's probably not smoke. His throat is dry, though, and he gags on the dust in the air and spits to the side to expel the grit from his mouth.

"What happened?" he says aloud. He loosens his tie and undoes the top button of his new shirt. The cracking and rumbling has diminished, though it hasn't entirely stopped — something, somewhere, creaks menacingly like ship timbers — and he can still hear that electrical smacking sound like someone cracking a whip. His whole body still shakes. Warm air courses all around him now, cutting the dust a little, and he lifts his head. Through the gap to the outside he sees the bleached Texas sky and the skeletal top of the nearest unfinished condo tower, the Tinkertoy crane above it still slowly turning. Whatever's happening over here, those guys over there are still working. Maybe what's happening isn't what he thinks it is. Maybe it isn't happening at all.

Above him the ceiling has stopped rippling, but from broken ceiling panels and twisted framing hang loose wires and bent pipes and an AC duct split at a seam. A crack in a concrete beam slowly drips a stream of dust, and it occurs to Kevin that maybe he should get out from under it. But he can hardly move. His entire body beats like a drum, and when he unclenches his fists his fingers tremble so alarmingly that he clenches them white again. What do you do in a situation like this? What's the first step? Should he pinch himself? Maybe this isn't real, maybe he's only nodded off in the cab listening to the radio, or maybe he's still on the plane from Michigan, maybe he's asleep high over Kansas with Joy Luck deep in her novel next to him, and he's worried himself into a nightmare. Maybe he's still in bed back in Ann Arbor, with more room to be restless than usual because Stella's away in Chicago and not pressed against him with her hair scraping his cheek and her humid breath against his chest. Wake up, Kevin tells himself. Computer, freeze program.

Then he remembers the receptionist, and he starts violently, as if he's been stung by that electric whip he keeps hearing. Oh God, where is she? He jackknifes to a sitting position without touching his hands to the floor, which is graveled with broken glass and shards of black marble. Before he can imagine the worst he sees the girl curled in a fetal ball on the floor a few feet away, just this side of a heap of crumpled wall where a corridor used to run deeper into Hemphill Associates. She's clenched like a fist, her knees drawn up, her fingers dug into her upper arms, her hair spilled over her face and jeweled with broken glass. Kevin tries to speak, but his mouth is dry and his tongue seizes up, and he hacks and clears his throat and spits again. Careful of the glass all around him, he sets his heels against the floor, one shoe and one sock, and drags himself on his backside a quarter-inch toward the girl.

"Hey," he rasps, then pauses to spit more dust. He can't tell if she's conscious, but at least her rib cage is rising and falling. She's just a couple feet beyond his stocking foot, and if he could only bring himself to unclench the muscles in his leg and extend his knee, he could nudge her with his toe. But he can still hear that nautical creaking, and he's wondering if he should move at all. What if the slightest gesture from him brings the ceiling down? What if he slides forward and the whole goddamn peak of the building comes down on top on them? He's not doing either of them any good if he does that. What if all it takes is the thunder of his pulse? Or a sharp intake of breath?

Another startling, electrical whip crack freezes him. It sounds like it's getting closer, as if the wire is snaking through the rubble, seeking him out, and he says aloud, "That's *really* getting on my nerves." At which the girl shudders all over, to Kevin's vast relief. "Hey," he rasps, "can you hear me?"

She stiffens, catches her breath, gingerly lifts her head. Fragments of glass tumble from the hair spread over her face.

"Careful." Kevin scoots another quarter-inch. "You've got glass in your hair."

Someone is shouting in his head that he should go to the young woman and brush the glass off her, but someone else is shouting equally loud, *don't you fucking move.* He's afraid of the glittering glass all around, afraid he'll embed it in his hands and his stocking foot. He's afraid the room will start lurching again, that the electrical snake will bite him finally and fry him to a blackened crisp like a cartoon cat, that the cracked beam overhead will split and pulp his head like a melon. Through the windowless gap a hot, steady wind is clearing the room of its haze of dust. He can breathe a little easier. Meanwhile the girl has propped herself on her elbow. With trembling fingers she parts the hair over her face, gingerly combing kernels of glass to the floor. Now Kevin's like the guy at the toga party in *Animal House,* alone with a passed-out sorority girl, a tiny angel on one shoulder and a diminutive devil on the other, but this time their roles are reversed. *Go to her,* says the angel. *Stay where you are,* says the devil.

"That's good," he says, trying to keep his voice steady. He manages to extend his feet toward her. "You're getting it."

Through her hair he can begin to see her more clearly; her face is bloodlessly white and her eyes are squeezed shut. She licks her lips, she blinks, she opens her eyes and looks up at him, and then the floor abruptly splits under Kevin's thighs with an almighty crack, expelling a puff of dust all along the seam, leaving Kevin's feet dangling in the air as the floor beyond it tilts violently away. On the other side of the crack everything—broken glass, office chairs, girl—slides toward the gap to the outside. Instinctively Kevin lurches back, heedlessly pressing his palms into glass, hauling himself frantically away from the split. Downhill from the sliding girl, the upright conference room chair rolls over the edge and out into the air, its seat still turning. One of the upended chairs slides after it. The girl meanwhile has erupted into frantic action, scrambling uphill on her hands and knees through the cascading glass and drywall and debris, her wild eyes fixed on Kevin from behind her jeweled veil of hair. Before angels or devils tell him otherwise, he twists on his bruised hip and thrusts his hand over the edge for her, his palm stinging with glass and already oozing blood, but before she can even reach for it she puts her foot on something sliding past her—it's Kevin's missing shoe—and loses her purchase, landing flat on her belly, sliding backward.

"No!" she shouts fiercely, her palms dragging against the floor. At the last instant she clutches the armrest of the one remaining chair, but the chair's sliding, too. Then she slithers over the edge and she's gone, followed by the chair, its little wheels spinning uselessly.

Kevin convulses away from the crack in the floor. He's really shaking now, it's not just his racing pulse. His palms are burning and dripping blood. Oh God, he thinks, oh God oh God oh God. He's trembling so hard he's afraid he'll vibrate right over the edge and out the window after her, so he curls his stinging hands over his chest and scrabbles with his feet away from the crack, banging past a leather chair on its side, plowing through the spilled soil of the potted plant, leaving a wake through broken glass, until his back is up against the inside wall of the lobby and his knees are drawn up to his chest, the soles of his feet—one socked, one shoed—pressing hard on the floor.

Oh God, he thinks, I just saw someone die. He presses the back of his head against the hard, merciless wall behind him and squeezes his eyes shut, but then all he sees is the girl splayed against the Austin skyline, just hanging there, arms and legs spread like a skydiver's. Which is not even what he actually saw, but it's what he sees now in the pulsing darkness behind his eyelids. One moment she was just beyond his reach, and the next she was over the edge. I almost had her, he thinks, but I waited too long, I hesitated. If I'd spoken to her sooner, if I'd nudged her quicker with my foot, if I'd gone to her right away . . .

. . . *you'd be dead, too,* says his fucking little devil, *you'd have been on the wrong side of the crack, and you'd be spinning weightless through the air, watching the pavement hurtling toward you.*

"Oh *God,*" he says aloud, but he's afraid to open his eyes for fear of seeing worse, for fear of seeing the crack widen and the floor tilt again, of seeing the Austin skyline framed by the maw of the shattered window, in the last minute before he himself is pinned against the sky like a specimen. Still not opening his eyes, he tugs his rucked-up pant leg down over his bandage and slowly lets his feet slide forward. As soon as his legs are spread against the floor, as if a passage has been unblocked, a damp warmth spreads through his groin. The skin of his inner thigh begins to sting lightly, and then he's stung as well at the back of his nostrils by the smell. He cracks an eyelid. The stain of his piss is darkening the inside of his left trouser leg. The ammoniac tang joins the other acrid smells, of fried chemicals and burned plastic and powdered concrete and Christ knows what else—ozone, maybe, whatever ozone smells like, from that loose, crackling, still-invisible wire. The stain spreads nearly halfway to his knee; it's all that tea he's been drinking since he landed, he thought he'd emptied his bladder in the men's room at Wohl's, but no, there's a reserve he hasn't tapped, and now his brand-new trousers are ruined. Second pair today, and he's damned if he's buying another. He starts to laugh and cry at the same time. Two ruined pairs of dress slacks in one day, that's his limit.

He slumps against the wall. Pissing himself has calmed him a little; the stinging warmth is reassuring. He's not dead yet. He plucks the wet cotton away from his leg and then remembers the glass in his palms, and he turns his hands over. Blood has darkened the cuffs of his jacket—I'm just leaking all over, thinks Kevin—but the glass in his hands doesn't look as bad as it feels. It's not in jagged shards, but rough little kernels, like broken auto glass, a few in one palm and even fewer in the other. He's tempted to just slap his hands together as if he has sand all over them, but even now he's still got enough sense to know that that would really, really hurt. So instead he licks blood off the thumb and first two fingers of his right hand, then lifts his knee and steadies his left hand against it as he attempts to pluck a fragment out of the heel of his palm. The glass is slick with blood and hard to get a grip on, and oh God, it stings like a bitch, but he pries the nugget loose with his nails and flicks it away, watching blood well into the tiny white hole it has made. He squeezes his eyes shut and shudders all over like a wet dog, then opens his eyes again and brings his trembling fingers to bear on another fragment of glass.

Something buzzes rhythmically nearby, over and over, like a wasp trapped behind a window screen. Fuck off, thinks Kevin, whatever you are—another loose wire, a shredded ceiling tile thrumming in the hot wind, some crumbling bit of masonry about to vibrate onto his head and kill him. Fuck *off*. You're in shock right now, says one of his little familiars—could be the angel, could be the devil, he can't tell the difference—you should pull yourself together, clear your head, start thinking about what you need to do to get out of here. Yeah, says Kevin back, but what about my *hands?* They *hurt.* He flicks another kernel of glass away like a booger.

The buzzing continues, angry, insistent, suspiciously regular, and Kevin lifts his head from his minor surgery to listen, holding his breath. It's a familiar sound, and he latches onto it, numbly wondering if the buzzing is proof that this is all a dream—it's his alarm going off and he's going to wake up any second now, disoriented and groggy, to see the pale green numerals of his clock glowing in the dark, he's going to feel Stella stirring against him, muttering for him to shut it off. The buzzing is like a rope thrown into his well of sleep, and all he has to do is grab on and haul himself to safety.

It comes in threes: *Buzz, buzz, buzz.* Pause. *Buzz, buzz, buzz.* It's quite near, and suddenly his devilish little angel says in his ear, *answer the fucking phone.* Kevin lowers his knee and drops his hands palm up in his damp lap and stares slack-jawed beyond his shoeless toes at a little black flip phone buzzing amid the glass near the crack in the floor. The phone rotates a quarter turn with each trio of pulses.

"Oh," breathes Kevin, and then, as if that electrical snake has at last sunk its fangs into him, he jerks his legs under him, curls his hands spastically against his chest, and slides knee by knee, his toes pressed flat behind him, toward the phone dancing on the edge of the abyss. The weight on his right knee revives the pain of his first laceration of the day and squeezes blood through the bandage into his brand-new trousers, *but then they're already ruined,* says his angelic devil, *so what the hell difference does it make?* His heart's pounding again because any second now another foot or so of the truncated floor is going to crumble off like pie crust and tilt him into oblivion. When he's within fingertip reach of the vibrating cell he sinks back on his butt and leans forward, but his hand trembles so hard that he jerks back, afraid he'll fumble the throbbing little phone—his lifeline, his ray of hope, his salvation—over the side.

He inches forward on his knees, heart thundering. *Not so fucking close!* The phone vibrates through another cycle, and Kevin snatches the cell and yanks it back to his chest. He rocks painfully back onto his toes, and plucking at his lapel with two smeary fingers he shoves the phone inside his jacket. Then he swivels onto his butt again and, crying out at the sting of glass pressed deeper into his palms, hauls himself back from the crack and up against the wall, his wake through the debris punctuated with bloody palm prints. The phone pulses against his chest like another heart. Braced against the wall, his legs splayed, he can hear someone whimpering, and it takes him a moment to realize it's him.

Then the phone stops and it's as if his own heart has stopped, as if whoever was calling has already given him up for dead. "No!" he cries, and thrusts his hand inside his jacket again, smearing his tie and his new shirt with blood. He holds the cell by the tips of his fingers, steadying his wrist with his other hand. The glossy black burnish of the phone is already dappled with red. He wipes his fingertips on his trousers and licks his lips. He tries to breathe more deeply, but it's as if his ribs are wrapped tight in gauze. He flips open the phone. The keypad is impossibly miniature and pristine and he nearly flips it shut again, not wanting to bloody this immaculate little artifact. And anyway, who's he going to call? What's he going to say? Then the phone starts to buzz again, and Kevin nearly drops it. After everything that's just happened, his startle reflex should be fried, but he's still jumpy as a cat. So jumpy, in fact, that for a moment he's not sure what to do with the phone, how it works, what it's for. The little screen has lit up with the message BLAKE CALLING. Blake who, Kevin wonders. I don't know anyone named Blake.

He licks his forefinger clean and presses Talk and shakily lifts the phone to his ear. He can't think of a thing to say.

"Hey sweetie, can you talk?" says the phone.

Kevin can't make a sound. His throat feels like someone's crushing it with both hands. He can't even grunt or groan or squeak. The inside of his mouth feels like it's coated with talc.

"Sweetie?" says a young man's voice. "You there?"

What Kevin feels like doing, what he wants to do, is start screaming. In fact he can feel a scream boiling up inside him all the way from his bowels, like vomit, and he actually pinches his lips shut.

"Leslie, c'mon." The guy on the other end sounds impatient. He's a just a kid, Kevin can tell. Just a boy.

"Lez?" says the boy. "Quit goofing around."

Kevin unpinches his lips and whispers, "Hello?"

"Hello?" Now the caller is puzzled. Even at a whisper, Kevin's voice doesn't sound like the person the guy on the other end expected to hear. "Who's this?" he says.

"Who's this?" answers Kevin, stupid as a monkey.

"Where's Leslie?" Right now the kid, wherever he is, is looking at his own screen to make sure he's got the right number. "Who is this?"

Kevin's exhausted. It's all he can do to keep his head up. He has no idea whose phone this is, for all he knows it could have bounded in from another room, but as he slumps in the dusty ruin of Hemphill Associates, as a sultry breeze blows in from the vast hole of the empty window and courses uphill along the fatally tilted floor, carrying the distant wail of sirens, Kevin figures he has to act on the assumption that the little black phone belongs—belonged—to the girl who just slid over the edge.

"I'm all alone here," Kevin manages to rasp through his tight, dry throat.

"I'm serious, dude," says the kid's voice, trying to sound tough. "Where's Leslie and why have you got her phone?"

"It was buzzing, and I picked it up."

"Okay." The kid's voice is noncommittal. The boy has decided to bank his anger because clearly he thinks the guy he's talking to is some kind of moron. "Where'd Leslie go?"

Involuntarily, Kevin's gaze drifts across the crack and down the tilted floor and over the edge, where, through the haze of dust and the glare of sunlight, he can see the condo tower with a ragged-edge hole in it, two floors laid bare like a doll house, a tangled venetian blind flapping in the breeze forty stories up. A thin haze rises out of the hole, but no gouts of flame or smoke. That's good, thinks Kevin.

"Where's Leslie?" the kid demands again, no longer disguising his anger. "Why have you got her phone?"

"She's gone. I'm all alone here." Across the street, on an upper floor of the neo-deco building with the Starbucks on the ground floor, a woman in a red blouse stands in a window, looking in Kevin's direction. She presses both hands to her mouth while someone behind her rubs her neck—Kevin can just make out the flexing hands. I'd get out of there, Kevin thinks, if I were you.

"Where'd she go?" Who is this idiot on his girlfriend's phone, and what has he done with her?

"Out."

"Out where?"

Kevin says nothing. He's not certain of much at this moment, but he does know that he doesn't want to be the one to tell this guy the worst thing he's ever heard. He's not getting this individually from either of his little *Animal House* familiars, he's getting it both from the devil and the angel, loudly and simultaneously, cowardice and compassion in equal measure. Keep Your Mouth Shut, they remind him.

"What's your name?" The kid tries another tack.

"Kevin," says Kevin, dully.

"Well, Kevin, you're kind of freaking me out."

"I'm sorry." Kevin's as monotone as a somnambulist. "That's not my intention."

"Can you at least tell me, is Leslie coming back soon?"

"I don't think so."

"Seriously, dude, who *are* you?"

Just hang up, say Kevin's voices, so he says, "I gotta go" and lowers the phone, searching for the End Call button with his trembling finger while the tiny voice of the kid chirps at him.

"Is she okay?" the boy is saying. "Can you just tell me that?" Kevin presses the button, the voice goes dead, the screen tells him helpfully CALL ENDED. He shuts off the phone, flips it closed, and sticks it inside his jacket. He sags back against the wall, bone tired. He closes his eyes.

I need to stay awake, he's thinking. I can sleep later, but there's something I need to attend to right now, if I could only remember what it is. It's a mix of feelings he's had before, a simultaneous urgency and lassitude, sort of like his competing angel and devil, but with no obvious moral component: *Get up and do something* in a tug of war with *Just let me sleep for a minute,* like the night his grandfather died on the Quinn family farm west of Lansing, a couple miles of dirt road north of the Grand Ledge Highway. Like courtiers hanging about the death chamber of a king, the family had congregated at Grampa Quinn's eighty-acre empire, in his sagging old farmhouse where the floors creaked alarmingly underfoot and all the doorways were slightly out of true. Kevin was a new graduate of Michigan and working at Central Café, and he had driven up from Ann Arbor through a late Christmas Eve blizzard in his deathtrap Pinto, braving whiteout on I-96, the snow finally limiting visibility to the fuzzy cones of his headlights. He saw no other cars, coming or going; no one else was stupid enough to be driving in weather like this. He crawled the last few miles up the unplowed county road to Grampa's at fifteen miles an hour—which was still too fast, but any slower and the Pinto would terminally stall out—and he watched for Grampa's drive through the snow streaking at his windshield, afraid that he'd never find the farm in the dark, afraid that he might already have passed it. Just when he despaired of ever seeing the mailbox, just when he thought he'd either freeze to death in a snowbank or drive all the way to Mackinac City, out of the blizzard crawled Grampa's indestructible steel mailbox on its sturdy length of iron pipe, with the family name, missing the *Q*, in sliding letters across the top. UINN said the snow-covered letters, making the name sound even more Gaelic than it already was. Kevin inched off the road and fishtailed up the snowed-in driveway, squeezing in between the weighty pickup trucks of his farm cousins. The trucks, the lawn, the leafless maples were all thickly blanketed by snow, and more snow fell endlessly through the yard light that hung from the roof beam of the barn.

From his car, Kevin tramped through the drifts in his Converse All-Stars and thin denim jacket. He stamped the snow off his sneakers on the porch and then hauled the storm door aside and pushed open the kitchen door without knocking. The overhead light cast a superfluous yellow glow over everything in the kitchen, all of which was already yellowed with age: the ancient Frigidaire, the Formica-topped table, the patterned linoleum that crackled under foot. The only remotely new thing in the kitchen was a yellowed Mr. Coffee on the yellowed counter, where Kevin's Aunt Mary, his father's sister, was fortifying herself with a huge cup for the night's vigil. She lifted her head at the scrape of his sodden feet on the mat and by way of greeting said, "Take off your shoes." And then, turning away, "Where's your mother?"

"She isn't here?"

"Nope," said Aunt Mary, evoking with a monosyllable a lifetime of tension between the Quinn and Padalecki families. "Kathleen's here," she added, and Kevin found his sister asleep under a garishly orange afghan on the swaybacked sofa across the living room from Grampa's old black-and-white Motorola. The TV and the little ceramic Christmas tree on top of it provided the only light in the room. The tiny red and white bulbs on the tree cast very little light, while on the screen Alistair Sim was trembling his way silently through *A Christmas Carol,* the grainy image hauled in through the storm from Channel 10 in Jackson by Grampa's skeletal rooftop aerial. Kathleen wasn't the only one not watching the redemption of Scrooge: his cousin Kyle in jeans and a huge cable-knit sweater sprawled snoring in Grampa's recliner, presenting in the flickering TV light a clear view of his basketball gut, the threadbare soles of his white socks, and his cavernous nostrils. One of Kyle's kids, whose names Kevin could never keep straight, curled on the ancient carpet before the TV with his or her blond head on an embroidered throw pillow. Standing in his wet socks under the oppressive woodwork archway between Grampa's dining room and living room, Kevin sensed that the house was murmurous with comatose Quinns; just below the threshold of hearing he was vaguely aware of snores and sighs and farts fumigating the clammy old farmhouse in the middle of the night. Only he and Aunt Mary were awake at the moment, and she touched him lightly on the arm as she passed, startling him a little.

"Merry Christmas," she whispered, perhaps to make up for her brusqueness in the kitchen, and she beckoned him to step carefully through the sleepers in the living room to Grampa's bedroom door, which stood open and which, in fact, was probably impossible to close in the humidity of all that snoring, sighing, and farting. In the doorway she stopped Kevin with another touch and tiptoed to the bed, bending over the figure on the right side of the mattress. Kevin's grandmother had been dead for nine years, so Grampa could've lain in the middle of the mattress if he wanted to, but even at the end he kept to the side of the marital bed he'd occupied for fifty years. Or perhaps it was just easier for his daughters to tend him there. A lamp on the bedside table cast a nimbus of yellow light around a bent straw in a half-empty glass of water, a little brown bottle of morphine with an eye dropper in it, and a box of baby wipes. The bed's usual blankets and bedspread were neatly folded on a chair, and its bottom sheet had been replaced with a fitted, rubberized sheet, a reminder along with the baby wipes that colon cancer was not a tidy way to die. Kevin had expected at least an IV drip, but the old man lay untethered under an incongruously new blanket, baby blue. His head was centered on a single pillow, his hands, as pale as exposed roots, curled on his chest, and his feet, in red woolen socks, sticking out beyond the end of the blanket. From the doorway, Kevin could not see or hear his grandfather breathe. In fact Grampa looked like he was already dead, and Kevin realized that his own heart was pounding, perhaps because he was seeing something that had been denied to him the night his father died. On that summer night in Royal Oak, still floating from the weed he'd smoked an hour before, he'd been shuffled into his own bedroom by his mother's awkward priest while his father's body had been bagged and gurneyed and wheeled down the hall. The priest hadn't even let Kevin peek through his curtains to watch the gurney being lifted into the ambulance, and the next and last time he saw his father he was looking surprisingly youthful in the coffin at the funeral home. But now Kevin was standing at the threshold of the inner sanctum, where the thing itself was taking place, where his grandfather's breaths and heartbeats were counting down to nothing, where each exhalation measured an increasingly large fraction of what remained of his life. Above the bed, at the margin of the dim lamplight, a pointillist blot of green mildew had been spreading slowly across the bedroom ceiling for years, and it looked to Kevin now like the stain of his grandfather's last, diseased breaths.

"Can you hear me, Dad?" Aunt Mary said, taking one of the old man's hands in both of hers.

Kevin heard no reply, but Aunt Mary nodded for Kevin to come to the bed, and he jerked into the room as if someone had pushed him. Aunt Mary slipped the old man's limp, waxy hand into Kevin's and stepped away. What do I say? Kevin almost asked her, but it wouldn't have mattered, because his throat tightened and his eyes watered and the best he could do was utter a tremulous "Hello?" Grampa Quinn's eyelids fluttered open, and his eyes, faded to a milky blue, fixed on Kevin. His face was as pale as his hands, and his lips were papery and blue. His tongue moved weakly inside his mouth, as if he couldn't even muster the energy to dampen his lips. Then, for an instant, his gaze brightened and his cold hand moved in Kevin's, and he managed to whisper, faintly but distinctly, "Frank?"

Kevin couldn't speak. He looked helplessly at his aunt, who slipped in beside him and took the old man's hand and said, "No, Dad, it's Kevin. Frank's son. Your grandson," and Kevin watched the light in his grandfather's eyes fade as quickly as a bright stone dropped into dark water. Then his aunt caught Kevin gently by the arm and escorted him to the door, and he left the bedroom feeling worse than he had when he'd come in, guilty that he wasn't the one his grandfather wanted to see at the end, then angry at his father for letting them all down by dying eight years before, then angry at his grandfather for not hiding his disappointment, then angry at himself for being angry at his father and his grandfather for things they could not control. Through the contention in his head he was dimly aware of Aunt Mary murmuring to Grampa Quinn, lifting his head to offer him water, dropping morphine between his lips with the eye dropper, and he pulled himself together when she came out of the bedroom and led him tiptoe through the living room and the dining room and up the cold, creaking stairs to the last empty bed in the house, in a unheated, high-ceilinged back bedroom, lined with peeling wallpaper and stacked all around with moldering old boxes of God knows what. With a farm wife's no-nonsense tenderness she turned him out of his denim jacket and maneuvered him onto a canvas cot, tucking him in like a child with a scratchy old army blanket.

"Don't take it personal, hon." She cupped his face with her cold hands. "It's all running together for him at the end. He don't know who's here anymore and who isn't."

Kevin was still too choked up to reply, so she just patted him and said, "You try to sleep, and we'll come fetch you when it's time."

But then they didn't. Aunt Mary, God bless her, had too much on her mind, and no one else knew that he'd arrived. Ever since that night Kevin has lacerated himself for not being present when his grandfather died, for sleeping through it. He could have stayed awake, he could have offered to sit up with his grandfather, but instead he'd let himself be stashed out of sight like one of those mildewed old boxes, so that when Kyle, who *was* awake at the time, said, "He's going," and a dozen Quinns all over the house rose from their beds or sofas or recliners like vampires from their coffins to troop into the bedroom and witness Grandfather Quinn's last, stertorous breaths, Kevin was fitfully asleep on the stiff old cot upstairs, still humiliated by his grandfather's undisguised disappointment. For years afterward Kevin was angry at himself, because out of all the nights he'd stayed up for no good reason—to finish a paper in college, to party until dawn, to fuck, to restlessly channel surf because he couldn't sleep even if he wanted to—this was the one night when he should've made the effort to stay awake and he didn't, and the old man died without his witness. And the worst of it was, he'd known that night, as he let Aunt Mary steer him upstairs and onto the cot, that it was his responsibility and nobody else's to keep himself awake. In the end his body betrayed him, clouded his consciousness, dragged his eyelids down, lied to him like a seducer by saying, "Just rest your eyes for a minute, you'll feel better afterward," so that when Aunt Mary finally remembered and shook him awake in the leaden dawn of Christmas morning, Kevin woke up angry at himself, at her, at the world.

"Why didn't you wake me?" he'd whined as he thundered down the stairs in his stocking feet, and Aunt Mary had said, "I'm so sorry, hon, I forgot all about you upstairs, I'm so sorry," leaving Kevin to face a houseful of cousins, glum and smug in equal measure, while Kathleen lifted her eyebrows at him, saying only "Hello." But the voice he's hearing now is louder, practically shouting, and the touch is rougher than his Aunt Mary's, fingernails digging into his arm. "Hello!"

"What?" He opens his eyes and clenches his stinging fists. A woman is squatting next to him, not his Aunt Mary, not Kathleen, but someone else. Disheveled brown hair, watery blue eyes, cracked lipstick.

"Are you hurt?" says the woman, gripping his shoulder. Her skirt is a little too tight for her to be squatting, and her touch is as much to steady herself on the toes of her pumps as it is to reassure Kevin.

"No," he says. Then, wincing and opening his fingers, "Yes, a little. I picked up some glass."

She lightly cups one of his hands with one of hers, and her

warm touch thrills Kevin like a lover's. He's seen her somewhere before, but where? He doesn't know anyone in Austin.
The woman says nothing, but looks away through the ruin of
the outside wall and into the hazy glare. She tightens her grip
on his hand and says, "Where did you come from?"

"Ann Arbor, Michigan."

The woman winces. "No. I mean, where did you come from
in this building?"

"Oh." Kevin doesn't want to disappoint her. He doesn't
want her to let go of his hand. "Nowhere. I mean, I was right
here, on this floor, with..."

"With whom?" Ever the copy editor, even now Kevin notes
the correct use of the objective pronoun. Then the full horror
of what just happened jolts him again, an electric shock to his
heart. "There was a girl," he says. "A young woman, I mean."

The woman glances around, still cupping his bleeding hand,
still steadying herself on his shoulder. "Is she going for help?
Did she find a way down?"

She did, thinks Kevin, but not what you have in mind. "No."
He wishes he hadn't mentioned her. "She's gone."

"Gone?"

Kevin lifts his chin toward the gap, over the edge. "I didn't
know her name."

The woman closes her eyes and sighs, twisting slowly down
on the toes of her pumps as if she's deflating, ending up next to
Kevin against the wall. There's soot on her face and her brown
hair is tousled. She's his age, maybe a little younger, though
it's hard to tell—she's a little too made-up for him to be able
to see the woman underneath clearly—and now he remembers
where he's seen her before. She's the woman from Starbucks, the
woman with the laptop and the little suitcase on wheels, the
woman who asked his opinion about letting some guy down

gently. The woman with the fancy coffee who'd never heard of Damon Runyon. The Yellow Rose.

Kevin starts to speak, but his throat tightens up. She turns her wide, cornflower blue eyes to him, not seeing him, her gaze entirely inward. He notices that one of her false eyelashes lies like a caterpillar just under her eye. "Where did you come from?" he says.

She gazes at him unblinking, He nudges her and says again, "Where did you come from?"

Her gaze snaps into focus. "Below. One floor down. I think."

Kevin notices her nostrils flaring, a little *Bewitched* twitch of the nose. She's sniffing the air like a mouse.

"I peed myself," he says.

"What?"

"I pissed myself." Kevin gestures feebly at his damp, stinging lap. "That's what you're smelling."

Involuntarily the Yellow Rose glances at the dark stain, then meets his gaze. "Hon, if that's the worst thing that happens to you today, you'll be a lucky man."

"Yeah."

Now she's tucking her heels under her again, balancing on the toes of her shoes and steadying herself against the wall. She combs the tangles out of her hair with her fingers, scowls at the soot on her palm. "I'm not exactly feeling fresh at the moment, either."

"Why are you here?" Kevin says.

She's got that directionless gaze again, the thousand-yard stare. Perhaps she misunderstood the question, the way he misunderstood the one about where he'd come from. Perhaps she thinks he's asking her an existential question. Aw hon, she'll say, why are any of us here?

"Why'd you come up," he says, "instead of down?"

She narrows her eyes at him. "How bad are you hurt? Can you stand?"

"I'm fine. It's just my hands."

"Come on." She hooks her fingers under his elbow and tugs, helping him slide up the wall to his feet. His knees are a little wobbly; she senses it and tightens her grip, but when she tries to pull his arm around her shoulders so that she can support him, he shakes her. I can *do* it, Mom. Still, she clutches his sleeve, and Kevin almost apologizes.

"Will you help me find a way down?" Her eyes struggle to focus.

"Sure," he says, "why not," as if he's doing her a favor.

She tugs him between the elevators, where the six doors, three on each side, are buckled to various degrees. The woman keeps close to Kevin, tightly gripping his arm; Kevin curls his bleeding hands spastically close to his waist, holding them stiffly so that they don't shake. The ceiling above is crumpled, too, but it hasn't fallen in, though Kevin can feel grit under his stocking foot. Together they scuff along like runners in a three-legged race. With only one shoe on, Kevin limps as if one leg were an inch shorter than the other. The hot breeze from the gap presses at their backs, carrying the smell of something burning. Kevin tries to ignore it. The Yellow Rose leads him up to one of the crumpled elevator doors and gingerly taps the warped metal with the tips of her fingers. Her nails are long and bright red, and she bends her fingers back, jerking them away and then touching the metal again. She takes care of her hands, Kevin notices; they look younger than her face.

"We probably shouldn't take the elevator," Kevin says, and the woman looks sharply up at him. She's petite; without her pumps she would come up only to his chin.

"They say don't take the elevator in emergencies," he says.

"I know." She's placed her palm flat on the buckled door. "That's good," she murmurs, then tugs him farther on, past the elevators into the hall beyond, which splits right and left. At the junction they each tug in a different direction, then stop and pull close again, the woman clinging to Kevin's sleeve. Each direction is the mirror image of the other: a narrow hallway with a high ceiling and a couple of tall, anonymous doors. The Yellow Rose's hall on the left is full of glaringly lit haze and dust. Kevin's hall, on the right, is hazy, too, but more fitfully illuminated by a flickering light around the corner.

"This way." She tugs him to the left, and they hobble together to the first door. The woman tests it nervously with her fingertips, then lays her palm against it before trying the handle, while Kevin hovers at her side. It's locked, so they scuttle to the next door, which is also locked, and then follow the hall around a sharp corner into the glare of twin emergency spotlights. They stop short, squinting into the white light at a door with a red-lit EXIT sign above it. The haze is thicker here, though not enough to make their eyes water, and without speaking Kevin pulls free of the Yellow Rose and hobbles, sock, shoe, sock, shoe, toward the door. The floor is cool under his stocking foot.

"That's the way I came up." The woman hangs back by the turn in the hallway.

Kevin stops inches from the door, hands still curled, hip poised at the crash bar. He looks back at her. In the harsh glare of the emergency lights, her disheveled hair looks like a wig, and her makeup looks like a mask.

"The stairway's full of smoke." She's squinting into the bright light, nervously opening and closing her hands.

Kevin lays the back of his hand against the door. It's not warm, so he licks his lips, glances at the woman, and nudges the crash bar with his backside. The door clicks open, and black, acrid smoke gusts out of the entire length of the opening.

Kevin can feel heat, too, and he recoils from the door. It swings slowly shut and pinches off the smoke, which gathers in an ugly thundercloud up under the high ceiling. Kevin's already running now toward the Yellow Rose, who has both hands clasped to her mouth, her eyes gone even wider. Forgetting the pain in his hands, he hooks her by the elbow and hauls her around the corner and back to the junction in the hallway, his one shoe grinding dust, his shoeless heel hammering the hard floor. The Yellow Rose's sharp heels clatter alongside him. They clutch each other panting by the elevators, not looking at each other. Her gaze has gone glassy again, and Kevin's is wild, glancing all around without seeing much.

"Was it like that before?" His throat is nearly too dry to speak, and when she doesn't say anything, he rattles her a little. "Was it like that when you came up?"

No, she shakes her head.

"Is it worse now?" Kevin's almost angry at her.

Yes, she nods.

"You might've said something before," he says. "About, you know, the building being on *fire*."

He's gripping her tightly despite the bitter stinging of his palms. She looks up wide-eyed, almost as if she's beseeching him.

"I couldn't go down, so I thought maybe I could come up" — she shakily glides her palm up, across, and down like an airplane — "and then go down the other way."

"Fuck," he says. "*Fuck*."

She flinches suddenly, looking past him, forcing him to wheel with her. He turns to see what she's looking it, and the cloud of smoke he let in through the emergency door glides like a shadow around the corner under the ceiling, as if it's following them. Kevin looks over her head down the other, darker hallway, with its sinister flickering light.

"Wait here." He lets go of her, leaving two bloody palm prints on the sleeves of her jacket, and he hurries up the hallway to another locked door and pounds on it with his hands. But it stings too much to ball his fists, so he backs up and kicks the door savagely with the toe of his expensive shoe, making black scuff marks along the bottom of the door. "Hello!" He kicks and kicks. "Can you hear me? Can anybody hear me?" He backs up and kicks the door flat with his shoe, like a TV cop, and his stocking foot slides out from under him and he ends up sprawled on his ass, grinding the glass into his palms again. He's on the verge of tears as the Yellow Rose stoops to haul at his elbow, helping him to his feet.

"We should stick together." She slaps the dust off his suit.

He ignores her, starting into the haze down the darker hallway, and she clutches at him, trying to hold him back.

"We have to check down here," he says, breaking free. "There's got to be another stairwell."

"Don't," she says, but she doesn't stop him, and around the corner he sees, in the flickering light, that the end of the hallway has collapsed. Not just the ceiling, but a concrete beam from the floor above has come down, along with most of a wall—a heap of rubble like an ancient ruin. A light fixture spits and fumes, floating orange sparks that fade and die in the haze. This is the source of the whip-crack he heard before. The emergency door and lights are buried behind the heap of concrete and drywall. In the maddening flicker of the fixture, Kevin sees an arm thrust out of the rubble a foot or two above the littered floor. It's hard to tell in the unsteady light, but he thinks it's a man's arm, from the blue dress shirt buttoned at the wrist. The arm sticks out from just above the elbow, palm up, the hand limp.

Kevin balances on the balls of his feet, ready to flee. He glances at the ruined ceiling, at the haze all around, anywhere but at the arm. Above the tangle of rubble he can make out the glow of the emergency lights, but he can't see the exit sign. And he's glad, because the word EXIT would read like a cruel joke. NO ENTRING is what it would really say.

"Come back!" cries the Yellow Rose from around the corner.

"Don't go," said his Aunt Mary from the porch of his grandfather's house, clutching her elbows in the cold. "Give 'em a chance to clear the roads first."

"I gotta get back," Kevin said. "I promised my mom I'd be there for Christmas."

But it was already early Christmas morning, and he knew as he scuffed through the snow of the farmyard to unbury his Pinto that he wouldn't get to his mom's until noon at the earliest, even if the roads were clear all the way back to Royal Oak. But he couldn't spend another moment in the house with all those rural Quinns and his dead grandfather. Not after having been mistaken for his dead father, not after having slept through the old man's death, not after having been the last to know. Kathleen loomed behind Aunt Mary, watching him blankly with the sleeves of her massive sweater pulled over her fists. He didn't even ask her if she wanted to come; she and their mother weren't on speaking terms at the moment. Go, stay, her look said, it's all the same to me.

So while his sneakers soaked up snow, he flailed at the accumulation on his car with the little brush on the end of his windshield scraper, until the faces watching from the farmhouse realized he was serious, and Kyle and a couple other burly farm cousins tromped out in their boots with the laces undone and helped manhandle Kevin's Pinto through the snow down the drive and into the road, then stood by the mailbox in their shirtsleeves and watched him fishtail down the hill. Kevin barely made it down the road, his wheels churning snow and gravel, but the Grand Ledge Highway had been plowed and the tires gripped the scraped gray pavement gratefully. A haze hung over snowy fields on either side, and a weak winter sun, just risen, hovered above the skeletal branches of some farm's woodlot. He fiddled with the radio but found only Christmas music, and every tune, from "Run, Run Rudolph" to the "Hallelujah Chorus," sounded like a taunt, so he drove with the radio off, listening to the rush of the heater and the clatter of his shitty little car.

East of Lansing on I-96, bored by the freeway, he got off at the Okemos exit and headed south through Mason, hoping that the storm the night before had passed mostly north of the freeway and that the back roads were clear. By now the sun had climbed higher into a crystalline blue sky, and the snow on either side of the road glittered so painfully that Kevin regretted not having brought his sunglasses. The road itself was clear and dry and the streets of Mason were empty early on a Christmas morning, so he decided to risk an even smaller road, Dexter Trail, that wound around small lakes and through woods and past ranch houses and farms. On a long, straight stretch of the Trail east of M-52, just north of Stockbridge, he impulsively pressed the accelerator to the floor and pushed his rattling little deathtrap as fast as it would go on the cracked pavement — which, luckily for him, wasn't very fast, so that when the road passed through a gloomy patch of woods where the low winter sun hardly ever shone, and the car hit some ice and began to spin, he wasn't instantly propelled into a tree. Tree trunks slid sideways past his windshield, then the road behind him, then trees sliding the other way. When he was facing forward again, his adrenaline kicked in and he stomped on the brake, screeching to a halt on a dry patch of pavement just beyond the woods and stalling out the car. As he sat panting in the sudden silence, he saw that someone else had hit the same ice and spun out not long before, only without as much luck as he'd had. In the steely winter light falling across a farmyard just beyond the woods, Kevin saw a pair of tracks plowing through the snow across the yard and past the front of a derelict farmhouse. The twin tracks ended at a green pickup truck tipped on its side at the edge of the field beyond the house.

His heart racing, Kevin sat in his ticking car in the middle of the road. The tracks looked fresh, unblurred by later snow or wind. The old farmhouse, though, was heaped with snow. Its front porch had long ago collapsed like a shopkeeper's shutter over the first-floor windows and the peak of the farmhouse roof had caved in, so that he could see bitter blue sky through the empty window frames of the second story. Across the weathered gray siding someone had spray painted, in huge letters, NO ENTRING. Even under the blanket of snow Kevin could see the tangle of untrimmed bushes across the farmyard, the angular heaps of rusting farm machinery, and the splintered uprights of a barn that had long since burned or collapsed completely into itself. The tracks of the overturned pickup seemed to aim straight through the only unobstructed path across the yard and into the field beyond.

Still trembling, Kevin restarted his car, checked his mirrors, and pulled the car as close as he could to the side of the road without getting stuck. He put on the emergency blinker, left the motor running, and got out. Clutching his denim jacket shut at his throat, he slipped and slid in his soaking sneakers up the track of the pickup, calling out weakly in the bitter cold, "Hello?" The empty farmhouse seemed bigger and gloomier now; through its broken windows he saw that the first-floor ceiling had also caved in, too, so that the interior of the house was stuffed full of splintered gray timbers like a box full of pickup sticks. Even if you wanted to, there'd be no entring that house, making the blunt warning across the front seem both superfluous and more menacing. Scuffing up the track on his icy feet, Kevin thought the handpainted warning might as well have read ABANDON ALL HOPE.

Kevin called out again, "Anybody there?" but his words froze and died, leaving only a ringing, icy silence. He was shivering, and his feet were beginning to sting. The snow around the truck was disturbed by the truck's final topple onto its side, and Kevin steadied himself with one hand on the freezing side panel as he edged along its rust-eaten and salt-rimed undercarriage. He kicked through the snow around the front of the truck, trailing gusts of white breath. The truck's hood was still warm under his hand, so he called out again, "Anybody in there?" The windshield was cracked but not shattered; it might even have been an old crack, an elongated *S* that snaked from one side to the other. The cold light fell across cracked black vinyl seats that were patched with duct tape and leaked sickly yellow foam stuffing. Kevin put his shaking hand on the cold, cracked glass and peered into the cab. The driver's door window was rolled up and intact, while the passenger door window, pressed into the snow at Kevin's feet, was crazed with fractures. His pulse throbbed in his throat, and he angled this way and that, peering into the foot wells and the narrow space behind the seats, briefly misting the glass with his breath. There was no one in the truck.

The hair rose on the back of his neck as if someone were watching him from behind, and he spun suddenly around. The field of snow glittered away into the distance, poked through with the dried stalks of last year's corn. No one there, either. He glanced at the gloomy house, gray wood heaped with white, then at the ruins of the barn, blackened uprights frosted with snow. He stepped back into drifts up to the calves of his jeans to get a wider view of the truck. There was no snow on it, so it must have crashed since the storm, but the only footprints around it were his own, coming up from the road. He trudged along the top of the truck, noting the empty bed and the intact window at the rear of the cab. Standing behind the sideways tailgate, he saw the truck's tracks and his own coming up from the road, saw his Pinto with its lights flashing dimly in the bright sun, saw its thin plume of exhaust rising straight up in the brittle, windless air. He turned completely around, stamping a hole in the snow. There was no one in the truck, and no tracks led away from it.

Suddenly the cold penetrated deeper, not just the freezing air through his thin jacket, but an all-encompassing cold that seemed to flow from the truck, the ruined barn, the decaying equipment, the slowly collapsing house.

"Hey!" he shouted, as loudly as he could, but the syllable disappeared into the cold as quickly as the mist of his breath, leaving no trace that he had ever cried out at all. The snow glittered painfully in every direction, except in the interior of the derelict house. Even though the roof had collapsed and the windows were all broken out, none of the relentless winter light seemed to make it into the house's interior, where all he saw were the shadows of shattered and upended timbers, curling peels of ancient wallpaper, sheets of water-stained lath and plaster, and where, he knew, with absolute certainty, that if he stared into the shadows long enough—trembling in the cold, up to his knees in snow—something would move and beckon him.

He started to run, clumsily, back toward the road. He threw his arms out for balance and let his jacket flap open, lifting his knees high to punch his sodden, freezing sneakers through the drifts. Halfway across the farmyard it occurred to him that he might tread on something sharp under the snow, that he ought to retrace his original path back around the truck, but there was no way he was going back there. He plunged through drifts up to his knees, caking his jeans with snow, and he struggled past the front of the ruined house without looking back, finally bursting through onto the pavement, gasping white clouds, his whole body shaking, his throat raw. He yanked open the Pinto's door, fell into the bucket seat, and put the car in gear even before he slammed the door or buckled his seat belt. The wheels whined in the snow, ratcheting Kevin's panic even higher, but then treads caught pavement and he skidded out onto Dexter Trail and rocketed away from the house and the empty truck, warmed as much by sheer relief as by the car's wheezing heater. He didn't look back, he never drove that road again, and he never mentioned what he'd seen to another living soul.

Now, as he hesitates in the smoky, flickering hallway, Kevin thinks, that's two tests I failed in twelve hours: not staying awake for Grampa Quinn and not reporting the overturned truck. The memory of that Christmas has haunted him for twenty-five years. He's imagined alternate versions, where his grandfather clutches his hand and calls his name, the last words Grampa Quinn ever said, or where Kevin pulls an unconscious driver out of the truck and drags him through the snow to his car and races him to the emergency room in Stockbridge or Pinckney. Sometimes he thinks he's exhausted the memories of that day, that they've stopped making sense, but now the hand sticking out of the rubble—motionless, fingers curled—is another test, and it's as if he were standing beside the truck again, in the cold, cruel winter sunlight. His eyes are beginning to sting from the smoke, from the flickering light, and he knows he ought to touch the hand, to see if the guy's still alive under there. But he's more scared of touching that hand than he's been of anything else, ever, in his whole life. What if it has a pulse, or, worse, what if it twitches? What can Kevin do? He can't lift the beam, he can't pull the guy out, he's not sure if even clawing at the rubble would do anything but bring the rest of the ceiling down on top of them both. What if it's still warm?

What if it clenches in pain, like a dying spider in its last throes? What if, in a moment out of a horror movie, it clutches him tightly and won't let him go?

"He's dead." The Yellow Rose is just behind him. She's edged into the hallway after Kevin.

"Did you check his pulse?" Kevin asks without turning around. When she doesn't answer, he turns to see her fingers plucking at the air near his sleeve, as if she wants to pull him away.

"Did you?" he says.

"Yes." Her eyes flicker side to side. "He's gone."

Are you telling me the truth? Kevin wonders. Or are you just trying to get me out of the hallway? Before he can think about it, he's pinched the thumb of the hand between his own thumb and forefinger and waggled it side to side. It's warm to his touch but completely limp. Kevin puts two fingers on the wrist, the way he's seen actors do it on television, feeling nothing and leaving a pair of bloody fingerprints. What if he's doing it wrong? What if the wrist has a weak pulse and he's just not feeling it, not with his own pulse racing and the woman tugging at his elbow?

"Come on," she says. "Please."

At last he lets her pull him away by his elbow, back around the corner.

"I told you not to go down there," she says, and for a moment Kevin and the Yellow Rose are a longtime couple, bickering but affectionate, strolling arm in arm. But only for a moment, because as they step between the elevators, they both see that smoke is now rising from the gaps between and around all six sets of crumpled doors and pooling in a cloud over their heads. The woman whimpers at the back of her throat, two descending notes, the sound she might make in another context, if she'd just discovered that her cat was on the counter, say, or that her cake had fallen, or some other vexing but minor quotidian disappointment. She sags against Kevin, and he has to slip his arm around her waist to prop her up, planting more handprints all over her nice suit.

"Come on." He urges her on rubbery legs past the smoking elevators and onto the ledge of flooring where she first found him. She's positively shuddering now, and the best he can do with his injured hands is grasp her clumsily by the elbows and lower her slowly to the floor against the wall, even as he tries to scuff the broken glass away with his shoe.

"It's okay." His own voice is breaking. "It's all right."

He drops her the last six inches and she thumps against the floor, nearly toppling onto her side. Her face has crumpled, her eyeliner is running. The stray eyelash is gone, who knows where, and she shivers against the wall, her hand pressed to her mouth, her cheeks streaked with black. Kevin squats unsteadily before her, wanting to dab at the inky tears, but his hands are still stained with blood.

"Oh God," she says. "I thought if I came up..."

The best he can do is brush her hair with his knuckles. She clutches one of his wrists with both hands and gazes at him with brimming eyes. "The floor was on fire," she says in a hoarse whisper, as if she's afraid of being overheard. "So was the floor below me." She snuffles, swallows. "I could hear people screaming."

"Jesus." Kevin strokes her hair with the back of one hand, while letting her cling tightly to the other. He's almost in tears himself now. "Why didn't you tell me?"

The woman's sobbing uncontrollably now, and Kevin folds her in an awkward hug, the two of them crouched in the intersection of floor and wall. He can feel her heart beating. Then her sobs subside almost as quickly as they started, and she looks up, their faces close enough to kiss. Behind her blusher and lipstick and runny eyeliner, she's very pale.

"I didn't want to lose hope," she says in a weak but steady voice. Her eyes are glistening, but no longer overflowing. "I believe hopelessness is a sin?" Her rising inflection makes her sound uncertain. Kevin swivels clumsily off his feet to sit beside her, his arm around her shoulders. He sniffles, gasps, knuckles his own tears away. She tips her head back against the wall, watching him.

"There's always hope in God." Her voice is weak but steady.

"Unless there isn't." Kevin's not looking at her, he's watching sunlight shafting through the smoke rising across the wide gap where the conference room used to be. He's already thinking, this is the last sky I'm ever going to see.

"Don't you believe in God?" She's watching him with a child-like intensity.

No atheists in burning skyscrapers, thinks Kevin, but she's still giving him that innocent look, so he says, "Maybe we shouldn't get into this right now."

"If not now," she says, with a directness that pierces him and annoys him in equal measure, "when?"

Acrid smoke penetrates to the back of his sinuses. He glances back. Black tendrils ripple along the ruined ceiling, struggling against the hot wind blowing from outside. Kevin looks at the woman.

"What's your name?" He tightens his arm around her.

She presses against him, twisting her knees toward him. "Melody."

"I've never met a Melody before," says Kevin. "That's a lovely name."

"What's yours?"

"Kevin."

She pats his lapel and sniffles. "I'm glad you're here, Kevin."

"I'm not," Kevin says before he can stop himself, and he starts to laugh. He squeezes her with his stinging palm.

She laughs, too. "Me neither, I guess." Then, "You didn't answer my question."

"What question?"

"About God?" Melody says, but before Kevin can answer, the phone in his jacket starts to buzz, startling them both. She recoils and clutches him at the same time, digging her polished nails into his jacket.

"You have a *phone?*" she says.

"It's not mine," Kevin says.

"For God's sake!" Melody yanks at his lapel and plunges her hand inside his jacket. "Why didn't you say you had a phone!" She plucks out the cell and turns away from him, expertly flipping it open and pressing Talk.

"Who is this?" she demands, her voice suddenly sharp, and Kevin, speechless, can hear the tinny voice of the boy he talked to earlier.

"Yes, I know. I'm in the building." She listens a moment, then says, "Hang on, I'll ask." She presses the phone to her chest so the guy on the other end can't hear.

"Leslie?" she whispers, and Kevin shakes his head and makes a diving motion with his hand.

"She's not here," says Melody into the phone. "I think she got out already." The tinny voice speaks, but Melody interrupts him. "Sir, what's your name? Blake? Listen, Blake, could you call 911 and let them know there are two people trapped on . . . what floor is this?"

Kevin gasps, stammers, says, "Fifty-one, I think. Maybe fifty-two."

"Go see if it says." She jerks her chin toward the elevators. Kevin stiffly levers himself up off the floor with his throbbing hands, and steadying himself against the wall, which is beginning to get warm, he peers around the corner into the elevator lobby. If the floor is marked, he can't see it. Now smoke is pouring out of the hallways beyond the lobby and out of the elevators themselves, trembling against the breeze blowing through the gap.

"It's the fifty-first or fifty-second floor," Melody's saying in a steady voice. "Tell them to hurry, please, won't you, Blake? We're counting on you."

Kevin slides to the floor next to her. "The smoke's getting worse."

But Melody's not listening; she's cut Blake off and is thumbing in 911 with intense concentration, biting her lip and splaying her legs before her. She lifts the phone, listens, groans in frustration.

"It's busy," she says. "How can that be?"

"I think they probably know by now what's going on."

She holds up her finger to silence him and enters 911 again, listens, cuts it off, enters it again, cuts it off again. "*Damn* it all! How can it be *busy?*"

Kevin feints feebly with his hand toward Melody. He'd like to have the phone back. He's thinking he might want to call his mom. He's thinking he might even want to call Stella. The idea that it might be the last time he'll ever speak to either of them is seeping into his mind like black water. Meanwhile Melody has closed the little phone within her trembling fist, and she's staring blankly into the smoky sunlight coming through the gap. "If 911 doesn't work now, when is it supposed to?"

I could ask you the same about God, thinks Kevin, but he doesn't say it. Melody's staring into space, sucking in her lips.

"Is there someone you want to call?" he says as he gingerly

reaches for her closed hand. He's wondering if he'll have to pry apart her fingers to get the phone.

"Take it," she says, and abruptly pitches the cell at him. He fumbles for the phone, but it thumps off his chest, clatters off the floor, and bounds over the crack in the floor, sliding toward the edge. Kevin and Melody simultaneously catch their breath. The cell phone glitters in the sunlight at the last moment, and Kevin's not sure, but he thinks it starts to buzz again as it sails over the edge and out of sight. Kevin turns to the woman beside him. She's pressed one hand over her open mouth, and with her other she's digging her red nails into his forearm. She looks at him wide-eyed.

"I'm so sorry!" she says from behind her palm.

Kevin just sighs. Now he's going to die alone, drowned in black water. He clutches her wrist and pries her fingers loose from his arm.

"I'm *so* sorry," she says again in a tiny voice. She lays her hand on his upper arm. "Was there someone you wanted to call?"

Kevin lets his feet slide out straight like Melody's, and he slumps against the wall. Only the friction of his new dress trousers keeps him upright, and any second now he could just melt like wax in the growing heat and ooze across the crack and dribble over the edge.

"Will you forgive me?" She strokes his arm.

"It's okay." His sinuses and throat are beginning to feel raw. Even with the wind from outside, the ruined lobby is filling from the ceiling down with black smoke. "I really didn't want to make that call, anyway." He looks at her. "You know what I mean?"

"I do." She wipes inky tears away with the heel of her hand. "I know exactly what you mean."

"Seriously, what would you say?" He can see Stella in her

professional suit, the slim, narrow-waisted one that attracted him to her in the first place that morning in Expresso Royale. He sees her striding in her heels across the imperial lobby of some convention hotel in Chicago, the vertiginous atrium of the Embassy Suites or the dim, clubby lobby of the Sheraton. She might even be sharing a midafternoon cocktail with some guy she's met at the convention; she may even be flirting with him a bit, because flirting is Stella's default mode, not that it would mean anything, it's just how she is. And because she's Stella, and not Beth, she wouldn't even notice the image of the burning Texas skyscraper on the TV over the bar, but she would interrupt the conversation if her phone rang, and Kevin sees her sly smile of apology to the guy with her at the bar as she dives into her bag for her cell. That's the age difference between him and Stella in a nutshell: he'd shut his phone off in a situation like that, but because she's younger than he is she answers the thing instinctively, no matter whom she's talking to. On one of their early "dates," after they'd already been sleeping with each other for three weeks, she kept answering her phone during dinner one night at a tapas bar on Main Street, so that finally, while she was in the middle of a call, he excused himself, went outside, and called her from his own cell, watching through the restaurant window as she said to whomever she was on the phone with, "Hang on, I have another call," then looked puzzled as she glanced at the screen and saw it was him. Then he heard her saying, "Kevin?" and he'd said, "Hi, remember me? The guy you're having dinner with? The guy you're sleeping with? The guy whose house you moved into?" On more than one occasion he's glanced at the screen on his own phone and, when he's seen that it's her calling, he hasn't answered, he's let the call go to voice mail, then lied to her later about leaving his phone turned off. But when she sees it's him, she always answers his call—always—and that thought pierces his heart.

Of course if he'd called her today from Leslie's phone, she wouldn't have recognized the number on the screen—"I don't know this number," she might even say out loud to the guy at the hotel bar—and then Kevin would have heard her saying her own name in a noncommittal, businesslike voice, and he pictures the mask she makes of her face when she's talking to someone she doesn't know. And then he'd've said, if he could choke it out, "It's me," and the thought of her mask relaxing, of her voice saying, "Hey, you," and then the thought of what exactly he'd say to her next—it all makes his throat tighten as if someone has just seized him around the neck with two rough hands. Either that, or the increasingly acrid air is choking him.

"Maybe they're already coming for us," Melody says.

Kevin coughs. "Who?"

"Rescuers?" Melody's tears are running clear now. Her eyeliner's all washed away.

"Didn't you say the floors below are on fire?"

She nods, weeping.

"Then how would they get to us?"

She's trembling again, so Kevin rouses himself, pushes himself up on his stinging palms, puts his arm around her.

"I'm sorry about the phone," Melody says.

"It's all right."

"I'm not sure I'd want to make that call either."

"Who would you call?"

"My kids." Melody coughs. "My father. My ex-husband."

The air is hotter and the smoke is thicker, black and roiling against the ruined ceiling above. It's slowly lowering, filling the room from above, and some of it is beginning to stream through to the outside. He doesn't hear sirens anymore. In the distance Kevin can still see the construction crane towering above the condo tower. The narrow catwalk alongside the cab, forty stories up, is lined with little figures in orange safety vests and yellow plastic hard hats. They look like figures from a Bob the Builder playset, little round-top wooden dowels painted with bright hard hats and happy faces, plugged into round slots on top of the Tinkertoy crane, watching Kevin die. You guys should get down from there, he thinks, you really, really should.

"I want to talk to my kids," says Melody, "but I don't."

"I know." He pictures Stella bloodlessly pale on a stool in the convention hotel bar, snapping around to look at the image on the TV. He hears her sharp incredulity: "What are you doing in Austin? Why didn't you tell me you were going?" If she didn't put it together right away, she would later on, and he's not sure what will hurt her more, that he's about to die, or that he was thinking of leaving Ann Arbor to get away from her. The guy at the bar with her is feeling awkward. He sees she's upset, but he hardly knows her. The decent thing would be to stick around, but all he really wants to do is make an excuse and hurry away. Kevin pictures Stella clutching the guy's sleeve the way Melody's clutching his, and he's grateful that she's not alone. He pictures her trembling uncontrollably. He pictures her knees buckling. Would she faint? Do people faint anymore?

"I wouldn't want this to be their last memory of me," says Melody, and Kevin says, "I know." He holds her tight, drawing her face to his chest. "I know, I know."

She mutters something against his shirt, and he relaxes his grip.

"You smell like coconut," she says.

He sighs and looks up. The ceiling of smoke is even lower now. If they were standing, their heads would be in the cloud. More smoke is coming from over the rubble that chokes off the hallways to either side.

"We need to get lower," he says, and before she has a chance to reply, he lifts his arm from around her and starts sliding on his butt toward the crack in the floor, clutching her wrist and pulling her with him. He no longer cares about the glass on the floor but pushes heedlessly through it as if it were sand, hauling with his heels, pushing with his other hand. He feels a resisting tug, and looks back. Melody is balling her fist and trying to pull her wrist out of his grasp.

"No," she whispers, ghostly pale. "I'm not ready for that."

"Neither am I," Kevin says firmly, not letting go of her, "but we need to get lower, away from the smoke. Okay?"

Without unclenching her fist, she looks up. The smoke cascading along the ceiling is a torrent now, a roiling, snaky, upside-down black river. She inches slowly alongside him, and sitting thigh to thigh they hang their legs over the crack and down the slope. Like a pair of schoolchildren they're holding hands. Kevin's hand still stings, but he doesn't loosen his grip.

"It's not as steep as it looks," he says.

"Maybe we should take off our shoes," says Melody. "For better traction."

Kevin nods, and without releasing hands, they each use a free hand to bare their feet. Kevin lets his remaining shoe drop and it skids to a stop halfway down the slope. He peels off his socks one-handed and tosses them limply after the shoe. Melody bends at the waist, demurely twisting her knees, and takes off one pump and then the other, placing them neatly side by side next to her, at the edge of the crack. They sit with their bare feet brushing the sloping floor, which, to Kevin's touch, is feeling warmer than it ought to. Waggling their backsides, they press closer together, shoulder to shoulder, thigh to thigh, their hands squeezed together between them. This, thinks Kevin, is the last time I'll ever touch a woman.

From behind them comes a rush of heat, as if someone has opened an oven door, and simultaneously they look back to see orange flame sheeting through the smoke along the ceiling, swelling like a tide up and back, up and back, a little closer to the gap with each surge. Kevin and Melody can feel each rising increment of heat on their backs, can feel it tightening the skin of their cheeks and foreheads. They look at each other, and neither of them speaks for a moment.

"You're a Christian?" he says.

She nods.

"I know a story about this martyred saint, I forget his name." Kevin had heard this from Father Vince, his mother's priest. "The Romans roasted him alive over a fire, and just before he died, he said, 'You can turn me over now, I think I'm done on this side.'"

Melody's eyes fill with tears. "This isn't a time to joke."

"If not now," says Kevin, "when?" He nudges her. He's crying, too.

"Will you pray with me?" she says.

What for? thinks Kevin. To whom? And suddenly he's angry at the God he doesn't believe in for abandoning them to this, for looking away when they need him, for lying down on the job. Way to go, lord. Nice work, asshole. Thanks for nothing, motherfucker.

"Why don't you pray for both of us?" he says.

Melody tightens her grip on his hand, making it sting almost unbearably, and as the heat from above begins to sting their backs and singe their hair, she closes her eyes and says, "Heavenly Father, please forgive my sins and the sins of this good man here—"

Actually, I'm not so good, thinks Kevin.

"—and take us both quickly to Your bosom—"

A-fucking-men. As quickly as possible. We're going to burst like water balloons.

"—and please, dear Lord, look after my family and this man's family and ease their sorrow and help them know that we reside in Your house now, with You, where there's no more pain and uncertainty and fear, forever and ever."

This is unbearable, thinks Kevin. I'd rather jump than listen to this. But at the same time, he thinks, keep talking. Don't stop.

"In Jesus' name," says Melody, opening her eyes, "amen."

Kevin's eyes are stinging with tears and smoke. The smoke's lowering slowly over their heads like a hood, and he can feel the backs of his ears blistering, can feel the heat pounding through his jacket and his shirt and scalding his back. Kevin grips Melody's hand, and without speaking they scooch over the crack and bump onto the tilted floor below. Right away gravity drags at their ankles, and they slide too fast, their bare feet scuttling like crab legs without purchase.

"No," whispers Melody, as if she's afraid of being overhead, "no no no no no no no." She grips his hand so tightly that his blood squeezes through their fingers. Their feet are scrabbling like cartoon feet, and the edge of the drop slides irrevocably toward them, but at the last moment Kevin and Melody simultaneously plant their feet and skid painfully to a stop, their momentum almost, but not quite, tipping their center of gravity over the edge. Instead they rock back onto their backsides, squatting barefoot a few inches from the drop like a pair of shoeless peasants. Kevin's heart is pounding, and he can feel Melody's pulse, too, through the warm, slick grip of their palms.

"Know any more jokes?" Melody says breathlessly.

Kevin starts to laugh, and for a moment he's afraid he'll never stop, that he'll laugh so hard that he'll rock them over the edge. A scrim of smoke rises from below, dimming the blue sky and obscuring the construction crane and the condo tower with a hole in it and the tiny white faces watching them from windows in the building across the street. Kevin can see past his knees straight down into the street below, and it makes his stomach churn. He sees the little oblongs of fire trucks and ambulances and cop cars, all at irregular angles to each other. He sees dots scurrying between them.

"Guy falls off the top of a skyscraper," he manages to say, and Melody catches her breath.

"No, listen." Kevin squeezes her hand. "Guy falls off a skyscraper, and halfway down, he passes the window of a guy he knows, and the guy in the window says to him, 'Hey, Bob, long time no see. How you doing?' And the guy who's falling says..."

"'So far, so good,'" says Melody. "Everybody knows that one."

Kevin shrugs. "I guess."

At least it's a little easier to breathe here. The sheet of fire is still some ways above them, and the smoke is being carried upward through the gap above them. Through the scrim of smoke Kevin can see a helicopter, its rotors sparkling in the sun. It looks like a toy. He's afraid to move, afraid to make the slightest shift, afraid to even turn and look at Melody. They're both trembling, and it doesn't seem to matter how tightly they cling to each other, they shudder like a pair of dry leaves in the wind.

"I'm sorry," says Kevin.

She's looking at him, but he can't bear to look back at her.

"For what?" she says.

"For everything." Kevin's mouth is very dry. He turns to her finally. Stella's not here, Beth hasn't spoken to him in ages, who knows where Lynda or the Philosopher's Daughter are these days, so Melody will have to do. "Will you forgive me?"

He realizes that he's left her an opening to bring up God again, but instead she dips her head and nuzzles him. Her hair scrapes his cheek, and she presses his hand to her heart. He takes her chin in his hand and lifts her face. Both their faces are sooty, and where they aren't sooty, they're sweating and reddened from the heat. But their eyes are dry, and she looks at him as if she's known him for years, knows everything about him, all his secrets, good and bad and in between, and loves him anyway.

"Yes," she says. "I forgive you."

He kisses her. Her lips are salty, and he feels the fingers of her other hand trembling on his cheek. They embrace at the edge, cheek to cheek, and through her singeing hair, Kevin can see the inverted river of fire, filling the space above where they'd been a few moments before. Kevin shuts his eyes and dips his head and whispers hoarsely in her ear, "Are you ready?"

"No," she whimpers.

"There's no more time."

"I can't do it."

"It's all right," Kevin says. "I'll do it."

She tightens her arms around him. "Don't let go of me."

"I won't," Kevin says, and in one sudden movement he presses their joined hands to his chest and jerks his shoulders forward, pitching them over the edge.

For an instant Kevin thinks, maybe prayer works!, because they just seem to hang there, buffeted by the wind. His eyes open to the whole Google Maps panorama of Austin turning slowly below them — the ant-busy street below, the buildings thrusting up toward them, the hammered verdigris green of the river, the sun-faded hills studded with red roofs — and for a nanosecond his heart swells with the hope of a miracle, that they will soar like angels, wafting hand in hand to the pavement below to land gently on the balls of their feet like the risen dead before the eyes of breathless office workers and astounded first responders.

But it's not a miracle, it's not a moment of salvation, and let's hope Melody didn't think her God was rapturing her at the last moment. She's not an angel—not yet, anyway—and Kevin's not either, he's just Wile E. Coyote, and he's overshot the edge of the cliff to hang there just long enough to make a mournful face and hold up a sign that says HELP! The next instant they're plummeting into a sixty-mile-per-hour wind, Kevin's jacket snapping behind him like a cape, his blood-stained tie whipping over his shoulder. Melody's hair is streaming, her skirt is pressed between her legs, her jacket puffed with wind. The two of them are pinned, no doubt, against the faded blue sheet of Austin's sky, or against the gashed, rectilinear facade of the burning building, by the lenses of cell phones and news cameramen, witnessed live over cable news networks and the Web, doomed to be replayed endlessly in a loop, YouTubed over and over and over again, the pair of them a tragedy or a rallying cry or a sick joke, stripped of their individuality in the three and a half seconds it takes for them to fall.

Then their hands are pulled apart and they're falling separately, from fifty stories up, at a terminal velocity of fifty-five meters per second. Kevin's got just three seconds to live, and he wants to know a lot of things all at once. Is this going to hurt? Why doesn't anyone stop this? What did I do to deserve this? Isn't my life supposed to be flashing before me? Where's my highlight reel? I want a fucking highlight reel! Turns out I was middle-aged at twenty-five, only I didn't know it. Where's Melody now? Did she let go of me or did I let go of her? He'll never know now, but so what? Everybody dies alone, but at least she's got a family, she's got children, someone's going to miss her. Who's going to miss me? Nobody I know even knows I'm here, and nobody here knows who I am. Who's going to remember me? Who's even going to notice that I'm gone, and how long is it going to take for them to notice, and how long is it going to take for them to figure out where I was when I died?

The wind is punishing his eyes, but Kevin keeps them open, watching the upturned faces below scattering from his descent. None of them know who I am, I might as well be a 180-pound sandbag as far as they're concerned. Who will mourn me? Who will write my eulogy and what will they say? Will I even *have* a eulogy? He was too young to give the eulogy at his father's funeral, and it fell to his father's brother Tim, who showed up drunk at the church and rambled and sobbed and lost his place in his notes. Later he typed up what he'd meant to say and mailed a copy each to Kevin and Kevin's mom and Kevin's sister, and now Kevin doesn't know where his copy is anymore, he never read it anyway, it's one more worthless piece of paper he's leaving behind for someone else to dispose of. Who? Kathleen, probably, he can't imagine Mom doing it, she'll slide deeper into her bottle of Gordon's, staring out through the glass while Kathleen shoulders the burden, which is what Kathleen always does, but then there's also Stella, his de facto widow; Stella will cry buckets and shudder with grief and no one will ever know how much she means it, maybe not even Stella.

Kevin writhes in the air, the wind thumping in his ears, the tower streaking past. He glimpses Melody one last time, her legs pedaling, her arms flailing, her face obscured by her hair. Still alive, though, as he still is, if only for another instant. So far, so good.

What's Stella doing right now? What is she doing *right this instant?* His watch is still set to Michigan time, but he's dying in the Central Time zone, and it's the same time in Chicago that it is here, and that brings her closer to him somehow. She's not in the bar with some guy, she wouldn't do that, Stella loves me, I'm pretty certain of it, she wouldn't do that. She doesn't know what's happening to me, she can't sense it, but she's thinking of me anyway, she's on her way out of the Sheraton on an errand that has to do with me, and it's poignantly ironic because she's passing the bar where a crowd is watching the breaking news on CNN and she's not turning to see what all the fuss is about as the growing knot of midday drinkers and conventioneers draws a collective breath at the video of two wriggling figures falling from a burning office tower in Austin, Texas. Déjà vu all over again. But Stella's too wrapped up in her thoughts of me at the moment, she's stepping out of the Sheraton briskly and expertly on her high heels, her purse slung over her shoulder, out onto the streets of Chicago where it's as midsummer hot as it is in Texas, and she's carrying herself with that lovely feral walk that I still love even though she annoys me and terrifies me, she's carrying herself purposefully in search of a CVS or a Walgreens, she's already got the address from the hotel concierge, and she marches up the fluorescent lit aisle of the store in search of a home pregnancy test, the one she used last month didn't tell her what she wanted to hear, but now she's missed her period again, and she buys the little box at the pharmacy counter from a bored young black pharmacy clerk, and Stella twinkles at the young woman, trying to get her to share in Stella's anticipation, but the clerk's not going for it, it's just another boring moment in the middle of her boring shift. But Stella doesn't let that bother her, she never lets the indifference of others bother her, and no, she doesn't want a bag, thanks, she just sticks the box and the receipt in her purse and sails out of the store into the sticky heat again, eating up the sidewalk in long strides like a runway model, though her legs are too short and too muscular for that, and she hardly notices the crowds on Michigan Avenue or the bleary sun or the odor from the sluggish river alongside the hotel, though it seems like a longer walk going back than it did coming, even though it's the same distance, silly, I know *that,* but even Stella understands the psychology of it, she's carrying a secret, or the promise of a secret and she can't wait to be back in her room, and that's where she is *right now,* her purse and her suit jacket dumped on the bed, her pumps kicked off on the carpet, the box of the pregnancy test ripped open on the bathroom counter along with the folded sheet of instructions, which she hasn't bothered to read because she's done this before, she knows the drill, and she's sitting on the toilet with her skirt tugged up and her panties around her ankles, and she's pigeontoed, holding the stick under her stream, concentrating with her lips pursed like it's painful. The bathroom door's open and the TV's on with the sound off, not CNN, thank God, that would be *too* poignant, but Bravo, probably, showing a marathon of one of those hideous housewives shows she likes so much, and apart from the upholstered hush of the room and the rumble of ventilation, the only sound is the patter of Stella's micturition against the stick and into the bowl. Then she sets it aside, pulls up her panties, tugs down her skirt, stands barefoot on the icy bathroom floor, washing her hands and watching herself in the mirror — is that the face of a mother? — and then she picks up the test and pads out onto the carpet, instinctively shaking the stick as if it were a thermometer or a Polaroid, and she sits on the end of the tall bed with her bare feet dangling like a little girl and watches the zaftig, bitchy housewives with the sound off, until at last the test is ready, and she reads the result by the light of the TV, then looks up at herself again in the mirror over the desk. *Hi, Mom!* Still holding the stick, her heart pounding, happily oblivious to the tang of her own pee, she plunges her hand into her purse on the bed and comes up with her phone, then rises from the bed and floats barefoot over the carpet to the window, where she gazes out at the sunlight glinting on the dirty water of the Chicago River below, then lifts her eyes to the glittering meniscus of Lake Michigan, in what she guesses is roughly the direction of Ann Arbor, and she starts to tear up at the thought of her boyfriend, her landlord, her lover, not quite her husband, the man she isn't entirely sure loves her. She flips the phone open one-handed, turns it on, cants her head to one side like Carrie Bradshaw, lets her middle finger hover over his speed dial number—think fast, Kev, you're going to be a father—but she doesn't press the button, because on second thought maybe it's not such a good idea to tell him over the phone, it's the middle of the day, he's at work, he doesn't always answer his phone and even if he does, he might not take it well. Because anyway you look at it, this is going to be a difficult negotiation. Stella's too savvy not to know that. Better work up to it and tell him in person, tell him after dinner tomorrow night, after a heavy meal, get a bottle of wine in him and cuddle with him on the sofa, where she can tell him face to face while she's touching him, reassuring him, coddling him along like the big baby he is, before she starts to remake him into the man she needs him to be. She flips the phone shut again and stands at the window hugging her secret to herself with her phone in one hand, her other hand cocked at the wrist and brandishing the pregnancy stick like a cigarette holder. I'm ready for my close up, Mr. DeMille. She's crying from happiness, sure, but from anxiety, too, and from anger, because what's that grump of a boyfriend going to do when she tells him?

Kevin's crying, too, but tearlessly, because the wind of his descent is sandblasting his face. I love you! he wants to shout, but the wind's also pummeling his lungs, he's dizzy and light-headed and he might even pass out before he hits the pavement, which would be a blessing, but he desperately wants her to know this one thing, he wants it to wing through the ether via some sort of telepathic wormhole, he wants to tell her that he loves her, that he always did and he always will, though the future tense doesn't mean much at the moment and is losing value fast, at fifty-five meters per second. But I want you to know that, Stella, I want you to remember that I loved you when you hear the news, I want you to remember that I loved you when you realize I went to Austin without telling you, I want you to remember that I loved you when you understand what I was doing there, I want you to remember that I loved you when you realize that I was thinking of leaving you—I want you to know that I loved you and was thinking of you at the very last moment of my life.

Will she forgive him? Is there time for that? Maybe not, that'll have to come later, if at all, and Kevin hasn't got any more time. What's he got to look forward to now? He won't be there when she comes home on Tuesday to an empty house, he won't be there when she gets a call from his sister, Kathleen, because when they pull his driver's license from his pulped remains, Kathleen's his emergency contact, he never got around to changing it to Stella, and Kathleen and Stella don't get along—Stella sets my teeth on edge, Kathleen told him in a rare moment of candor, and Stella's always offering to help Kathleen lose some weight, if, you know, she really wants to make the effort—Stella's going to have to hear it from her, maybe even off the answering machine or voice mail, as she stands in Kevin's empty house, carrying his child. Oh, she's gonna hate me, she's gonna despise me, she's going to be mortally wounded, well, maybe not mortally, since Kevin is getting a sudden, instantaneous tutorial in what "mortally" really means, and in this last, infinitesimal moment of his life, as the litter in the street and the grain of the pavement rush at him, he's hoping that she takes it in stride, and he's pretty sure she will, Stella is nothing if not a survivor, Stella's a fighter, Stella has an uncanny way of landing on her feet, Stella keeps her sunny-side up, Stella makes lemonade. Stella's going to be okay, Stella will get another man, even though that might be harder to do if she has a kid, and not just a kid, but a kid by a man who died in some spectacularly public and horrible fashion, who's even a kind of minor celebrity now, one of the two jumpers from the tower in Austin. Look at the mess I'm making, and I'm not even dead yet. But even if she doesn't get another man, she'll raise the kid all by herself, she'll buy every baby book in the baby book section and she'll clean out Baby Gap and Ikea and stuff the house to the rafters with kid paraphernalia—no, it's the kid he ought to be worried about at the very last, the son or daughter who right now is only pee on a stick and few thousand cells in Stella's belly, it's the kid who's going to have to face life without a father, it's the kid who's going to learn at a tender age that his father died before he even got the news that he was going to be a father, it's the kid who's going learn that her father's death will have been seen by millions before she was even born. Deal with *that,* munchkin, it's bad enough to lose your dad at a young age, and I ought to know, but my own kid will have to live with the knowledge that the most important fact he'll know about me is the way I died.

I'm sorry, thinks Kevin, please forgive me, winging that through the ether, too, and into the future, to a kid who won't understand any of the circumstances of her birth for years yet, and who may never understand them at all, because who does, really? But I'm sorry for that, I'm sorry you'll never know me and I'm sorry I'll never know you, it's all my fault, I should have stayed in Ann Arbor where I had it good, where I had a woman who loved me, where I had friends and a history, where I had a job I was good at, where I didn't realize just how good I had it until it was gone. I'm sorry that I've hurt you, even before you're born, but I want you to be happy, I want you to be strong, I want you to love your mother even if she gets a little frantic and needy at times, I want you to understand that you're the center of her life, you're all she ever wanted, and I know it's asking a lot, but I want you to live up to that responsibility, though of course if you do live up to it, you won't have gotten that from me, but that's the nature of fatherhood, isn't it, that you want your kids to be better than you were? I wish I believed that I'll be looking over you and your mother, but I don't, though who knows, I could be wrong, perhaps I'll come to you in a dream, looking younger and fitter, perhaps, without the hair in my ears and the laugh lines and the enlarged prostate, perhaps I'll come to you both, I'll hover over your crib wearing a white linen suit, smiling down as your mother tucks you in, saying, sleep tight, your daddy loves you, he's watching over you, he'll keep you safe, that's just the sort of thing Stella will believe, a little anxiously, perhaps, but that's what she'll tell herself. And she'll never, ever tell you I was planning to leave her, that I was, without knowing it, planning to leave you both, instead she'll tell you that I was in Austin because I knew you were coming and I wanted to be prepared with a better-paying job, I wanted to do the right thing, and you'll believe every word of it, because Stella's your mother and a good saleswoman, besides, and because there's no reason for you not to believe it, and anyway, it's true, I would have adored you if I'd known you were coming, I would have stepped up and done the right thing, I would have made you the center of my life and happily paid for clothes and shoes and tennis lessons and ballet classes and baseball camp and orthodonture and trips to Europe and college tuition, and I'd gladly have given up all the pointless things I stupidly thought made my life worth living, because I'd realize that *you* made my life worth living, and I'd have laughed with you and lost my temper at you and burst into tears at the sight of you and begged fate or God or the universe to deal you a better hand than they're dealing me, and I'd have done my best to make sure you turn out okay, that you had a good start in life, because I'm here to tell you, kiddo, there's nothing certain about it, and you make all the preparation you can and then hope for the best. It's a little late for me to be doing "My Boy Bill"—the way my dad, your grandfather, whom you'll never know, either, used to sing it in the shower—but I'd have laid down my life for you, and who knows, maybe that's what I'm doing right now, but it's not so bad, it's not so hopeless, I'm not so far gone that I can't wish you every good thing, every happiness, and all the love in the world with my dying breath.

And as the ground rushes up to meet him, Kevin Quinn, for the first time in a long time, for the first time in years, and maybe even for the first time in his life, is looking forward to what comes next.

About the Author

James Hynes is the author of *The Wild Colonial Boy, Publish and Perish, The Lecturer's Tale,* and *Kings of Infinite Space.* He lives in Austin, Texas.